Summer
with ELISA

Johanna Hurwitz

Summer with ELISA

ILLUSTRATED BY
Heather Harms Maione

HarperCollins*Publishers*

For my granddaughter—
Juliet Elizabeth Hurwitz
I wish you joy every season of the year

Summer with Elisa
Text copyright © 2000 by Johanna Hurwitz
Illustrations copyright © 2000 by Heather Harms Maione,
based on the original drawings created by Lillian Hoban
(original illustrator of the books about Russell and Elisa),
by permission of the estate of Lillian Hoban
For information address HarperCollins Children's Books, a division of HarperCollins
Publishers, 1350 Avenue of the Americas, New York, NY 10019, or visit our web site
at http://www.harperchildrens.com.

Library of Congress Cataloging-in-Publication Data
Hurwitz, Johanna.
Summer with Elisa / by Johanna Hurwitz; illustrated by Heather Harms Maione.
p. cm.
Summary: During the summer between first and second grades,
Elisa struggles to write to her brother Russell at camp and then enjoys
a family vacation in the country.
ISBN 0-688-17095-1 (RTE)
[1. Summer Fiction.   2. Vacations Fiction.   3. Family life Fiction.]
I. Maione, Heather Harms, ill.   II. Title.   PZ7.H9574Stm 2000
[Fic]—dc21   99-32514   CIP

10   9   8   7   6   5   4   3   2   1
❖
First Edition

Contents

Summer Plans

It was the twenty-fourth of June. Two minutes ago Elisa Michaels had finished the first grade. But even though she was cheering with all the other boys and girls as they rushed happily from the building, she still wished school weren't over. She could hardly wait until September, when second grade would begin. Second grade was much more grown-up than first!

Elisa's mother was waiting outside the school

to walk her home. "You have a whole long summer vacation ahead of you," Mrs. Michaels said. "We'll have to think of some good things to keep you busy."

"Marshie, I'll be home to play with you every day," Elisa told her baby brother, whose real name was Marshall. He was being pushed along in his stroller. Marshall was only twenty months old. He still didn't say very much, but he could walk and run and follow Elisa around the house. He could dig in the sandbox at the park and build with blocks at home. Elisa thought it would be lots of fun to help take care of him during the summer.

Marshall banged on his stroller with the bagel he had been chewing. He was busy teething, and he didn't care about school and vacation time.

When they got to their apartment building, Elisa's big brother, Russell, who had his own key nowadays, was already home.

"Just four more days, and I'm off to sleepaway camp," he announced proudly.

Elisa had watched early in the month as her mother had packed and shipped off a big trunkful of clothing for Russell to wear during the three weeks he would be away from home. There were new T-shirts and new shorts, new socks and new underwear. In every piece of clothing Mrs. Michaels had attached a small label that read RUSSELL MICHAELS in bright red letters.

Elisa wished she had a trunkful of new clothing with her name on every piece, but she was glad she wasn't going away from New York City to sleepaway camp. She wouldn't like to be separated from her parents and Marshall for so long. But Russell was much bigger. He was eleven years old, so he wanted to go away. At least he *said* he wanted to go away. Elisa wondered if he really and truly meant it.

Elisa thought it would be strange not to have Russell home for three whole weeks. But in a way it would be fun too. For three weeks she would be the oldest child in the family. For three weeks Russell wouldn't be around to boss and tease her. For three weeks she and Marshall would have their parents to themselves.

"I won't get homesick," Russell told his parents confidently.

"What's homesick?" Elisa asked.

"Homesick means that you miss your home," Mr. Michaels explained to his daughter.

"Won't you miss your home?" Elisa asked Russell.

"I don't think I'll miss *you,*" he said. "It will be fun to live in a cabin with a bunch of other boys who are my age. We're going to have big adventures together."

"You may feel a tiny bit homesick at first," Mrs. Michaels told Russell. "But it will pass, and then you'll be home again before you know it."

"Be sure to write to me," Russell instructed his family on the morning he was leaving for camp.

Mrs. Michaels surprised him by saying, "I already did."

4

"Why did you write to Russell when he's still here?" Elisa asked.

"I mailed a letter to the camp. I knew it would be fun for him to get mail as soon as he arrived."

"What did you say in it?" Russell wanted to know.

"You'll have to wait and read the letter," said Mrs. Michaels.

"I wish you'd write me a letter," Elisa said to her mother.

"Someday when you go to camp, I'll send letters to you there," her mother replied. But Elisa wasn't at all sure it would be worth going away from home for so long just to receive mail of her own.

"You write to me too, Elisa," Russell requested. "I want lots of letters."

"Okay, I will," she promised her brother. She hoped something exciting would happen so she could write about it.

As soon as Mr. Michaels took Russell to the

bus terminal, Elisa ran to get a piece of paper and a pencil. She sat down at the kitchen table and began writing. "Dear Russell," she wrote. "I hope you are having a good time at camp." She stopped to look at her words. That's silly, she thought. How can Russell be having a good time? He hasn't even gotten on the bus yet. Elisa scrunched up the paper into a ball and threw it in the garbage. She would write a letter to Russell tomorrow.

Supper without Russell wasn't too strange. It was as if he were having a sleepover at a friend's house. But when Russell didn't come home the next day, it felt different.

"I wonder what Russell's doing at camp," Elisa said to her mother.

"You could write him a letter and ask," Mrs. Michaels suggested.

Elisa pulled out a sheet of paper. "Dear Russell," she wrote. "Is camp fun? I've been having fun playing with Annie." Elisa stopped writing. Russell wouldn't care that she had gone to the playground yesterday. She went to the playground all the time. She wished she had something new and special to write about. She scrunched up the paper into a ball and threw it in the garbage.

That morning Marshall was due for a checkup at the doctor's office. Elisa went along. She was glad the checkup was not for her. Instead she could watch the iguana in the waiting-room terrarium while Marshall had to get a shot. She remembered that once, when she was little, Russell told her that the iguana was going to get out of the terrarium and bite her. She had believed him and gone running to her mother for safety. Of course Russell had just been teasing her. He had always teased her, since she was as little as Marshall was now.

Elisa smiled and tapped the glass of the terrarium. These days it was much harder for Russell to frighten her. The iguana turned its head slightly, and Elisa stuck her tongue out at him. She knew he couldn't get out of the terrarium! Still, she sort of missed having Russell around to tease her. On some days she only pretended that she believed him. It was a game they played together.

During the following days, nothing special happened. Sometimes Elisa played with one of her classmates. Once she went to the library with her mother. She had her hair trimmed at the barbershop, and her mother bought her a pair of open sandals that she could wear without socks. None of these was anything that would interest Russell. So Elisa put off writing to him while she waited for something really important to tell.

One day, when Russell had been away at camp for almost two weeks, Elisa received a letter from her big brother.

Dear Elisa,

I am not homesick for you. I go swimming every day here. I've learned how to dive off the low board. Maybe before I come home, I'll even be able to dive from the high board. There are twelve boys in my bunk. Their names are Ted, Larry, Sam, Evan, Ethan, Noah, Bobby, Keith, Chris, Mike K., Mike P., and me. The food stinks, but otherwise camp is fun.

From,
Russell

P.S. Keep out of my room or you'll get in big trouble when I get home.

Elisa read the letter over and over. It wasn't often that she got a letter. It was also exciting that her reading skills were good enough that she understood almost every word without help.

"The food stinks," she read aloud, giggling. "The food stinks." *Stinks* had never been a reading word at school, but she was able to sound it out.

Elisa had actually gone into Russell's room a few times since he had been away. Once, just a day or two after Russell had left for camp, she had run into the room looking for him. At that moment she had forgotten he was away. But usually she went to look at his shelves of books and toys. She never touched anything. Russell's things just reminded her comfortingly that he would be back again. She wondered how Russell was able to guess that she had been inside.

Now that he had written to her, Elisa knew that she *must* write to him.

Dear Russell,
    I am glad I don't go to camp if the food stinks there. The food is good here. I helped Mommy make chocolate chip cookies yesterday. we had spaghetti and meatballs for supper last night. And the night before we had corn on the cob.

Elisa stopped to look at all she had written. Her mother had helped her by spelling aloud the

words *chocolate, yesterday,* and *spaghetti.*

Maybe Russell would get homesick if he heard about all those good foods here at home, she thought. She scrunched up her letter into a ball and threw it in the garbage. She would start again.

Dear Russell,
I am sorry that the food stinks at camp. Since you have been gone, Marshall got another tooth. Yesterday he fell in the park and hurt his knee. Mommy put a Band-Aid on it, but he pulled it off. I am fine. I am a little homesick for you even if you aren't homesick for me.
Love,
Elisa

Elisa was tired from so much writing. She folded her letter and put it inside an envelope.

Her mother had put the address of Russell's camp on the refrigerator. Elisa removed the magnet and took down the paper with the address. Carefully she copied all the information. Then she put the paper back. She got a stamp from the little box on her father's desk where he kept them. She licked the stamp and stuck it on the corner of the envelope. All she had to do now was lick the flap that closed the envelope and put it inside a mailbox.

Just as Elisa was about to do that, she had a thought. Suppose something very exciting happens later today, or tomorrow? She'd better wait to seal the envelope. Then she could add the information to her letter. Elisa put the envelope inside her library book. That way she wouldn't lose it.

That evening at supper Elisa's parents told her some big news. "Soon after Russell comes home from camp, we're going on a vacation together to the country," Mr. Michaels explained.

"To the country?" Elisa asked with wonder.

"Yes. We are renting a house with a big garden for you to play in. It will almost be as if we're living inside the park," said her mother.

"We're going to another country!" Elisa shouted. "I can't believe it."

"No, no. It's not another country," said her father. "It's our country. But it's not in the city. There will be trees and flowers and plenty of room for you to play outside. We'll have a lake nearby for swimming."

"That sure sounds like another country to me," said Elisa. "What is it called?"

"Connecticut," said Mrs. Michaels.

"I will write it in my letter to Russell," Elisa exclaimed. Finally she had some really big news to tell her brother.

When supper was over, Elisa ran to get her library book. It wasn't on her chest of drawers. She looked all over her room. "I lost my library book," she told her mother.

"Oh. Don't worry about it," said Mrs. Michaels, laughing. "I knew you'd finished read-

14

ing it, so I returned it when I took Marshall there for Toddler Time."

Elisa gasped. "You returned my book?"

"That's right," said Mrs. Michaels. "It was while you were in the playground with Annie Chu and her mother."

"But I left my letter to Russell inside it," Elisa said.

"Oh, I'm sorry. I didn't notice it. But you know what? I bet someone will find it and mail it to Russell," her mother said consolingly. "The chances are very good that he'll still get the letter from you after all."

But a week later, when Russell came home with a trophy for Most Improved Swimmer, seven mosquito bites, and a trunkful of dirty laundry, he said he'd never gotten a single letter from Elisa.

Elisa was very happy to see her big brother after all this time. But she was very sorry to hear that the letter never arrived. "I wrote a letter, but I left it in my library book," Elisa explained.

"What good is that?" Russell wanted to know. He looked taller, and he was suntanned, but he sure sounded just like the old Russell.

"It doesn't really matter," said Mrs. Michaels. "You're home now. Elisa can tell you all her news in person."

Elisa tried to think. What had she written in her letter to Russell? She couldn't remember anything at all. But she did know the one thing she hadn't written. "Russell!" she shouted. "Guess what? We're all going on a trip together. We're going to the country for our vacation."

"All of us? What fun is that?" asked Russell.

"I think you'll have a good time," Mr. Michaels told Russell. "I hope it will be just as much fun for you as camp."

"It can't be as much fun as camp," Russell told his father. "All my new friends won't be there. Just us." Then he turned to Elisa. "You'll see. Next summer, when I go back to camp, I'm not going to send you a letter."

"Please," Elisa begged him. "Pretty please."

"Next summer is a long way off," Mrs. Michaels pointed out. "I wouldn't worry about it now."

"If Elisa cared about me, she would have sent me a letter. I sent one to her."

"I can't help it if my letter was inside the library book that Mommy returned."

Mrs. Michaels leaned over and whispered something quietly in Elisa's ear.

"Secrets aren't polite," grumbled Russell. It was something he'd been told many times.

Marshall banged his spoon against his plastic dish. He didn't care about letters or secrets. But he liked to make a lot of noise.

The next morning Mrs. Michaels took Elisa to the library. At supper she had whispered that perhaps the letter Russell never received was still waiting inside the library book. Luckily Elisa remembered both the author and the title. She ran to the shelf and found the book. Inside, there was her letter, just where she had put it for safe-keeping.

"I found it!" she shouted with delight.

"Now you can give it to Russell," said Mrs. Michaels.

"Oh, no, no. I have a better idea," said Elisa excitedly.

And that is why, just one day later, Russell received a letter in the mail from his sister, with his camp address crossed out on the envelope and his home address penciled in. Elisa had mailed the letter on her way home from the library. The news in the letter was old by now, and Elisa had forgotten to add the P.S. about their trip to the country. But it didn't matter, she thought. The important thing was that Russell felt important getting a letter. It proved that his sister cared for him.

"From now on, when you write letters, you should mail them right away" was all Russell said to Elisa after he read it.

"When we go to the country, I am going to write lots of letters," Elisa said. "And then I'll go and put them in the mailbox right away," she promised.

Marshall banged his spoon on the table. He was too little to care about mailboxes and letters. He wanted more chocolate pudding.

A Pet for Elisa

Traveling to the country seemed to take forever. First there were many trips from their apartment down to the street to load the car with all of the family's suitcases. In addition to clothing, Mrs. Michaels had packed sheets and towels. Russell and Elisa were each allowed to fill a small overnight bag with other things they wanted to bring.

Russell brought his camera, a pair of binoculars, two paperback books, and a box with a new jigsaw puzzle. His parents also permitted him to bring his kite, even though it didn't fit inside the overnight bag.

Elisa brought Airmail, her old rag doll that she liked to sleep with. The other things she put inside the bag were a package of colored markers, a notebook of unlined paper for drawing, a book of paper dolls, and a pair of scissors.

Of course Marshall couldn't pack a bag, so his mother selected a few of his favorite playthings for him. Everything was squeezed into the trunk of the car. Russell and Elisa sat in the backseat with Marshall in his car seat between them.

"We each have a window," Elisa said to Russell. "But not Marshie," she added thoughtfully.

"Marshall is happy to go for a ride," said her mother. "He doesn't care where he sits." She placed a large picnic cooler on the floor of the backseat. It was filled with sandwiches and fruit and juice for them to eat along the way.

21

Elisa waved good-bye to their apartment building. She was sorry that none of their neighbors like Nora and Teddy Resnick or Mrs. Wurmbrand was around to see them go off. Nora and Teddy were still at their sleepaway camp, but Mrs. Resnick had offered to water the Michaelses' plants and feed Russell's fish until they returned home.

The trip took four hours. It would have taken less time, except along the way first Elisa and then Russell needed to take rest stops to go to the bathroom.

"It's a good thing Marshie wears diapers," said Elisa. "Otherwise, we'd have to make a stop for him to go to the bathroom too."

At last they pulled up in front of a white house on a road with only a few other houses and many trees nearby. "This is the place," announced Mrs. Michaels, who was holding a map.

Elisa couldn't decide if she wanted to see the outside or the inside first. But when her father opened their door of their vacation house, she

22

ran inside with the other members of her family.

Everything about the house was interesting to her—the carpeting on the floor; the furniture, which was different from theirs at home; the rooms and stairs. Imagine! They could go upstairs and downstairs inside this house. In their city apartment all the rooms were on one level. In the bathroom there was a sliding door attached to the tub instead of the shower curtain with fish on it that they had at home. Elisa opened the door and looked inside. The bathtub looked just like a bathtub, but it would be fun to be inside it with the door closed.

"Oh! There's a fireplace," Elisa shouted with excitement when she looked around the living room. "Remember how the wolf tried to climb down the chimney to catch the three little pigs?" Then she thought of something. "Are there any wolves around here?"

"No, not a single one," Mr. Michaels reassured her.

"I sure wish a wolf would come down this

chimney," Russell said. "That would be something really exciting to tell my friends when I got back home."

Upstairs there was a bedroom for Russell and one for Elisa to share with Marshall. The TV set was in the biggest bedroom, where Mr. and Mrs. Michaels would sleep.

Elisa opened all the closets, but they were empty except for the hangers. She opened the drawers in the chest in her bedroom. They were empty too. It would have been fun to find something inside, she thought.

In the kitchen Elisa examined the dishes on which they would be eating their vacation meals. She liked them. Unlike the white plates with blue and green stripes that they had at home, these dishes had pretty flowers all around the rims. Even string beans would taste good on a plate with flowers, she thought.

When Elisa finished exploring inside, she asked if they could go outdoors.

"I want to make the beds," Mrs. Michaels

said. "But if you stay nearby, you can go outside by yourself."

"Alone? I can go outdoors all alone?" Elisa asked in amazement. In the city she never went outside unless a grown-up was with her.

"It's different in the country," said Mr. Michaels, who was bringing in the last of the suitcases.

Elisa rushed outside and looked around. There was grass surrounding the house just like in the park back home, but there were no benches. They could sit right on the ground, she thought. That would be much more fun than an old bench. Back home she rarely sat on the grass. Too many people walked their dogs and didn't clean up after them. But here the grass looked very clean. Elisa sat down, and the pieces of grass tickled her bare legs.

Suddenly she saw a motion in front of her. She looked carefully. The small green creature near her was a frog. Even though she'd never seen a *real* one before, she recognized it at once. She

wasn't afraid of it at all. The next time the frog jumped, Elisa tried to catch it. The little frog was too fast for her.

Elisa didn't give up, though. Three more times the frog jumped, and twice more it got away. Elisa followed after it, and on the next jump she grabbed it in her hand. She put her other hand over the first to make a little cup. It felt funny to have a frog inside her hand, but she held it carefully, so it couldn't escape.

"Look what I found! Look what I found!" she shouted, running into the house. She opened her top hand cautiously so Russell could have a peek.

"Aw. It's only a little frog," said Russell. "Can I hold it?"

"First take our picture," demanded Elisa.

Russell ran and got his camera out of the overnight bag. "Smile," he told them.

"I wonder if frogs can smile," said Elisa. She removed her top hand so the frog was visible, and she grinned for the camera. Only after the picture was taken did she let Russell hold the frog in his hands.

"Be careful. Don't let it get away," said Elisa. "I want to make it into my pet. I always wanted a pet."

"You can't have a frog for a pet," said Russell.

"Why not?" Elisa wanted to know.

Russell couldn't think of an answer, but he was sure he was right.

While Russell was holding the little frog, Elisa looked for something that could be made into a frog home. Her mother came to the rescue with a large plastic container that was meant for storing food. It was deep enough that the small frog couldn't jump out.

The container needed something more to make it a good home for a frog. Elisa took a tablespoon from the kitchen drawer and went back outside to dig up some dirt to put on the bottom of the container. She found a few small stones, and she tore up a bit of grass to put inside the container as well.

"He'll need water to drink," Russell pointed out.

"Use this," said Mr. Michaels. He handed Elisa the lid from an empty jar. It was big enough that, once it was filled with water and put inside the container, it almost looked like a small pond.

"What will he eat?" asked Elisa. She'd heard of buying cat food and dog food and fish food. But she'd never heard of frog food.

"Frogs eat bugs," said Russell.

Elisa made a face. "That's disgusting."

"Not if you're a frog," said Russell.

"Well, where can I get bugs?" she asked.

"If you leave the container outdoors, in some shady spot, bugs will probably come to the frog," suggested Mr. Michaels. That solved the feeding of Elisa's new pet.

"He needs a name," Elisa announced.

Everyone except Marshall had a name to offer.

"Prince Charming," said Mrs. Michaels.

"Kermit," said Mr. Michaels.

"How about Mike?" suggested Russell. "Then he'll be Mike Michaels."

Elisa shook her head at every idea they gave her.

"It's your frog. You found him—you name him," said Russell, shrugging.

So Elisa spent the rest of the afternoon thinking about names. She thought of the names of her favorite book characters and the names of her first-grade classmates. Finally she hit upon the perfect name. "Freddy the Frog," she announced to everyone. "That's his name."

The frog didn't pay any attention to all this. He stayed in the container without moving much. But when she watched closely, Elisa could see his chest move in and out as he was breathing. "He likes privacy," she told her family. "He doesn't want to hop around when everyone is looking at him."

Even so, Elisa could not take her eyes off her new pet. When Mr. Michaels headed for the nearest supermarket with a shopping list and he invited Elisa to join him, she didn't want to go. Freddy might start hopping or doing some other frog activity while she was away.

"Could I take Freddy with me?" she asked.

"Supermarkets have rules about bringing pets inside," said Mr. Michaels. So he went off by himself to buy all the things the family needed to fill the empty refrigerator and cupboards.

Later that evening Elisa could hardly bear to say good-night to Freddy. "Can't I bring his container into my bedroom?" she begged.

"I think he'll be happier outdoors," said her mother. "You'll see him in the morning."

Elisa had been looking forward to sleeping in her new bed, so she blew good-night kisses to Freddy and came inside the house. She had a bath in the tub with a door and got into bed.

Marshall was so pleased to see her that he stood up in the crib and began calling, "Leese, Leese." That was how he said Elisa's name.

Mrs. Michaels came into the room to kiss the children good-night. "Have a good sleep," she

31

told them. "We'll be busy doing many things tomorrow." Then she turned out the light.

In the dark Elisa was glad to have Marshall across the room and soft, cuddly Airmail in her arms.

When Elisa woke the next morning, Airmail was on the floor and Marshall was no longer in the crib. She ran downstairs and found her mother fixing some breakfast for her little brother. "Can I go see Freddy?" Elisa begged.

"Sure," Mrs. Michaels answered. Elisa had already forgotten that her parents said things were different in the country. They certainly were. At home she never went outside in her pajamas!

The ground made Elisa's bare feet wet, but that didn't bother her. She rushed right to Freddy's home. He was sitting near the jar lid of water.

"Did you eat some bugs for your breakfast?"

she asked him, making a face. It sounded yucky to her. Toast crumbs would be so much better. She picked Freddy up and held him gently.

That day the Michaels family took a drive to see the area. The lake was nearby, and people were swimming and picnicking. Mr. Michaels said he would rent a rowboat and take the children out on the water one day soon.

They went to a nature museum with loads of real animals that had been preserved for them to admire: beavers and bears, porcupines and skunks, and many, many birds of all sizes and colors. "But they don't have a frog," Elisa pointed out. "I have a frog!"

"Big deal," said Russell.

The reunion between Elisa and Freddy at the end of the day *was* a big deal. She greeted her pet with a detailed description of all that she'd seen and done.

At suppertime, as they sat around the table in the vacation house eating hamburgers and fresh corn on the cob, Elisa began talking about where she'd keep Freddy when they returned to New York City.

"I don't think the city is a good place for a little frog," said Mrs. Michaels. "It would be better to play with Freddy now and to let him go when we return home."

"Oh no," Elisa replied. "I can't do that."

She thought about places where Marshall couldn't reach. Maybe the top of her chest of drawers in her bedroom would be the safest place for Freddy.

Four days after the Michaels family had settled into their vacation house, Elisa woke to a terrible discovery. Freddy had disappeared from the container.

"He's gone! He's gone!" She wept.

"I bet he jumped out," said Russell. "It must have been boring for him to sit in the same place day after day."

"It wasn't boring. It was his new home," Elisa

said, whimpering. She crawled along on the grass, trying to find her lost pet.

Mr. Michaels came outside to help her search. They looked through the grass and under the bushes nearby, but there was no sign of the little frog. Elisa sobbed. "I wanted to take him home with me. He was my pet. I wanted to show him to my friends and take him to school and everything."

"Elisa," said her father softly, "Freddy must have gone back to his mother and father. That's where he belongs, not inside a plastic container with a jar lid for water. It wouldn't have been right for you to take him all the way home to New York City. You wouldn't want to live so far away from Mommy and me, would you?"

Elisa sat on her father's lap and sobbed quietly into his shirt.

"Do you think he'll miss me?" she asked.

"Of course he'll miss you. But he'd miss his family even more," said Mr. Michaels.

"Maybe he has a big brother and a little

brother frog like I've got Russell and Marshie," said Elisa thoughtfully.

"Maybe he does," said her father. He pulled a tissue out of his pants pocket so Elisa could blow her nose.

"I'll always miss him," she said.

"Of course you will," he answered.

And of course she did. But it helped that during the day Mr. Michaels found a little beanbag toy in the shape of a green frog to buy for Elisa.

"I'm going to call him Freddy," she said, holding the soft toy in her hand.

"You won't have to worry about feeding this Freddy any bugs," Russell observed.

Even though Russell teased Elisa, he thought of her when he discovered a small ceramic frog in a gift shop two days later. He gave it to Elisa at suppertime.

"Is this for me?" asked Elisa delightedly.

"Of course," said Russell.

"I'm going to name him Freddy."

"What a surprise!" said Russell.

August 3

Dear Annie,

we are on a vacation.

we drove very far in our car. It took a long time. Russell kept teasing me. we had two fights. Marshall slept almost the whole way. Mommy says she hopes all of us will sleep on the way back home—but not Daddy. He has to drive the car.

Your friend,
Elisa

38

Up a Tree

In the country Elisa felt as if she were Little Red Riding Hood and Goldilocks and Hansel and Gretel and all the other fairy-tale characters that lived in the woods. At first she worried a bit about wolves and bears and witches in Connecticut. All the trees around the house made it easy to imagine that one of those nasty creatures might be hiding there.

"I think I just saw a wolf in the bushes," Russell would say.

The first time he said that, Elisa ran inside the house for safety.

"We would never have come here for our vacation if there were wolves," said Mr. Michaels, looking up from the newspaper he was reading.

"Maybe you didn't know about this wolf," Elisa suggested.

"Who is smarter? Russell or me?" he asked his daughter.

"You!" said Elisa.

"In that case, take my word for it. There are no wolves here." He smiled at Elisa. "Do you think Russell would have stayed outside if he thought there really was a wolf in the bushes?"

Elisa laughed. Her father was right.

"Russell likes to tease you. It's the way big brothers act," Mrs. Michaels reminded Elisa.

"I'm a big sister, and I don't tease Marshie," Elisa pointed out. Since he had come home from camp, she noticed that Russell seemed worse than ever. Besides teasing all the time, he liked to brag and show off.

"I can eat three ears of corn," he boasted at suppertime. Elisa couldn't eat more than one ear. "I can stay up later than you," he gloated when Elisa had to get ready for bed that evening. Now that she was going into second grade, it didn't seem fair.

The next day at lunch Russell continued to brag. "Be sure to put mustard on my sandwich," he instructed his mother. "Mustard used to tickle my tongue, but at camp we all ate mustard. Now I love it," he said. "Babies don't like mustard," he added, looking at Elisa.

Elisa didn't like mustard. It was worse than tickling on her tongue. It burned. But she didn't want to let Russell know that. "Marshie doesn't like mustard. But I do," she said. "Put some on my sandwich too," she told her mother.

"Are you sure?" asked Mrs. Michaels.

"Yes," said Elisa. "Just a little." Maybe if she ate a little every day, her tongue would get used to it.

"I want *a lot* of mustard. I love it!" said Russell.

"I love it too," said Elisa. "I could eat a whole jar of it."

"You could not."

"Yes, I could."

"Could not."

"Could."

"I'm going to buy you a jar of mustard, just for yourself. I want to watch you eat it with a spoon," said Russell.

"No one eats mustard with a spoon," said Mrs. Michaels.

"Elisa said she could eat a whole jar, so I'm going to buy one for her," Russell insisted.

Elisa drank a lot of apple juice with her bologna sandwich to cool her tongue from the burning taste of the mustard. She didn't know how she was going to eat a whole jar just to show

Russell that he didn't know everything.

Because it looked as if it would rain, the family hadn't made any plans that day. Elisa didn't mind. Vacationing in the country was a big enough plan for her. But Russell was restless. He sat on the step outside the house complaining. "I can't fly my kite because there's not enough wind. I finished one of my books, and I'm saving the second one. I don't know what to do."

"You could take some pictures with your camera," Elisa suggested.

"There's nothing special to take pictures of," he told her.

"We could play checkers or a card game together," she offered.

"Boring," said Russell. He looked around. "I know what," he said. "I'm going to climb a tree. I climbed some trees when I was at camp. It's a lot of fun. You get high up, and you can see far off. And you feel like you're a bird or a squirrel," he added.

Russell looked at the trees around the house

and selected a fat one nearby. It was much taller than the house. Elisa watched with amazement as he began climbing .

"Won't you fall down?" Elisa shouted up to him anxiously.

"Not if I hold on tight," Russell called back. Already he was on a limb far over her head.

"Russell, Russell! Come back," Elisa called. She could hardly see her brother now because there were so many leaves hiding him. She began to worry. Elisa knew there were no wolves and bears and witches here in Connecticut. But maybe if Russell climbed really high, he'd enter a magic kingdom like in "Jack and the Beanstalk" and there'd be a giant waiting to eat him up. Elisa wasn't certain that she believed in giants, but she didn't like her brother to take dangerous chances.

"Russell. Please, please come back," she called again.

"Okay, okay. Here I come," said Russell.

Slowly he began to descend from the tree. Then he jumped down and brushed himself off. "That was fun," he said.

"It looks hard," said Elisa.

"It's hard if you're just a little girl. But it's easy for me," Russell bragged.

"I'm not a *little* girl," Elisa protested.

Russell laughed at his sister. "Even if you were big, you couldn't climb this tree," he told her. "There are lots of things boys can do and girls can't."

"I don't believe it," said Elisa. "Girls can do anything boys can do," she insisted. "I'll show you right now."

She went over to the tree that Russell had just climbed. "I'll climb this tree too."

"Hey, Elisa, you'd better not," said Russell nervously. He suddenly remembered how a few years ago he had dared Elisa to jump off the chest of drawers in their apartment back home and she had broken her arm.

"I can do it if I want," said Elisa.

"No, you can't," Russell said. "You'll get hurt, and I'll get blamed."

"You're just saying that because you want to be the only one to climb trees around here. But I can do it too," said Elisa. She tried to hoist herself up the trunk of the tree the way she had seen Russell do. It wasn't easy at all. But there was a small branch growing out of the tree that was low enough for her to stretch her leg and put her foot on. Then she put her foot onto another branch. It was sort of like climbing stairs or a ladder.

"Come on down, Elisa," Russell shouted to her.

"You went lots higher," Elisa shouted back.

"I'm lots older," Russell reminded her. But it was the wrong thing for him to tell his sister. She was more determined than ever to climb just as high as he had gone.

Then Elisa looked down. It was scary. If she looked up, she was okay, but looking down made her worry about falling. She put her leg over a

tree limb and sat hugging the trunk of the tree. Climbing up hadn't been so hard after all. But she realized that it was going to be tough work to climb down.

"Come on down," Russell called to her again.

"I'm not ready," said Elisa.

"Come on down before you fall!" Russell yelled.

The door to the house opened, and Mr. Michaels came out. "What's going on?" he asked Russell. "I could hear you shouting from inside. Marshall is taking a nap, so it would be a good idea to keep your voices down."

"Okay," said Russell.

"Hi, Daddy," a voice called from the tree.

"Elisa? Where are you?" asked her father.

"Here I am. I can see you. Can't you see me?"

Mr. Michaels looked around. Then he looked up. "Elisa Michaels," he shouted when he spotted her, "get down here on the ground at once!"

"Don't shout, Daddy. You'll wake Marshall," Russell said.

"Never mind Marshall. Elisa, how did you get up there?"

"I climbed, just like Russell," she called down to him.

"Russell, did you dare Elisa to climb this tree?" asked Mr. Michaels.

"No, I didn't! It was her own idea," said Russell. "I even told her not to climb up there."

"Well, Elisa, I'm telling you to climb down now," said Mr. Michaels.

"I can't," Elisa said softly.

"What do you mean you can't?"

"I'm scared. I'm scared I'm going to fall."

"Don't look down," said Russell. "Just put your feet on the limbs the way you did going up. But don't look at the ground."

"I'm scared."

"I'll come get you," offered Russell.

"No, you won't," shouted Mr. Michaels. "Those limbs can't hold the weight of both of you. I wish we had a ladder," he said, sighing. "Russell, you watch Elisa and I'll run down the road and see if the people at the next house have a ladder we can borrow."

He returned a few minutes later without a ladder. "No one was home there," he said.

Elisa began to cry. "I don't want to stay here forever," she said.

"Elisa, you made it up there. I bet you could make it down again," Mr. Michaels told her.

"I'll catch you if you fall," Russell promised.

"Don't scare her more than she is already," Mr. Michaels whispered to his son. "Wait a minute, Elisa. I have a new plan."

Mr. Michaels ran into the house and returned holding two sofa cushions. Then he ran back and got two more.

"I can't believe it," said Mrs. Michaels, following him and holding the cushions from the living room chair. "I turn my head for one minute, and you're up a tree."

"It was easy going up," said Elisa, sobbing, "but it's hard coming down."

"I felt a drop of rain," said Russell.

"I'm going to get all wet," said Elisa.

"Not if you come down," said Mr. Michaels encouragingly. "Turn around and put your right leg on the limb that's underneath you. Look at the tree trunk, not at the ground."

"The cushions are going to get soaked," said Russell.

"Hush," said Mrs. Michaels. "Who cares about wet cushions? Come on, Elisa. You can do it."

Elisa held on to the rough bark of the tree trunk as she managed to turn and face the tree. She put her right foot down on the limb beneath her.

"Thata girl!" shouted Mr. Michaels. The rain was coming down a bit harder now. "Now put your left foot on the next limb. You can do it."

Elisa's face was all wet. She didn't know if it was rainwater or tear water. She sniffed hard and put her left leg down.

"You're halfway down now!" shouted Russell. "Come on. Keep going."

From inside the house there came a loud cry. Marshall had awakened from his nap.

Usually Mrs. Michaels would have responded by going and picking up her young son. Today she didn't even seem to notice. "Come on, honey," she called.

Elisa put her foot on the limb below.

Elisa's father encouraged her. "You've almost made it."

Elisa looked down. She saw all the cushions lined up to soften the ground. The earth didn't look so far away anymore either. Carefully she put her foot on the next branch. One more, and she was practically down. She let go of the tree trunk with her right hand and wiped it on her jeans.

"Here I come," she shouted, and she jumped onto the cushions. She landed with a soft thud.

Mrs. Michaels gave her a big wet hug. Then everyone grabbed cushions off the ground and rushed inside with them. Marshall had a wet dia-

per, but everyone else was wet all over and had to change into dry clothes.

Afterward, while Marshall was sitting in the booster seat drinking milk from his training cup and eating a cookie, Mrs. Michaels went to get her hair dryer. This time it wasn't for drying her hair. She aimed it at the sofa and chair cushions to dry them.

Russell told Elisa that he'd play a game of checkers with her.

"Good," she said. "Checkers is more fun than climbing trees."

"It's a whole lot safer," said Mr. Michaels.

"And drier," added his wife.

"Not if you play checkers outdoors in the rain," said Elisa.

"But we're not," said Russell as he double-jumped his little sister.

Dear Nana and Granpa,

Today I climbed up a tree.

I also made a bet with Russell. I said I could eat a whole jar of musterd. Russell bet me a dollar that I could not do it. He bought a jar at the supermarket. But guess what?! I never said I would eat all that musterd IN ONE DAY. Every time Mommy makes sandwiches, I am going to put a tiny bit of musterd on mine. When the jar is all finished, Russell is going to owe me a dollar. Ha, ha on him!

Love,
Elisa

P.S. Too bad it's going to take such a long time to get the dollar.

At the Beach

One day instead of going to swim at the lake, Elisa and her family took a longer drive to Ocean Beach.

"Have I ever been to the beach before?" Elisa asked as they were getting into the car.

"When you were a little girl," her mother replied.

"As little as Marshie?" asked Elisa, pointing to her small brother, who was already strapped into his car seat and busily trying to untie the laces on his sneakers.

"Marshall is twenty-one months old," said Mrs. Michaels. She counted on her fingers. "You were over three or four years old when you went to the beach."

"I don't remember," Elisa said.

"I do," chimed in Russell. "I made a castle out of sand, and you knocked it down."

"You're just making that up," said Elisa. She turned to her mother. "Did I knock down Russell's sand castle?"

"Could be," replied Mrs. Michaels. "It's the sort of thing little sisters do."

"Sure. And today if I make a sand castle, Marshall will knock it down," said Russell, sounding annoyed before anything bad had happened at all.

Luckily Mr. Michaels came out of the house carrying the big cooler with the family's lunch. He put the cooler on the floor of the backseat, just under where Elisa was sitting. Then he checked that both Russell and Elisa had put on their seat belts.

"We're off," he announced as he got into the front seat next to Mrs. Michaels.

"What else happened at the beach?" Elisa asked.

"You waded in the water," Mrs. Michaels informed her.

"And you splashed me all over," Russell told her.

"Did not."

"Did too."

"You're just making it up. Mommy? Did I splash Russell when we went to the beach?" Elisa wanted to know.

"I can't remember," said Mrs. Michaels, turning around to face her children in the backseat. "But it's possible. Anyhow, splashing is part of going to the beach. You're wearing a bathing suit, so it's fine to get wet."

"What else happens at the beach?" Elisa asked.

"You can look for shells," her mother told her. "Sometimes you can find wonderful seashells along the water's edge."

"Last time I had a whole pile of shells, and Elisa threw them into the ocean," Russell remembered aloud.

"Did not."

"Did too."

"You're just making that up," Elisa protested again. She didn't think that she would ever have done *all* those bad things to Russell.

"Elisa is older now, and Marshall is too young to get into much mischief," Mrs. Michaels reassured Russell. "I'm sure everyone is going to have a great time today. We're lucky that it's such a beautiful, sunny, perfect-for-going-to-the-beach sort of day."

Elisa nodded.

"We'll see," said Russell.

"Why don't you just look out the window now and watch the scenery?" suggested Mr. Michaels.

"Okay," said Elisa. "Are we almost there yet?"

"It won't be long," said Mrs. Michaels.

Before they even saw the beach, the fresh, salty smell of the ocean came in through the car's open windows. Then Elisa gave a shout. "I see it!"

They had to drive for several more minutes until they reached the beach entrance. Mr. Michaels paid the admission fee and drove to the crowded parking area.

"There are millions of cars!" Elisa proclaimed. "Will there be room for us?"

"The beach is very big," Mrs. Michaels said. "There will be room for everyone."

"Don't forget anything," Russell called out as he jumped from his seat.

Mrs. Michaels took Marshall. Mr. Michaels took the lunch cooler. Elisa took her shovel and pail; Russell took the blanket to spread on the sand. Everyone, except Marshall, had something to carry.

"Who will carry the towels?" asked Mrs. Michaels.

"We can each put one over our shoulders," Russell suggested.

"Great plan!" said his father, patting Russell on the back.

Finally they were ready to walk onto the beach. The sand squished between Elisa's toes through her open sandals. It was finer than the sand in the park back home, and paler. Even though there were so many, many people walking all over it, the sand looked cleaner too.

They walked past other families who had spread out their blankets and towels. They walked around children digging tunnels in the sand, teenagers throwing balls and Frisbees, and adults sleeping in the sun. At last they found a spot that seemed just right.

Mr. Michaels put down the cooler and helped Russell open the big blanket. Then Mrs. Michaels put Marshall right in the center and sat down beside him. Elisa began pulling off her clothing. Underneath her shorts and T-shirt she was wearing her new green bathing suit.

61

"Don't move until I put suntan lotion on you," her mother instructed. So Elisa had to wait.

First Mrs. Michaels put lotion on Marshall. It must have tickled him because he laughed as she rubbed the white cream on his arms and legs.

Mr. Michaels went off and returned with a big umbrella he had rented. "Let's be careful not to get too much sun," he told his family.

Because Russell was so grown-up, he was allowed to run into the water by himself. Elisa had to wait until her father walked down to the water's edge with her. She didn't mind. There were so many people around that she worried just a little that she could get lost. All those families, all those blankets, all those umbrellas looked very much the same. Probably they all had peanut butter and jelly sandwiches inside their coolers too.

Now, without her sandals on, the sand felt hot under the soles of her feet. But when Elisa and her father reached the point where the water washed against the sand, it felt cool and damp. A

small wave lapped the edge of the shore and splashed Elisa's toes. Then a second and bigger wave came, and the water reached her ankles.

"This is fun!" Elisa told her father.

The two of them walked into the water until Elisa was wet all the way up to her middle. The ocean was so exciting that Elisa didn't care that it was freezing cold.

After a while, when Elisa's teeth started chattering, they returned to the blanket. Marshall was sleeping under the umbrella, and Mrs. Michaels was reading a book.

"Your turn," Elisa's father said as he took a towel and rubbed Elisa to warm her up. Mrs. Michaels closed her book.

"See you in a few minutes," she said, and walked off toward the water.

Elisa sat down on the blanket. "Where's Russell?" she asked her father.

"He's probably made a new friend or two," Mr. Michaels said, lying back on the blanket.

Elisa picked up her shovel and started digging

in the sand. She wished Russell were there to dig with her. He might spend half his time picking on her, but it was still more fun to be with him than to play on her own. So every minute or so Elisa stopped and tried to find her brother among all the other children she saw on the beach. Russell was wearing bright red swimming trunks. But about a hundred other boys were wearing red trunks too.

Then Elisa spotted him. He was walking by himself and picking up shells.

"I see Russell," she announced with delight. "Can I go to him?"

"All right," Mr. Michaels said. "But do *not* go in the water. Okay?"

"Okay," Elisa said, nodding.

She jumped up from the blanket and made her way toward Russell. But when she got closer to him, she realized that the dark-haired boy with red trunks who she thought was her brother was actually someone else. Elisa stopped short and looked around. She saw another boy who looked

like Russell and ran toward him. Oh, dear. That wasn't Russell either.

Suddenly someone put a hand on her shoulder. Elisa swung around, startled, only to discover that the someone was none other than her brother.

"What are you doing walking around all alone?" Russell asked.

"I'm not alone. I'm with you," Elisa answered. Then she added, "I thought I saw you, but it was someone else."

"You want to take a walk with me?" Russell asked.

"Sure," said Elisa.

"Look," said Russell, pointing off toward their left. "That part of the beach has hardly any people. Let's go that way."

So Russell and Elisa walked along together, passing children digging tunnels, teenagers throwing balls and Frisbees, and grown-ups sleeping in the sun. But after a bit there were no blankets on the ground and fewer people around.

The sand was coarser, and there were more pebbles underfoot.

"It hurts my feet," Elisa complained.

"Don't be a sissy," Russell told her.

"I bet the reason there aren't any people here is that no one wants to walk on all these stones," Elisa said.

"They're all sissies," Russell said.

Elisa looked back in the direction from which they had come. It seemed a long way to the blanket with her parents and Marshall and the cooler with their lunch.

"I'm hungry," Elisa said.

"It's too early for lunch," said Russell, moving ahead.

"It is not."

"Yes, it is."

They came to a large trash can. There were strange noises coming out of the can. Russell and Elisa approached cautiously.

"What do you think it is?" Elisa asked nervously.

Russell shrugged his shoulders. Elisa thought he looked a little bit scared too.

"Do you want to look inside?" Elisa whispered.

"Sure," said Russell. He moved very quietly toward the can and peeked inside.

"Oh, look!" he shouted to his sister.

Elisa came forward slowly. She was still a little frightened of the can's contents, but she was curious too. She peeked inside and was amazed by what she saw. There was a large seagull inside the trash can.

"He must have flown inside to reach some food," Russell said. "But he can't get out."

"Why not?" asked Elisa.

"Because he can't open his wings inside the can," Russell told her.

"Will you pull him out?" Elisa asked.

"Sure," said Russell. Then he looked at the seagull again, and he paused. "His beak looks pretty strong," he said.

"Are you afraid he'll bite you?" Elisa asked.

"Oh, no," said Russell. "But maybe I'll hurt him when I try to pick him up."

"He'll be so happy to get out of the can he won't care if you hurt him," Elisa said.

"He might be happy afterward, but he'll be scared and angry first," Russell responded.

The seagull let out a loud squawk, and both Russell and Elisa jumped away.

"Maybe it *is* lunchtime," Russell said.

"You said it was too early," Elisa reminded him.

"I could have been wrong. I'm feeling hungry now too," Russell said.

"We can't leave the seagull. If no one comes to let him out of that can, he'll die in there," said Elisa.

"I know," Russell said softly.

"I know what!" Elisa shouted suddenly. "We can tip the can over. Then the seagull can get out by himself."

"Right!" Russell exclaimed. "I was going to say the same thing myself."

The trash can was very heavy. It took all of Elisa's and Russell's strength to tip it over. Finally it crashed to the ground with a loud thud.

A moment later the seagull came walking out. He strutted a bit on the ground before letting out a loud cawing sound and flying off.

"We saved him!" Elisa said.

"Yeah! We did!" Russell agreed.

Walking back toward the blanket, Elisa was so excited about saving the seagull that she didn't even notice the pebbles cutting into her feet. She didn't notice the beach attendant who approached them either.

"Hey, you kids," he called out. "I saw what you did."

"You did?" asked Russell.

"Yes. We want to keep the beach clean. Did you know that knocking over trash cans is punishable by a large fine?" the man asked in an angry voice.

"We don't have any money to pay a fine," said Russell.

"Anyhow, we didn't do anything bad," said Elisa indignantly. "We did something *fine*. We rescued a seagull that was stuck inside the trash can."

"That's right. He was trapped in there," Russell told the man.

The beach attendant paused for a moment, then nodded, "That's all right then," he said. "We don't want the seagulls to come to harm."

"We rescued him," said Elisa.

"Good work," the beach attendant said, smiling. Then he turned and walked away.

"I was more scared of him than of the noise in the trash can," Russell admitted.

"He's not a real policeman," Elisa pointed out. "He didn't even have a gun."

"Besides, we didn't do anything bad," said Russell.

The sand grew smoother, and soon they were back in the crowded area of the beach again.

"Where in the world were you?" Mr. Michaels asked when the two of them reached the blanket.

71

"We took a walk," Russell explained.

"We rescued a seagull," said Elisa.

"In fact, we're heroes," Russell said.

"And we're hungry too," said Elisa.

So they sat down and ate their peanut butter and jelly sandwiches and told the whole story to their parents.

They drank lemonade and smiled at each other. "It's a good thing you were with me," Russell said to his sister. "It was hard work tipping over that trash can."

"I know," said Elisa.

After lunch Russell and Elisa made a sand castle together. Elisa was much too grown-up to knock it down, and just as their mother had predicted, Marshall was too young to be a nuisance.

It was a wonderful day for all the Michaels family. And for the seagull too.

Dear Nora and Teddy,

Did you come home from camp yet?

We are having a good time in the country. It is almost like staying in a house in Riverside Park. There are hundreds of trees, chipmunks, birds, a frog (I caught him, but he got away), and a snake (I didn't want to catch him).

The best thing about the country is that we can go outdoors by ourselves. But the second day I got into big trouble. I took a walk and picked some flowers for Mommy. There were all different colors. Later a lady came to our house and scolded because I had picked the

best flowers from her garden.
I didn't know they belonged
to her.

I was very sorry to do
something so bad. But I made
a big picture of the flowers,
using all my markers. It was
the best drawing I ever made.
I brought it to the lady's
house. She gave me a hug and
said she was going to hang up
my picture so she would have
flowers all year long.

Love,
Elisa

It's Raining, It's Pouring

The summer vacation was passing quickly. There were so many things to do in the country. Some days they went swimming at the lake. One day they drove to a petting farm. The children had a chance to see farm animals close up and to touch them. Russell tried milking a goat, and Elisa found an egg hidden in the hay of the chicken house. She was disappointed to learn that the egg wasn't hers to keep.

"I bet they hide the same eggs over and over," said Russell.

"How could a chicken do that?" Elisa asked her brother.

"Not the chickens, silly. The people who own the farm. They want you to find an egg, so they hide some in the hay."

Even though she had to turn in the egg, Elisa had a good time at the petting farm. She had never touched a cow or a horse before. She'd never seen a real live pig, or chickens, except on TV or in the movies.

Another day, just before their vacation was over, they went to an amusement park. Elisa rode on the merry-go-round. Even Marshall went on the merry-go-round. He sat with their mother and laughed and laughed the whole time.

"Merry-go-rounds are for babies," Russell claimed. He went with Mr. Michaels on the Ferris wheel.

"Do you want to come too?" their father asked Elisa. "There's room for you in the seat."

"Oh, no," said Elisa. She would love to go home and tell her friends that she had been on the Ferris wheel, but it wasn't worth the scare of actually doing it so she could talk about it afterward. She would just have to tell everyone about all the other things she had done in the country instead. Elisa stayed below and watched with awe as her father and brother got higher and higher in the sky. She was very relieved when they were safely back on the ground again.

"What are we doing tomorrow?" Russell asked as they were driving back to their house.

"Tomorrow's our last day," said Mrs. Michaels. "Then it's back to the city for all of us."

"I thought we'd take a nice ride in the car," said Mr. Michaels. "There's a waterfall about an hour away, and it's supposed to be very dramatic."

"What's a waterfall?" Elisa wanted to know.

"Don't you know anything?" Russell asked her. "It's water rushing down a mountain, sort of like a big faucet that's turned on and never turned off."

"I never saw a waterfall," said Elisa. "Did you?" she asked her brother.

"I saw it in a movie," said Russell. He shrugged his shoulders. "It's not such a big deal."

"Well, it's something Mommy and I would enjoy," said Mr. Michaels. "I thought we'd pack a picnic and have a relaxing last day in the country before we return home."

"What kind of sandwiches?" asked Russell.

"Whatever you like," said his mother. "We'll stop at the supermarket on the way to the house. I can buy cold cuts or whatever you want."

"Fry! Fry!" shouted Marshall, remembering the french fries he had eaten at lunchtime in the amusement park.

"We can't have french fries, silly," Elisa told her little brother. "They'd get cold in the cooler."

The next morning the sky was very gray. "It looks like it's going to rain," Russell announced.

"Maybe it will clear up," his mother called from the kitchen. She was already making the picnic lunch: roast beef on rolls for Russell and his father, tuna fish for Elisa and herself, a cheese sandwich for Marshall, and chocolate chip cookies for everyone.

"Don't forget the grapes," said Elisa.

"I won't."

Mr. Michaels opened the door and walked outside. "It sure looks like rain," he said.

"Maybe it will shower and clear up," said his wife hopefully.

"We could still go even if it's raining," suggested Elisa. "We could eat our picnic in the car."

"How can you see a waterfall in the rain?" Russell asked. "It won't look special if water is falling *everywhere*. We can stay home and watch TV."

"No TV," said Mrs. Michaels, shutting the cooler with all the food inside.

"Finish up your breakfast, and then you can write some postcards. Maybe by the time you finish, the weather will have improved," said Mr. Michaels.

Elisa wrote a postcard to old Mrs. W., their

neighbor back home. And then she wrote a letter to her friend Annie Chu. Russell wrote to his two best friends from school. "How many *r*'s in *Ferris*?" he called out. Elisa knew just what he was writing when she heard that.

By the time they finished their cards, it had begun to rain.

Elisa rushed to the window to look out. First the rain came down gently, but it seemed to get harder and harder the longer she looked.

"This doesn't look like a good day for our drive," Mr. Michaels admitted when he joined her at the window.

"Good," said Russell. "I didn't really want to go see an old waterfall anyhow."

"I did," said Elisa.

"Then keep looking out the window," Russell replied. "That's a waterfall out there too."

"Well, at least lunch is all ready whenever we are," said Mrs. Michaels.

"I know," said Elisa. "We could still have a picnic."

"Big deal," commented Russell. "We're going to eat sandwiches for lunch and call it a picnic. Yippee."

"We won't sit at the table," Elisa informed him. "We'll pretend we're outdoors. And we'll take the blanket and spread it on the floor and sit on it. Just like we were outside."

"Outside. Outside!" Marshall crowed happily.

"That sounds dumb. Where will we put the blanket?" Russell asked grumpily.

"Daddy. Get the cooler," Elisa instructed her father.

"How about saying please?" he reminded her.

"Please get the cooler," Elisa said. "And, Russell, please get the blanket. And, Mommy, you can hold Marshall's hand. And I'll lead the way. We'll pretend we're walking in the woods."

"Boy, this is really dumb," said Russell as they all lined up.

"Be a sport, Russell," said Mr. Michaels.

Elisa led the way. First she walked through the kitchen area. Then she walked into the living room–dining room space. All her family followed behind. Next Elisa went up the stairs to the big bedroom where her parents slept. This took a while, as Marshall was still perfecting his stair-climbing skills.

"I wonder what the name of this mountain is," Mrs. Michaels said.

"It must be Staircase Mountain," her husband responded.

When they reached the bedroom, Elisa said, "I see a hill." She pointed to the center of the room.

"It sure looks like a bed to me," said Russell.

Elisa ignored his comment and moved on. She left the bedroom and walked into the room where she and Marshall slept. "Look at those beautiful trees," she said, pointing to a painting of evergreens that hung on one wall.

"It sure looks—," Russell began, but his father gave him a poke.

"Like trees," Russell concluded.

Elisa turned and went to the bathroom.

Everyone crowded inside with her. In the bath-room she turned on the faucet in the sink.

"Look!" she exclaimed. "There's a waterfall."

"Well, so it is," agreed Mrs. Michaels. "It's not quite as big as Niagara Falls or even the falls we were originally planning to visit. But it certainly is a waterfall."

"Too bad they don't sell picture postcards here," said Russell.

Elisa turned off the faucet. "Follow me," she told her family.

They went back down Staircase Mountain and into the living room–dining room area. "This looks like a perfect spot for a picnic!" Elisa exclaimed. "Let's spread our blanket here."

"This is nuts," Russell muttered. Still, he opened the blanket and spread it on top of the carpet.

"This is a lovely spot you picked, Elisa," said Mrs. Michaels as they all sat down. "Look at that beautiful green bush over there." She pointed to the green armchair across the way.

"I'd rather sit in that bush," said Russell, getting up.

"No. It might be full of thorns or prickles," said Mr. Michaels, grabbing hold of his son and pulling him back down again.

Mrs. Michaels opened the cooler to remove all their sandwiches for lunch.

"May I have a napkin?" Mr. Michaels asked his wife.

Mrs. Michaels looked inside the cooler. "Oh, dear," she exclaimed. "I forgot to pack the napkins."

"I'll go get them," her husband said, putting his sandwich down and standing up.

"Daddy, we're in the woods. There are no napkins in the woods," Elisa shouted.

"Oh, I forgot," Mr. Michaels said, and sat down again.

Russell let out a snicker. "I hope no one has to go to the bathroom here in the woods."

"More. More," Marshall called out. He had

eaten his quarter sandwich and was ready for the next segment.

"I love tuna fish sandwiches in the woods," said Elisa, chewing happily on her lunch.

"Roast beef tastes good anywhere," said Russell.

They ate their sandwiches, and the grapes and the chocolate chip cookies. Russell and Elisa and Marshall drank apple juice while their parents drank iced tea.

"Now what?" asked Russell when all the food was consumed. "Can we go *home* now?"

"It's too early," said Elisa. "Let's play some games. And tell stories."

So they played I Spy and Animal, Vegetable, Mineral. Then Mr. Michaels told them a story about the time he went on a picnic when he was a little boy and how he'd gotten lost.

"I wish I could get lost on this picnic," Russell said.

Mrs. Michaels remembered a picnic that

she'd gone on when she was young when the food had gotten lost.

"How could you lose the food?" Elisa asked.

"Everyone thought someone else had brought it. And when we sat down to eat, there was nothing except a roll of Life Savers that my aunt Virginia had inside her pocketbook."

"What did you do then?" asked Russell.

"We all pretended that we weren't hungry. But after about half an hour we all got into the car and drove to the nearest restaurant we could find."

"Well, that proves that this was a great picnic," Elisa said. "No one got lost, and we had real food to eat."

"We could still get in the car and go for a little drive," suggested Mr. Michaels.

"Aw, Dad, that waterfall just isn't going to look very special in the rain," Russell protested.

"You're absolutely right," his father agreed. "I was thinking about a shorter ride. Who'd like to go to the ice-cream shop in town? I thought there might be some people on this picnic who would enjoy an end-of-vacation-didn't-we-have-a-good-time ice cream."

"I would!" shouted Russell, jumping up at once.

"Me too!" shouted Elisa.

"Me too!" shouted Marshall.

They gathered together all the trash from the picnic and put it inside the cooler. Russell and Elisa and Marshall put on their rain slickers, and they all made a run for the car.

"That was a pretty good picnic," said Mr. Michaels as they drove along in the rain toward the ice-cream shop.

"There was just one thing missing," said Elisa.

"Napkins," said Russell.

"No," said Elisa, shaking her head. "Something else."

"What was that?" asked their mother.

"Bugs," said Elisa. "You're supposed to have bugs at a picnic.

August 13

Dear Annie,
    Tomorrow we are going home. I'll tell you all about our vacation when I see you. I'll show you the picture Russell took of me with my pet frog before the frog went away. Vacations are loads of fun, but I'm glad I'm going home. I love home the best.

Your friend,
Elisa

HARRY SYLVESTER BIRD

HARRY SYLVESTER BIRD

Chinelo Okparanta

MARINER BOOKS
Boston   New York

HARRY SYLVESTER BIRD. Copyright © 2022 by Chinelo Okparanta.
All rights reserved. Printed in the United States of America. No part
of this book may be used or reproduced in any manner whatsoever
without written permission except in the case of brief quotations
embodied in critical articles and reviews. For information, address
HarperCollins Publishers, 195 Broadway, New York, NY 10007.

HarperCollins books may be purchased for educational, business,
or sales promotional use. For information, please email the
Special Markets Department at SPsales@harpercollins.com.

FIRST EDITION

Designed by Emily Snyder

Library of Congress Cataloging-in-Publication Data has been applied for.
ISBN 978-0-358-61727-3

22 23 24 25 26   LSC   10 9 8 7 6 5 4 3 2 1

For all our people.
For our pasts, our presents,
and for our tomorrows.

Begin with art, because art tries to take us outside ourselves. It is a matter of trying to create an atmosphere and context so conversation can flow back and forth and we can be influenced by each other.

—W. E. B. Du Bois

We have fought hard and long for integration. . . . But I've come to believe we're integrating into a burning house.

—Dr. Martin Luther King Jr.

What if the ways we respond to crisis is part of the crisis?

—Dr. Bayo Akomolafe

PART I

1

Kizimkazi, Tanzania
December 2016

WE ARRIVED AT THE RESORT IN THE AFTERNOON WHEN THE sun was rising above the army of palm trees, lined and fanning in the breeze like windmills in the brightening orange and blue. Chevrolet and Wayne (I refuse to call them Mom and Dad) had remained silent for the forty-five-minute drive from the airport, except for brief responses to the white-capped, white-gowned driver (such as when the driver asked if they'd be needing the Wi-Fi access code, and they both nodded and said "yes" and "thank you" at once). In the spirit of solidarity, I nodded too.

But the signal had been weak and the connection elusive, and soon Wayne and Chevy leaned onto their separate windows (I in the middle) and zoned out as if they were sleeping with their eyes open. When the driver pulled up to the resort's gate, the Maasai warrior—with his red-and-pink shuka, his cowhide sandals, and his wooden club—rose from his bamboo stool and inspected our car before waving us in. All in an instant, the resort emerged before us like a tropical paradise. Behold, before my eyes: conical thatched makuti roofs flanked by the green fronds of the palm trees, white hammocks dangling between the stems, gold-trimmed lounge chairs with rolling arms and claw-foots, wide-beamed umbrellas, and, in every direction, lush and low-lying tulip and hibiscus bushes.

Wayne and Chevy had fought on the plane, and before getting on the plane, and before that, and I had begun to think that perhaps for once they had grown satiated with their fighting for the day, but as we stepped out of the cab, a new fight materialized: the taxi service had been included in the booking, but who would pay for the tip, and how much to tip? I was only fourteen and without any income other than the occasional allowance, but knowing them, they would have had me pay if they thought I could have somehow managed it.

My stomach knotted with their bickering, palms sweaty, head full and woozy. As if the car sickness were not enough, now this fight.

Wayne said, "Honey, it's Africa. One dollar is enough for a year's living. You don't need to give them more than that."

"Fine, I'll get it this time. But it was nearly an hour drive," Chevy said. "I don't see what giving five dollars will hurt."

In the end, they settled on two dollars. Two years' income, Wayne said, for less than an hour's drive. Chevy narrowed her eyes at him then walked away, dragging her luggage along. I followed Chevy. Of the two, she was the one to follow. Wayne often erred too far on the side of harshness, of cruelty. Treat others the way you would not like to be treated, it seemed to me, was his motto. No golden rule for him. With Chevy, at least sometimes there were surprises. As I rolled my luggage away, I heard the driver softly say, "Asante," and maybe the driver truly was grateful. Gratitude in principle and by practice. I knew a bit about that: this was late December, and our Christmas tree had been an oversize mother-in-law's tongue in a tall maroon urn. It was a houseplant that we'd owned for the preceding half decade. Wayne had insisted it was the perfect segue into our Africa safari trip. Chevy had insisted that Christmas was its own event and deserved its own tree.

Why spend the money after he had doled out so much on the impending trip? Wayne had asked.

Well, Chevy answered.

We laid our three gifts under the plant. My Christmas gift from them had been a nail clipper wrapped in an empty matchbox. Nothing to brag about. Still, I had made a practice of gratitude—a notion that I had stumbled upon on the Internet—and so I was grateful for the gift. And after all, nails grew and would always need clipping. Maybe this was how the driver saw it too. A practical sort of gratitude.

THAT FIRST DAY on Mchangamble Beach, after we had all dragged our luggage to reception, and after Wayne, Chevy, and I had been greeted with coral-colored drinks with miniature umbrellas, and after we had checked in and inquired about the Serengeti excursion (which Wayne claimed would be the highlight of the trip), we settled in our executive room. Wayne and Chevy placed their luggage at the foot of their queen bed, and Chevy hurried into the bathroom. I knew what she was doing in there: washing her hands and her face, and maybe more, before she would as much as touch anything in the room. She emerged disinfected, in a robe, and snaked her way through the opening of the mosquito netting that surrounded the bed frame. Pink flower petals had been arranged in the shape of a heart at the center of the coverlet. With one wave of her hand, she dispersed the petals onto the floor and sat on the bed. Wayne said, "But, sweetie, why?" To which she rolled her eyes.

"Harry, your area is all set up. Make yourself comfortable," Wayne said from the archway between the room and the expanse of space leading to the adjoining walk-in closet. He waved his hand as if to wave me toward him. When I approached, he headed back to the main bedroom.

The closet was large enough that, even with my cot, there was enough space for me to move around. I placed my luggage in a corner. There was no door separating the main room from the closet, but the arched doorway provided me semi-privacy. I sat quietly for some time on the cot, breathing in intentionally from one nostril, holding it for five seconds, breathing out the other nostril, until my head and belly settled, and the car sickness vanished.

"Breakfast?" Wayne asked Chevy cheerfully over in the main bedroom. It was afternoon, which meant that it was actually lunch-time, but earlier Wayne had argued with the hotel staff until they agreed to make a special exception and serve him breakfast. Travel delays, Wayne had said, and "It isn't fair for us to miss breakfast due to no fault of ours!" I turned my head away, embarrassed that he was beginning again. Wayne was doing what he did best—being a cheapskate. Breakfast was included in the price of the accommodation. Lunch was not.

"Breakfast, indeed!" Chevy said, leaping off the bed. But then she sat back down. "You two will definitely need to clean up first! What time did they say again that breakfast would end?"

"That's the beauty of it!" Wayne replied. "No time at all! Whenever we arrive, they will serve it to us!"

I walked over to the desk not far from where Wayne stood celebrating his win. Win upon wins. Even this trip was a celebration of a different win: the Purists, the third political party said to have splintered off from the Republicans, but who everyone knew also included many Democrats, had won the presidential election. All over our hometown of Edward, Pennsylvania, yellow-and-red elephant stickers, posters, and bumper stickers decorated front yards, windows, and cars. This trip, Wayne insisted, was a celebration.

Well. I picked up the hotel's restaurant menu, leafed through it. "It's usually over at ten o'clock," I said to Chevy. I brought the menu to her so that she might see for herself, but as I held it up, she whisked it away.

"Don't you dare!" she said sternly, flinging her hand at me but also keeping it from touching me. As if I were not her very own child, as if I were not flesh of her loins, as if I were instead some

foreign pathogenic prototype! Her mouth was a bag of knives. All
my life, she'd been cutting me with her words.

"You're covered in filth!" she scolded. "Have you washed your
hands?" My skin felt the slash and the stab of shame. I walked to the
bathroom to wash up, though I knew that even after I was clean,
she'd still recoil at my touch.

At breakfast, Wayne was jovial and whistled loudly as he weaved
between the people like smoke between stacks. Servers also laced
through the crowd, their greetings of "Jambo!" and "Mambo?" and "Na
wewe?" filling the room. By the time Wayne had decided on what
he'd eat, it seemed to me that he'd picked up quite a bit of the
language. But what business did he have speaking the people's
language, I wondered, much less being in these people's country
when he despised them so? But of course. The answer was clear
to me even then. Wayne saw them as beneath him, as servers, as
people to be exploited, and so it made sense that he'd come to their
country to exploit their services.

There was a frenzy to Wayne's manners—the frenetic movement
of his arms and the sharp way he jutted his head as he ordered his
meal: a vegetable omelet breakfast from the grill. He ordered the
same for Chevy and me. I had long ago learned not to protest.

We sat quietly, Wayne whistling a song I did not recognize. My
thoughts flashed in and out so quickly, I could not have articulated
them. All I knew was that they left me feeling anxious.

When our omelets arrived, they were decorated with carrot
pieces shaped so that they read "Karibu" and "From USA to Zan-
zibar" and "Hakuna Matata." I nibbled at my food, looking out
the open sides of the restaurant. Trees like windmills. Hammocks
like thick ethereal clouds. Empty spaces. In all of that beauty, I felt
hollow. "It is beautiful," I whispered to myself. "This resort is very
beautiful. This omelet is very tasty. These flowers are very pretty."
On and on I went, because something in my heart told me that
what is true must be said. Because if I didn't say it, then I didn't

think it, and if I didn't think it, then I didn't feel it, and if I didn't feel it, then it didn't happen. And surely, all of this was happening. Whether I liked it or not, all of life was going to keep on happening.

The resort manager arrived at our table the instant that I was coming out of my thoughts. "Jambo!" he greeted. His tall, olive-skinned body towered over us. "How are you finding everything?" he asked. His wet, dark eyes moved purposefully from Wayne to Chevy to me, his gaze perching on each of us.

"Oh! It's so wonderful to be here! Lovely food, lovely servers, lovely everything!" Wayne said. I cringed. The effusive praise wasn't what made me cringe, but the knowledge that certain topics seemed to gravitate toward Wayne, or he seemed to gravitate toward certain topics, like a magnet to iron, or like an object falling toward the earth. It was only a matter of time before the conversation arrived at one of those.

"Glad you're finding it so good," the manager said in a thick French accent. "You know, the workers here can be very lazy. Maybe it's the Zanzibari culture, but I'm glad you're happy with what you see." To Chevy, the manager said, "And you, madame? How are you finding things?"

"Very well, thank you," Chevy said rigidly.

"She's having a splendid time," Wayne declared.

"So, you arrived from the States this morning?" the manager asked, turning back to Wayne.

"Early this afternoon, actually," Wayne said. "And, yes, from Pennsylvania."

"Near Philadelphie?" the manager asked.

"About two hours away," Wayne said. "Have you been to the States?"

"Aahh," the manager said. "If memories could talk!"

"But they can!" Wayne said with alacrity. "Tell us! What took you to the States?"

"Long story, but let's just say I once had a nice life in the States. In Californie, actually. It all started as a holiday visit, but I fell in love with Californie." At this, he brought the tips of his fingers together to a point at his mouth, for a kiss. "Loved the place like I've never loved a place before. Long story short, I ended up over-staying my visa so that I could build myself a nice life there. Had a nice job, worked as a chef, managed restaurants, then things got interesting . . ." he said. "Not a very easy country to live in without papers."

"Oh my," Wayne said, visibly disturbed.

"We should be finishing our breakfast and heading out to the beach," Chevy said matter-of-factly.

"You're French, from France?" Wayne asked, and I could tell in that moment that a new thought had come to him, something that would make things more orderly in his mind.

"Yes, from a small town by the name of Soulac-sur-Mer. Have you heard of it?"

"Oh, I thought as much," Wayne said eagerly. "That you are French, that is. Then you're not really one of those illegal immigrants we find all over the place in the States."

"Ah, oui, but I was illegal for seven years," the manager said, chuckling.

Wayne stared at the manager, his mouth agape.

"When things began to get too difficult, I resorted to working under the table at the very restaurants I used to manage. You wouldn't believe, but I also had a period of a few years when I sold drugs just to make a living—pay rent, maintain my Porsche, put food on the table."

Wayne's mouth was even wider now, but then the manager said, "Ah, don't worry, I didn't use; I only sold."

Wayne's face lifted as if this were the beginning of a redemption. "So, how did you end up all the way here? All the way from California to Tanzania?" he asked.

"I'll have to tell you another time," the manager replied. "Like I said, it's a long story. My life has been one long adventure, and I'm afraid you don't have the time for it." As he spoke, he pointed to Chevy, who had already stood up and was walking away from the table.

"She's a bit particular with people," Wayne said, apologetically.

"No problem," the manager said. "Hakuna matata." His teeth glistened nearly enough to mask the wrinkling of the tawny leathery skin around his smile.

At the jungle spa, inside the massage pagoda, no one spoke. I sat with my feet dangling at the edge of the veranda, outside the curtains that separated me from my parents, waiting until the ninety minutes were up. My eyes hovered at a vanishing point somewhere on the Kizimkazi Bay. The ginger and papaya aroma of the massage ointment crept into my nostrils. Occasionally, I kicked up the sand with my feet. Why did adults even need massages? I wondered. Especially Chevy. Why was it acceptable for a stranger to touch her when she didn't allow her own son the very same right—or was it a privilege? She hadn't asked the masseuses if they'd washed their hands first, or if they'd showered before administering the massages.

Some months back, I had eavesdropped on one of Chevy's exposure-response-prevention sessions, and I had heard the therapist remind Chevy that the goal of the sessions was to get her to fight against the force. "Everything is contaminated, as you know," the therapist said. "Whatever force is keeping you so preoccupied with contamination—keeping you so restrained from life—you owe it to yourself to fight. You fight it by making one thousand correct exposure-driven choices. One thousand correct choices and the force will no longer have a hold on you!"

Needless to say, the force still had its hold on Chevy at the resort. Yet, the massage!

The dolphin tour was next on Wayne and Chevy's agenda, so I reasoned that if I could just make it through the massage session, then I could at least swim with the dolphins.

2

Kizimkazi, Tanzania
December 2016

INTO THE LITTLE BOAT WE CLIMBED WHEN IT HAD ARRIVED AT the jetty. The guide gave us large towels to wrap around ourselves. "You will definitely get wet," he said. That would turn out to be an understatement.

At first, the boat was like a boat, to be expected, speeding through the water, its engine revving louder and louder the faster it went. How shall I describe the water? Suffice it to say that it was bluer than anything I'd ever seen, and clear, like a watercolor painting. The way the line divided the sky from the briny deep must have been an image taken right from the Creation narrative. Rewind in time, the boat would have been an ark, and we, the animals.

But then the waves grew larger and water poured into the boat in what could not have been but appeared very much to me to be a deluge. Suddenly, I was sick. Sick like a dog. My stomach tightened; my muscles contracted. "I'm sick!" I called out.

Wayne looked at me and laughed. "Isn't this amazing?" he asked. The tour guide smiled with satisfaction.

"Wayne, I don't feel well," I said softly. Then, in a moment of vulnerability, I used the D-word. "Dad, we have a situation!" I said, tugging at Wayne's shirt. But Wayne was busy pointing somewhere far away, at the beach houses or the boats, and asking the tour guide a question that I could not quite decipher.

"We have a situation," I repeated, turning to Chevy. I reached out to tug at her, but I immediately retracted my hand, certain that if I did in fact touch her, a scolding would follow. I lay my hand back over my stomach. "Mom, I feel sick," I said as loudly as I could muster. But she, too, was busy with the blue expanse and with the wind in her face and with the beauty of so much nature.

Should it not be natural for people who call themselves parents to check in on their very own spawn? You, perhaps, can now understand why, for the most part, I defaulted to referring to them with a certain detachment—as mere wardens: Chevy and Wayne, Wayne and Chevy, certainly not Mom and Dad!

In any case, as they would not hear my pleas, I laid myself down on the boat's bench. The tour guide was busy lecturing on the dolphins. Chevy and Wayne had by now taken out their cameras and were snapping photos left, right, and center. I wrapped my towel tightly around me and over my face. This must be what people mean when they talk about seasickness. I told myself to breathe, and I began counting down from ten, nine, eight, seven, six, five . . .

When I woke up, we were on the pier, and the tour guide was calling out to me, shaking me by the shoulders.

"But the dolphins," I protested weakly.

"We already saw them," the guide said. "Ask your parents." I looked around and saw that my parents were a great distance ahead of me, walking in the direction of our hotel room.

I turned away from their diminishing figures to look back at the guide. "I missed the dolphins," I whined, like a question.

The guide smiled apologetically at me. "I tried to wake you up, but sleep had caught you bad, my man."

I trudged toward the hotel room, dreading what lay ahead: tomorrow, the trip to Stone Town and Prison Island, where I would see the old town and some giant old turtles. The trip would require us to take a car and then a boat. At least with the dolphin tour, I had been spared half the torture—only a walk to the jetty and then the boat ride. And even without the car sickness brought on by the gravelly, bumpy inner roads, still, the misery!

In this moment of lament, I remembered a series of thoughts I'd had on our drive from the airport. I recount them with a great deal of shame. The thoughts occurred after we had turned off the main road. They began with a memory really—of *Uncle Tom's Cabin,* tucked away in Wayne's office at the university. Those summers when he taught summer courses, I spent hours of my weekdays reading book after book from his shelves. In the cases where the words were above my intellect, there was always the oversize dictionary on Wayne's desk to which I referred. I found that I rarely needed the dictionary, though. I had, after all, been subjected to the gifted and talented program of the Edward Public School System as early as elementary school—at the Center for Enriched Studies at Wayne's university. I had taken, by that time, a number of advanced summer literature courses. I had become an established member of the Edward Community Ingenuity Project by then. Forget video games and cell phones. Wayne's motto was "Say no to screens!" And so, back in those days, I shied away from screens.

Academic intelligence aside, I must also have possessed advanced emotional intellect. For beyond the basic act of comprehension, I found myself utterly caught up in the emotional turmoil of the characters in the books I read.

Uncle Tom's Cabin was the book I read with the greatest interest. I was still young then, but I'd understood enough of it to be taken by its sentimentality—from the escape of Eliza and her son to the friendship between Tom and Eva, and even the eventual killing of Tom. I was not taken by the religiosity of the work. What struck me the most was the loss. Of course, at this point in my life, I only had the feelings; I did not yet have the language to express those feelings. It was only years later, as a teenager, that I found the words. Still, in my own nonverbalized way, I was keenly aware of the repeated trauma the slaves must have undergone each time they had to be sold. The persistent terror of being separated from loved ones in the blink of an eye. I must have loved Chevy and Wayne then. Certainly, I had tender feelings toward them in those earlier years. Enough tender feelings that I could not have imagined being separated from them. I was, after all, only seven years old.

In any case, as I read *Uncle Tom's Cabin* that day, I had not seen myself in the written description of Sam's character—what Wayne would have referred to as "the lazy, happy darky." But there was an illustration of Sam on a loose sheet of paper, folded in half and tucked away in the pages of the novel. I saw my aspirational self in this physical depiction of Sam.

And so it was that Wayne returned to the office at his usual time to find seven-year-old me staring at Sam. I did not notice the moment Wayne entered. I imagine he must have called my name once or twice, but I was so absorbed by the illustration that I did not hear.

He was standing right in front of me by the time I finally noticed. "What the hell is wrong with you?" was the first thing I heard him say before he snatched the picture from me and examined it. He lifted his eyes and regarded me thoughtfully. I remained silent. "What?" he asked.

"Nothing," I said. "It's a good drawing." I held his gaze.

Wayne continued to look at me, then, slowly, he began to rip the picture into shreds. We held each other's gaze. Each long strip of paper fell to the floor until the entire image was destroyed. Who knows how old the illustration was, or its value. Whatever Wayne saw in me as I looked at Sam must have been dreadful enough for him to sacrifice even a thing of great worth.

The simple truth was that I had lost myself in Sam's features—his full lips, his coal-black hair, his dark, penetrating eyes that seemed as if he were also somehow seeing himself in me. His jawline was sharply defined in a way that mine wasn't. His body was perfect. In that illustration lay a key to my selfhood, and I had stumbled upon it purely by accident. And just as soon, Wayne had snatched it from me. Till today, that incident remains the most keenly distressing memory I have of my childhood, and I can't exactly say why.

I'd thought of Sam that day on our drive from the airport. Sam, whose features somehow reminded me of the driver's, or vice versa. In fact, because of their resemblance, I had at first admired the driver. But then, with my admiration came fear. The driver was, after all, an African, and I thought: What if he is kidnapping us and leading us to a human sacrifice? I immediately became embarrassed by the thought and by the possibility that, as much as I had been trying to distance myself from Wayne, perhaps I had already been corrupted by him. Despite my best intentions, perhaps I had already become his son.

For the remainder of the ride, the two fears battled each other in my mind, a tug-of-war—the fear of the African driver and the fear of having already become like Wayne. And then, go figure, just as the two fears were about to reach a panicking point, an illness crept in—the malaise from the bumpiness of the road. Luckily, we arrived at the hotel's gate soon after.

Back at the hotel room following the bungled dolphin tour, the memory of that car ride descended upon me like a wet, dank, prickly second skin. I covered myself with my blanket and slept for the remainder of the day, not having any energy or desire to join my parents for lunch or dinner. Not that they had asked.

✳

THE NEXT MORNING, Chevy brought me a box of breakfast—one boiled egg, a croissant, a plastic container of yogurt, a banana. There were times when it seemed she suddenly remembered she was a mother, and I was her son. I was grateful for these moments. Yet they didn't make up for the lack of touch. Perhaps this was why, that morning, I decided, sick as I was feeling, that if she would still not touch me, not even to assess my body temperature, as I'd seen parents do on TV and at school, and as I was sure she must have done to me when I was a baby or toddler (I had faint memories of this), then I would not set foot on another tour.

"Come on, Harry," Chevy said, after she'd set the breakfast box on the floor by my cot. Her voice was softly flowing through the archway that separated my closet-room from the main room. When I didn't respond, her tone grew harsh. "Get up! You must get dressed now!" She began to stuff items vigorously into a polka-dotted tote. "Bring the breakfast box. You can eat in the taxi!"

Her footsteps thudded. I felt her aura hovering over me. "Harry? Do you hear me?"

I remained motionless. Touch me now, I thought. I am your son. Even the tour guide was not afraid to wake me by touch. Go on, shake me awake.

But she simply stood there. "Harry? Get up, Harry, or we'll be late!" Her voice bellowed. "Your father is already waiting for us in the taxi, Harry!"

Still, I did not move. It wasn't as if they'd miss me on the trip. She was only adamant about my going along because she did not want the hotel staff to find me alone; an unaccompanied, unsupervised minor was always some kind of liability. I was old enough to know this.

When she finally slammed the door and then fussed with the knob, locking it behind her, I breathed with equal parts disappointment and relief. I'd researched Prison Island on the Internet before we'd even gotten on the plane to Tanzania. I would have loved to see the old turtles, their ages marked on their shells. But I didn't mind being spared the history of the old town, where I would have had to endure the narration of the slave trade and a tour of the old site of the slave market, right there on the Cathedral Church of Christ. We'd be taken into the dungeons where the slaves were housed and we'd be shown the rusting metal shackles, the real thing from over a hundred years ago! And surely, surely, we'd be told of Bishop Edward Steere and of his work in the abolishment of slavery. As if that were really any sort of restitution for such a terrible institution. Never mind the bazaars with the colorful fruits and vegetables all stacked neatly on the covered earth—the lime greens of the bread-fruit and bright reds of the shoki shoki and yellows and purples and dusty brown potatoes unlike those in the supermarkets in the States. The beautiful reddish warmth of the place, and the pretty wooden doors that I'd seen online and would have loved to see in person. And yet, again, never mind all of that because there was also the matter of the whipping tree and the statues of the slaves with the metal chains around their necks, just like it had been, right there in Stone Town, over a hundred years ago. Yes, I would have loved to see the turtles, but I could not have borne to see the rest. It would have reminded me too much of Wayne, of the kind of people who were capable of capturing and whipping and enslaving other human beings.

I devoured the boiled egg, croissant, yogurt, and banana within the first hour of Chevy's departure, though I'd initially told myself that I'd be miserly with it, that I would ration it out the way the African slaves must have rationed out their morsels of food.

I passed the time roaming between the bed and the bathroom. Time moved as slowly as I had ever known it to move.

Whenever I relieved myself in the bathroom, I noticed a mounting hunger in me. Slowly I grew angry, angrier at Wayne and Chevy, but especially at Chevy, for she was the one who came the closest to caring about me, and she had fallen short once again.

Sometimes, I thought of the ways I could cure her. How to *cure* my mother of her inability to touch me?

By the end of that afternoon, I'd grown so angry that on my last trip to the bathroom, just before Wayne and Chevy returned, I looked at myself in the mirror but pretended it was her that I saw, and I said, "Listen, it's not real! Dirt is not real! Soap exists to clean you, not to give you a false sense of security."

I gathered myself and left the bathroom. As I walked through their room, my eyes landed on Chevy's luggage, which was, of course, zipped protectively closed. I unzipped it with a vengeance and touched all the clothes that I could readily see. "See?" I shouted. "You wouldn't even know that my hands have been on your things! It's all in the mind!"

Still unsatisfied, I picked up her garments one by one, rubbed my hands all over them. "If you won't touch me, then I will touch you by force! Take this!" I screamed.

I walked over to the pull-out drawers, where I knew she'd placed other items. The first one was her underwear drawer. I rubbed my hands all over her lingerie, her panties, her bras. I opened the next drawer and found her scarves, and I did the same. On and on I went until I had rubbed myself all over her leggings and socks and all the things I'd rather not have touched.

Finally satisfied, I huffed back to my cot. What kind of parents were they? To abandon their child like this?

In the midst of my outrage, I found myself wishing I'd brought some of my Tastykake snacks or at least some of my Little Debbie Swiss Rolls with me on this trip! All my rage had rendered me ravenous.

Seated on my cot, I remembered *Uncle Tom's Cabin* again, the forced isolation that the slaves endured in the hands of their slave masters, and I wondered, Have I become like a slave? For, if Chevy had only treated me more humanely, like her own child, not as a source of fear or disgust, then I'd not be in this position in the first place. I had essentially been imprisoned in this hotel room by a mother who saw me as contaminated, the way slave masters must have seen their slaves. And now, here I was, alone in a foreign country, at the hands of masters who had not taken care to provide me with sufficient food in their absence.

It seemed to me that my case was even a tiny bit worse than the average slave's, because my very own loved ones were the people responsible for my imprisonment. It was, of course, wrong of me to rationalize my circumstances in this way, and I rebuked myself for the inappropriateness of the comparison. Yet, I thought it still. I was, after all, suffering, and I could not shake this image of myself as a slave from my mind.

It is blasphemy to compare yourself to the slaves, my first mind told me.

But *I am* suffering, my second mind insisted.

But your suffering is nothing like the suffering of slaves.

I'm just saying that I know what it is to suffer, my second mind said.

I'm just saying that there's nothing special about your suffering, my first mind said. It's not even suffering. It's like comparing apples and ants.

In the end, I really did hate myself for allowing such a comparison into my mind. It was surely a consequence of having a father like Wayne. Wayne, who was always saying that Blacks had no real reasons to complain, that their plights were not much worse than the plights of everybody else. We were all suffering, he liked to say. To be alive was to suffer. I knew enough to know that Wayne was wrong, that not all suffering was the same. And yet, back and forth my two minds went, shuffling my reasoning, casting dark, streaming veils of doubt on the walls of my consciousness, until finally I fell into a deep but restless sleep, the stale flavor of umbrage hovering on my tongue. I had no idea when Chevy and Wayne returned and, of course, it did not occur to them to wake me up for dinner.

★

MORNING CAME, AND Chevy towered again above me. "Harry? Get your lazy butt up!"

This time, I obeyed. I went to the bathroom as instructed, washed off and brushed my teeth hurriedly, slapped on a T-shirt and shorts.

Chevy's voice was a strong wave, hauling me forward, and so I prepared myself for the Serengeti as quickly as possible. The old jerky road beckoned menacingly, and I did not resist.

We would take the fifteen-minute bumpy taxi ride out onto the main road, and then another forty-five minutes to the airport. I sat in the front passenger seat and inclined my chair so I could lie down. As the car sped on, I closed my eyes and listened with trepidation to the weight of my parents' silence.

3

Kizimkazi, Tanzania
December 2016

THE COASTAL AVIATION PLANE WAS A 5-H JOE GRAND CARavan, but it was anything but grand! It could have sat at most sixteen people, and that would be with everyone tightly packed as in a mob of giant gladiators in a miniature amphitheater. But, of course, this was Africa, nothing like ancient Rome. The great outdoors versus the Colosseum. Wildlife migration versus elegant and majestic Roman arches. Not saying that Africa was somehow less, of course.

"Make sure to look out for Ngorongoro Crater," Chevy was saying to Wayne. "You can see it from the plane. The wildebeests and all the animals we'll see at Serengeti live in the crater too."

"Isn't it also a UNESCO World Heritage Site?" Wayne asked smugly.

From the cockpit, the Tanzanian pilot answered, "Yes, indeedy, it is. A UNESCO site since the late seventies."

"The largest inactive volcano in the world, is it?" asked another passenger with the blondest hair that I had ever seen. He turned to a woman by his side and explained something in what I imagined to be German or Dutch. The blond man's skin had a thick and leathery appearance to it, like the French manager's at the resort.

"Indeedy!" the pilot said. "The largest, indeedy!"

Soon the passengers were asking and answering all their questions at once. Their voices trickled, poured, splashed around me like dirty puddle water. All that talk about UNESCO and the wildebeests, and yet they'd glossed over the most obvious—that there might be no wildebeests in the crater had the pair of German brothers who used to farm there succeeded in their mission of chasing all the wildebeests away. I had read it on the Internet. It was there for anyone to see, with even the most minimal of research, and yet. Either they truthfully did not know, or they were pretending not to know to spare their guilty consciences. If they *did* know, I decided, it was a lesson: One could have one's cake and eat it too. All one had to do was to cultivate a selective form of amnesia.

If they didn't know, no problem. Simply wear your ignorance with confidence, like a God-given and indisputable birthright.

On the descent onto the Kogatende Airstrip, the wildebeests, of course, and the antelopes were the first to welcome us, racing in the near distance, gently scattering the tall green elephant grass on the sprawling open plain that was Serengeti. The animals' bodies slid in and out of the grass with grace. Then off we were, into the safari vehicle en route to the wilderness camp, the sun and the breeze kissing our faces through the open sides of the truck. I soaked up the freedom that was perceptible in the open air. My lids became heavy with something like peace, and whatever resentment I'd held for Chevy and Wayne and for all the passengers on the Coastal Aviation plane was, for all intents and purposes, gone. No weight. I marveled at the power of a place to heal.

What were Chevy and Wayne saying to each other? It didn't matter. I closed my eyes and listened to their bickering voices. As the tall green and beige grasses of the plains swished this way and that, the sounds merged into something like soft humming, almost like a lullaby, and there I was, falling into a peaceful slumber.

We stepped off the jeep and onto the rich red earth after what seemed to me thirty minutes of bliss. The men who greeted us at the entrance of the wilderness camp were finely shaped jars of honey—you could sweeten your whole life with droplets of them. But especially the man with the darkest skin. He, not Ngorongoro, should have been voted one of the seven natural wonders of Africa, maybe even of the whole world. I had never seen anyone like him before. The softness of his eyes. The dimple in his right cheek when he smiled the most beautiful smile I had ever seen. It was not at all a sexual attraction, though it might have been as strong.

"Welcome to Camp Nala!" the darkest man said, stepping forward with a bowl. "My name is Benson, and this here is Abdullah, and to my right is Moses."

In the bowl was a stack of sage-green terry washcloths, and with a metal tong, the darkest man handed Chevy, Wayne, and me each a towel. The cloth was warm in my hands and smelled of mint. A fresh welcome.

I rubbed the soft cotton over my hands and had just brought it up to wipe my face when I heard, "You can't even see him."

Wayne added covertly, his lips barely moving, "If that isn't ugliness, I don't know what is."

Chevy laughed a little, like a cough.

Benson was still smiling.

Oh God, I thought. Not again. The way Wayne and Chevy liked to go on and on about people. Now they would surely go on about these men. "These Africans . . ." I recalled jokes that Wayne was fond of making, like "Don't you know, my boy, they're dark because they're dirty!" And he would laugh at the top of his lungs. Wayne sometimes claimed that his jokes were based on fact. This dirt joke, for instance. But from the movies I watched, I knew well that the "dirty" Africans washed themselves far more than Wayne or I did. The only one in the family who was sure to take a shower every day was Chevy. Left to myself, I might only shower twice a week. Especially in the winters when I didn't go out much and there was no heat to cause me to sweat. The fact was that showering took up more time and energy than I sometimes wished to give it. Not that there was much else that took up my time or energy. In any case, the Africans seemed different. Even in the "Save the poor African children" commercials that sometimes aired on our TV at home, the African villagers were often carrying buckets of water and washing themselves.

But Wayne was certain of their filthiness. I rejected his certainty and the complete confidence with which he (and Chevy) aired their opinions. This was how they paraded through the world. I had never identified with that sureness of self. My life was a perpetual question mark. Am I good enough? Are my motives pure? How can I make them see my goodwill? With this uncertainty of my own goodness in the world, I wondered how I could really be their child.

The darkest man put his hand on me and said, "G-Dawg, are you doing OK?" Looking back, this must have been the moment I began my slow journey into a new me. Of course, I did not know it at the time, but the mere question "Are you doing OK?" was a revelation—of kindness, of concern—and the benevolence made an impression. There was also the fact of the hairs on his arms. I noted them and wished I could be them, to be so close to the man, to be, even, a version of him.

"I'm OK," I stammered.

The darkest man withdrew his arm and said, "Great!" He went on to address the group as a whole. "Welcome again to Camp Nala! Here you will find the main lounge, with snacks and water and juice. You may come here whenever you like. This will be the meeting point when we set off for our safari adventures. Next door is our dining hall"—he pointed away from the group—"where dinner will be served every evening at eight p.m., after Camp TV session."

"What's Camp TV?" Wayne asked.

Chevy raised her hand as if she were in a classroom and said, "Excuse me, where are your lavatories?" She proceeded to mutter to Wayne and, of course, I heard, "I'm expecting to find it dirty and perhaps even unusable, but still I'll try."

I immediately thought, Dirt trepidation in a wilderness camp? Why did she even bother to come in the first place?

One of the men who had greeted us led Chevy halfway to the bathroom and then pointed her toward it.

"I'm glad you asked," the darkest man was saying. "As you will notice, there is no television on-site, but Camp TV is our version of a sitting room in the outdoors where we all gather to talk about our safari adventures, what animals we saw, what animals we still wish to see, and to generally get to know one another. There will be snacks, alcoholic beverages, and nonalcoholic beverages, all at no cost to you."

"Wonderful," Wayne said. "Lord knows it's gotta be a crime to turn down free drinks!"

The darkest man continued. I admired everything about him: the way he stood, the velvety texture of his voice, the salient whites of his eyes.

The clock struck eleven thirty, making me aware of the many more hours that remained before Camp TV would commence. I longed for the hours to race by. What better place than in the dark to consume with my eyes this new man, to be with all his beauty?

By the time the darkest man was preparing to show us to our tent, Chevy had returned from the bathroom. "Not bad," she sighed with relief, in a whisper. "Amazing, even. Especially for Africa."

"Really?" Wayne asked, without irony.

"Yes. It's a real flushing toilet and running water." Her voice was increasingly high-pitched and loud, but she must not have been aware of it. "I was expecting a hole in the ground and water in a pail!"

We all heard her. I cringed, moved my weight from one leg to the other, shifted my glance around. I observed the camp workers shake their heads in a rebuking sort of resignation. As if they'd heard it so many times. I imagined that this was the nature of their job: to be forced to coddle even the most misbehaving clients so that they might favorably review the experience and potentially bring in more clients. My jaw clenched, incensed as I was on their behalf.

Then soon enough the darkest man was leading us to our massive tent, which was nothing short of a five-star hotel room. The floors were wooden, and a net-like construction at the front allowed us to feel like we were in the open, as if on a patio, except enclosed and protected from flying insects and things. We'd only have to roll down the solid tent wall on that side to be completely shielded from the outside, but at night, if we chose not to, then we could look out and be with the stars, all within the comfort and protection of the net.

Chevy, of course, exclaimed as soon as we entered. "Wow! WOWOWOWOWOWOW!" she kept saying. Every once in a while, Wayne joined her, "WOW!"

I was also impressed, but I chided myself for being impressed. "Not you too!" I said to myself. Was I racist like Chevy and Wayne for expecting the tent to be less than what it was? I rejected the thought of my possible racism. No, I was nothing like Chevy and Wayne. I did not share their morals, their values, their worldview. I had almost nothing in common with them. I identified with people who were nothing like them. The place was just fancier than I would have expected for a campsite—fancier, not only for Africa, but for anywhere.

After he had shown us to our tent, the darkest man led us back out. We sat together and ate a picnic-style lunch near the area where Camp TV would be held. What was lunch again that day? Yes, a salad of fresh romaine, carrots, radish, and tomatoes. To go with it, some well-seasoned broiled chicken, the kind of chicken that looked like it once belonged to a chicken, which was to say, chicken on the bone, not the ground-up masses of patty that Chevy took out of a bag in the freezer and slapped on a plate and into the micro-wave. Those patties were supposed to be chicken, but, really, they could have been anything.

"Now you may get some rest," the darkest man announced after lunch was through. "A reminder that at two p.m. sharp, your driver will arrive to take you on your safari drive. Please meet him at the main lounge. You will be out on the drive until five p.m. At six, please join us for Camp TV, if it is your desire!"

✹

THE DRIVER WAS a short, wide-toothed man named Salim. He greeted us quickly and led us to his jeep. The decal on the bright yellow trunk hatch declared: LIFE, LOVE, AND THE PURSUIT OF WILDERNESS. Inside the automobile, Salim handed me, Chevy, and Wayne stainless-steel water bottles and blankets. The sun would begin setting by 4 p.m., Salim explained, and we would need the blankets then, when the wind picked up and the temperature dropped. "Now, let's all buckle up!" Salim instructed, cheerfully.

Wayne began just as soon as Salim turned on the engine. "The Big Five, Salim. I'll have nothing short of that." He proceeded to name them for Salim: "African elephant, lion, African leopard, Cape buffalo, and the black rhinoceros."

"Yes, sir," Salim said. "I will do my best."

But of course, that answer would not suffice. I knew Wayne, and even before he opened his mouth to speak, I could tell a retort was coming. "What do you mean by 'You'll do your best'?" he asked.

"Sir, sometimes the animals go on journeys or hunts and are hard to track."

"Well, then," Wayne said, "you really will have to do your best."

Chevy shook her head admonishingly at Wayne. "I'd really love to see the wildebeest crossing," she said, delicately, as if to pacify Salim.

The road was bumpy and clouds of dust powdered our faces. For several minutes the jeep sped along the open landscape. Out of the blue, Salim lurched to a stop, turned off the engine, and pulled out his binoculars. A moment later, he started the engine again and the jeep accelerated but the ride was gentle this time, cautiously inching closer, like an arrow homing in on the bull's-eye.

About twenty minutes had gone by at this point, and then Salim said, "Over there!" He pointed his finger to where the water glistened like silver tinsels beyond the grassland. My eyes descended on the rhinoceros.

"Sometimes it looks like a termite's mound," Salim said. "See that one eating? *Euphorbia candelabrum* is what he's eating. But it's poisonous for humans. If you touch it and then touch your eyes, you can go blind."

Wayne was already adjusting the focus of his Canon. "Can you move the jeep closer?" he asked. With that fancy professional camera of his, one would think that Wayne would have been able to get a good shot from a distance.

"Euphoria candleabrium?" Chevy chuckled, mispronouncing it. "Sounds like 'euphoria' and 'candle' and 'arboretum.' A euphoric arboretum of candles!" She laughed louder.

"Can you move the jeep closer?" Wayne asked again.

"Wow!" Chevy said, scrambling in her handbag to find her iPhone. "I forgot—I need to get a photo too!"

"Move closer!" Wayne shouted at Salim.

Salim startled at the raised voice, fumbled with the key in the ignition, and jerked the car forward. But then reason returned to him. He stopped the car and said in a nervously joking way, "Any farther and we might be in the water!"

✳

AFTER THE RHINOS, along the way to the buffaloes, we saw the zebras. "Zebras have horns in their upper and lower teeth and lead the way, eating the tall grass in order to pave the path for the wildebeests," Salim said. "The wildebeests don't enjoy the tall grass like the zebras do, so they rely on the zebras to eat those. In this way, they have a symbiotic relationship with each other. One gets to eat first, the other gets to see clearly in order to protect themselves from predators."

"Who protects the zebras, then?" I asked.

Wayne and Chevy looked at me with astonishment, perhaps because I hardly ever spoke, or perhaps because they found my question intriguing.

"Zebra skin is black and white like shadow and light to absorb and reflect light. This skin pattern also protects them from predators," Salim responded.

At a distance, a tall pink-capped stork was acting like a referee, perched at the sidelines while smaller vultures picked at a dead baby wildebeest. The stork hung calculatingly, waiting for the right moment to pounce.

"Salim," Wayne said, "I don't care very much for these zebras. How about we try for the leopard?"

"Yes, sir," Salim said. "But there are so many other animals to see along the way."

"Yes," Chevy shrieked in agreement. "It's important that we see all the animals along the way!"

"No. Absolutely not!" Wayne said.

"I think it's important that we do!" Chevy insisted.

"Weren't we on our way to the buffaloes?" I wondered aloud in a whisper.

"I prefer we go for the leopard," Wayne said.

"I don't see why we can't just continue with the buffaloes," Chevy replied.

Salim drove by a waterhole where dozens of hippos wallowed. I returned to a complete silence in the awkwardness of things.

"Have you ever seen two hippos fight?" Salim asked, nervously chuckling. "Very brutal and bloody. They fight until the death."

"Hippos?" Chevy asked, effectively distracted from her debate with Wayne.

"Who cares about hippos?" Wayne exclaimed, raising both hands above his head.

"You're a hippo!" Chevy hissed.

"All right," Salim said. "No need to see any more of the hippos. Why don't we try for the leopard now?"

I might have liked to see these two hippos fight to their death, I thought.

★

THE JEEP SPED through the potholed roads. Salim drove up a small hill and then descended. He backed out onto the main roadway only to drive up and around the hill again. He raised his binoculars, put them back down. He took out his walkie-talkie and whispered in Swahili over the line. I wondered who he was talking to. The darkest man?

Salim put the walkie-talkie back down. After what must have been at least an hour, the leopard emerged from a cavity in the sausage tree. At first none of us were able to see it, the way its spotted body blended in with the bark and branches. The leopard emerged even farther, leaving the shaded canopy of the sausage tree. Less than a yard from the Kigelia trunk lay its prey, a full-sized doe with its head hanging on its body by a thin tissue, the rusty-red blood flowing from the gash in its neck like ribbons.

"Amazing!" Wayne exclaimed.

"Will it eat the whole thing?" Chevy asked.

"Yes," Salim whispered. "It will eat it bits by bits, day by day, until there's nothing left of it."

"Aren't they supposed to be some of the strongest animals on the planet?"

"How can you say that?" Chevy asked loudly. "What about the lion or the tiger?"

Wayne's and Chevy's voices continued to rise, and I watched as the leopard perked up in their direction.

"Hush!" Salim whispered, sternly. "Do you two want to get us killed?"

"She says some utterly ridic—" Wayne began.

"We can't be so loud when we are seeing these animals," Salim whispered. "Either you will chase them away, or they will chase you for their meal."

The whole jeep fell silent.

The evening roared ahead of us between fits and starts of the engine and the arguments. When we finally returned to the camp, the first thing on my mind was not the darkest man, but rather how to nurse the throbbing headache that hours with Wayne and Chevy in a jerking jeep had given to me.

Back at our tent, Chevy showered first, then Wayne, at Chevy's insistence. The water had been warm for their showers—I'd seen steam creeping out from above and under the bathroom door—but it was cold by the time my turn rolled around. I let the water trickle over my body, then turned off the faucet to lather. I turned it on again only to rinse off the suds. The tent was quiet. Wayne and Chevy had already departed for Camp TV. My pajamas on, I ran to my bed and buried myself in the blankets. I was pleasantly surprised to find a heated water bottle at the foot of my bed. A Camp Nala notecard taped to the water bottle read "Enjoy the warmth!" It was signed by Benson. "Thank you," I whispered, and breathed with relief and pleasure as thoughts of the darkest man filled my mind. Benson. If I were to see him tonight, what would I say to him? How would I thank him for the water bottle? But first, it seemed sensible to ascertain whether the water bottle was a thing that he had given specially to me, or if it was something that everyone at camp received.

I climbed out of my bed and flapped open the covers on Chevy's mattress. Immediately, I felt deflated, for her bed also had a water bottle. I walked over to Wayne's side. Also a water bottle. Words could not have expressed my disillusionment.

At that point, it was past 6 p.m., and Camp TV was surely underway. At 8 p.m., dinner would be served. I decided to avoid the whole charade and stay inside, under my warm blankets. I climbed into bed, but the pit in my stomach was large: I was hungry. More than that, I wanted to see the darkest man.

Climbing back out of bed, I shed my pajamas for some evening clothes. Long sleeves, to fend off the mosquitoes and flies.

✶

OUTSIDE, THE STARS sprinkled the sky like grains of salt. The air smelled crisp like an open freezer, or like that gap in seasons between the Pennsylvania fall and winter.

At Camp TV, the oily scent of the triangular snacks that looked like spanakopita drifted in the air. I grabbed a handful of them, then found a spot by two empty chairs at the edge of the Camp TV setup. The food had a kick to it, and some heat, like the swelter of a McDonald's or Burger King spicy crispy chicken sandwich, except more. More pepper, more fire—an African twist, I supposed.

Voices rose and fell as the hosts took drink orders. The food was causing me to sweat a little. I asked for a glass of water, glancing around in search of Benson, but he was nowhere to be seen. My eyes landed on my parents just as I placed my order. It was the anarchy of Wayne's mannerisms, like a body and a mind at war with each other, that caught my attention. He had clearly had too much to drink. Chevy sat rigidly, like a block of ice refusing to melt.

I devoured the hors d'oeuvres, especially the spanakopita, despite its heat. After some time, I decided that I was sufficiently full and that I should head back to bed and try my best to forget about what I'd just witnessed. I might, of course, have stayed if the darkest man had been there. I would have loved nothing more than to be in his presence, the way people crave to be in the presence of their heroes, the way we all crave to be in the presence of our aspirational selves. But alas, Benson was not there. All I needed now was that glass of water. I'd hardly risen from my seat when Wayne's voice boomed, "Young lady, I said, could I have another beer?"

There was a silence before a camp host, a bald young man, approached with a beer on a tray.

Wayne refused the server's beer. "Young lady, I said I'd like another beer!"

The young woman whom Wayne was addressing now turned to face him. "Sir, I've told you before, I don't work at the camp." Near her sat another young woman. They looked vaguely alike. They must have been around the same age—in their early or mid-twenties. Old enough to be the ages of any of the younger teachers in my school, say, Ms. Rice, but not old enough to be the age of Mrs. Smith, the school librarian, and certainly not old enough to be my parents' ages.

"Where're you from?" Wayne asked.

I shook my head in horror.

"We're from Ghana," the second young woman said.

"Ghana?" Wayne asked.

"Yes," both women said at once, seeming bemused.

"Why're you here if you're from Africa?"

"Excuse me?" the first woman asked in what appeared to be an honestly inquisitive sort of way. For a moment, I thought that perhaps she really had not heard the question.

"I said, 'Why're you here if you're from Africa?'" Wayne repeated.

"Ah, I see," the woman said. "Probably the same reason you're here. To see the animals, to experience the beauty of Serengeti."

"But you're African," Wayne said.

"Sir, can I offer you this beer now?" the Camp Nala host asked.

"Are safaris only to be enjoyed by non-Africans?" the second Black young woman asked.

"But you can see for yourself," Wayne said, extending his hand in an expansive way as if to show the audience to her. "You're the only Black guests here."

"Oh, Chale," the first Black young woman said. "Pardon me, it must have been written somewhere in the book of life that safaris are to be enjoyed only by whites, yeah? The beauty of Africa is something to be experienced by white people alone?"

"Please, sir," the host begged. "Take your beer."

The first Black young woman stood up at her friend's urging.

Together they walked away from Wayne until they reached the area on the edge of the camp where I sat, cringing, my thighs so stiffly joined together that they ached. The first woman's body seemed made of prickly things. She shook herself off as if to dislodge some pesky burs, so agitated was she by the whole incident.

"It's all right," the second woman was saying. "He's drunk. He doesn't know what he's saying."

"He knows exactly what he's saying," the first woman said.

After a while, the first woman seemed to have calmed down and then her eyes landed on me. "Oh," she said. "I didn't realize you were there."

"Yeah," I croaked.

"What's your name?" she asked.

"I'm Esi, and this is my sister Nana-Ama," the second one said, smiling.

"I'm Harry," I said.

"You're not here by yourself, are you?" Esi asked.

"No," I said, pointing dejectedly to my parents. "Those are my folks."

"Ah," Nana-Ama said. "Poor thing!" she exclaimed softly, almost in a whisper.

4

Kizimkazi, Tanzania
December 2016

Night fell and night passed, and after we got ready for our second day on the safari, Salim met us at the main lounge. The sun had not yet risen when he drove us off in the jeep. As a bright morning replaced the darkness of dawn, Salim pulled the jeep off to the side of the road, under the shade of an umbrella tree, and turned off the engine.

"What's going on now?" Wayne asked. The birds were singing, and the sky was orange and blue like a flame or a flat-headed agama lizard.

Salim leapt out of the low, open doorway of the jeep and began to set out a picnic: egg sandwiches, muffins, jam, yogurt, coffee, and tea. "Breakfast is the most important meal of the day," he said cheerily. "First breakfast, and then off to see the wildebeest crossing."

"That's actually a myth about breakfast," Chevy said. "There's no proof of that claim. Check your sources."

"I don't see why we need to eat breakfast first," Wayne said. "We just woke up. We haven't even had a chance to be hungry yet."

Already, they were at it again.

"We are only wasting time with all this food," Wayne said.

"Yes, sir. We won't waste any time," Salim said. "We will go as fast as you can eat."

Salim was pouring the hot water into the tin cup for Chevy when we heard the rumbling of the jeep's engine. Salim, Chevy, and I looked up all at once. Wayne was nowhere to be seen. Then, the realization descended upon me: He was in the driver's seat. Salim must have had the same realization in that moment, for he immediately rushed around the back of the jeep in an attempt to regain control of the vehicle. He had hardly reached the back of the jeep when the automobile pulled away. Chevy dropped her teacup of hot water. Splashes landed on my arm and legs, and I screamed. The jeep sped off. Salim raced after it, his hands lifted high in the air, waving and shouting at Wayne to stop the car. Chevy began screaming after Wayne too, dashing after Salim, shouting curses. "You little cunt! What the hell do you think you're doing?!" I stood by the picnic table watching the scene: a thin dark man chasing a zooming jeep, and Chevy running after them, her brown hair flailing because her sun hat had tumbled off and was floating like a beige balloon in the breeze. Perhaps this was fine, I thought. Both God and the universe knew that I would have loved nothing more than an opportunity to do without Chevy and Wayne.

Under the shade of the acacia tree, I stayed quiet and unmoving in the hopes that remaining this way would keep the lions or leopards or elephants or wildebeests from coming for me. My eyes fell closed. Each time sleep threatened to overtake me, I shook myself awake, understanding the need for at least some form of vigilance, not that there was much, short of climbing up the tree, I could do if an animal came for me.

When I opened my eyes next, the sun was setting, and I thought, This is what it must have been like for Rip Van Winkle—to wake up and discover that the world had continued to revolve and rotate and spin on without him.

I blinked my eyes as if to clear them of the billowing darkness, but it was true, the sun was indeed setting. Why had no one come for me all this time? How had I managed to sleep so many hours away without feeling even a pinch of hunger, or any discomfort from my upright sleeping position?

The questions were still swirling in my mind when I saw a different jeep—a dark green one rather than the cardboard box brown of Salim's—pull up. The darkest man hurried out of it, calling me to him. "Harry, my man, you doing OK?"

I nodded and rose from the earth.

"Your parents, they gave us a scare. It's been an all-day affair getting back the car from your father. Salim and your mother . . . Well, everyone is safe now."

I saw my parents inside the jeep through the vehicle's low glass windows. The darkest man led me to the automobile. The look on his face was one of commiseration, pity. At the door of the jeep, he said with remarkable tenderness, "I'm sorry, G-Dawg." He proceeded to reach into his deep vest pocket, and the next thing I knew, he was pulling out a beautiful vivid blue, almost violet, crystal. "Rarer than a diamond," he said, holding out the shining rock to me. "This beauty can only be found here on the continent. It's yours, G-Dawg, from me to you, so that you will always remember Tanzania."

I was stupefied, incredibly grateful but unable to say anything. I simply reached out and accepted the gift. My eyes were heavy with tears, but I did not let a single drop fall.

As we pulled away, I fumed at the realization that Wayne and Chevy had actually gotten themselves kicked off the safari, and that thanks to their awfulness, I was now being forced to head back to Kogatende Airstrip with them. How I wished I could free myself of these terrible humans who called themselves my parents, but I remained taciturn, holding my words in like a pressure cooker not quite at full pressure. All of the hissing and rattling, but the steam release valve was still very much in place.

At least I had the crystal rock. I held it in my palm and stroked it gently, then turning from it, I looked out the window. Darkness had fallen but I could see the darkest man still, a sole shadowy figure in a beige khaki uniform standing a few yards away from a jeep, waving his arm slowly in the air. I imagined that look of pity, of sympathy, still on his face. I knew that his wave, like the rock, was for no one other than me.

PART II

5

Edward, Pennsylvania
January 2017

Iɴ ᴛʜᴇ ɴᴇᴡ ᴡɪɴɢ ᴏꜰ ᴏᴜʀ ᴇxᴘᴀɴᴅᴇᴅ sᴘʟɪᴛ-ʟᴇᴠᴇʟ, I ᴡᴀᴛᴄʜᴇᴅ them fight. I stood in the living room, the recently replaced maroon carpeting sprawling like a vast bloody ocean beneath me. I knelt on the landing that led into their room, my head curving like a question mark, my eyes peeking through the thin gap between the door and the wall.

Wayne and Chevy stood in the bedroom, positioned in the lounge area between the armchair and the ottoman, adjacent to their eastern king bed. Chevy's words were a stream of fiery ribbons flowing from her blazing red mouth. Wayne's arms were like an ax as it chopped down a tree. First create a notch, then hack at 45-degree angles, each strike opposite from the one before. Aim higher for the second notch. Strike again. Step aside and watch the tree fall. These were the instructions my grandfather once recited to me as I watched him work in his backyard in Centralia a few years after Chevy and Wayne moved to Edward, and long after Centralia had started burning, long after most of the town's residents had thrown in the towel and vacated, long after the trees began to die.

There my grandfather had been, weathered by life, all wrinkly and covered in age spots and folds of flesh, adamantly taking up space in his dear Centralia, the still-burning town. I must have been eight years old at the time.

Our home—which is to say, Wayne and Chevy's and, I suppose, my home too—was not in Centralia, but in Edward. When visitors came, Wayne sang praises of the new wing—the new master bedroom, complete with a bay window, high ceilings, and a marble en suite. The bathroom had a whirlpool tub and a sit-in shower, its stall large enough to house a family of five, as well as two expansive his-and-her sinks. Again and again, Wayne shepherded his colleagues to the wing, and I waited patiently for their *ooohh*s and *aaahh*s as the tour came to its end point at the old living room. There, I was often made to sit, pretending to be invisible—a fixed element, like the leather couch or the crawling English ivy in the white lace ceramic vase.

In the preceding years, the house had been a rectangular box of burgundy wood planks and dusty brown bricks. The carpeting, which ran through the entire interior except the kitchen and bathrooms, was a dirty beige. Even the staircase wore the dirty beige like a tired old wedding gown. That carpeting must have been there from the day the house was first built, in 1983. The original owners had eventually sold the dwelling and moved far, far away from Edward. They had predicted, due to the increasing torpescence of the citizens—already manifest in the economic downturn of the place, combined with the town's excessive production of waste and the mounting costs of municipal trash disposal—that soon enough the town would burn down like Centralia. They had predicted that Edward would inevitably be turned off by the government, that it would be taken off the revenue and funding maps, its schools and churches and local parks and post offices—all of its community buildings—officially closed, until it disappeared altogether like a defunct language off the surface of mouths, and of the earth. Of course, Centralia was further along on this path, having dropped from a population of one thousand people in 1980 to sixty-three ten years later. Now, only seven. All that remained was for Centralia to disappear from our collective memories and then from our lips.

But Wayne and Chevy had stayed near enough to Centralia because family was blood, and blood was love, they said. I disagreed. Despite my brief existence on earth, I knew enough to know that blood was not in fact love. Love was love because of memory. Love without memory was null. Blood with the wrong kind of memory was also null.

But Wayne and Chevy had insisted that blood was love, and all these years later, there was talk that Edward would soon be turned off as well—jobs were now hard to find, an increasing number of homes were going into disrepair and then eventually abandoned, even the town hall and the once-thriving Edward Hotel had boarded-up windows. Garbage abounded. People had begun fleeing the town, and no new residents were coming in to take their place. Imminent death, so the word on the street went.

Wayne was not interested in the rumors. Rumors were like the heartbeat of an old man on his deathbed. One moment a flurry of activity, the next moment a flatline. He was interested in the house, and in the fact that he had finally managed to renovate it.

"What a beautiful renovation job," the visitors often said. But what Wayne must have heard was *We clap heartily for you, for you must be responsible for it!*

But I knew that, fundamentally, Wayne was not responsible for the new wing. The batch of itinerant Mexicans were, with their yellow hazard hats and their browning gloves and their quick paces. Wayne had chosen the Mexicans because he knew he could squeeze labor out of them like juice from an orange, and for much less pay than a documented crew. He said so himself. He was always so proud of his schemes.

With their large white van and their pickup trucks and their shovels and their wheelbarrows, the Mexicans were the ones who tore the place apart and then put it back together again so that it was exponentially more beautiful than it ever had been. The Mexicans were the ones who deserved to be clapped for—or Wayne's money, at the very least—but certainly, *certainly,* not Wayne.

"Fuck you!" Chevy screamed.

"Fuck you!" Wayne screamed back.

My hate for them grew considerably every day. I know a child ought not to feel this way toward his parents, but what other option did I have? As you can gather, their behavior gave me no other choice.

In the moment that Wayne spit on Chevy, the pounding in my head began again. Chevy wiped off the spit with a fan of her pale hand, then spun on her feet like a ricochet. Her dirty sage-green robe sashayed around her calves. She stormed away. She wrung her arms around her body as she huffed her way toward the bathroom.

I had just returned from school when I walked in on their fighting. It was evening, and as I had not eaten since lunch, I was famished. Their fighting made me even more famished. I turned gently away from their door, my backpack in tow, careful not to drop any of the books that I carried in my hand. I walked with my weight barely on my feet, quickly back to my room on the far end of the old wing of the house.

The full-length mirror that hung at the back greeted me when I shut my door. I stood in front of it, my backpack dangling ponderously from one hand, the extra stack of textbooks in the other. I'd fretted over my image in the mirror for as long as I could remember, undoubtedly for all the years I'd been in Edward Elementary and in Edward Middle School. I was nearly fifteen years old and midway through my first year at Woodrow Wilson High School. And having met the most beautiful man in the world just a month back, I scrutinized my image even more.

If I'm being utterly candid, what bothered me was the prominent paleness of my skin, which in my mind, predisposed me, at least if my parents were any indication, to wickedness. For one thing, my respect for people who looked like my parents, clearly, had been diminished by the overwhelming fact of their persistent crudeness. For another thing, I had by this time lived long enough in the world to know that it was people like them who were responsible for much of the damage and destruction and hate in the world. They and their kind were the reason I could hardly bear to look at myself anymore. I would have switched for a crooked nose or misshapen eyes or brown teeth. I would have switched for any of the hair types that Chevy ridiculed as being wild and stray and out of control. I could take down the mirror to altogether avoid looking at myself in it, but the mirror was also a savior. It fueled my desire to become other than I appeared to be. Paradoxically, it was the vehicle through which I could envision myself in a different form.

I'd been just about to fade out, to descend into my aspirational self, when Wayne's voice cut through the air like a knife. "Harry, you back yet?" he hollered from the hallway leading to my bedroom. "Harry? Don't forget to steer clear! Happy hour in an hour!"

It should not have surprised me that Wayne and Chevrolet intended to carry on with their get-together even after all the fighting, but it did. Should there not have been some acknowledgment of what had happened? Some period of time during which everyone could catch their breath and make up? There never was. Not with them.

I ignored his call, and when he had returned to his room, presumably to finish getting ready for their happy hour, I laid my backpack down on the floor. Tiptoeing quietly back into the kitchen, I made myself a peanut butter and jelly sandwich, then snuck out of the house, trekking a few streets over, just to get some fresh air.

A long time ago, Edward Elementary School had been a paradise for children. In the spring and early summer, the tulips and grasses and all the other flowers grew bright in the bushes around the giant redbrick building. The wooden sandpit in the corner of the asphalt playground was still there, back when people still saw the health benefits of playing in the sandpit—development of motor and social skills, mental relaxation. The world had already begun to grow rigid when I was in elementary school—everyone proclaiming the negative consequences of this, that, and the other—and the sandpit would eventually fall victim to the "everything is going to kill us" manifesto.

Other playground equipment had already fallen victim. The horizontal ladders had been banished because the children's hands got blistered, or at least I had heard Chevrolet and Wayne say as much. The kids had sometimes tried to knock each other off the bars, and the ladders were deemed at fault for what the children did. Also gone were the seesaws, which were blamed for causing everything from splinters to broken ankles and broken noses.

But at least for a long time there remained the purple tulips and white asters, and the path rushes and the pigweed and the mugwort; and the honeysuckles climbed the fences, leaving trails of green and yellow; there were also the dodgeballs, because the dodgeballs were soft enough, and parents had not yet gotten around to complaining about the occasional black-and-blue marks left on their children's flesh. And of course, there were the basketballs because, somehow, those were also deemed safe. The girls still had their colorful chalks, because the parents had not yet gotten around to complaining about the toxicity of those. Thanks to the chalk, the dark gray asphalt was covered in beautiful pink-and-orange hopscotch boxes and Avoid the Shark drawings and chalk mazes and the expanding concentric circles of their bull's-eye target games.

Edward Elementary had still been a paradise. And those evenings when I left our house to escape Wayne and Chevy's fighting, sometimes it was to the Edward Elementary School playground that I went.

It was to the playground that I went on that particular day. Being January and frigid cold, the flowers were gone and only a handful of children were around. I sat on one of the swings and slowly ate my sandwich.

A sharp whistling from the corner of the playground where the honeysuckles had grown announced the advent of some boys, about half a dozen or so of them, shuffling rapidly and then settling into formation, their hands up, trying to get ahold of the basketball or to block or to defend or whatever it was.

I watched the thudding of feet with dispassion, watched dirt-stained shoelaces whip up and down; listened to the sounds of their voices, panting and fighting over the ball. I could not be bothered. They dribbled the basketball by the sandpit, a low dribble here, a speed dribble there, a crossover dribble, a half-reverse dribble.

The hand on the back of my shoulder sent shivers down my spine. I turned around to see the face of a girl my age and immediately I felt relief. Something about her made me feel like there was a gate I could step through, like there was a warmer world I could belong in, and she was the channel leading to it. If she would only come closer, I thought, my life would feel just a bit better.

There I was, Harry Sylvester Bird, and as I looked at her, I wondered who she might be. She must have been new to the neighborhood, for I had never seen her before.

"The swing," she said. "I been waiting. You mind if I swing a bit?"

"Oh, sure," I said, at ease with her but flustered at the same time. I had lost track of how long I'd been there, and I had not at all noticed when she arrived, or how long she'd been waiting.

"I'm Flora," she said sweetly.

"I'm Harry," I replied, then I found myself overcome with the urge to say something else. What exactly, I did not know. I could not make my mouth utter a thing. Eventually, after I had stood by her and helped her to the swing, I said, "Well, I better get home," though I would have liked to stay with her longer. I chided myself silently for not having the guts to remain with her. How could I have known by then that, already, our lives were two separate lines moving at two different speeds, heading to two faraway points, and that nothing I could have done—staying or not staying—would likely have made a difference?

By 8:30 p.m. that night when I returned home, Wayne and Chevrolet were guzzling down liters of alcohol with their colleagues and friends for their Friday happy hour. I stood in the foyer listening to their conversation.

"The enrollment goal for the incoming class was eight hundred students," a man whose voice I did not recognize said. "It's never happened before—to fall completely short of our goal! Six hundred and fifty?!"

"OK, so you're well behind on your enrollment, what difference does it make? You can focus on the students that you do have. Smaller class sizes, a better education experience for you and for them," Chevy said.

"My dear," Wayne interjected, "you're completely missing the point. A whole hundred and fifty less than the expected deposited students? What happens over the summer after the summer melt? We could be as low as five hundred and seventy-five! Do you know what that means?"

"An utter crisis!" another man chimed in. "A shortage of a mere fifty students could mean a $1.5 to $2.5 million deficit for the university!"

"This is the very downfall of our education system!" Chevy cried. "Since when did we start treating education as a business? All this focus on numbers! You'd think we were speaking about the finances of a Fortune 500!"

"Fair point, but what happens to our jobs?! We need the students to keep us employed! We need full classes to ensure our salaries!"

"Perhaps we need to start rethinking our higher-education system, then! Shouldn't we ask ourselves what factors are causing the students, and their parents, no longer to look toward an elite private institution for their educational needs? Maybe the system needs revamping?" Chevy asked. "If you ask me, the students deserve more."

I had once loved her for exactly this, the way she seemed to value children and their welfare. There was a time in my life when I was certain that she loved me the way a mother loves her child—fervently. How old would I have been then? No more than five or six. But still I had the fading, thin, intangible memory of her love. This was one instance in which she was demonstrating, it seemed to me, remnants of that love. Surely she was aware that in fighting for the welfare of other children, she was also fighting for mine.

"It isn't like the medical field," Chevy was saying, "where the patients are beholden to the doctors for their very health, sometimes in life-or-death conditions. There's no life-or-death here. Pharmaceuticals mess with the medicines for capitalistic gains because they know the patients will still have no other option but to return to the medical institutions for care. Pharmaceuticals breed addiction crises because of exactly that—both the addiction and the cure for the addiction will amount to profits for the pharmaceuticals. Higher education does not breed dependency in that way, and even the status it offers is arguable. Everyone knows that status is a capricious beast of a thing and, anyway, status comes in many forms. Higher education is not the only path . . ."

When I was surfeited with listening, I climbed up the entry stairwell, turned right toward the hallway leading to my bedroom. They were on the left side of the house, glasses clinking, voices rising. As I opened my door, I heard Chevy. "Harry, is that you? Harry?"

"Let him be, Chevy," Wayne said. "What're you gonna do, offer him some booze?"

"I said, Harry, is that you?" Chevy said again, this time in a more singsongy fashion, and it was in that moment that I realized that she was drunk. Laughter and the sound of bottles knocking against one another filled the living room. The house smelled of dankness and stale beer, and it was only evening yet.

6

Edward, Pennsylvania
March 2017

THIS RITUAL OF WAYNE'S TO TAKE ME ALONG TO ALL HIS lectures began when I was a child. "Our special father-son outing," he used to say. Afterward, Wayne would stop by the grocery store and buy each of us a newspaper. We would then sit in the car for half an hour, flipping through the pages. At ages seven, eight, nine, and even up to twelve, it felt like a treat, to be invited to engage in this grown-up activity of newspaper reading in a car with my father. But by age fifteen, it was like being trapped in a pen with a large farm animal—a hog or a goat—whose ambient scent you couldn't bear. By fifteen, Wayne's aura was worse than a farm animal's. It could make even a strong-gutted person nauseated.

That particular day, it was cold outside and the prospect of sitting in a lecture room full of boring academics postulating about things they knew or pretended to know made me feel even colder. When I opened the door of my bedroom and walked down the hallway to meet Wayne, he was already standing by the front entrance of the

house. The door hung open. He was dressed like Mr. Rogers—
a zip-front maroon cardigan over a cotton dress shirt, and a black tie.
His winter coat hung on the briefcase that he carried in one hand,
his keys in the other. His hair was slicked back, also Mr. Rogers
style, its salt-and-pepper gray shining with too much gel. Something
about him looked contrived, like a Stepford husband.

I wore my usual black hoodie, which I'd pulled over my black
baseball cap, which I wore over my black do-rag, which I used to
hide my hair from onlookers, Chevy for one and, if I'm being
honest, primarily from myself. Over my hoodie, I wore my gray
winter coat.

"What the hell are you doing with that rag over your head again?"
Chevy screamed from the kitchen doorway.

I was astonished at her ability to see it even under all my layers.

"It's like a fat black rat's tail is coming out of your baseball cap.
What are you now, a hood rat? You want to embarrass your father?"
It never changed. This was the same line she used on me each time
she caught me with the do-rag.

I ignored her like I always did. She could not be expected to
understand.

In the car, neither Wayne nor I spoke. Wayne simply whistled as
if everything was fine in the neighborhood. At least Chevy wasn't
with us, or else they'd surely have gotten into it about his decision
to allow me to accompany him despite the do-rag.

There was always one sort of meeting or another, usually part of
a lecture series, or if not that, then what Wayne referred to as a
Town Hall, in which the community members aired their griev-
ances. An opportunity to postulate on issues they knew they'd
never be able to agree on unanimously, it seemed to me. There was
never a solution for how to distribute work more equally among
the junior and senior faculty, or how to improve the process of
ascertaining student evaluations or the current system of faculty

merit review. The list went on and on, and many proposals were written, but year after year, it seemed to me that nothing changed: the conversations remained the same.

What would have been a better use of their time? I couldn't have said with certainty, but I knew that it would have been far better to fix something than waste time in these idle lectures. Do a measurable, visible good in the world. Once, for instance, I must have been ten or eleven at the time, a man had given a lecture on Centralia. I was utterly fascinated by his lecture, for until then, I had only known of the town as my grandfather's town. But the man had charted the history of the place and, for the first time in my life, I understood what a tragedy the fall of it had been, how many families had lost their homes and livelihoods as a result. What caused it to burn? The issue of garbage—what to do with a town's trash? Burn it! Well. The landfill fire had caused a spark in a live coal vein, and soon enough the fire had spread through the old underground mine tunnels under the roads and streets of Centralia.

Even after the lecture was done, my mind continued to fixate on a possible solution: How to put out a fire in the veins of a town? That was something all the lecturers should have worked on. That was what they should have done: Come up with a plan and then enact a measurable, visible good. Put out the fire and revive the town. Instead, all they did was talk.

In any case, on that particular day in March 2017, we attended another lecture series. The lectures were to take place in one of the large university auditoriums where many of these lectures routinely took place. The space fit around 150 people.

As usual, fewer than half of the seats were taken. We snaked our way through the aisles, Wayne stopping to make small talk with several of his colleagues, before finally taking his seat, me by his side, in the very front of the room. As we sat, he leaned toward me and whispered that there would be four speakers. He would be the last one up. "Save the best for last," he said, winking at me.

I wanted so much to feel tenderness or pride toward Wayne in this moment. But this was the period of my life when his behavior so repulsed me, and I failed to feel anything kind toward him. I do not regret my feelings, and I'm sure you'll see why soon.

The first speaker was Latino, tall, looked like a person who smelled good, fancy perfume, maybe.

"Typical wetback. Can't even speak English properly," Wayne whispered to me. "This country is going to the dogs."

This was not an unusual comment for Wayne. It seems astonishing that a man would utter such a remark to his son, and in a public place nonetheless, but perhaps he believed that most people saw it his way, that they just weren't openly owning up to it. Why he should have such animosity toward people unlike us in the first place, I couldn't grasp. His abhorrence of others, which was already unbearable on our Tanzania trip, had only grown worse. I reasoned that he must have seen something in me—that is, something resistant to what *we* were and, as a consequence, he must have felt it necessary to double down on his efforts to make me see the higher status that we, by his lights, occupied in society.

But again, that particular day, I simply thought, What in the world is a wetback?

On the screen, the title of the lecture gleamed: "Memory, Trauma, and the Struggle for Citizenship in Latin American Narratives."

The Latino man's voice was silky rich. His lecture focused on the field of epigenetics and the ways in which trauma and social struggles had the ability to cause chemical modifications around genes, just as much damage as genetic defects did.

"They always wanna play the victims," Wayne whispered again to me. "If the struggle for citizenship is so hard, then why don't they just go back to where they came from?"

I thought about his question, and while I couldn't say for sure, I had followed international news and skimmed enough political books—*Breach of Confidence: How America Stepped on the Smaller Countries in Order to Rise* and *Corruption of the Promise of America* and

It's a Dog-Eat-Dog World: Well-Kept Secrets about the Rise of America—to suspect that America was often causing messes in developing countries around the world. Destroying other countries' governments and hospitals and schools and religions with the pretense of having something better to offer. Anyway, if Americans could go and stay in these people's countries freely, why shouldn't they be allowed to come and stay in America freely?

But I remained silent and busied myself by picking at my lips, sore and flaking from all the times in my life that I'd bitten them to keep from talking back to Wayne and Chevrolet.

The next speaker was a woman. As she took the stage, the screen flashed with her lecture title: "The Ethics of Food in Contemporary America."

She talked about M—Corp, the company that was destroying the planet by creating genetically modified "Frankenfoods" that could lead to greater incidents of hormone-related diseases, cancers for instance.

From an ethics perspective, she argued that the supposed goal of using genetically modified crops to feed the world's poor was simply a false promise. She read statistics that showed that genetically modified foods were pricier than the world's poorest populations could afford and not all that much less expensive than the "natural" or "organic" foods. M—Corp's real goal, she claimed, was to eventually have a monopoly on all foods, and so theirs was no humanistic cause, but rather a capitalist endeavor disguised as benevolence and philanthropy.

Being a rather precocious fifteen-year-old, I managed to follow her arguments. The Internet had schooled me already on many of these topics, and it was a fact that, though Wayne and Chevy had done not much else to encourage me academically, they had made sure to provide me with a laptop and a smartphone, via which I consumed much of what the Internet had to offer, for better or for worse.

I knew nothing of M—Corp, but I made a mental note to go back and read up on it.

As I sat digesting the lecture, I heard a pesky, fly-like voice at my ear. It was Wayne again, whispering rather loudly to me, "Lazy broad!"

Eager to create space between us, I eased myself like a lever to the other armrest of the chair. I leaned my head on my hand and pretended that I had not heard him speak. All I wanted was to be as far away from him as possible without drawing attention to myself, but then Wayne made a lever out of his torso too and leaned toward me, our bodies now diagonally parallel, and he continued whispering: "Probably couldn't get herself a man so here she is, talking about food instead of cooking it for her husband and kids."

I shut my eyes as if to shut him out.

When I finally opened my eyes, a man was walking to the rostrum. His presentation was entitled "Bridge Between Two Cultures: The Colonial Predecessor Dandy and the African Tastemaker—Narratives of Sapeurs in African Literature."

"It's possible that some of you have never heard of sapeur culture," the man began. "In short, it consists of men dressed extremely nicely. Think Versace, Giorgio Armani, Louis Vuitton. The idea is one of peace. That is, in order to preserve such delicate niceties, there is simply no room for violence or for things like war. A neat, orderly presentation is always utmost for the sapeur."

The lecturer appeared to be a sapeur himself. He wore a short cloak with tapering sleeves and a large tumbling collar. Around his neck was a polka-dotted white-and-lavender bow tie, and a matching lavender handkerchief peeked out like a miniature hand fan from his breast pocket. His feet were clad with the shiniest crocodile shoes I'd ever seen (the only ones I'd ever seen). They could have lit a dark room.

"Lazy bastard," Wayne whispered, as if echoing his previous accusation regarding the M—Corp woman. "Shouldn't he be eating watermelons in some shack somewhere and collecting welfare?"

He went on muttering something about the difference in water-melon consumption between Africans and African Americans. Same difference, he seemed to be saying, but I could barely hear him because I was suddenly so taken by the sapeur lecturer, whose dark rich skin reminded me of the darkest man.

When Wayne's turn finally arrived ("Literature of the Romantic Tradition"), he stepped onstage with alacrity, head lurching forward with each stride like a man on a mission. Beaming wide, he cleared his throat, adjusted the microphone with one hand so that it made a squealing static sound, and began:

"A number of studies have henceforth compared Coleridge to Keats. But alas, we know that no two more incongruous personalities ever existed on earth! Such incongruity can easily be perceived in their poetry, and I do hereby quote Coleridge:

It is an ancient Mariner,
And he stoppeth one of three.
'By thy long grey beard and glittering eye,
Now wherefore stopp'st thou me? . . .'
. . .

He holds him with his skinny hand,
'There was a ship,' quoth he.
'Hold off! unhand me, grey-beard loon!'
Eftsoons his hand dropt he.
. . .

'I fear thy skinny hand!
. . .

I fear thee and thy glittering eye,
And thy skinny hand, so brown.'—

Fear not, fear not, thou Wedding-Guest!
This body dropt not down. . . .

And I hereby quote Keats:

Who hath not seen thee oft amid thy store?
Sometimes whoever seeks abroad may find
Thee sitting careless on a granary floor,
Thy hair soft-lifted by the winnowing wind; . . ."

On and on he read, quoting various excerpts from Keats and Coleridge, giving the impression of a person going around in circles, digging himself deeper into a hole.

Finally, he said, "Alas, you, dear audience, might feel free to draw your own conclusions, for I hereby rest my case!"

His lecture ended with the same sort of force it had begun, his body lurching forward with self-satisfaction. I lowered my head, quite a bit embarrassed by him. For the first time since I began attending his lectures, I sensed that Wayne was not very intelligent. It seemed to me that he was rather happy to simply recite excerpts from old works, for his lectures always consisted of relentless quotes from classic poets. Where his colleagues' lectures consisted of matters that felt more socially urgent, Wayne's felt a bit, well, vapid. And yet, I admit that, though I was embarrassed by him, I also pitied him, so much so that it seemed my pity outweighed my embarrassment. He was my father, after all.

When Wayne began walking off the stage to retake his seat, I at first imagined myself gently grabbing his hand and leading him out of the auditorium to somewhere private where he would be safe from inevitable ridicule. But the farther away from the rostrum he walked, the more his look of self-satisfaction seemed to grow. By the time he stepped off the stage, his shoulders appeared almost levitating.

"That should teach them a little something!" he whispered to me as he took his seat. All of my pity fell to the wayside like a bad idea. Of course! I thought. Of course!

The event came to an end. The lecturers and audience members began to mingle. Servers walked around with their silver trays of hors d'oeuvres, carrots and celery sticks, cheeses, and small clear plastic cups of wine. As the adults reached for the alcohol, it occurred to me that I could do the same. I reached for the wine, but my fingertips had hardly touched a cup before the server said, "Young man, how old are you?"

She was an older graying woman who looked like a cross between a librarian and an airline attendant. "You know very well that what you're attempting is out of the question. May I offer you some Coke instead?" She smiled like making amends.

It wasn't as if I intended to drink the wine to get drunk. I was simply eager to imitate the laissez-faire attitude of the adults. My goal was to, in sipping languorously on the wine like they did, more comfortably admire the sapeur from a distance.

Suddenly, Wayne's voice arrived from nowhere, and I felt his hand descend on my head. "What exactly do you think you're doing?"

He dragged me out by the tail of my do-rag. "Have you lost your mind?" he hissed.

Through the auditorium doors, down the long, empty hallway, then outside the building's main doors, and finally out into the open air, the wind slapped our faces with a burst of late-afternoon March cold. "You think it's all right to embarrass me like that?"

"I didn't mean anyth—" I began.

We stayed quiet for some time while he revved up the engine and sped out of the university campus, down Market Street and then left onto Twelfth Street. As I've said before, the ritual surrounding our post-lecture activities involved the stop at the Giant supermarket. But it was unusual when, after parking in our usual spot, Wayne placed both his hands on the steering wheel and exhaled deeply. "All right, all right," he said. "Wayne, you've got to get a grip. You've just got to!" He then leapt out of the car a bit too eagerly like a happy kangaroo.

I waited, confused, in the car. In a few minutes, he was back with two newspapers in hand. One he handed to me, the other he kept for himself.

"There you go, Son," he said. But I left the newspaper where he'd set it on my thighs.

"Son, am I talking to a wall?" he asked. "Go on, take a read. Believe me, these things will soon be extinct. This is a real privilege that I'm providing you with. You'll thank me one day for giving you the experience!" On and on he went. "Harry? You're gonna read it or what? . . . Harry?"

Whether to shut him up or because I knew it to be true—that newspapers were indeed going defunct, and it was a sort of treat to get to read them next to him—I exhaled and silently began flipping the pages.

Only five minutes must have gone by before I heard the sounds—soft at first, barely there. The day had been cold, and the wind made it feel colder. The sound might have been the wind smacking the body of the car with thick gusts of air. At this point, I should say that Wayne was called Wayne, as in the Amish name for "wagon driver." He was not, and to my knowledge had never been, a wagon driver. But he did drive a Ford, which was the SUV in which we now sat. Chevy, incidentally, was named Chevy, as in Chevrolet, as in the American motor company. Her parents had named her after their greatest desire, which was to one day own a Chevy. Later, years after she was born, they purchased a blue Chevrolet Monza (this much Chevy once told me), and they'd then considered having another child, just to have the opportunity to name that child Monza. Poor child, but wise child too—it seemed to me a sign of its wisdom that it had refused to come. It isn't easy having to live one's life answering to the wrong name. Alternatively, sometimes I wondered why my grandparents hadn't aspired to a Bentley or a Lamborghini, or even a Toyota—those might have made for more interesting names for a child.

But I digress.

I heard the sound, coming from Wayne's side as we sat in his Ford SUV. I turned to regard him. He was holding the newspaper way up so that the open pages flanked each of his cheeks. His face was covered, but I recognized the sounds. He was sobbing.

Since our return from Tanzania, "Dad" was a word I had firmly decided not to use for him, just as I had also decided never again to call Chevy "Mom." But there were moments of vulnerability—his, hers, mine—when I reflexively reverted to those words. This was one of them. In all my life, I'd never witnessed the man cry. I looked at his body, molded dejectedly as it was around the steering wheel. Accompanied by those sounds, I could not help myself. "Dad?" I said softly. "Dad, are you OK?" His sobbing grew louder. His body trembled under the newspaper, and the newspaper trembled with him.

Alarmed, I moved toward Wayne, shuffled myself so that my body was spread over the console, the gear stick jutting into my ribs. I leaned my body on my father's and wrapped my arms around him. By now the sobbing was becoming tremendous and I *shhh*ed Wayne as gently as I could manage, and I whispered words that seemed to come out of me from nowhere—"I'm so sorry, Dad. Please don't cry, Dad. Everything will be all right." But how could I say that everything would be all right if I wasn't even sure what the issue was? I chided myself, ordered myself to shut up. I assured myself that there was no need for words. Better not to say anything at all than to give false reassurance. I resigned myself to simply holding Wayne. We remained quiet together, son leaning against father. "Please, Dad," I said again. But his sobbing would not cease. There he was, Wayne, unlike the Wayne I'd ever known, shockingly vulnerable, naked with his emotions in front of me. I was moved by his crying, so profoundly that I suddenly felt I should let him be, turn away to give him some privacy. I had not yet shifted when his sobbing finally began to ease up. Between sobs, he said, "What a crying shame, Son. What a crying shame."

Then we sat once more in silence. I straightened myself and shifted back to the passenger seat. Finally, his body ceased its quivering. When he turned to me, his face was pink and blotchy like the inside of an unripe seedless watermelon. He took a few deep breaths to steady himself, then he said, "Son, I've been robbed. Just trying to pull myself together, finish out my obligations, but the truth remains—I've been robbed."

I listened with concern, not quite understanding.

"What this means, Son, is that things are gonna be difficult for us for some time." He broke down into an even more profound fit of sobbing, muttering about the failure of the academy.

There was a silence before Wayne said, "How dare they give it to him and not me? How dare they? Tell me, what difference will one more tenured Black man make for the larger world?"

Goosebumps rose on my skin. I was suddenly aware of myself. My face flushed. It seemed clear to me in that moment that the blood that flowed in my veins was of a different variety than the blood that flowed in Wayne's veins.

Giant supermarket was less than two miles from our house. Pedestrian walkways lined the roads. I didn't say anything to Wayne. I simply tossed the hood of my sweatshirt over my head, opened the passenger side door, and climbed out of the SUV. Behind me, I gently shut the door and began the cold walk home.

✱

THE NIGHT HAD been relatively quiet, but by morning it was as if their voices had grown talons. Even with the television in the background—F*X News, I was certain—their voices reverberated through my walls.

"Shouldn't you have thought of that beforehand?" Chevy was asking.

"It was worth it for the equity alone," Wayne replied.

"Equity?! How does equity help us if you will soon be jobless? It isn't even enough that you'll be jobless—now we also have a new loan on our shoulders? Equity?! What difference does equity make?"

"I don't expect that you'll understand," Wayne said calmly, like a reasonable non-concession.

I myself did not understand, though I had tried very hard to understand. Wayne was always throwing out that word, and so I had looked it up one day. Even with all my reading, equity still seemed to me an abstract concept, a virtual, intangible marker of wealth that in the end amounted to zero dollars in your pocket unless he sold the house on the spot. And as Wayne had no intention of selling the house anytime soon, what use was equity to him? Either way he'd be stuck paying for the house; and either way he'd be stuck with a loan.

"But I'm telling you, it's the problem with the country," Wayne was saying. "Don't blame me. *They're* the ones taking away our jobs. Soon they'll come for yours too."

Years ago, Chevy had traveled to Stockbridge for her Ayurveda certification. A few hundred hours of coursework in Massachusetts had rendered her a master of a thousand-plus-year-old traditional ancient Indian medicine. Her clinic was at the corner of Eleventh and Market, near the coffee shop and at the same plaza as the Giant supermarket. The opening banner still hung over the entrance: GRAND OPENING: EDWARD AYURVEDA HEALING CENTER. WELLNESS SPRINGS FROM US. The irony, I always mused, whenever I regarded the sign.

"Always blaming them for your failures," Chevy said. "Look, they certainly should go back to where they came from. But if they don't? And it doesn't appear they will!"

I was suddenly aware of a patch of wetness on my bed. At fifteen I should not be doing it still, but I had done it again, wet the bed. I will not. No more, no more. And yet, there I was, pissing all over my New Year's resolution.

"And if you don't find another job?" Chevy was saying. "Where will we live? Under a rock?"

I stripped my bed of its sheets. I gathered the pile and went into the hallway. In the laundry closet, I stuffed the sheets into the washing machine, trying my best to shut out Wayne's and Chevy's rising voices. Back in my room, I walked straight to my en suite bathroom, showered quickly, dried myself off and walked, naked, back into the bedroom, where I found myself standing in front of the mirror. I listened to the sounds coming from the kitchen, and I wept softly at the overwhelmingly pale image of myself.

7

Edward, Pennsylvania
June 2017

THE UNIVERSITY SEMESTER ENDED IN MAY, AS IT ALWAYS DID, and almost immediately Wayne leaned into his despondency. Each time I returned from school, I found him in the living room, leafing morosely through old photographs.

"Look here, Harry! Remember this one?" He always stood at the junction where the split-level entryway stairs met the living room. Always, he stood holding the photo album to his chest and a single photo in his other hand. He'd pull up an old sepia-toned snapshot of himself as a baby, or of his parents as young adults, or of his and Chevy's wedding, or of me as a baby.

"Look how young we used to be! Remember this one?"

"Yeah, Wayne," I'd always say, barely looking. I'd climb the steps, which was my signal for him to step aside. As soon as I reached the top of the stairs, I'd make a beeline for my room. "Yeah, I remember," I'd call out.

The truth is that despondency is as infectious as a yawn. I am, of course, naturally prone to melancholia, but Wayne's despondency always had an additional effect on me, and as such, I sought to avoid him.

This particular day, he stood by the door frame, not quite leaning into it. I sat on my bed, my AP Physics textbook on my lap. If every action had an equal and opposite reaction, then what did I need to do to get Wayne back to himself? I wanted to fix the situation: give him back his job, along with his confidence, but at the same time, I acknowledged that I did not agree with his entitled perspective on the loss of his position. I acknowledged, too, that it was simply not my place to fix this, and, anyway, I did not have the means to do so. What was clear, I repeat, was that his despondency was having an effect on me. It was June and afternoon, and the sunlight should have drawn me outdoors, but I found myself wanting to crawl under the covers and sleep.

"I made some spaghetti and meatballs out of your favorite sauce—Francesco Rinaldi Sweet and Tasty!" Wayne said. "I even baked some of those Pillsbury crescent rolls you used to love. Whaddya say?"

"Not sure," I said. It annoyed me that he was pretending to care. Plus, the last few times I ate tomato sauce, Francesco Rinaldi or whatnot, my stomach writhed in agony, and so I was no longer eating any tomato products. I had complained about it over and over to him and Chevy, but he had clearly forgotten.

Wayne stepped into my room and went straight to my dresser. He picked up the stone that sat atop it. "Interesting," he said. "Where'd ya get that?"

The way he carried it, so nonchalantly, made clear he didn't understand its value. I rose from my bed, trying to keep cool. I walked over to him and smoothly took the stone from him. "Just an unexpected find," I said.

He walked over to the window. "The lawn's due for a mow," he said. "Better get to that sometime."

"Sure," I said. "I'll do it maybe today."

His presence in my room was agitating.

"Wayne?" I asked.

"Yeah, Son?"

"Turns out I'm hungry after all. Why don't we go eat the spaghetti and meatballs?"

That afternoon as I mowed the lawn, my stomach grumbled and twisted and turned inside and out. I mowed hastily, my mind numb as I left uneven strips across the grass. It was a Friday, and as it was also summer, the sun was still spreading its sharp hot wings all over Edward. I felt a growing emptiness in me, a practiced sort of vacancy. I enjoyed the moments of silence, but as always, it was a slippery, slipping vacancy, and soon the smoke was rising, thick rolls of gray thoughts. Burnt logs littered the ground of my mind. What were those sounds coming from the side of the house? What was all that hammering?

I finished up, completed my last strip, and turned off the lawn mower.

Wayne had settled himself by the side of the house equidistant from the browning hedges and the oak trees, not quite the back-yard. He'd pulled out an old folding table and a matching folding chair from the garage—the set he'd purchased years ago when he and Chevy had thought that the house might truly become a home, tender love and all. (At least, this was how Wayne had one day told me the story.) But with the passage of time, the metal legs of the folding table and chairs had rusted to a terribly dull brown, and in all the nineteen years they'd been married, Wayne and Chevy had only managed to fill the garage with a mountain of junk: ugly miniature furniture, an old, torn-up full-sized sofa, broken end tables, gnomes holding watering cans, and Christmas figurines including Mary, Jesus, and the Magi. Chevy refused to go into the garage anymore because she'd begun to see the garage as a virus; if she were to step into it, she claimed, it might infect all parts of her body, leaving her . . . well, she didn't know what. Didn't matter. She would just avoid the garage.

For a while—between the ages of twelve and thirteen—I had tried to clean up the rubbish, but it was clear that Wayne was determined to continue to pile up his mountain of old broken things. And now, like Chevy, I could no longer enter it.

"My, my," Chevy said, coming from the front yard, just as I was arriving to Wayne's setup from the backyard. "What's going on here?" She ran her red-tipped fingernails across the perimeter of her Hello Kitty lunch box, which she always carried to work. At this time of day, she was returning from the Ayurveda shop. "Lucinda mentioned you were out here. What exactly—"

"Please don't start with me," Wayne said.

"I'm not starting anything," Chevy said. "But what exactly . . . Is this what you've been doing all day?"

"Drop it, Chevy," Wayne said.

"I'm just saying, you've got to be careful, Wayne. Remember Centralia? The entire town burned down. You don't want to be the person who accidentally sets the whole of Edward on fire!"

"Just drop it, Chevy. I'm not starting a fire. Do you see a fire here? Plus, that was a garbage dump fire. Whole different thing."

"I'm just saying," Chevy said.

"I don't need anything to stoke my anger," Wayne said. "I've already spent the whole day being angry. Enough." The way he said it, it was as if being angry had suddenly become an activity in and of itself.

"You know, dear," Chevy said, "I'm too tired for whatever this is. I just hope you're not up to another one of your stupid projects!" There was a measured sharpness to her voice. I could tell that she was fighting to control her temper.

"A man must earn his keep. If they won't have me at the university, then I'll make my living on my own," Wayne said.

Chevy walked closer to him and peered curiously at the object that he was tinkering with.

The contraption started to buzz. His laptop sat on the folding table next to the contraption, and he tapped some commands into it. He pushed buttons on the machine, which made loud beeping then whirring sounds. The machine's parts moved up and down and molten plastic dripped down its metal lever. Once it was finished, Wayne unscrewed the case and retrieved his 3D object.

"Everybody needs one of these," Wayne said. "It's a market waiting to take off. I'm gonna be the one to set it off. You know how much I stand to make off the sales?" He rubbed his hands together and laughed in his self-congratulatory way.

"All right," Chevy said. "You know what—" She raised her hand in defeat. "Whatever it is, just clean up your mess when you're done." She rolled her eyes at Wayne, pivoted on her maroon suede heels, and headed back to the house.

I didn't stay to watch Wayne or see what products he was making. Had I, I would have had reason to take matters into my hands. But my desire to leave was so overwhelming that I set off on an aimless walk around the neighborhood.

This was the point in my life when I began to romanticize Centralia, by virtue of my desire to get away from Chevy and Wayne. That day, I imagined myself for the first time potentially taking refuge in the empty, still-burning town. If I could slowly fix it up, even just a tiny part of it, really fix it up—not just like a Potemkin village—then maybe I could one day move there. A one-man town, or close to it. There was a certain peacefulness at the mere thought.

8

Edward, Pennsylvania
August 2017

SUMMERS IN EDWARD WERE BUSTLING. CHILDREN RODE THEIR bicycles and scooters up and down the roads, toddlers dragged along balloons from summer parties, shirtless men sat in the front seats of their cars, honking loudly as they drove by. Adults laughed as they strolled the streets that led downtown. Sometimes Wayne and Chevy joined the next-door neighbors—Lucinda and Jake—on their well-furnished front patio, and after they'd all had their fill of beers, it seemed possible to hear their laughter clear on the other side of town.

In those summer days, Edward smelled like barbecues and cotton candy—sweaty and moist, of smoked meat, fat drippings, charcoal, and caramelized sugar. In the river, people revved the engines of their boats, and the odor of the gasoline mingled with the smoke of barbecues. Still, the water gleamed like a coronation.

I walked around town more aimlessly than ever that summer. It would seem that a fifteen-year-old should by this time have at least one bosom friend, but I did not. I had not managed to make any close friends. At Woodrow Wilson, it was clear I was even too geeky for the geeks.

I did have one almost-friend, and that was Flora. We ate our lunches together when school was in session and when Flora was not tucked away in the computer lab, researching universities— she was already convinced that she would be going to "the best of the best," with a major in chemistry. Her own father was a research chemist whose work focused on the botulinum toxin. She planned to focus on biochemistry and study genetic mutations, especially those that possibly led to cancer. She wasn't interested in drug therapies, she said. She was interested in getting to the fundamental source of the problem in order to find ways to prevent cancers from ever beginning. When she spoke in detail about her plans, I felt like I was melting. It was her voice, the sweet tenderness of it, but it was also her strength of character, her sureness. It was also the dark rich color of her skin and the way her hair formed tight short curls around her head. It was everything about her, everything that I could perceive, anyway.

During the school year, I had continued to run into her at the Edward Elementary School playground, but now that it was summer, I missed her presence. I had not run into her at the playground all summer long.

One day I set off on a mission to walk all around town until perhaps we ran into each other. I had no idea where she lived, but I reasoned to myself that if I walked as far out as possible along the roads leading to both the high school and the elementary school, I might come across her.

I set off briskly on my mission. The sun being too strong, and my sweating too intense, I did away with my do-rag within the first twenty minutes. By the time I hit the forty-minute mark, I had taken to wiping the sweat off my head and hair with my bare palms.

After walking for about an hour, I found myself in a neighborhood I was convinced she lived in. Something about the aura of the place reminded me of her.

The house was a corner town house, with a black front door and two rosebushes standing on either side like guards.

I heard the lawn mower long before I arrived, from a couple of houses away. From an even greater distance away, I saw a shadow of a person. As I approached, I saw that the person pushing the lawn mower across the grass was an older Black man, and that as he pushed the equipment, he formed the most uniform tracks I had ever seen.

Around the block, another row of six town homes stood in a small enclave, only a little recessed from the road.

A couple of boys were playing basketball in the front driveway of one of the town homes. Behind them stood a girl who resembled Flora from a distance. My nerves began to rise, like a dead body, heavy, coming up, floating on the surface of water. But when she turned around, I saw that she was not Flora. Her face was thin and long where Flora's was full and round. Her lips were flat where Flora's were always in a pretty pout. In this girl's eyes, there was an obsequiousness where Flora's eyes were assertive, almost defiant, always seeking, always curious.

One more time around the block, I promised myself, and then I would leave. One more time just to see if maybe she did in fact live in this particular part of town.

As I came up to the corner where Front Street met Dennis Street, the lawn-mowing man stopped his mower and stood, watching me curiously. I made to walk away, faster, but it was as if my feet were confused—to move faster or to slow down? I paused, picked up my pace, then paused again.

"Child, you looking for someone?" the man asked me, walking up to the curb of the street to meet me.

My mouth would not move, and in trying to get it to do so, I found myself stuttering and stammering. In that moment, a car pulled up to us.

"Child, you OK?" the Black man asked again.

The siren turned on once, twice . . . Blue and red lights swirled. "Son, that man bothering you?" the gruff voice peeking out of the window asked.

The siren went off.

There was a moment during which I could have considered which question to answer or could have decided firmly not to answer either question. Or considered, better yet, how to frame my answer to either question. But I was only fifteen, and the questions had become muddled in my mind. And as my mouth was still refusing to open, I simply nodded. That evening, and for all the years that followed, I would console myself by reasoning that the second question was an interloper, and that I'd only meant to answer the first.

Before I knew what was happening, the white officer had rushed out of the car and was shouting at the Black man, cuffing him, shoving him into the back of the car. I screamed at the officer, telling him that the man had not in fact been bothering me, and that I'd come simply on a walk to maybe see a girl I missed, that none of this was supposed to happen.

But it was too late. The officer would not hear, and, anyway, the Black man had been repeating loudly, "Trespassing? Trespassing?! In my own front yard?! You're just gonna arrest me? Right here in front of my own house?"

The Black girl and Black woman who appeared to be his daughter and wife rushed out of the house and pleaded with the officer to let go of her dad, her husband.

So much chaos. My head swirled, swelled like a balloon that would soon burst from too much pressure. Off I ran.

That evening, I returned home crying. My face grew puffed from all that crying. If you can believe it, Chevy, drunk from alcohol, pulled me to her chest and cradled my head against her bosom when she happened upon me in the hallway. That was the benefit of the alcohol—it helped her forget her fear of dirt; it gave her the permission to be the mother that I had long ago known, the mother who clearly still existed somewhere in her, buried deep within. I welcomed her embrace and imagined that the alcohol scent of her bosom and breath was instead of warm bread pudding or warm cake—anything comforting and sweet.

Why exactly was I crying? I could not have said, but I do know that I felt the weight of guilt; I had inadvertently contributed to injustice in the world. The understanding that I could be complicit in a thing like that was more than my emotions could handle. Maybe this was why I would eventually care so much about the swastikas and White Power signs of Centralia, and about the raping of the old woman by the disappearing man. But more on that later. For now, still, the dithering, the fumbling, the inability to change anything. That summer evening in 2017, I had managed to create disaster for a family on the other side of town. And then, I had done the cowardly thing and reverted to tears.

9

Edward, Pennsylvania
October 2017

In the months since Wayne pulled out his machine by the side of the house, he worked steadily, perched on the folding table and chair, clacking away at what he called his "design." Sometimes he whistled as he worked. He rarely took a break once he had set himself up out there, didn't even pause to relieve himself or to eat until hours later, when he was finally done with the machine for the day. He simply sat, prodding and poking the contraption, trying to make it spit out the exact image of the design that he was trying to duplicate.

"He's up to no good," Chevy said one morning. Wayne had set his table in the front yard instead of by the side of the house. It was not yet 8 a.m., and it seemed to me that he must have finally finished with his products. He put up a large sign that read: EMPOWER YOURSELVES, GET YOUR LIBERATORS HERE!

Chevy stood in the kitchen juicing celery and kale in her Nutri-Bullet. I was cutting up a banana into my Irish oats, getting ready to leave for school. Any luck, I thought, and maybe the pesky Jehovah's

Witnesses who sometimes came around would stop by his table, but hopefully no one else.

"It's been months now. I wonder what took him so long," Chevy said.

"Maybe he wanted to perfect it," I said. "Better quality, more money, I guess."

"You can bet your bottom dollar those products will be no good," Chevy said. "I know enough about your father to know that. Can't count on Wayne to create anything worthwhile."

I gulped. But did she mean it that way? Was she oblivious to the implications of her statement?

I set off to school, cutting across the lawn, trying my best to catch a glimpse of the so-called products. But the way Wayne had packaged them, I did not succeed in seeing what they were.

By the afternoon, when I returned from school, Wayne was still out there. I went up to the table, aiming to catch a glimpse, but Wayne purposefully kept me from discovering what they were: the way he followed my movements with his eyes, then swatted my hands each time I moved to lift up the tarp that covered the objects.

That night, I tossed in bed. I had a long dream of waves rising from a river and slapping the metal railings of a bridge. I woke up with a start when the largest wave hit the highest point of the bridge. "You can afford not to care, Harry," I said to myself. "Harry, this is you not caring. This is what it looks like not to care." And yet, I *did* care! The idea came to me then. Get up and check on Wayne's products. Get up and see what exactly your father is up to.

In my Star Wars: The Future Generation pajamas, I snuck down the stairs and out the door that led to the garage. I flipped on the light switch. The garage was as packed as a dumpster on pickup day, but I spotted the folding table and chair, and by its side the boxes and bags of Wayne's items. At first, I made out the 3D printer. Then, in horror, I lifted up a green pistol. This product that Wayne had held with such pride in his eyes was a gun. Oh God, I thought. I understood then that my father had a murderous mind. The most violent offenses could be carried out in the minds and backyards of the most innocuous-looking of men. My pale, peachy-skinned, middle-aged father would have called himself a good man, but only because he could not see himself clearly.

I put the items back down, a dozen in all, plus the machine. I walked gently back up to my room, where I mulled over the situation on my bed.

The town of Edward was bounded by the Susquehanna River, and our house, while not exactly a stone's throw from the banks of the river, was close enough that I could reach it in under a thirty-minute walk. I stripped off my Star Wars: The Future Generation pajamas and put on a sweatshirt and jeans, then snuck back down to the garage, where I found a large black garbage bag and one of Chevy's old oversize roller suitcases. First, I stuffed the dozen pistols into the garbage bag, and then I stuck the bag into the luggage, along with the machine. I walked down our street, then to St. George's, until I arrived at Front Street. The road was quiet and the air cool. The moon lit up the night like the dimmed lights in all the nightclubs that I had ever seen online and on television. My heart pounded like a gavel on a sounding block. I went all the way to the center of the bridge, unzipped the luggage, took out the black garbage bag, and tossed it into the river. Next, I took out the machine from the luggage and tossed it also into the river. Any luck and they would drift far, far away and no one would speak or hear any more of them.

Back in my bedroom, I fell into a deep sleep, my whole body filled with bloody shame. I didn't wake up again until I heard their voices coming to me from the kitchen.

"Just what did you think you were going to do with them?" Chevy was asking.

"Really? Really?" Wayne replied with annoyance. "You're the one who was complaining about money! I found us a solution and now you ask me that question?"

"Oh my gosh, Wayne!" Chevy screamed. "Anyone could have told you it was a stupid idea! What a stupid idea! What a stupid, stupid, stupid idea! And now you've gone ahead and lost them. How do you lose a dozen guns? What's wrong with you?"

"Harry!" he called. "Harry! I said get your butt out here now!"

"Now you've gone and wasted money we don't even have! And you'll be totally unable to recoup that money because your products are gone! GONE! We have bills! BILLS! No one can pay our bills. I sit around at the shop, and there are hardly any clients. I sit around all day waiting for clients to come. Meanwhile, we have bills, and you think it's OK that you squandered our money this way? And you lost a dozen guns?! Is this a bad dream? Am I in a bad dream? What—"

"Harry!" he shouted, almost frantically.

"Coming!" I called back.

"Did you happen to go into the garage? Have you seen . . ." Wayne's voice was shaking. He paused awkwardly. "Have you seen any gun-looking items or a printing machine?"

"What's a printing machine?" I asked.

"Son, just answer the question," Wayne said. "Have you seen them?"

"Stupid!" Chevy interjected. "What kind of person even comes up with such an idea?"

"Oh my God!" Wayne said. "Will you stop for a second? It's not like I managed to sell a single one of them!"

"Still!" Chevy said. "Still!"

"Harry?" Wayne said. "Answer me. Have you seen them?"

I shook my head. "Sorry, Wayne. I don't know what you're talking about."

"All right," Wayne said. "All right." His hands came up to his head in exasperation. He began pacing the kitchen. "All right. I'll figure it out from here."

Did I feel a little guilty for lying? Of course, but I was confident in what I had done. It was far better that I'd discarded those awful things before either Wayne killed someone or sold the gun to someone who'd kill someone. Sure, there were probably plenty of other Purists making molten guns, but at least now there were twelve fewer guns in the world.

10

Edward, Pennsylvania
December 2017

It usually took Wayne and me about thirty minutes to drive into Centralia in his Ford, a straight shot at first on Market Street, past the houses with their strung-up decorative lights, Christmas trees visible from the living room windows of the ranch and Craftsman-style homes. We passed the McDonald's, then the Home Depot, and finally the red and blue and yellow sign of the Wendy's restaurant, the russet-haired, freckled, pigtailed girl smiling blankly at us. We passed a series of billboard advertisements boldly advertising Jesus and sex toys. "Fantasy Boutique" and "Sexy Cherry" right next to "Shackled by Lust? Jesus Saves!"

We turned onto the highway from Market Street, then continued about twenty minutes through the rural sloping plains, all the stacked-up, rolled-up hay in the small towns along the way, before finally arriving at our destination. Even in the winter, rumor had it that it burned.

We didn't go to Centralia to visit anyone. It was simply that Wayne needed somewhere to go, and he liked to give me driving lessons on the town's empty roads. He'd convinced me that it would be the perfect prelude to the Driver's Education class that all students at Woodrow Wilson were required to take in the second semester of their sophomore year. I didn't exactly need convincing; I wanted the freedom that comes with having access to a car. More than that, Centralia had by then become a pull in my mind. I had fully begun to romanticize it, to make it the potential site of my escape plan in progress.

I was also aware that I was doing Wayne a favor. He had still not managed to find a job, and at least in driving me around, he was occupying himself.

The roads were clear and bare. The only trails of snow were those that lined the roadsides. Wayne drove like a turtle, like a geriatric man who felt the need to be cautious even on an empty road. But I had the sense that his slowness was just a way to prolong the trip, to make it so that he didn't have to return home and face the emptiness of the remainder of the day.

Fleeting clouds hung above us like a distant blanket. I imagined a time when the town was bustling with life, women and men walking hand in hand, the wind blowing their hair; children teetering about under the sharp rays of the sun. There would have been movie theaters and floral shops and dress shops and all the shops that an old town could have. In those days, no one must have ever imagined that the town would one day burn down.

At Centralia, Wayne always pulled the car to a stop in one of the abandoned parking lots. We switched places, and he instructed me to put on my seat belt, lower the parking brake, check the rearview and side mirrors, and the lights, before turning on the ignition. Reverse, both hands on the wheel, stop completely at the stop sign.

There was no greater feeling than being on the highway, speeding down it but making sure to stay within the speed limit. Wayne was the worst imaginary driver. He would wrap his hands around an imaginary steering wheel and slam his foot on an imaginary gas pedal. Instead of urging me to stay within the speed limit, he'd scold me to go faster.

"Son, what the hell are you going so slow for? The road is all yours and still you're moving like a snail!"

"But, Wayne—" I always began.

"But nothing. Just drive. Seize the day!"

I'd slam my foot on the accelerator. I never mentioned how slowly he always drove into Centralia. Speeding, I was gathering, was an exploit that he reserved solely for me.

Several weeks into our forays, in what would have been the old downtown area of Centralia, I had pulled the car to a stop and was practicing parallel parking when my eyes fell on a million graffitied swastikas and penises and White Power signs sprawled across the highway. Wayne didn't appear to be bothered by any of it, as he did not react. But in that moment, I first felt the itching all around my body—a persistent feeling of defilement. How had I missed all of this on our previous driving excursions? The more I regarded the road, the dirtier I felt, and the more my skin begged to be scratched. I looked around and my eyes fell on the skeletal remains of a burnt tree. My entire head began to itch, and my arms, my genitals, and even the space between my butt cheeks. I turned from the tree and looked to the other side of the road, but all I saw were huge craters and smaller gouges in the earth, weeds crawling from them like a horde of termites. In front of us, the only remaining house on the road was covered in what must have been black mold and green algae. Wooden boards shut up its doors and windows.

"We gotta go," I said to Wayne. "I'm not feeling so great."

"Come on, Son," Wayne said. "We only just got here. We've got so much time before we need to get back home."

"Wayne, I'm not feeling so great," I said.

"Come on, Son. It's not like you want to go back and have to spend all day with Chevy. Lord knows, I don't!"

"I'm OK with that, Wayne. I just want to get back home," I said.

"That reminds me," Wayne said. "I gotta show you how to position the car when you park on a hill. There's a hill right up there." He pointed at the hill. "Come on, let's go."

Seated there in the driver's seat, my skin crawled more than I'd ever experienced before. I felt on the verge of madness. When I started the car, I'd no intention of speeding and thereby cutting the thirty-minute drive in half. Wayne screamed at first in anger, and then with glee at the speed.

Back at home, I parked the car in a fury, left the keys on the driver's seat, and hurried into the house. Somewhere in the middle of that trip, the idea of what the town could look like if cleaned up implanted itself in my mind. But in the moments after I got home, all I could think about was jumping into the shower. As soon as I did, I rubbed the soapy loofah all over my body, scrubbed and scrubbed and scrubbed, and finally it seemed that I had washed the filth of the town off my skin.

It was Christmastime, but there would be no Christmas for us, as I'm sure you've already gathered. Wayne was broke. Chevy was broke. And I was still an unemployed child. It's true that at that age I could have gotten myself a job at the McDonald's or Wendy's or even at the Giant, but no one had raised the idea, and I certainly was not going to bring it up myself. The thought of having to work in close proximity to people with whom I was sure I would have nothing in common terrified me.

We sat around the living room together as a family and celebrated the strangest, most lackluster Christmas I had ever celebrated up to that point in my life. Wayne and Chevy and I pulled open gifts that we'd wrapped in last year's gift wrap. From Chevy, I received a pair of socks, which I imagined she'd bought at the CVS by the Giant. I'd seen a pattern like it there before. From Wayne, I received a winter-themed (snow and pine trees) coffee mug, which I imagined that he, too, must have bought from the CVS. I did not drink coffee, but it was large enough that I could use it for my cereal, and I was happy for that. For each of them, I had made a lavender-scented candle, using the empty mason glass jars of Chevy's almond butter containers. The Internet was my friend in those days, and I ordered some wax and the lavender essential oil with my year-old allowance money. At home, one evening when both Chevy and Wayne were in their room, I took over the kitchen, melting the wax, adding the lavender oil and the purple dried petals from the small floral bouquet that I had found at the Giant, attaching the wick to each container and securing it in place, and then pouring in the floral-patterned wax and allowing it to set for four hours. Afterward, I cut the wick at about half an inch long and tied two of the white ribbons that had come with the bouquet around the candle jars. I chose lavender because tensions were always running high in the house and I wanted something calming for us. I could have done with some calm myself.

"Hmm, interesting," Wayne said, looking at his candle in a jar. "I suppose there could come a day when we might need a candle."

"These might work very well for my Ayurveda shop," Chevy said. "If you don't want yours, I'm sure I can make some kind of practical use of it," Chevy said.

"Practical use of it?" Wayne asked. "Practical use would be using it for its purpose—to provide light. This is the United States of America, for God's sake, Chevy. This isn't an African village where there is no electricity."

"Oh, not again," Chevy said. "All I meant was—"

"Even the wilderness camp had electricity," I muttered under my breath.

"Try going to a village then next time and come back and tell me you—"

"Wayne, just drop it," Chevy said. She stood up and announced that she had had enough of Wayne, that she'd take this opportunity to go next door and give Lucinda her Christmas gift.

I shook my head. So much for calm. But all of their jabbering did remind me of my time in Tanzania, the wilderness camp, and, most of all, the darkest man. All of that seemed a lifetime ago, an entire world away. How I longed to go back. My mind leapt to Flora. The whole summer and that first semester of the academic year, I had not seen Flora. By December it was clear that I would no longer be seeing her. She and her family had likely moved out of town. I wondered where she was now. How was her family celebrating the holidays? Did they celebrate? The more I thought of her, the more I mourned her loss and, of course, the loss of Benson, the two people who had made me feel at ease with myself. The darkest man was all the way in Tanzania, and now, Flora, too, was gone.

11

Edward, Pennsylvania
March 2018

Outside, the March snow was already melting into muddy puddles all over Edward. The sun was bright, like an invitation to go out, but it was a lazy Saturday, so we all stayed in.

Chevy slithered into the living room from her bedroom, then relaxed onto the couch before the television, rubbing her feet. I watched her from the dining table where I sat eating a bowl of Special K. According to her mandate, I was no longer allowed to be in the living room, let alone eat in it. Chevy had made the executive decision that I only come to the living area on special occasions and by her specific invitation. What I surmised from her decision was that my constant mingling with other students in a place like a high school—and the close proximity to other people's germs and dirt—had become a new threat.

In any case, I sat slurping up the milk in the dining room as quietly as I could, making sure not to smack as I chewed, for I knew that any smacking at all, like my presence in the living room, would infuriate her. I had always been such a quiet boy, and in some ways, my quietness had spoiled her: now she had the expectation that

I should be perpetually quiet, not even the smack of my mouth as I chewed. It wasn't just the chomping sound, she claimed. She minded sounds in general, she said.

But Chevy didn't mind the loudness of her television. I could have heard the news broadcast clearly from outside the house all the way at the edge of the lawn. From my close proximity in the dining room, it was painfully loud. And yet, somehow, she could still hear my smacking.

"Headaches got you down? Try Mequsiqir," the commercial was saying. "When taking Mequsiqir, do not drive or drink. Side effects include shortness of breath, dizziness, depression, worsening depression, thoughts of suicide, pulmonary fibrosis, heart attack, stroke, blood clots, high blood pressure, bleeding and ulcers, aneurysm, and on rare occasions death. The risks outweigh the benefits. Tell your doctor if you experience any of these side effects while on Mequsiqir. Do not take if pregnant . . ."

The commercial came to an end, and the news broadcast began. "The Purists, the new political party made up of a large number of former conservative Republicans and Democrats, are rapidly becoming the most influential party in the country. Following last week's report of trespassing, during which a group of Purist boys traveled into liberal territories in the Philadelphia area, those university campuses east of the Susquehanna and of coal country—Temple, Drexel, Haverford, Swarthmore, Bryn Mawr, and others—destroying property and posting signs on every building, the liberals are now calling for reparations . . ."

The sound of the drill came from somewhere in the garage. Chevy jumped in her seat. "What the heck was that?" she asked.

"No idea," I said.

The hammering came next and then the sound of what must have been a chain saw.

"Oh God," Chevy said. "What now? What brilliantly stupid idea has he got this time?"

Just then Wayne walked up the stairs, a wide smile on his face. "Either of you ever guessed how much a park bench goes for? I bet you haven't! How about upwards of three hundred dollars! The way I figure it, everybody could use a park bench in their yard, back or front. I'm gonna be the park bench supplier. You know how much I'd make?"

He flew back down the stairs.

"Oh God, oh God, oh God," Chevy said. "I'm just gonna pretend I didn't hear that."

I continued to eat my cereal and browse on my phone. Skin care and hair care products for men.

Another commercial came up for pajama jeans. "Want to look great even in the comfort of your own bed? Pajama jeans look just like designer jeans, so you can go to bed feeling just as stylish as you would feel in the daytime!"

I shook my head. The world flabbergasted me sometimes, though it occurred to me that those pajama jeans were something Chevy might be interested in. I looked over at her. She'd fallen asleep and was snoring softly on the couch.

I went back to browsing on my phone. Hours must have gone by before Wayne entered like a hurricane and woke Chevy up.

"You gotta come take a look. I actually got it done. It's a real beauty."

In her sleepiness, it might not have occurred to Chevy that the beauty of which Wayne spoke was located in the garage, which she abhorred. Drowsily she followed him down the stairs and into the garage, and I trailed behind.

In Wayne's defense, he had tried. Two-by-fours and 2½-inch pocket-hole screws were scattered all over the garage floor. Pieces of wood were arranged in a pile, and the leg assemblies of the benches were also piled up on the side wall of the garage. Wayne's chain saw and jigsaw looked like they'd seen enough work for the day. And true to what he had claimed, from a distance, the bench was a beauty. But, though still drowsy from her nap, tugging with one hand at the arm of the bench, Chevy said, "Now, Wayne, did you actually screw the nails in?" She sat carefully on the bench, and at first the only issue was the wobbling of the legs. No matter how she adjusted herself, the legs wobbled. When she stood up, dust shavings rose like powder.

"Ugh," she said, coughing and wiping her face. "You got me all dirtied up on this thing, Wayne. What were you thinking?"

"Take a seat," Wayne said to me. "You try it out."

Chevy fled the garage. I knew she'd run to the bathroom to wash herself.

"Come on, Son," Wayne said. "Never mind her. You try it out and see!"

My weight had hardly settled on the bench when it crashed to the floor and I found my butt flat on the ground.

12

Edward, Pennsylvania
August 2018

Bʏ ᴍʏ ᴊᴜɴɪᴏʀ ʏᴇᴀʀ, Wᴀʏɴᴇ ʜᴀᴅ ɢᴏɴᴇ ᴛʜʀᴏᴜɢʜ ᴀᴛ ʟᴇᴀsᴛ ᴀ dozen bad moneymaking ideas, from buying fledgling lemon and avocado trees on Amazon and selling the fruit in our yard, to mailing the Pennsylvania snow to warmer climates. None of the ideas proved lucrative, and whatever remaining hope he had declined precipitously. For one thing, global warming was having a deleterious effect on the Pennsylvania snow.

My very first day of junior year began with a visit from my Aunt Fern, but let's just say that, like the plant, there was nothing flowering about her. The visit was unexpected. The unexpectedness of it was not in and of itself significant, for in my sixteen years, I had only seen Aunt Fern come to our house a handful of times—to drop off money owed that either Wayne or Chevy had lent to her, or to drop off mail that the USPS had accidentally sent to her instead of to Wayne.

What was significant about this particular visit was that I had no idea that Aunt Fern had even stopped by until a loud ruckus came from my window, the sound of things crashing into other things. At first, I wondered if Lucinda and Jake were having some kind of construction work done, but then I heard Aunt Fern's voice, as loud and pitchy as a whistle. I had just returned from school. As it was the first day of the academic year, it had also been an early dismissal day. My backpack still hung in my hand. I dropped it and ran back out the front door to see what was going on. Wayne was away somewhere, and Chevy was at her shop. It seemed the responsibility to sort out matters rested solely on me. At the moment that I reached Lucinda and Jake's patio, Aunt Fern lifted one of the fancy outdoor stools and threw it at the woman. The glass scattered to the floor. "Stay away from her," Aunt Fern screamed. "If you have any respect at all, you'll stay away from her!"

By the time I was finally able to pull Aunt Fern away from Lucinda, my baseball cap and do-rag had fallen off. That August, the sun scorched. Everywhere people were murmuring curses about global warming, both the believers and the nonbelievers. My hair must have gleamed its strawberry blond in the hot sun, for even as I dragged her away, Aunt Fern said, "Look how handsome you're becoming, taking after your father more and more every day!"

Despite everything going on, I still managed to take offense at Aunt Fern's words.

In any case, I noticed a portion of Aunt Fern's cheek was bleeding, so I led her by the elbow back into the house, where I found Chevy's stash of rubbing alcohol and a small, round Band-Aid.

She was gone from the house long before Chevy and Wayne returned. She did not say much to me about what had triggered the fight, but she did keep repeating, "That double-crossing bitch of a woman. What kind of woman does that to a man?"

That evening, I brought up Aunt Fern's visit with Wayne and Chevy at the dining table, where we sat eating lasagna and spring salad. The television toggled between commercials and news. Pantene Pro-V, Ricola cough drops, Purina Puppy Chow.

"Is that right?" Wayne said.

Chevy looked luminous in her bathrobe. Her face and lips glowed pink, freshly scrubbed, for she had just come out of the shower. "I wonder what she would have come all the way here for in the first place," she said.

The newscaster said, "A bag containing a dozen molten guns was found in the Susquehanna River this morning at five a.m. A 3D printer was also found—"

"Oh God!" Chevy exclaimed, dropping her fork into the heart of her barely eaten lasagna. "Did you hear that? Wayne, did you hear that?"

"What?" Wayne said.

"Oh God!" Chevy said, pointing at the television.

"Dive crews and officials who were sent out to investigate—"

"Oh God!" Wayne said.

Chevy stood up from her chair and held her wet hair up in a bun on her head. She began pacing, looking panicked, her face completely flushed pink.

"Honey, I swear I have no idea how they got there," Wayne began, walking toward Chevy, pleading. What he thought his pleading would accomplish, I didn't quite know.

"What if? What if the police . . ." Chevy started to say but didn't finish.

My heart was beating. It felt like it was going to explode. My palms began to sweat. I wiped them off on my jeans. What if the police traced the items back to us? What if we all took the blame for Wayne's bad idea? Was it a crime to make guns with a 3D printer? But no one was killed, and it appeared none of the guns were missing.

"I'm so sick of your bullshit," Chevy said, breaking down in tears. "I'm so sick of all your bullshit! Why I'm putting up with any of it, I can't even say. I swear, Wayne, you better find a way to fix this. I don't want any part of it!"

"If you'll remember, several months ago, a group of Purist boys' bodies were found in the river, a large Purist sign plastered on their boat. God rest their souls . . ."

Chevy was full-on crying at this point, cursing the day she married Wayne.

"Police have linked the items to the Purist young men, who, several months ago, were found drowned in the river with alcohol intoxication . . ."

Chevy and I must have looked wide-eyed at the television at the exact same time, then she squealed, and when I turned to look at her, her mouth was hanging open from shock.

"No way!" Wayne said. "No way, no way, no way!" He fell to his knee and sighed the longest sigh of relief I'd ever heard. "Thank heavens!" he said softly. After a moment, he began to laugh softly, but it sounded a little like crying.

And that was that.

None of us talked or moved for what must have been at least an hour. The whole incident with Aunt Fern was completely forgotten.

13

Edward, Pennsylvania
October 2018

TWO MAJOR THINGS HAPPENED THAT OCTOBER. THE FIRST was that, one cold morning as I headed off to school, I opened the front door to a pair of people who I at first believed were Jehovah's Witnesses, only to find that they were a pair of Purist young men handing out flyers around the neighborhood. They explained that they'd seen me around and asked if I was interested in joining their mission. They were seeking my pledge. Of allegiance. After all, I looked like I was one of them.

You might think that it would be a clear decision for a person like me to make, an obvious decline, but I had begun to think of college and related expenses, and I knew that I could not count on my parents for help, so there was the strong financial allure of their proposal: four years' room and board to any university of my choice. Their plan was to bring things back to the way they used to be by infiltrating the national education system. Make our nation great again. In exchange, I would be a Purist body adding to the growing army of Purists. More numbers, more power. There would be no further commitment required on my part, at least not in the foreseeable future. My presence alone would be their re-compense.

But the pull of their offer was mitigated by my ideals. I was more idealistic then than I am now. I weighed two things—power and integrity. What they were offering me was power. What I stood to sacrifice was the freedom to believe in what I wanted to believe, the freedom to be whom I wanted to be, to love whom I wanted to love.

At the end of it all, I declined as politely as I could.

The second major thing was that I walked in on Chevy and Wayne in the middle of something I still cannot quite understand.

Chevy was sitting on the edge of their bed, the door wide open. I'm not sure if it was that they had forgotten to close the door, or if they'd expected that I'd already be asleep. It must have been around 10 p.m., and generally, on weeknights, I was fast asleep by 9 p.m. Also, as I've said before, I was an exceptionally quiet child, so they'd have had no reason to believe that I was awake.

That particular day, their arguing had been loud, not unusual for them, but what was unusual was that it immediately turned to deaf-ening silence, no gradual decline. After not hearing a single sound from them for several minutes, I thought to go check and see that they hadn't, perhaps, resorted to actually killing each other.

From beside their doorway, I watched as Chevy tucked her hair behind her ears, turning her back to Wayne. He went to her, tugged at the belt of her robe. She just sat there, allowing him to continue to tug at the belt, but she would not allow him to pull it open. He stood a long time, begging silently with his eyes to open the robe. Finally, Chevy allowed him to do so. Then she just sat and allowed him to gaze upon her naked body.

I stood by the door a long time waiting for something to happen. A strange sort of dread fell upon me. When I remember the scene, I can still feel the heaviness of the air that night, the way that time seemed not to move for a while.

Her breasts hung bare, her nipples alert, and when Wayne knelt before her, she only protested weakly, like a person who felt that she owed it to him, despite her own wishes. "Not now, Wayne."

He was fully clothed in a T-shirt and jeans, but his feet were bare. "I can do it just the way you like it," he said.

"Not today," she said.

He used his hands to gently push open her legs, and then he bent his head between her legs and stayed there, his head moving slightly up and down and side to side.

My palms began to sweat. I was aware that this was a thing that I should not be privy to, that I was intruding, and yet I could not get my legs to carry me away.

The back of Wayne's head moved more as he worked between her legs. Her legs began to shake.

"That's how you like it?" he asked softly. She moaned and made to get up. He extended his arm to keep her in place. He kept doing whatever he was doing. I watched. She tried to get up again.

"Just give me a chance," he said, looking back up at her. "Yeah?" he asked softly. Then he put his head back between her legs.

"Wayne, not . . ." she said.

"Please, yeah?" he asked. And he went gently back between her legs. "You like it like this?" he asked.

She moaned unexpectedly.

"Yeah?"

She remained silent.

"Yeah?" he said.

She let out an even louder moan, and her legs seemed to buckle. I held my breath. My hands folded into fists, perhaps to steady myself in all the discomfort of the scene.

"Yeah?" Wayne asked again, still ravaging her. "Yeah, Chevy?"

"All right, all right," Chevy moaned. Her body lurched and curved in the middle.

"Yeah?" he asked one more time.

"Giving it a chance," she said. "Giving it a chance," she moaned louder, and the loudness of it sent shivers down my body.

I know that it is unusual for a child to witness such an event between his or her or their parents and stay to behold the entirety of it. I do not know why I remained, but if I had to describe it as an adult, I'd say that, perhaps, I was taken by their song and dance in a detached sort of way. I didn't exactly see them as Mom and Dad, but more as wardens, so there was something oddly scientific about my observation. I noticed the way in which Chevy had one foot in and one foot out. I was astonished by the act itself, the power of Wayne's head between her legs.

When finally I was able to move my feet, I tiptoed quickly back to my room, shut my door, and it was only then that the weight of what I had just witnessed caught up with me. I attempted to wipe the image from my mind. But it was too late.

Imagine my shock when, later that night, I watched Chevy from my bedroom window cutting across the back lawn. Lucinda's back porch lights came on, and as soon as they did, Chevy ran to her. They stood together within the frame of the outdoor globe lights. Both women's faces were bare, devoid of any makeup, but there was something luminous about them. They were even more beautiful than with their makeup on, fresh, almost like teenagers. An outside observer might have called them both gorgeous, not just their faces but also the curves of their bodies—the arcs of their breasts and backsides, the dips in their waists, all of which was visible through their clothing. They were both wearing leggings and tank tops. It was October and nighttime, but neither of them seemed to notice the chill.

Lucinda wrapped her arms tenderly around Chevy's waist, then after a moment, she pulled herself away to inspect Chevy's face. She stroked Chevy's cheeks gently, wiping the tears away. She said words I could not hear, and Chevy nodded softly. Lucinda pulled Chevy back in a soft embrace, and she began to very slightly sway with Chevy in her arms in a mollifying, palliative sort of way. Chevy's arms were also wrapped around Lucinda's body. They stood that way for a long while, their bodies swaying together. A gentle love song could have been playing in the background, and they could have been dancing to it. Lucinda stroked Chevy's arms, over and over again, as if this tender approximation of a dance was something they'd been doing for years. She was about half a head taller than Chevy, and it seemed a perfect fit when Chevy leaned her head in the crook of Lucinda's neck. Their light brown ponytails mixed together so that it was hard to tell where one woman's hair ended and the other's began. It was strangely the most intimate thing—which is to say, the most romantic thing—I had ever witnessed up until that point in my life.

I'd never seen Chevy that way before. I had no idea where Jake could have been. When Chevy raised her head from the crook of Lucinda's neck, she reached her face up toward Lucinda, and Lucinda reached her face down toward Chevy, and their lips locked in a slow and sensuous way. There was longing in the kiss, their eyes open at first and then slowly closing as the kiss deepened.

I heard my doorknob turning, and then the opening of my door behind me, and yet I could not bring myself to turn away from the women. By the time my brain processed the sounds, Wayne was already standing by my side, also looking at Lucinda and Chevy, not saying a word. I looked up at him for one long moment, and he just stood rigidly, watching the women.

"Dad?" I said in an almost whisper. He looked sternly at me, a slight imperceptible shake of the head, like a command, which I knew meant that I was not to say a word about this ever. Instantly, I knew that he already knew. That this had been going on for some time. Together we turned back to the view outside my window, and we stood there, watching Chevy and Lucinda kissing each other passionately, tenderly, and lovingly—nothing like I'd ever known my mother to be. Never had I seen her this way with Wayne. If she could feel this way with someone, then what was she doing with Wayne? And, by extension, what was she doing with me?

I don't remember exactly how the night ended. I know that at some point Wayne left my room. I also know that at some point Chevy must have returned home. What I remember is that the next day, Wayne and Chevy resumed their bickering, and life as I knew it went right back to normal.

14

Edward, Pennsylvania
May 2019

MAY OF JUNIOR YEAR AT WOODROW WILSON, WAYNE AND
Chevy pulled out one of the hoarier dining table chairs for me to sit
on. They both sat in the living room too, but on the spotless leather
couch adjacent to the crawling English ivy, and then Wayne twitch-
ingly asked, "How far exactly?"

Chevy followed with "Is there a scholarship involved?"

It could have been that they were happy with the idea of my
being far away from them, my being no longer their responsibility
(their financial crisis had only continued to spiral out of control;
Wayne was still unemployed, and it appeared that Chevy's shop had
completely worn itself out on the small-town clients—either that,
or Ayurveda was a luxury that even the richest of them could no
longer afford).

"California, maybe. Who knows, maybe somewhere in Africa.
I'll figure it out," I said. I had no idea how far away I would go or
if there'd be any scholarships involved, and, truth be told, I had not
applied to anywhere in California, let alone Africa.

Chevy cleared her throat. "Africa?"

I swallowed air, a dry aching gulp. I pondered nervously over what had prompted me to lie. It would be at least another semester before I heard back from the universities to which I had applied.

"On the other hand, Africa would be rather inexpensive," Wayne said thoughtfully. He stood up. "Excellent plan, Son!" he said, patting me on the back.

I noted the look of despondency on his face. Beneath the mask of approval was an unambiguous look of gloom.

"I'm just gonna grab a quick coffee. Pardon me. I'll be back in a few," he said, and walked out of the house. The door closed behind him.

A lot can happen in the span of a coffee run. A crater can form in the already-deep gorge between a mother and a son. A boy can dig in his heels about his dislike for his father.

"Well, we'll have to take this one step at a time, won't we?" Chevy said.

"It's not as if you actually want me here," I responded, petulantly. Days sometimes went by when she and I didn't so much as exchange a word.

"Harry, I'm just saying that we'll have to take it one step at a time. Where exactly have you applied? Can I get a list?"

"What does the list matter?" I asked.

"I'd like to know." She began to say something else but then she grew quiet, and in her silence the TV droned: "In other news, in Colorado frustrated students walk out of the vigil, claiming political exploitation. 'We are people, not a statement,' the students chanted today. Also, 'Mental health! Mental health! Mental health!'"

"What a tragedy," the female TV anchor said.

"People are increasingly difficult these days," the co-anchor replied.

"No wonder some of us choose animals," the first anchor said.

"With all the breeding we do, though, soon all of humanity will be overrun by animals."

"Speaking of animals, how about that Danny? Serious error in judgment, wouldn't you say?"

"Just a gag, an innocent gag, a stupid unthinking gag," the co-anchor said.

"But seriously, how many babies have been born into the royal family of late—George, Charlotte, Louis—and yet, it never occurred to him to use the chimp photo until now? A mere coincidence?"

"Call it what you will, they're just being sensitive," the co-anchor said indignantly.

Just being sensitive? Such a cruel justification. This, I knew, was the custom of white magic—the most exploited of all magic. It excused itself without consequence and often laid the blame for its own shortcomings elsewhere. But then again, why hadn't white magic worked for Wayne? Maybe Wayne was just too daft even for a gift like that. Or perhaps Wayne's fears were coming true—was white magic losing its power?

"Sloan, Springfield, Medfield College, even Edward Community College . . ." Chevy was reading off her own list as if wrangling with the words, tucking loose strands of hair behind her ears. Her red nails glowed like pained determination. "These are all right around the corner. They all have strong work-study programs. You could work part-time, earn some money, give back to the family—"

"You mean, like, get a job?"

"Given the circumstances," Chevy said, "don't you think college would be a good time to start contributing to the welfare of the family? Depending on your class schedule, you could combine work-study with part-time work at, say, Starbucks, Giant, wherever."

"Work-study is already a part-time job," I said. "You want me to get two part-time jobs plus college?"

"Worse things have been asked of people," Chevy scoffed. She rose from her seat as if to declare herself the winner of the debate.

"No," I said. The force of the word from my mouth was like a vigorous spit and was shocking, even to me.

"Oh, Harry. Don't be silly. You will get a job starting this summer," Chevy struck back, the pleasure of her win evident in the supercilious "Oh? You think you're any match for me?!" look on her face. She lowered herself onto the couch. "In fact, no better time than now to break the news to you: Your father and I have both decided. We're requiring that you work for the duration of your senior year. Like I said earlier, you may choose where you work. You may also choose your own schedule. We will, of course, help you with the job applications." She paused and leaned forward in her seat, her eyes narrowing, as if examining my face, or as if to make sure that I understood the terms of the challenge: that she would forever be on the winning end. Then she stood up to leave.

The clock on the wall was ticking, each second in time with my heartbeat. I felt tension in my temples. But I was not done. They hadn't bothered to help me with my college applications, hadn't even bothered to ask me about my plans until I brought them up myself. I would certainly not be needing their help for any job applications, because I did not need their help for any applications at all, but also because I was not planning to take a job, much less two. "I'm adopting Centralia this summer, and I'll be working on it for the entirety of my senior year. It's my senior-year project," I heaved, laying what I believed would be my final triumphant card on the table.

"Meaning?" Chevy asked, her face scrunched with a look that was a mixture of frustration and ire.

The crawling ivy had grown so much that its twines reached farther than I had ever seen it. Soon the whole corner of the living room might be filled with its sooty green.

"Harry, I said, 'Meaning what?'" Chevy barked.

"Meaning that I can't get a job this summer and I definitely can't get a job senior year," I said as clearly and as confidently as I could. "I've committed. The school has already invested a lot of money in the project." Yes, I was playing the only hand I had available to me, but what I had said was also true. Despite the torment of that last foray into Centralia, the notion of cleaning up a town—creating an idyllic new home—had won, and I had found myself, one day in class, moved to propose the renovation as my senior project. "Is it even possible?" I asked Mr. Kopp, my senior project adviser. He arched his brow, pursed his lips, nodded slowly, and then said, matter-of-factly, "Trying to fix a broken—or rather—burning world, sure, why not?" And that was that.

"Goddammit, Harry!" Chevy roared, and before I knew it, she was towering over me on the dining table chair, stretching her hand and smacking me on the head, and then again, each smack stronger than the one before. And I thought: Now you touch me? This is how you touch me? My arms rose from the sides of my body and shoved her with a ferocity buried somewhere deep inside of me. Everything paused, an utter stillness as I looked at my mother crouched on the floor, staring in horror at me, a thin trail of blood trickling from her lower lip. We stayed that way for a while. It was as if time had somehow stopped.

When I finally snapped back to reality, my remorse would not allow me to apologize, to embrace her, to help her back up. I simply stood there, towering above her, and in that moment, I wondered just when did I—Harry, the little boy—become so much bigger than my mother, this woman? When did I gain power over Chevy, whom I'd always imagined far more powerful than me? "Remember this, Harry," I told myself, "that moment when your power overtook your mother's."

I looked at how small she was, almost girl-like, as on the day I had first watched her kissing Lucinda. There was an astonished innocence in her face, and this time a quiet disbelief radiated from her eyes.

I admonished myself and promised to look out for this. Never again to accidentally do anything to hurt a woman, even one like Chevy.

When the doorbell rang, I decided to ignore it. Purists or Jehovah's Witnesses, it didn't matter. But then the bell rang twice more, three times, and finally I climbed out of bed.

At the door, Wayne was carrying a cup holder filled with three cups of coffee. The sun was brilliant and, at first, I lingered in the sad paradoxical brightness of it, the way it beamed with effervescence when everything in my life felt so dreary.

"I'm sorry, Son," Wayne said. "I couldn't open it with the key with my hands full of these cups." He extended a coffee cup to me.

"No, thanks," I said.

"Come on, just take it," Wayne said. "Coffee is good for you. Aids digestion. Your stool will tell you as much!" He chuckled, and the sound of it was like constipation, full of unease.

"No, thanks," I said again.

Wayne emitted a quiet wailing sound, and I peered at him and saw tears in his eyes. Though he was not full-on crying, the whole thing reminded me of that day long ago in the Giant parking lot when he cried over his tenure denial. I held his gaze. His cheeks glowed like oil.

We both stood silently, then he looked away, as if embarrassed. "It's just coffee," he said with a tumbling sigh. "Why can't you just take it?"

As I climbed back up the stairs, the television news was blasting. "Explosion sends flames and smoke into the sky in Deer Park plant fire. The massive tank fire occurred at the petrochemical storage facility and is putting much of Deer Park and its surrounding communities, including Houston, under alert. The occurrence has led to shelter-in-place orders due to spikes in benzene levels. The industry is referring to it as a mere blemish . . . But disasters such as Deer Park, or the Deepwater Horizon tragedy, or even the Arkema plant explosion are proving to be serious concerns and have now led to fear and negative attitudes about the industry. Only nine percent of college graduates surveyed in the area expressed a desire to work for energy companies, according to Petro Consulting . . ."

Not surprising, I mused. How could anybody be expected to accept food from a hand determined to take lives? Even the money—money that, in the grand scheme of things, amounted to only a measly series of meals and conveniences. Fickle, ephemeral money in exchange for the lives of people! What abuse! What cheap recompense!

I turned at the landing to head back to my room, tears falling down my cheeks. In the moment, I wasn't quite sure why the tears came. Later, I would decide that they were a kind of a commemoration of my budding resolution. Remember this, Harry. Never to accept favors from the hands of your oppressors. Never to pander to your oppressor's guilt.

But I knew already that I would break my resolution. I'd not accepted his coffee, but there was the matter of food, shelter, and the clothes on my back. I felt my uselessness as an individual very deeply. Perhaps Chevy was right. I needed to get a job.

Back in my room, I rummaged in my nightstand for a pack of my Little Debbie oatmeal cookies. I assuaged myself with each bite.

15

Centralia, Pennsylvania
Summer 2019

As I've mentioned, Centralia was off Route 61—Graffiti Highway—with roads filled with potholes and littered with swastikas and White Power signs. Every so often a handful of sunflowers and peace signs made unexpected cameos, and long, hardy-looking penises, too.

At one point in time, Centralia was full of single-family homes, duplexes, and row houses. Long ago, if my research serves me right, Centralia had had a lace shop adjacent to its only theater. At the windows of the shop, A-line dresses hemmed with lace hung from pink velvet hangers. There used to be a school and a church, but the school was gone, all but one sole house gone, the church gone. The trees, formerly majestic, had burnt to ashes, most of the roots rotted away. No new trees could ever grow in the soil. If one walked attentively over the roads and pathways and trails, one could still see the smoke rising from the earth, and wearing thin-soled shoes, one could feel the heat. This was the truth of the place—a vision of truth beyond the American Dream: The town was a disappearing act. So much of the country was a disappearing act, all these people afraid of fading under the glow of so many brighter stars.

I had a dream to rebuild the town, but not in any way to resuscitate the old America, for I was not of the Purist mentality that claimed that we needed to make America great again. It was simply that my natural tendency was to fix broken things. Plus, the project would take me out of school and give me time away from home, as well as allow me the opportunity to do away with the horrible graffiti. This project would help me feel like a productive member of society. I would brush the town's grimy, diseased teeth; I would water its dry heart and loins, dress its tattered and balding head of hair, mend and clothe its disfigured, naked body, do my best to nurse it back to life.

A boy whose life feels decrepit and in need of reconfiguring goes on to rebuild a decrepit town. It's true, and I might as well say it, that a part of me did identify with the town. I was broken. More than that, I felt a dissonance between who I was and what I looked like. If I could somehow give the town a more fitting appearance, then perhaps I could one day also do the same for myself. I was hopeful that I could create a brand-new exterior for myself—revised, re-envisioned, and very much unlike those of my parents, and of people like them.

I divvied up the days of that summer and made an elaborate plan, which I followed almost to a T, and which I shall quickly re-count in the pages that follow (a rundown that is, of course, as true as my memory serves, as haphazard as the notes and reminders I kept on my phone, and as accurate as my high school senior project binder dictates). This period in my life, unexpectedly, was the start of strange psychological manifestations in my life. To this day, I cannot decipher which parts were real and which parts were not.

Day #1

A Main Street is its own justification, its own rationale for existing. It is the thesis statement. But even a thesis is indebted to its supporting paragraphs. Make them do their

job; both the thesis and the buttresses must count. For a neat
and orderly Main Street, think of lace, like a skirt's hemming.
Apply wrought-iron lampposts like road trimmings, like lace.
Make the lanterns higher than the highest heads, though not
as high as the soaring birds. Make them glow all at once in
that moment before dusk sets in.

Early that first morning, Chevy had given me the silent treatment.

"I'm leaving," I had said at the top of the stairs after I'd eaten my
bowl of Cheerios. Wayne stood loading dishes into the dishwasher.
Chevy sat at the kitchen island holding her palm-sized vanity mirror
to her face and adjusting her lipstick with the tip of her pinkie finger
in place of saying a word. The sun caught the side of her face. It
was mornings like these that the creases on her aging skin shined
in the light.

"Have a good day, Son," Wayne said in a daze.

I walked around the front of the gray Dodge Ramcharger and
placed my Centralia renovation plans on the passenger seat. I
had wound up passing my driver's test after all those lessons with
Wayne and after taking Woodrow Wilson's mandated one-semester
class. The Dodge Ramcharger belonged to Woodrow Wilson High
School and was one of the vehicles I had used for Driver's Ed. For
my senior project, the school had agreed to lend it to me (at no cost)
for the duration of the town's renovation.

Centralia's Main Street, the straight road that was no more than
half a dozen small-town blocks long, was a manageable focus for
my first day. I parked the car in front of the one house still standing,
took my shovel out of the trunk, and started digging to set up the
power supply.

Harry, Harry, dig, dig, dig, dig, dig, I sang. *Harry, Harry, Harry, digging
for a pot of gold.* I worked tremendously and tirelessly, only stopping at
3 or 4 p.m. to drive to McDonald's for lunch. For dessert, I ate a pack
of the Little Debbie Swiss Rolls that I'd brought from home.

I returned to Main Street and spent the remainder of the day mixing cement and pouring the mixture onto the base of each of the sites of the two dozen lampposts. Overnight, the cement would harden.

As I poured the last bucket of mixed cement into the final lamp-post base, I saw a man approach. In the evening light, the man at first appeared like a shadow. I looked up at him, surprised that he should be there. It was a hot summer day, but the sight sent cold shivers down my body. All day, I had seen only a couple of cars pass by. The population of the town was down to seven. I had no idea where the seven lived. Certainly not on the cavernous, decrepit Main Street.

"What you doin' there, kid?" the man asked. His voice was gruff and old.

I contemplated the man silently, and in my contemplation forgot to open my mouth and speak. A thought is the shadow of speech. Gather your thoughts and spit them out into words. I ordered myself to speak, but the words did not come.

"Kid, I said, 'What you doin'?'"

If you're looking at something you don't like, avert your eyes. Maybe your eyes are the problem.

I turned away from him and focused on the lamppost base.

"You deaf, son?" he asked.

"Just finishing up," I said finally.

"All that sand," the man said. "Why you pouring sand on the street, man?"

"Cement," I replied. "Cement for light posts."

"Hey!" the man said, snapping his fingers, the thumb and middle of both hands.

I remained silent.

"Hey!" the man said again, waving his hands in front of my face.

I looked up at him with irritation. "What?"

"You should have poured water instead."

"Water?" I asked. "Water won't hold lampposts."

"There's nothing stronger than the tendency of water to reach the earth."

I crouched down to pick up the remaining bag of unused cement and put it in the trunk of the car. I did not understand what the old man was going on about.

"You have a good evenin', now," the man said.

I began to wish him a good evening too—a mutter of a greeting— but before the words had alighted from my mouth, I looked up to see that the man was gone, disappeared in the blink of an eye.

★

BACK AT HOME that evening, I had barely entered the foyer when Chevy's voice leapt at me. "Shoes off at the door!" She hollered as if she'd been waiting all day to gather together and dump all the gravity that her voice could muster on me.

I removed my shoes as instructed. As I walked up the stairs, her voice came again from the living room. "Better make sure to stay off this couch," she said to the wall, not turning to face me. "Better stay out of the living room altogether. No telling what germs you've brought with you."

DAY #2

> How to set up a lamppost:
> Drill holes into the cement base. Put your post in place, followed by your bolts. Drill the base of the lamppost to the cement base. Make them firm like a strong opinion, hardheaded so they refuse to change their minds.

This particular morning, the sky was splayed with sunlight, blue and yellow and bright, and on any other day I might have been lost in the rapturous but stagnant beauty of it all. Those vibrant colors. But instead, for three hours I trudged the drill and all the cable lines along with the bag of bolts, drilling holes into the lampposts.

The wiring of the lampposts and the drilling of the bolts were more arduous than I had anticipated, and so after lunch (I'd driven to McDonald's again), I returned to the lampposts and soldiered along. Nearing 6 p.m., with only a half dozen lampposts up, I gathered the items into the back of my car, ready to head back home.

"Why you standin' there like a lost cause?" the old man I'd seen the day before said.

Startled, I screamed. Why hadn't I heard his footsteps? An elephant-sized man like him should have announced his presence long before he came into full view, but his steps were light. Invisible, diaphanous steps. Cobweb steps. "Are you blind?" I shouted. "You don't see me working?"

Zebras have horns in their upper and lower teeth and lead the way, eating the tall grass in order to pave the path for the wildebeests. The wildebeests don't enjoy the tall grass like the zebras do, so they rely on the zebras to eat those. In this way, they have a symbiotic relationship with each other. I reasoned that I was certainly the zebra, and the man, the wildebeest. If the man were to keep reappearing and disappearing, then how best to form a symbiotic relationship with him?

Or else, the man was a predator—a lion or a leopard. Zebra skin was black and white like shadow and light to absorb and reflect light in order to protect the zebras from predators. "Make like a zebra," I said to myself. How best to protect myself?

"Kid, let me tell you something," the man said. "Decorate all you want, these coal mines, they ain't never gon' stop burnin'." The man laughed until he lurched into a deep-chested cough, and then coughed until it seemed he was choking. I did not know if I should be concerned. Suddenly the man cleared his throat.

"Make yourself useful," I said, a reproof but also an invitation. "I still have to put up the lamps."

"Lights in a town in danger of being turned off!" the man exclaimed. "What you think your tiny little lamps gon' do?" He broke into another laughing-coughing fit. "All over the damn country, those surly mechanisms already be turning towns off, making them disappear off the surface of the earth. What, you think you any competition for government machines?"

"What government machines?" I asked.

"Boy! Boooooy!" the man snickered. He was tall—several inches taller than my five feet eleven—with earnest light blue eyes, the same color and inclination as mine. If it was true that growth continued until the age of twenty-six, then perhaps, I thought, in a few years I would grow to be the man's height, maybe even slightly taller. But, hopefully, never the skin! The man was white and as wrinkly as old wallpaper! And as he snickered, his wrinkled leathery white face furrowed further until it looked like the folds of an armpit. An armpit for a face!

"What machines?!" I asked, increasingly impatient.

"Son, it's just like you said." The man lifted his arm. His shirt-sleeves were folded up to his elbows. He pointed at the skin of his arm, but the rest of him remained unnaturally still. "All of us, you get? Anybody with this same skin, we're a disappearing act."

The statement struck me. I myself had had those same thoughts. Had the man somehow read my mind? But I couldn't waste time wondering; there was, after all, an entire town to be rebuilt.

I returned to drilling, dragging the black metal of the streetlamps I'd purchased from Edward's Home Depot back and forth across Centralia's Main Street. I dragged the load until all the lampposts had been drilled into the cement bases. The man simply stood and watched. He never offered a hand.

For the next three days, I worked on the lampposts. By day #5, the lampposts were up, with no thanks to the man. And yet, every day that I worked on the lampposts, he continued to materialize and, at the end of the workday, disappear much the same way that he arrived.

Day #6

Rebuild and paint the exterior of the abandoned house. Only the exterior, of course. (It was a superficial fix, but I was, after all, only one man.)

Fill up the empty spaces. Make the town come alive.

The home that remained standing looked more like a shed than a home. I set off to build a handful of simple log cabins. On YouTube I had found a video published by The Outsider, with instructions on how to build log cabins for less than five hundred dollars each, no permit required. Between Centralia's fallen lumber and the money provided to me by the school district, I could build six and paint their exteriors to beautify Main Street.

I struggled to gather the logs and the lumber for the roof of the cabins in and out of the back of the Dodge Ramcharger. I also struggled to gather any unburnt lumber from Centralia's woods.

"You need some manpower?" the man asked again. He had taken to asking this question every day at the same time—just after I returned from lunch.

"Sure," I replied. But, always, when it came time to do the work, I found myself working alone.

Day #7

For a less disastrous, desolate look, highlight the features, enhance the contours of the place the way a sapeur might use a razor to highlight his brow, the way a sapeur's red bow tie might square his sagging shoulders. All the beauty that is worth having requires some form of determination.

Unlike the proverbial God, on the seventh day, I did not rest. Instead, I spent the morning at the Edward Home Depot picking out vinyl siding for the exterior of the one remaining Centralia shack. I picked out a light butter-yellow and a blue-gray paint for the siding. I would paint the exteriors of the log cabins to match.

"You really think you can do this all on your own?" the man asked as I struggled to gather the siding and the buckets of paint from the trunk of the Dodge Ramcharger.

I ignored him.

"You need some manpower?" he asked.

"Sure, whatever," I said. I ignored him again and set off. Upon completing each front, I imagined that the man might finally join in and help. But he did not!

When I was done rebuilding the siding of the houses, I turned to painting them, not bothering to ask him for help.

Each day, when the sun began its descent in the sky, the man vanished as he always did.

Day #8

On day #8, I stood at the town's very heart—where the block of row houses that used to be the drugstore, post office, liquor store, hardware, and grocery store stood. Now the place was overgrown with pigweed and finger-grasses. I cleaned the area as best I could, pulled out the weeds, cut the grass.

Days #9–10

Examine the doors. Doors are the gateway into the home.
A first impression goes a long way.

I had planned to paint all the doors of the remaining shack and the log cabins red. On one of these days, the old man watched and yapped away about his long-lost family fortune in the coal mines of Pennsylvania. "In another world, I coulda been rich!" he exclaimed as I painted the final coat on the last door. That small expanse of Main Street now appeared like an assembly of red-uniformed school students.

"In another world, we all could have been rich," I muttered.

Day #11

A town is only as good as the roads that run through it.
Examine the roads and their signs. Take the unsavory signs down.

"You're free to go," I said. I'd had enough of the man.

"I'm free to go?" the man asked. "Go where?"

"I don't know!" I cried. "Wherever you want!"

"Damned if I don't know your type by now!" the man said, laughing.

"My type?" I asked, wondering what exactly he saw in me. Could he see that I did not fit into the skin I was forced to wear? Could he see that somewhere on that other continent, between the great mountains, was where my heart lay?

"You sure is the wrong kinda introvert!" the man chortled, an accusation. "You know, I done read the research. Don't nobody ask me why. But . . ." (and now he transitioned into a formal, almost-rehearsed voice, like an ad clip by Stephen Hawking): "Psychology tests show that introvert CEOs are better leaders and own better-performing companies than extrovert CEOs. But that's only if you are the right kind of introvert."

I was stunned by the man's register change. But beyond that, I had questions. "Meaning what? What exactly would be the right kind of introvert?"

"It's all about the collaboration, kid!" the man said, in his normal voice.

"Meaning what?" I asked again.

"You wanna be a good introvert CEO, kid, you've gotta learn to collaborate!"

"What?!" I asked, fuming. "If you wanted to help, you could have already helped!"

The man returned to his formal voice: "Introvert CEOs are more collaborative and don't need to be the center of attention, certainly don't need to be the ones doing or talking all the time. They take the time to listen to the ideas of others and watch others work."

"You had no ideas! You did no work!" I bellowed.

"Don't you know, kid, that the best companies are the ones where everyone's ideas are allowed to flourish. Everyone's ideas, son, not just the ideas of the loudest people!"

As I walked to the car, I resigned myself to silence. I wanted nothing more than to be rid of the man and his incessant prattle. But just as I put the car into drive, he opened the passenger door and jumped in.

"Get out!" I shouted. He grinned mischievously at me. "Please, just get out. I have things to do."

"Come on, man," he said. "I'm at your service. Just drive."

I sat fuming for some time, but my resolve was slippery that afternoon and, in only a matter of thirty minutes, all that remained was the ghost of my conviction. In the end, I yielded and drove, around Centralia, down Graffiti Highway. The air was parched like a sore throat. The trees—what trees? It was a careless thing to do, allowing this stranger in the car with me.

At the first giant penis painted on the road, I stopped the car. Beneath the blush-pink phallus was WHITE POWER in bold print. Next to these, a triage of swastikas. I shook my spray can.

"Paintin' over your very manhood?" the man asked.

This was the renovation I had looked forward to the most: getting rid of the penises and the White Power signs, no question about it.

"It's not *my* manhood," I said quietly.

"Sure is somebody's manhood, and somebody with a blush-pink cock like yours!" The man laughed.

"Shut up!" I shouted.

"If anybody's pecker we needa be paintin' over, should be one of them's!" the man said.

"One of whose?" I asked.

"You know, one of them's! You know, them blackies or whatever they callin' themselves these days!"

"Shut up!" I screamed, dropping my spray can.

"You ain't fittin' to be defendin' them folks, is you, kid? You ain't a nigger sympathizer, is you, kid?"

I grabbed my head with my hands. The world closed in on me. "Shut up! Shut up! Shut up! Shut up! Shut up!" I screamed, walking around frantically in circles.

"Hahahaha! What, boy? You cain't take a joke?" He continued chuckling, and soon he grabbed me by my shoulders, forced me to stay put, and began play-boxing with me.

"Stop!" I shouted, but the man would not stop.

I took a swipe at him, a sucker punch to his gut. I was stunned by his lack of reaction. For every action, an equal and opposite re-action, but the man did not budge. My second spray can of water mixed with white vinegar and baking soda hung on my tool belt. I grabbed it and sprayed the man.

"Hey, whatchu do that for?" he screamed, wiping his eyes.

"Get away from me!" He backed away. I followed him, still spray-ing. He retreated more quickly, and then off he went, away, away and out in the great bland expanse that was Centralia.

I tried to steady my breath. "Deep breaths, deep breaths," I told myself. I needed to compose myself if I would ever succeed in making any kind of headway on this godforsaken highway. Racism won't have a hold on you after you've made one thousand correct choices in a row. One thousand anti-racist choices and, surely, some-thing was bound to change.

DAY #12

"What're you doing here again?" I stomped toward the man, pumping an irate fist at him. "I don't need you. I don't need your help anymore." Not that the man had ever been of any help.

The man held his hands up, palms facing me, as if to say, "Hands up, don't shoot!"

"All right. Sure," he said, bringing his hands back down. "You gon' be that way, then be that way."

I had gotten a third of the highway cleaned by the time I left the night before, a wild, hysterical scrubbing. I hoped to get at least another third done.

I pulled out my cell phone and checked the time. Quarter after nine. A solitary brown leaf tumbled in the wind. I observed the leaf, turning away from the man. "Ignore him and he'll go away," I repeated quietly to myself. I began spraying the wall of the highway with my spray can. Only a few minutes must have passed before the man opened his mouth again.

"But seriously, kid. Know what a coast guard is?"

I remained silent.

"Used to be one." The man flashed a wide smile. "Bona fide US Coast Guard officer!" Now he popped his collar. His gaunt cheeks suddenly looked stuffed with pride. "But seriously, kid."

"Seriously what?" I asked, exasperated.

"Ever done the research?"

"What research?"

"Ever gone on Google?"

"Everyone and their father's been on Google," I muttered.

"Ever Googled how to kill a blackie?"

I screamed now and the wind carried it like murder.

"Hear me out, kid."

More screaming.

"OK. What about them Jews? I got myself a list. Wanna see?"

One by one, I threw the items from my waist belt at the man, first the spray can, then the chisel, my carbide scraper, even my keys. Anything I could get my hands on. Minutes passed. When I finally stopped screaming, I looked to see the man running into the road, faster and faster. I was stunned at first, but then after a moment, I wondered if I shouldn't also be running away from something. I started slowly behind him, unsure of what was going on. Out of the blue a truck seemed to appear, slow at first, and then speeding, then disappearing back into thin air. The man disappeared in the truck's wake.

The man reappeared unexpectedly out of the cloud of dust that the truck had left behind. I saw the woman then, old and weak, seventy or eighty years of age. Her brown skin was yellowed, jaundiced. A stigmata, a sign of physical illness. I'd read of this before: ancient red blood cells, forcing themselves into tissues, refusing to exit the body as waste. How long could she survive?

"Don't worry your young self," the man said. "I'mma take care of her."

"Take care of her, how?" I asked.

"That's for me to figure out, and for you to find out," the man said, holding the woman so that her arms hung around his shoulders and his own arms held her up. Her head leaned sideways into the groove between his shoulders and neck.

I shook my head. "Where will you take her?" I asked. "I have a car. I'll drive her to the hospital."

"Don't worry about it young'n," the man said. "I got this."

The woman moaned softly.

"Man, just let me take her to the hospital," I said more adamantly. He refused.

The woman moaned again—a sound like water rushing over rocks.

The man walked off with her. Her bare, cracked, blood-caked feet dragged on the rugged asphalt of the road. Where he was taking her, I did not know. I should have done something to stop them in their tracks—gotten in my car and cordoned off the road with the Dodge Ramcharger. Used my cell phone to call the police. Screamed at the top of my lungs. Anything. But the car was too small to serve as a roadblock. And my voice—when had I ever succeeded in using it to call for help? I did nothing to stop the man. One thousand correct choices, but *this* was not one of them. There the man went, escorting the woman down the road, and then they both vanished where the road curved, disappearing like dissipating smoke. And all of that because I had been unable to make the next correct choice in a series of choices. Now, how to begin again?

Day #13

Begin again. But before you spend any more on the houses, examine the land. Pull out all the remaining weeds. Pick up trash and all the burnt things. Apply fresh mulch.

"Feeling left out?" the man asked again.

I remained silent, forced myself not to react. I crouched and began pulling out the weeds.

"C'mon, kid. You ain't got no reason to be peeved at me. My house is far from here, or else I woulda taken you too," the man said. Then he laughed. Hahahahaha. The sound of his laughter was like a mockery of all things good.

"Go to hell," I muttered.

"Ever heard the story of two teens stranded at sea?" the man asked. "Flat-out stranded with nothing better to do than pray their ever-lovin' minds out to their ever-lovin' lord of a God. Get this, kid, two kids jus' sittin' there in that craggy-ass broken-down boat of theirs, countin' the minutes till the water swallowed the boat! Jus' prayin' and prayin'. And then outta the blue a boat named *Amen* jus' slide right on up, I mean right on up to their rescue! A-m-e-n!"

Silence.

"Ain't I just like *Amen*?" the man asked in a self-congratulatory way. "Savin' that woman like I did! My goddamned name oughta be Amen! Don't you reckon, kid?"

I scoffed, a mixture of derision, umbrage, and anger.

"I promise it's real," the man said. "I didn' make up that story neither! Happened off the coast of Florida! Now all them religious fanatics jus' gon' have a party!"

"What're you going to do with her?" I asked.

"Kid, kid, kid!" the man said, laughing like a rascal. "See the way you be takin' care of the whole of Centralia? Takin' care of this whole damn town! These days, ain't no doubt in my mind that you got a point. And seein' things as I do now, I ain't got no choice but to take care of her neither! We gotta, gotta, gotta take care of her! Without her we ain't nothin', and without her we got nothin'!" He laughed mischievously.

If he would only quit talking, I thought. He was the devil inside the devil's heart with an engine of a mouth. Even as I poured the new mulch onto the earth, the man continued talking, following me around, vomiting all sorts of nonsense.

But after I returned to my Dodge Ramcharger and to the small lawn mower I'd bought for the desiccated grass, after I'd checked the gas and oil and spark plug and primed the carburetor of the mower, and just as I pulled the starter cord, the man vanished into the thin, prickly air. It was nearing noon, and I breathed with relief and spent the remainder of the day finishing the landscaping.

Days #14–28

For a livelier atmosphere, plant some trees.

But the land was burning, and no trees would stand.

At the onset of the renovations, I had bought giant terra-cotta planters and had built giant wood planter boxes. This particular day, I began building boxes out of concrete, which I knew would provide its own insulation and be a great buffer from the burning Centralia earth. The high lime content of concrete was toxic to many plants, so I allowed the boxes to sit outside for two weeks, each passing day watering the concrete to allow the lime to drain out.

After two weeks, I poured soil into all the planters. I'd made sure to cover the bases of the boxes so that the plants grew in the new transferred soil, not in Centralia's soil. Even on burning land, perhaps there could be living trees.

"Ever heard of holy oats?" the man asked.

"Holy wh—" Before the question had tumbled out of my mouth, the man had already begun to describe a concoction involving boiling oats in water, boiling and boiling and boiling as if to boil the hell out of the grain, as if to turn the entire porridge into holy water.

"Oughta buy her a few more weeks. Before she crosses over . . ."

"Crosses over where?"

". . . Into the night . . . You know what I'm sayin'? Before she goes right on back to her maker!"

The sky went mad, spewing rain like rods.

"Crossing over . . . crossing over . . ."

Longing for something solid, steady, secure, I ran into the Dodge Ramcharger. If I were to be struck by lightning, and if I screamed out for someone, would anyone other than this man hear?

The sky was falling, and the man was yapping away. The firmament above was a stream of fireworks . . . Staying alive takes practice. Deep breaths. Fix your eyes on sturdy landmarks. Believe in the power of your voice . . .

DAY #29 . . .

It was nearing the end of July when I finished planting the saplings. Only then did I gaze into the flat gray landscape and realize that all the colors of the houses and their doors would do nothing to implant a soul into a place so somber, so forlorn.

The sun had descended, like a fire quenching, when I saw that same man in the front doorway of the third log cabin. I walked briskly away.

"Kid, come back here!" he called. "I was finna let you . . ."

I ran.

"Kid, don't be that way," the man shouted. "Come on, kid!"

His voice stuck to me hard and fast like a tick on skin. Run toward your fear. At first, it will grow. At first, it will become giant, gigantic. Run toward it still. Run, run, run. Closer. Before your very eyes, it will fizzle away like smoke. It will disappear. But the man had become an unshakable presence.

What happens when your fear doesn't disappear? What happens when it only continues to grow? A gigantic monster. Larger than Hercules.

Lightning struck. Another storm was brewing. The wind preached its indignation. "Be still with it," I urged myself. "Be still with it."

And so I was.

16

Edward, Pennsylvania
April 2020

THE ANTI-MASKERS WERE FLOUTING THE RULES. "MASKS required?" Becky Hanson laughed. "No problem!" She stretched out the cloth in front of her face so that everyone could see the mesh fabric. The holes were so huge, I could have stuck whole fingers through them.

Becky flipped her hair behind her shoulders. "Should be our choice whether to wear them or not. That's what my parents say, and for once I agree!" She chuckled a bit here. "We have rights. Nobody should take away our rights!"

"Hear, hear!" a handful of students chimed in.

Brandon Thomas said, "My dad has a beer mask. Just for laughs. It has a hole in it. He drinks beer through it. He wouldn't be caught dead with a real one!"

"That's right!" Patrick Chandler said, leaning on one of the red lockers. "Things gotta breathe! You know what I'm saying?" And they all fell into collective laughter.

Only the first few months into the new year and already the numbers were exponentially rising. No one at Woodrow Wilson seemed perturbed by this fact, though. Teachers still stood in front of their classrooms, holding their fingers and pointing sticks and metric rulers at students, tinkering with their computer projection systems and interactive white boards, like any other day.

I walked through the hallway carrying my plastic blue binder and the Dodge Ramcharger keys. I had just arrived, the morning bell had not yet rung, and already I wanted out. From my locker, I grabbed the stash of receipts for all the items I had bought for the renovation. Since having completed the physical renovation in the summer, I had stored the receipts for safekeeping in my locker while I prepared the binder portfolio for submission. The binder alone had taken me the entirety of the fall and winter to put together, longer than the renovation itself! In all my life, never would I have thought that mental work was a tougher beast than physical work, but this was proof. Now that I was finally finished with the project, I was eager to submit and be altogether done with it.

I shut my locker and left, dodging Brandon and Becky and Patrick where they stood in the hallway, maintaining what I measured to be at least twelve feet of social distance. I could not take any chances. At eighteen years old, I was aware of my mortality the way a middle-aged man is. I sensed, viscerally, the reality that was death. I felt it looming. I did not believe in my own exceptionalism, not at all, and certainly not where death was concerned. I did not want to die.

Already, in my mind, I saw the droplets from their laughter, from their breaths, those little infested bubbles hanging in the air like mini parachutes, descending slowly.

When I reached my senior project adviser Mr. Kopp's office, I laid the binder down on his paper-littered desk.

"Mr. Bird, mission finally accomplished?" he asked, looking up at me from the stash of papers that he was grading.

"Mission accomplished," I replied plainly.

I was proud of the work that I had done. Inside the binder, I had included initial sketches of the "before" along with what I hoped would be the "after" of various locations in Centralia. For the final section of the binder, I included the real-life photographs of the "before" and "after." In the pages between, I detailed the steps I took toward renovating the town, every section cleaned, every bit of graffiti erased, every edifice built, every tree planted. The only aspect of the project that I had not included was the Centralia man. I had no idea what to make of my experiences with him.

"Looking forward to reading!" Mr. Kopp said, and then went back to grading papers.

I ran into Mrs. O'Neal on my way to the Driver's Ed classroom.

"Wanted to hand these back to you," I said, giving her the keys.

"Great!" she said. "And no accidents to report, right?"

I shook my head.

She led me to the sign-out book, where I signed the keys back in.

"Where's the car parked?" she asked.

In the parking lot right outside the Driver's Ed classroom, the same place I had picked it up, I told her.

Together we walked outdoors where she conducted the inspection.

I was only going to submit the binder and return the keys because I was done with the project, not because I was done with school, but in the moments after Mrs. O'Neal and I reentered the classroom from the parking lot, and just as I stepped foot into the hallway to begin heading to homeroom, a sneeze descended on me with such ferocity that I felt dizzy and fell against the wall. Whose sneeze was it? I couldn't quite say, for the student had continued on his way, and I was left to deal with the potential repercussions of it. And what did I do? I ran out of the school! Why? Because the news reports of the virus were rolling nonstop in my head, and the sneeze felt like a terrible attack. Outside the school, images of Chevy and her germ trepidation began playing on the reels of my mind, suddenly justified. Of course, I had my own mask on—a cloth bandanna that I had begun to wear everywhere I went. But the dude had not had a mask on! What a relief it was, then, that I had submitted my senior project. I was effectively done with school, for as I had completed all my credit requirements, only taking electives in my final semester, graduation was guaranteed. Better safe than sorry. I made up my mind no longer to return.

17

Edward, Pennsylvania
May 2020

By May that year, the signs were already up. I saw them each time I went out on a walk, masked, of course, around town. All over Edward, blue, white, and orange signs read:

PRACTICING #SAFESIX?

Below the question, two masked stick figures stood six feet apart, a double-sided arrow between them to indicate the distance. Below the image of the stick figures, the words:

MASKING FOR A FRIEND.

And below that:

STAY SAFE.
#MASKON.

"Six is an arbitrary number," Wayne said one evening.

"It's been confirmed that the virus is like an aerosol spray that lingers in the air," he continued. "Which essentially means that we're all doomed."

Chevy said, "That's a bunch of baloney! They're droplets. They DROP to the floor! The hoopla is all just fearmongering. Droplets drop. It's not like it's airborne or something. If so, we would all be dead already! Do you know anyone who has died of the virus?" She was still cavorting with Lucinda, who continued to spend long hours training with clients. With the fitness centers closed, she had turned her garage into a private gym. Perhaps Chevy needed to believe that the risk of transmission and death was less than what some news sites said. "So, do you?" she asked Wayne.

"Not yet, dear. But ever heard of six degrees of separation? Honey, it's really just a matter of time."

"All right," Chevy said. Even from where I was, all the way in my bedroom, I could sense her irritation. "Six degrees, you say? Then, do you know anyone who knows anyone who knows anyone who knows anyone who knows anyone who has died of the disease?"

Wayne did not respond.

"Well, then," Chevy said, resting her case.

All day, I had been feeling ill, and by this time, I was feeling ill enough that I had the urge to say something. I could not have brought myself to go to Chevy, for our relationship had only continued to deteriorate.

I left my room and promptly found Wayne in the kitchen at the sink washing dishes. Chevy had by now retired to their room.

"Does my head feel hot?" I asked Wayne, who swiftly rinsed the soap suds off his hands, wiped the wetness off on his trousers, and felt my head with the back of his hands.

"No warmth outside of the ordinary," Wayne reported.

"I feel like I'm having trouble getting air," I said.

"You can't breathe?" Wayne asked, his forehead wrinkling with concern.

I shook my head. "It's difficult to, anyway."

We both stood silently for a moment. Wayne appeared to be thinking.

"Your color looks fine to me. Your lips are nice and rosy. No blue that I can see."

"But, Dad," I said.

"Can you jog in place for me? Just for one minute?"

"What?" I asked.

"You know, try and jog in place for me."

I began to jog in place. When I stopped, Wayne's eyes fell to my chest, then rose back to my face. "You seem to be fine," he said.

"But, Dad—" I said.

"I suppose . . ." Wayne started. "I suppose . . . Well, I don't know, Harry. You haven't by any chance lost your sense of smell or taste?"

I shook my head.

"Any coughing?"

I shook my head.

"Just to be safe," Wayne said, excusing himself. I watched him go to his laptop.

"What are you doing?" I asked.

"Ordering an oximeter machine. Next-day delivery."

"What for?" I asked.

"We can monitor your oxygen intake this way. It should be able to alert us when we absolutely need to go to the emergency room."

"Emergency room?"

"Don't worry, Son," Wayne said. "We're not there yet. We'll cross that bridge if the time comes."

★

THE FOLLOWING DAY when the oximeter machine arrived, Wayne called me over. I stood and watched as he wiped down the package with the alcohol wipes he had snatched from Chevy's Ayurveda shop. Trying to find alcohol wipes—antibacterial wipes, in general—was like trying to find an albino alligator, he said. They weren't available anywhere.

"All right," Wayne said. "Your index finger, please."

I extended my finger to Wayne.

A long minute went by, and the thing still did not produce a reading.

"It's not working," I said nervously.

"Hold on, Son," Wayne said.

Red numbers began to flash.

"Oh my God!" I screamed. My oxygen read 88%, with a pulse rate of 34. "I knew it! I'm dying!" I screamed.

"Hold on, Son!" Wayne said, frantic, turning the thing over, checking it to see if it was somehow defective.

Tears had begun to form in my eyes. "Dad, am I gonna die?" I asked softly. How long before death took its hold? What would dying be like? Would I have the strength to fight? Would I have the strength not to fight?

"Hold on, Son," Wayne said again.

I wanted to say that I was holding on as tightly as I could. But my mind was spinning. My bladder felt full.

"Son, let's try it again," Wayne said. "Son, your hands are freezing. Why don't you rub your palms together and warm yourself up before we try again? Maybe the sensor doesn't work as well with your hands so cold."

I rubbed my hands with fervor across my thighs, above my khaki cargo shorts, and then against each other until I felt the heat rising in them. After I had warmed them up, Wayne slipped the device onto my finger.

I let out a frantic, fear-filled moan as I awaited the reading.

"Come on, Son," Wayne said. "It's gonna be all right . . ."

The thing flashed numbers. This time the device read 96% with a pulse rate of 70.

"There you go, Son," Wayne said. "There you go. See, it's perfectly all right, you see? You're getting enough oxygen."

"But why isn't it one hundred percent?" I asked.

"I don't know," Wayne said thoughtfully.

"Do you think I need a pulmonologist?"

"What I think, Son, is that it isn't a good idea to be in the hospital right now," Wayne said. He rose from his seat, patted me on the arm, leaned over, and kissed me gently on the forehead.

I had never given much thought to Wayne's opinion of me, but suddenly I cared to know if Wayne was appalled by me, if the man was disappointed by my weaknesses the way that I was appalled by his. Involuntarily, my face scrunched up until I felt on the verge of crying. I truly thought I was at death's door. If a person wanted to die, he could just as easily give in to it. I could preempt it with a flourish. Plan my final exit, my departure from life, in style. But I did not want to die. I wanted to live more than I could explain. People said that those who chose suicide were cowards. I felt the opposite. I felt myself a coward for not being brave enough to yield gracefully to death.

✳

AT THE DOCTOR'S office the following week, I explained, "My chest feels tight. For a week, it's been a struggle to breathe." Even there in the office, I could hardly breathe out of the two masks on my face. I was also wearing the widest-framed sunglasses (Chevy's abandoned Jackie O's) I could find so that my face felt as protected as possible without having to wear a full helmet.

The doctor, who was careless with his mask-wearing, allowing the bottom strings to hang loose instead of tying them in place, rolled the cuffs of the blood pressure monitor around my left arm. How irresponsible, I thought, to expose your patients to your droplets in this way.

We waited quietly for the machine to take the reading. Finally, the machine beeped.

"Have you ever been accused of having high blood pressure?" the doctor joked. The bottom strings of his mask shook. I thought of the droplets, how easily they could spray out from his loose mask and make their way into my air passageways.

"Usually low: nineties over low sixties," I managed to reply.

"Well, then," the doctor said. "A little elevated. These things happen. You're at the doctor's office, you're probably worried."

My eyes darted back and forth from the blood pressure monitor to the doctor's face. I felt like I would break down right there in the examination room. Surely this was a sign that I was ill with the disease.

"Why don't we dot our i's and cross our t's today?" the doctor said. "I'll order up an EKG."

"All right," I said, nodding desperately.

I waited in the room in a gown that opened to the front. Practically naked and factually cold, I felt incredibly vulnerable. The technician came in and placed even colder strips of tape all over my body, and my insides trembled.

"Now, sit still. Don't move," the technician said.

When the EKG machine had beeped and stopped, the technician looked at the printed sheet. "One moment. I'll have to run this by the doctor," he said.

Again, I waited, my chest growing even tighter. If the printout had been normal, surely there'd have been no need for him to check with the doctor. My belly filled with a sensation of nausea. My head spun like a top. I was dying. I knew it.

I was certain that the EKG results were nothing but a death announcement when the technician returned. "Is everything OK?" I asked, trying hard to keep my voice from breaking.

"Yeah, yeah, definitely," the technician said, smiling slightly, tenderly peeling the tape tabs off my skin. "All set now. Just let me pack up my things and get out of your way. You'll be good to go before you know it!"

Why was he acting so nice, so compassionately? Fear rose even more in me. His compassion was surely a harbinger of death.

"But was the EKG normal?" I asked.

The technician did not stop his packing. As he wrapped the wires, he said, "If the doctor says it's fine, then I'm sure it's fine. In the grand scheme of things, this pattern is nothing to worry about."

I broke down in tears.

"Mr. Bird?" the technician asked, looking up abruptly, dropping the wires on the desk, rushing over to me. "Mr. Bird, are you OK?"

I bawled like a boy trying his hardest to fill a river. In the midst of the bawling, I managed to speak. "I'm dying, aren't I?" I sputtered. This was surely what dying was like. Dying always began with doctors' visits, which spiraled into more doctors' visits, which spiraled into more discomfort and more pain. Even though the doctors called you back, there was likely very little they could do for you. And yet they continued to poke and prod and force their strange medicines on you, which inevitably would speed up your decline until you were just plain out of life.

But maybe, I mused, dying was not the worst thing. Maybe living was the worst. Living was suffering. Being alive had to be the worst. Being alive was the dangerous thing. If you were dead, there was nothing left to fear.

"No, no, son! You're not dying! What would make you think that?" the technician asked.

I looked up at him, at the man's sincerely worried face.

"I'm not dying?" I asked. "Really?"

The man nodded. "Well," he said. "Technically, we're all dying. But you're gonna be fine." He tapped me gently on my thigh. "You'll be just fine, Mr. Bird."

"Thank heavens," I whispered with an exhale. I wanted so much to live.

Finally, after I'd caught my breath, the technician said, "You're good now?"

I nodded.

"OK. I'll send the doctor in. He'll talk with you and explain. You'll be fine, don't worry."

When the doctor came in, he was more jovial than before. "I hear you had some concerns," he said, smiling.

I nodded, feeling self-conscious. "My pattern was abnormal," I began.

"Nothing to worry about!" the doctor said. "Ninety-five to ninety-eight percent of the time, it's no cause for concern. Actually," he said, smiling cleverly now, "we see this pattern a lot in young muscular men."

There was nothing particularly muscular about me at that point in my life, but this statement did do a lot to assuage my worry. "So, I'll be fine?"

"Indeed, it seems you will live," the doctor said. "But if you want to be safe, we could have you come in for a stress test, an echo test, and a Holter monitor. I don't say this just to make money off you—or your insurance." The doctor chuckled a bit here. "But if it eases your concerns."

I had no insurance. With Wayne's unemployment, all three of us had been uninsured for some time. Wayne refused to enroll us in Medicaid. At first Chevy insisted that we should, but then she gave in to Wayne. I had attempted to enroll us without their knowledge, but I had found that I could not supply much of the necessary information without consulting them. This was the only problem with the country, Wayne liked to say. It would have been nice to be like Sweden or was it Norway or Canada, he said. And yet, he refused to enroll us in Medicaid.

In any case, knowing that I could not return for the extra set of tests, I had to believe that the doctor was right and that my heart would fall into the 95–98% category that was, in fact, just fine. I readied myself to head back home. Who knew what other patient had been on the examination table before me? Who knew whether the patient had the virus? I eagerly returned home to disinfect myself. Safety was fundamental. A safe home is a safe life. A safe life is a happy life.

One would think that this period of my life—in which I acknowledged the reality of the threat of germs—would have somehow endeared me to Chevy, but it did not. Neither did this period create any lasting bond between Wayne and me. I simply went through the motions of living, trying my best not to die, and they went through theirs, all of us dipping in and out of one another's lives in that sometimes vulnerable and intimate and other times distant and detached way that we were accustomed to.

18

Edward, Pennsylvania
June 2020

Bᴜ Jᴜɴᴇ, I ᴡᴀs sᴛᴀʀᴛɪɴɢ ᴛᴏ ꜰᴇᴇʟ ᴄᴇʀᴛɪꜰɪᴀʙʟʏ ᴏᴜᴛ ᴏꜰ ᴍʏ mind. I was getting no relief from my breathing condition. The doctor seemed certain that there was nothing of concern, and so Wayne and Chevy also believed that I was fine. But for peace of mind, I took matters into my own hands once again.

I arrived at the testing center as the sun was coming up. I had walked there briskly, for it was summer and Edward was filled with anti-maskers, and I had the persistent thought that if I somehow paused long enough to look around, I might become contaminated. I did not even stop at the pedestrian stop signs.

The testing center was a walk-up, like a drive-thru bank. I identified myself to the person behind the glass screen, showed my Real ID driver's license, the one that confirmed that I was a bona fide citizen. The health worker—in a mask, clear plastic visor, isolation gown, and plastic booties—extended their gloved hands out of the glass aperture, handing me two small packages.

The first package was filled with leaflets and flyers containing information on how to avoid getting sick—wash your hands with soap and water for as long as it takes to sing "Happy Birthday," disinfect counters and doorknobs and home surfaces regularly (never mind that we couldn't find disinfectant wipes, rubbing alcohol, or bleach anywhere), maintain social distance of at least six feet. Stay home except for essential reasons.

That first packet also contained a batch of free masks, those light blue surgical masks along with one white KN95 that felt soft like cotton.

The second package I was instructed to take to the next window, where they would use it to identify me and my test sample. There, at the second window, they stuck out their hand again, this time with a long apparatus that looked like an extended cotton swab. They asked me to keep my face forward. Reaching their hand out of this window's aperture, they stuck the swab-like instrument into my nose, pushed it, pushed it, pushed it. It was not terribly painful, but the discomfort was real. My tender, tender nose. How they assaulted it with this device! They held the device inside my nose, swirling around each nostril for fifteen seconds, but it felt like an eternity, and I thought, Noses are not meant for sticking things into—they are meant to push things out.

Finally, I was free to go. They would get back to me with the results in two to seven days.

By the time I started heading home, the streets were growing dark and then light again as if hours had passed and also had not. I felt myself growing agitated. A strangeness was creeping up inside of me. I roamed. I reasoned with myself that I should return home to wash myself. But I did not.

What follows now is a series of scattered memories. For much of it, I rely on the notes section of my phone, where I kept a sort of rough and scattered diary of this period of my life. As far as my memory of this stretch of time, it comes in and out, sometimes detailed and other times, remarkably less so.

My first set of notes, on the very same day as the testing day, reads as follows:

Ladies and Gentlemen, I stand here before you in honor of Love!

Love is love because of memory. All memory is meaning.

Good morning, good morning. It's an excellent day to be alive because you woke up on the ground and the ground did not wake up on you!

Good morning, good morning! It's a great day to be alive because it's raining from the sky, and not from your eyes!

On the second day, I was deeply uncomfortable, congested, feeling again that something was lodged inside my chest. I do not exactly remember where I must have been, but I do remember vividly the image of a tall pink-capped stork, acting like a referee, perched at the sidelines on an asphalt road while the smaller vultures picked at a dead baby fawn, waiting for the meat to drop and then, only then, did the stork pounce.

My next set of notes reads as follows:

A rhinoceros. Sometimes it looks like a termite's mound.

Euphorbia candelabrum for rhinos to eat. But poisonous for humans. If you touch it and then your eyes, you can go blind.

Cliffspringer. Klipspringer?

Like an ostrich moving its neck back and forth for balancing.

Life, love, and the pursuit of wilderness.

Have you ever seen two hippos fight? Very brutal and bloody. They fight until the death.

Like a giraffe, waving her tail like something between a swatter and a whip. This is how you keep the flies away!

Orange and blue like a flame, like a flat-headed agama lizard.

How does a leopard catch its prey? A swift, nearly bloodless kill. Powerful, muscular leopard. Selfish, too, always wanting to eat the entire prey by itself. Going as far as to sling it high above on a tree branch to ensure that it lasts him days. Like Shrek, a butcher bird, hanging its prey in the branch like a butcher's meat.

You know the most beautiful of sights? The wildebeests crossing the Mara River in Tanzania!

Everybody has a cross to bear. Even you, Harry! Even you!

I am me; I am dependable; I am a trusty sidekick! As faithful and as monogamous as a klipspringer!

Do you remember the day your country began to fall apart? You do? You do?! And what did you do to stop the falling? What?

My next memory is of running like a hyena, running as if limping! But I was lithe too, as lithe as a leopard's tail! My mind, I tell you, was a series of colorful swirls! Swirling words, swirling images. There was freedom in all those wonderful iridescent swirls!

Wandering aimlessly, wandering aimlessly . . .

You're a fool to allow yourself to get in trouble. But if you do, you're an even bigger fool for telling your trouble to anyone who cannot help you solve it.

When I find myself in a difficult situation, I ask myself, "What did your younger self teach you?"

"Love will cure an abundance of ailments!" I remember shouting, at some point, at the top of my lungs. "Love, LOVE, LOVE!!!"

The night wind had claws, and I shouted as if to combat it. "Love will cure . . . an abundance of ailments!!!!"

By this time—how many days now?—I had found a resting place by the dumpster near the Giant supermarket, across from the CVS Pharmacy. Some protesters had gathered there.

"My body, my choice!" On the surface they were all people like me—the women with their silk scarves flung across their shoulders, the men wearing white slacks in the rain as if to say to hell with practical things. All the young ones with their Veja and Adidas and Puma tennis shoes. In the back, a young man carried an American flag over his shoulder. Another young man in army cargo pants carried a sign that I could not quite read. A mother dragged her little child in a wagon. Another one carried her baby on her body in a baby sling. None of them wore masks. The rain beat hard. A little girl carried a sign made from a cardboard box. "Our body, our choice!" her young voice roared. Such power, I remember thinking. Such power, such power, such power.

I closed my eyes. I would do anything to blink away the sight.

When I opened my eyes, like a miracle, they were all gone. The moon was high above me. There was a wind, and combined with the rain, I felt a chill in my bones. But I could not bring myself to rise. Instead, I fell into a deep slumber.

In my next memory, the sun was shining again. Such glorious bright sunlight! The road was clear. What time was it? I could not have said. Where was my cell phone? I reached for it in my pocket only to find it dead.

A strange, overpowering sadness came over me. I was inert. My head felt laden; my eyes were suddenly overcome with fatigue.

I closed my eyes. When I opened them again, the road was full of people.

"No masks for us!" they chanted. "Our body, our choice!"

Two stragglers, a young man and a young woman, had severed from the group and were walking past me, oblivious that I was even there. "Hey, hey," the young man said. "You can't spell virus without U and I!" And he burst out laughing at his own joke.

The young woman said, "All right, all right, get this: Baby, do you need toilet paper? Because I am more than happy to be your Angel Soft!"

"OK, OK," the young man said, "check this out: If Corona doesn't take you out, may I?" They both laughed loudly. My head dropped. To make light of such a disaster. The protesters continued on. I thought about catching up to them and talking some sense into them, but my lethargy was greater than my desire to change anything. God forgive me, I did not have the breath to give.

19

Edward, Pennsylvania
June 2020

Be careful he doesn't rub against the walls . . . or the railing, or any of the furniture for that matter." I recognized the voice—the woman, my mother. "Filthy! Utter filth! How does a person allow himself to get this way?!"

"He's been roaming the streets for days, dear. God only knows all the places he's been. It's understandable that he'd be in this condition. At least we've finally found him . . ."

"Is that supposed to be a good thing?" she asked.

The living room looked like a morgue, white sheets spread over the couch, over all the furniture in the living room, even over the hand railing that led up the stairs into the hallway.

Chevy came out of the kitchen with a large plastic garbage bag. "I assume you'll go into his bathroom with him and wash him off? Once you remove his clothes, throw them into this bag and tie it up. Take it outside to the trash bin right away. Bring him back out here to the living room while the sheets are still spread. He can eat out here. I'll make him something."

———

How long had I been roaming the streets?

What of those protesters? Was there still a virus? Were people still refusing to protect themselves and others? How much of the country was dead or dying from it?

What had become of my Centralia renovation? And now an even more troubling thought arose in me: What of that old Centralia man? A shudder ran through my body. If I didn't get him out of my mind, I was certainly going to lose my mind again; I could feel it. I shut my eyes tightly.

When I woke up, I was clean and on my freshly made bed. The television from the kitchen was loudly yakking. A female news-caster's voice was saying, "They had B—, S—, and W—. Those were the front-runners. Now, they're down to—"

A male voice from the television interjected. "We must be unified and not allow ourselves to get angry. Anger never helps anything."

"And what exactly is wrong with anger?" the female voice asked. "Did we not witness firsthand what anger was able to accomplish for us the last time? Anger might get us even further—"

"That's right," Wayne said. "With all our anger, they don't have a shot!"

"But at least they're finally starting to see the benefits of anger," Chevy replied.

"So they should be grateful for our anger! Our man's an un-deniable genius! Look what he's already done for the country!" Wayne said.

Undeniable genius, indeed. I knew from Literature and Philosophy class that two diametrically opposed notions could simultaneously be true. A person could be clever and stupid at once.

"Look what he's done for the stocks, for one thing," Wayne said.

If executing the greatest con job in America was a sign of genius, then Wayne was right. For shouldn't it be obvious to the naked eye that attacking huge corporations and beginning trade wars in order to incite drastic falls and rises in the market were all part of a great con? Everybody knew the value of having the market crash over and over again! Simple: he and his cronies could buy shares for the extremely low market prices. Nothing as sweet as an inexpensive investment. Step 2: Renege on the convictions that led to the crash. Step 3: Incite the market to rise sharply again with new, paradoxical convictions. Step 4: Make millions from next to nothing.

It was also possible, however, that none of the ups and downs were curated. It was possible that all of it was a series of serendipitous accidents. It was possible to be an accidental genius, I thought. Still, if not a genius, the man was certainly intelligent. It was a mark of his intelligence to know the power of diversion tactics. But what was the value of misplaced genius?

"Those who don't like him can burn in hell for all I care," Wayne was saying. "They and their off-the-boat friends cost me my job!"

An unfortunate circumstance hurt you somewhere along the line of your life, I thought, and you decide to use that as an excuse to hurt others? But also, I thought: Not every crisis deserves to be engaged with. It is the nature of power to shift hands. Sometimes the best thing to do is wait your turn.

The news droned on. An abortion ban was underway in Alabama. No exceptions for rape or incest. Women were protesting. "It's as if Iraq has taken over Alabama," a voice from the television exclaimed. "America, the new third world country," another voice said.

It seemed to me then that the world would just continue falling apart, and what was I even doing?

I rose from my bed where I'd been lying in my white briefs and walked out of the bedroom, down the hallway, descended the stairs. My parents' voices were swelling and shrinking like waves behind me, and then calling, "Harry? Is that you, Harry?"

I continued to walk. The summer heat on my skin was an embrace. The streets were quiet for a while, and then the cars began to honk. Sometimes I heard the chortling of people driving by, stalling for a moment to look at me, before speeding off. Voices. What were they saying? No matter. The street smelled voraciously good and bad: the faint scent of cigarettes, the aromas of mowed hay, garbage, sweat. A blazing heat.

I walked toward the Giant supermarket, past it, toward the CVS. Inside the CVS, I heard the cashier snicker and then call out to me, "Sir, without proper attire, without a mask, I'm going to have to . . ."

I continued to walk through the aisles, perusing the items as if it were my first time in a pharmacy: Maybelline cosmetics, Claire's brand hair accessories. The next aisle: gift cards, wilted roses and carnations, the poor man's orchid. Chrysanthemums. OxiClean laundry detergent, Scott paper towels, multivitamins.

I heard the television broadcast again in my head, and I saw the old man from Centralia in my mind. By this time, I must have been standing at the medical supplies aisle. The incentive spirometer called out to me, and I picked it up, tore open its wrapping. I was no longer experiencing the tightness of my chest. I inhaled deeply and then breathed out measuredly into the small handheld device—a gradual, pacifying exhale. I breathed deeply again and exhaled into the thing, that same slow and measured way.

The cashier was approaching me, speaking to me. "Sir, I must ask you to leave. Sir, did you get that from . . ." The plastic package was lying on the floor of the aisle.

I stomped off, ignoring the cashier, still holding the spirometer in my hand.

Back into the blazing heat. I marched in the direction of home, but the old bitternut hickory not far from the Giant supermarket's parking lot was calling out to me. I went to it and sat beneath it.

How did I finally manage to get home? I do not remember. It was morning, that part I remember. The only other thing I would remember, years later, would be racing into my bathroom, tearing off my white briefs, brushing my teeth.

Harry, Harry, brush, brush, brush, brush, brush.
Harry, Harry, Harry, brushing for a pot of gold.

Harry, Harry, brush, brush, brush, brush, brush.
Harry, Harry, Harry, brushing for a pot of gold.

The splattering and splashing of the water on the sink drove me crazy. The wet splattering splash. My mouth felt contaminated. I put more toothpaste on my brush and began again.

Harry, Harry, brush, brush, brush, brush, brush.
Harry, Harry, Harry, brushing for a pot of gold.
Harry, Harry, brush, brush, brush, brush, brush.
Harry, Harry, Harry, brushing for a pot of gold.

My muscles tensed. My ankle made a cracking sound as I drew water from my cupped palm into my mouth. I rinsed, and again the water splattered loudly onto the sink bowl. Too much noise. Too much splattering. I needed it to fall down smoothly. I needed it to be calm and quiet and peaceful. Without that, I could not stop with the rinsing. I could not move on from the sink into the shower.

I must have been at the sink for at least a couple of hours by the time the water descended perfectly. My gums had begun to bleed. My shoulders had grown painfully fixed. My back ached. I felt as if I'd been there for as long as the time it took cement to set.

Finally, I patted my mouth dry and trudged into the shower.

Harry, Harry, wash, wash, wash, wash, wash.
Harry, Harry, Harry, washing for a pot of gold.

The protesters came to mind, holding up those signs and demanding their right to spread their droplets. Next, the vanishing Centralia man. "Come on, kid!" he was saying. I shivered. Formication set in. I had to wash away the words, wash away the sights altogether. If I could also wash away the memory . . .

Harry, Harry, wash, wash, wash, wash, wash.
Harry, Harry, Harry, washing for a pot of gold.

Even then, I must have known the futility of my efforts. All my labor rebuilding a burning town was pointless. All my enhancements, superficial. Centralia would keep on burning beneath the bright colors and the new face, even beneath the cleanliness and the sheen. And if the town were a metaphor for a body, and if the body were mine, then what to make of me?

Harry, Harry, wash, wash, wash, wash, wash.
Harry, Harry, Harry, washing for a pot of gold.

I could not coax the water to behave, to fall smoothly to the shower tub—it was the nature of water, after all, to splash, to ricochet, to make a splattering sound. More time passed while I began my shower afresh, each time struggling to control the water—its splashing and its sounds.

When I had finally managed to stop my showering, I climbed out of the tub and dried myself.

Back in my room, I slumped on my bed. My stomach hurt. It had begun to burn these days. A hot sensation that rose to my chest. The heat, the heat.

"Shut up, Wayne!" Chevy's voice came from the kitchen. "Just shut up! You're not helping the situation."

"Honey, I'm just saying that maybe we're to blame. He's a mess. Do you think he became a mess all by himself? Look at us!"

"Speak for yourself!" Chevy shouted. "You're the mess! You think you've set a better example for him than I have?"

"Yes!" Wayne shouted. "As a matter of fact, I have! At least I'm not a hypocrite!"

"What are you talking about?!" Chevy shouted. "Name one thing I was hypocritical about! Just name one!"

"Really? Really? You really want me to go there? Well, for one thing, you go around telling your friends and clients that the whole mask thing is a hoax, that the virus is a hoax, but then why do we have all these masks? You have all the PPE in China in your closet! And you *do* wear masks. Yet you tell people to forgo them! That is hypocritical!"

"They do not need the masks!" Chevy shouted. "I only wear them for my germ aversion, and you know it!"

"But you weren't wearing them before the pandemic!" Wayne shouted back.

"You know what? You know what? I'm so sick of you!" Chevy shouted. "So you think you're better than *me* now?" Her voice came out in a screech.

"This isn't a competition of who gets the 'Worst Parent of a Lifetime' award!" Wayne shouted back.

By now I had lain down on my bed. I should have eaten something, but Wayne and Chevy were at it again in the kitchen, and I did not want to be in the midst of their pandemonium. My chest tightness was somehow worse, my stomach burned, my head ached. I remembered my Tastykake stash. As I stretched out my arm to open the nightstand drawer, my eyes caught a glimpse of the shiny blue crystal seated on top, that singular gift from our long-ago trip to Tanzania. I picked up the radiant blue rock, suddenly forgetting the state of my stomach. I rose from my bed and boldly led myself to the front of my mirror, where I observed my naked self. "Look, location is an accident of birth," I told myself. "Paternity is an accident of birth. You had no control."

There was a clanking of dishes and silverware coming from the kitchen, and in that moment, I felt the change in me. I rooted myself in the change, in what seemed to be a new mind and a new body. A warm and good-humored presence enveloped me, and a new skin, thick and dusky like protection.

The morning light danced from the window like a bird or an angel of truth and tapped my shoulder. I didn't realize I was laughing, and why should I be laughing? Good morning, Good morning! Of course, you'd be laughing! It's an excellent day to be alive because you woke up on the ground and the ground did not wake up on you!

"Harry? Is that you?" Chevy's voice asked loudly all the way from the kitchen.

"G-Dawg," I whispered to myself. "G-Dawg."

"Harry?"

Still holding the crystal in my hand, I heard myself lightheartedly utter the words, "And thus do rocks determine the affairs of man!"

PART III

20

ALL OVER THE COUNTRY, PURISTS WERE LOUDLY LAMENTING their loss. All over the city, pockets of them carried on with their rioting, proudly defending their insurrection from the month before wherein they'd attacked law enforcement officers, stormed into and vandalized the Capitol, with intentions to harm chosen members of the nation's governing body: the senators, House members, the Speaker. I was beside myself. The veins of Centralia were still burning, and now the veins of the whole country were burning. But even in a burning world, I owed it to myself to forge ahead.

The doorway led to the basement of a nondescript coffee shop. It was still the tail end of afternoon, but between the short days and the shop's location under the dark shade of a pair of tall cedars, one would have thought it was deeper into the night.

Transracial-Anon met in the largest storage room of the coffee shop. DBT FOR SELF-ACCEPTANCE, a small sign read.

Another sign read: NO MORE GUILT.

"Looking at one's white self in the mirror can often be a stressful experience," the facilitator said, his mask hanging floppily from his jaw, covering his mouth but not his nose.

I was far enough away from him to be not threatened by his droplets. Lucky that the storage room was so large that it extended from one end of the building to the other, and there were hardly any supplies stored in it, so there was space enough.

"Emotional regulation techniques will help you identify a primary emotion and block out secondary emotions," the facilitator said. "Emotional regulation techniques will help you validate your primary emotion. Emotional regulation techniques will help you treat your primary emotion. Using praise and encouragement, I will reinforce your use of DBT skills. Let us begin again with positioning our-selves before our mirrors."

All of us participants exhaled almost at once while staring at our reflections in the mirror.

"What are you all feeling right now?" the facilitator asked.

"Repulsion," a bald-headed man spat. He was wearing no mask. I jumped and repositioned myself so that I was closer to the doorway.

"What are the rest of you feeling?" the facilitator asked.

"Sadness," a woman said. She was wearing a red polka-dotted bandanna as a mask.

"What are you repulsed by?" the facilitator asked.

"My body," I said. My KN95 mask was snug around my face. "It doesn't match who I see in my mind."

"Uncomfortable," another man said. No mask.

"Any other feelings besides sadness, repulsion, discomfort?"

"I'm afraid of what will happen if I remain this way and don't start to match the version of myself in my mind," I said.

"When's the last time you did things to match the self in your mind?"

"Not since I was a child," the bald-headed man said.

"I don't remember. Such a long time ago," the woman said.

"Never," I said.

"You've been avoiding your true self all your life? I can certainly understand why you are feeling repulsed by looking in the mirror!" the facilitator said.

"I just see whiteness, a big, bland, destructive soul," the bald-headed man said.

"That's a judgment," the facilitator said. "We always aim to steer clear of criticism and judgment. Remember, simply describe."

"I just want to drop this mirror and get out of here," I said.

"I understand how hard it is for you right now," the facilitator said. "But try to move toward your white self, toward the emotions. Go toward the fear. It is a big, bland white body reflected back at you. But look at it. Confront it. If you run away from it, your fear of it grows. If you stare at it enough, over time your discomfort will decrease. So, can we all move closer to our reflections right now and try to sit with them?"

Fifteen minutes passed. The bald man was crying.

"Perfect. How does that feel?" the facilitator asked.

"Painful," I said.

"I get it," the facilitator said. "But you did it!"

"Yes," I said. "I suppose I did."

"Good. Once you've all made peace and are no longer terrified of that self, we can work toward becoming your Black selves. A two-minute break, then let's try again."

This was the way my life went those days: at 10 a.m., I reported to work at the specialty shop (more on this later); at 4 p.m., I took my one-hour lunch break by attending my Transracial-Anon meeting; at 7 p.m., I left work and returned to my hostel.

After a long and arduous eighteen years of being confined with frenzied and unloving parents, I had been eager to be elsewhere. The particular night in June 2020 after which I had suffered my series of breakdowns, when I by chance picked up my Tanzanian crystal, my path forward suddenly became clear to me. What followed were days—no, weeks—of Internet research to set up my plan. I won't bore you with the details, but as soon as I could, I packed a duffel bag with some clothes and a third of the KN95 masks Chevy had ordered from Xinxiang and headed for the train to New York. I arrived in Manhattan in August.

It was fortuitous that I was eighteen and could legally inherit the money left to me by my grandfather. After settling the inheritance tax with the help of the executor, I was left with a cash sum of just under $40K. With this, I found lodging in an Upper West Side hostel, complete with two twin beds (a curtain between them), an in-room bathroom, free Wi-Fi, a restaurant café, and a sunken garden, just a ten-minute walk from Central Park, all for sixty dollars per night. It was supposed to be a shared room, but perhaps because of the pandemic, no roommate arrived. Moreover, due to the pandemic, common areas were closed off, buffet-style service was altogether done away with, and one had to wait in line, six feet apart of course, to pick up bagged breakfasts and bagged lunches. I was grateful to be lodging alone. I imagined that all other would-be lodgers had either chosen to remain safely in their own homes, or had been sick and confined in their own homes, or had been confined sick in some hospital somewhere, or, sadly, had died from the disease. This last thought always caused my arms to twitch and my breath to catch. If I did not immediately ward off the thought, I sometimes felt the urge to vomit, so I became efficient at suppressing it.

Unfortunately, even my grandfather's money would not be enough to live on past one year in the city, and I was well aware of this from the get-go. By the end of that first year, by my calculations, I would have spent over $20K in hostel costs. Food would be at least another $5K. Incidentals at least another $5K. I would be down to under $10K in the first year with no way of making it through the second if I did not do something. This fear of destitution was what, finally, gave me the courage to find a job.

And so by February, I had already taken a job at the first place that would hire me—a specialty shop that sold kangaroo meat for the persnickety cats of elite New York City cat owners. It was a solitary-enough job that did not make me too anxious. At least it was a job that I did alone, no coworkers or customers to worry about. The cat food was mailed directly to the clients. I was simply the middleman.

I had no idea who butchered and packaged and sent the meats. I didn't ask questions. What I knew was that the meat came all the way from Australia. The demand remained throughout the pandemic, even rose. I could have tried to learn more about this enterprise, but I didn't care. I only wanted to survive—as far away as possible from Edward and Centralia, and from my parents, and so I did not ask.

Memories of my days back then are blurry, with the exception of T-Anon and the specialty shop. But I'll say that the one consistent routine outside of T-Anon and the job was my daily visit to the park. After work and support group, I roamed the grounds alone, sat idly by the trees, listened to the audiobooks I'd borrowed from the library on my phone. Most days I ate only two meals (the bagged hostel breakfasts, which consisted of a box of Cheerios, a box of milk, a hard-boiled egg, and a banana; and the bagged hostel lunch, which was a Gala apple and a turkey or ham sandwich). Whenever I ate, I ate slowly, so that my stomach did not have the opportunity to be completely empty. After nearly a year of daily stomachaches, and much money spent on over-the-counter gut medicines, I had begun to look for alternatives. The helpful pharmacist at the Duane Reade had cautioned me that those over-the-counter medicines caused a rebound effect. The rebound effect, he explained, was the aspect that got people stuck on the medications for the remainder of their lives. "You can fight through it," the pharmacist said. "Constant food, eat like a mouse, but constantly. Might take some time, but the body knows how to heal itself." I never forgot those words. I powered through the pain and discomfort after that. Constant food in my belly was certainly more affordable than a lifetime of medication.

21

Manhattan, New York
May 2021

ONE AFTERNOON, I RETURNED TO THE SPECIALTY SHOP AFTER my Transracial-Anon meeting to find a flyer tacked on the door advertising full tuition and a housing stipend for white males aged eighteen and up who wished to enroll in the city's top universities as part of the white reaffirmation national plan.

This was, of course, part of the Purist agenda. I felt only repulsion for it. I ripped the flyer down and tore it into small pieces before throwing it into the trash.

A few days later, the flyer was up again. I looked around to see if I could ascertain who was responsible for it. All day, I had not seen a single person come up to the door.

Outside, masks of all colors littered the road and hung from the rearview mirrors of parked cars. I tore down the flyer, ripped it to shreds, and threw it in the trash.

The flyer did not return until the very last day in May.

Perhaps I had been too vulnerable that day. Perhaps I had been having a hard time inhabiting my new skin, or perhaps it was simply that a clarity had begun to descend upon me—that the specialty shop was a path leading to nowhere. I took the flyer with me, folded it neatly, and placed it in my pocket.

With my vaccine appointment that evening, my stress about the flyer quickly shifted into worry about the vaccination. I had elected the single-shot option, for fear of the shot somehow hijacking my already-fragile enteric nervous system. In choosing to get vaccinated, I knew I was doing my part in curbing the virus. Additionally, I could finally stop wearing masks.

It didn't escape me that there was the issue of the variants. That very morning, I'd read an article from a reputable medical journal which claimed that, according to recently performed research, vaccinated individuals had a significantly greater risk of becoming infected with variants of concern. Vaccinated individuals infected with the disease also had higher viral, more transmissible loads. Which was all to say that, though this particular pandemic was generally under control, another variant-driven pandemic was still looming.

The article was enough to boggle my mind. Why, then, was I even getting vaccinated? The best thing to do was still to mask up, carry on social distancing, carry on washing hands. Perhaps the anti-vaxxers had a point?

At the vaccination appointment at Yankee Stadium, where the jabs were being administered, I was given a fact sheet, listing the ingredients of the vaccine, who should and should not get vaccinated, possible side effects, its safety data summary as well as information on its clinical trials. Also included were helpful tips for post-vaccination and information on when to call the doctor.

The nurse shot the vaccine up my arm in a second. I almost did not feel it at all. Afterward, he monitored me for fifteen minutes during which I was sure I would immediately experience all the symptoms listed on the sheet: pain, redness, swelling, headache, chills, fever, nausea, fainting. But none of that happened, and after my fifteen minutes were up, the nurse discharged me.

Back at the hostel, I settled in for the night, still feeling very much myself. As I removed my clothes, I remembered the flyer. I took it out of my pocket and allowed it to sit undisturbed on my desk.

June came and went, and I did not experience any vaccine side effects. Same with August and September. Neither did I do anything with the flyer. October came and went, and still I did not touch the flyer. In November, however, and with the growing awareness that the flyer was in fact offering me a better opportunity than the one I was currently living and that if I waited any longer, I'd miss this year's application deadline, I revisited the flyer and, against my better judgment, I applied.

22

Manhattan, New York
October 2022

I STUCK A FINGER INTO MY CONTAINER OF BLUE MAGIC pomade, rubbed my palms together, then rubbed it all over my hair. Of all the beautiful scents in the world, bergamot was high on my list.

Now well into my first semester in college, I was settled in a new home—my first New York City home outside of the hostel. The scholarship's housing stipend was more than generous. Owing to it, I was able to rent my very own studio apartment in Upper Manhattan and quit my job at the specialty shop.

I had by this time rolled up all memories of Chevy and Wayne, dumped them into the garbage can of my consciousness, and taken the trash out. I was embracing my new self and reasoned that all of the discarding was warranted—of Edward and Centralia, of the home and landscape of my upbringing. Pennsylvania would, from 2021 forward, exist only as a reference of someone else's memory, never of my own.

"I am my body's healing," I said to myself as I stood before the mirror. "How unputdownable are you to yourself now?"

In the background, *The Vegetarian* played on Audible. It was early evening, nearing 5 p.m. The blinds of my windows hung open. Rain had fallen all afternoon and was still lightly falling, and now the cobblestone pathway and the trees were heavy with moisture. The sun was still up, hidden somewhere behind the thick blanket of gray clouds.

"Good evening, good evening!" I said to myself. "It's a great day to be alive because it's raining from the sky, not from your eyes."

"As for women who were pretty, intelligent, strikingly sensual . . ." the Audible narrator read, and I thought of Maryam. I could just picture her now, seated at the Midtown Diner, waiting for me. Strikingly sensual, indeed. Nerves sent shivers like lightning through my body. What if she realized her folly and immediately turned around to leave when she saw me?

"I am. I am meaning," I whispered to myself. "I may not always fit in, but in this new self, I belong."

I'd fallen for Maryam almost immediately, that very first meeting in Shephard Hall. I had just taken my seat in Rhetoric and Composition class when my eyes fell on her, and I promptly lost my breath. Every Tuesday and Thursday after, I continued to lose my breath. For the first six weeks of the class, I was always losing my breath.

What was it I liked about her? Quite simply, it must have been the way she wore her Africanness proudly—the way she walked, the way she spoke, the way she dressed. Her beaded bracelets and necklaces reminded me of my one and only trip to the continent. She even had an outline of Africa tattooed on her wrist. I loved her for this.

One day, at the exact same time as she was making her exit, I hurried to meet her at the door. She looked curiously at me. Her eyes must have scanned me up and down for no less than five ripe seconds. Meanwhile our classmates rushed out of the room, pushing and shoving their bodies through the doorway. Maryam took her time scanning me. And just like that, she asked me out! You can imagine that I lost my breath some more!

Two weeks had since passed, and now the date was upon us.

It was a quarter past five as I stood before the mirror, rubbing Blue Magic into my hair. The date was not until 7:30 p.m.

At around 5:30 p.m., I exited my apartment and locked the door behind me. Temperatures were warm—record warm—those days, but at least the most terrifying period of the pandemic had finally fizzled out, and having been fully vaxxed, I could look forward to moving about the city without as much worry.

★

THE TREK FROM 167th to 44th had been longer than I'd imagined it would be because of the random checkpoints—police officers checking pedestrians, subway and bus riders, and automobile drivers and their passengers for their vaccination cards (or, for those whose medical conditions or religions did not allow for it, their doctor's and clerical notes). The officers also checked my pandemic bubble registration. The purpose of the bubble was to attempt to contain social interaction to specific, identifiable bubbles. In the case of a sudden new outbreak, all bubbles would be essentially contained, or at the very least, more easily traceable. One could never predict when one would run into these checkpoints—they were in different parts of the city every day.

At that time, Damian was the only other person in my bubble, so I was cleared more quickly than several other pedestrians. Still, I practically had to run to make up the time I had lost.

I arrived at the Midtown Diner drenched in sweat. At the front of the restaurant, away from the doorway, a masked couple was arguing after being turned away for having no vaccination cards. I flashed my vaccination certificate at the pandemic security officer and was immediately granted a maskless entry into the diner.

Without looking for Maryam, I made a beeline for the restroom. I tore off some paper towels and frantically wiped my face, my neck, my palms. I unbuttoned my shirt and wiped down my underarms, my perspiring belly, my chest.

I tripped on a customer's foot, nearly falling on my face, as I walked back out of the bathroom. I gathered myself quickly, and when I searched the horizon of the restaurant, I found her seated only steps away from the man whose foot I had tripped over.

"Sorry," I said, as I approached her. "It's so warm today."

"Global warming, right?" she said with an assuaging smile. Then she looked more closely at me and added softly, "You OK?"

I was hovering over her at the table, and she said, "Why don't you take a seat and decompress? Are you coming from a meeting or something?"

I sat down.

"The walk was just much longer than I expected," I said, like a supplication.

"You walked from where?" Maryam asked.

"Wash—" I began.

The waiter arrived, interrupting us. "Can I get you both some drinks?" We must have looked of age, because he did not ask for our IDs.

I perused the drink menu. It's laughable that given how much Wayne and Chevy drank, I myself did not drink, and despite my close encounter with alcohol that day long ago—after the sapeur's lecture—I had in fact never ordered an alcoholic drink before. I was, after all, underage. I had to think fast. It occurred to me that if I should order any drink, it should be fruity—something sweeter and less acidic for the safety of my stomach. And yet, in practical terms, I had no idea which drinks were sweet. I carried on staring at the menu.

Though she, too, was underage, Maryam ordered a G&T with the confidence of a much older adult.

"Something to drink, sir?" the waiter asked me directly this time.

There was a silence in the space following the question.

"G-Dawg? Are you OK?" Maryam asked.

I remained silent, silently panicking. I remembered my phone. "Give me a second," I said. "There's a drink I had once that I liked. Let me call my friend Damian and see which one it was." I began to call a friend. The truth was that Damian and I were not truly friends. We'd only met briefly on campus, at the student union, where I had accidentally collected Damian's coffee. That was how I knew his name. Damian had been so forgiving that I had wished we were friends. We exchanged our contact info and, every once in a while, I called Damian with a question, just to keep the relationship from fizzling out. One day I had brought up the idea of, with his consent, registering him as part of my pandemic bubble. "Sure, bro. Makes perfect sense," he'd said. It was as easy as that. Later, I had invited him to happy hour drinks at the diner. I didn't actually have a drink that day. It was Damian who'd had a drink (he was the one of legal age, after all; though we'd also not been carded then either). In any case, the drink he'd ordered had looked really good to me from a distance, the way, I suppose, fire or lightning storms always look beautiful from afar.

"If you describe it to us," Maryam was saying.

But how could I describe a drink I'd never actually imbibed?

"I can come back in a few minutes," the waiter said.

Their voices were starting to overwhelm me—Maryam's and the waiter's. The phone continued ringing and then finally it went to voicemail. I left a message. "Hey, man, it's me, G-Dawg. I just wanted to know what drink you got the other day . . . Call me . . . You got my number . . ."

"Sorry," Maryam said to the waiter. "Yes, please. Can you come back in a few minutes?"

The waiter nodded and left.

"Need help deciding?" Maryam asked.

"On second thought, I think I could just use a glass of ice water," I said.

"You sure?" Maryam asked.

"Yes," I said, clearing my throat and wiping the sweat off my forehead with the napkin on the table. "Very sure."

———————

Handsome man, beautifully strong build, Maryam would tell me later, when she recalled her thoughts of me on that first date. But as she watched me use my napkin to wipe down the rim of my glass of ice water, and as she watched me gulp the water down, her face remained inscrutable.

The plates of burgers and fries arrived, and, of course, I wiped down each one of the utensils, though I knew I'd only be needing the knife to cut my burger in half, and the fork to eat my fries. No use for the spoon. We ate silently for a few minutes.

"So, where'd you get a name like that from? Like, is it your real name?" she asked. "Pretty sure it's just a nickname, but you let me know."

"My name?" I retorted, at first startled by the question. Then I registered why such a question might be pertinent. I said, "It's a long story."

"A long story?" Maryam asked, sipping on her G&T. I must have looked completely white to her at that point, for she said, "You seem completely white."

"Long story," I said again.

"We've only just arrived," she said. "You have all evening to tell it to me."

"Next time," I said.

Later she'd ask me how it was that I could have been so sure that there'd in fact be a next time. My saying "next time" had apparently given me an air of confidence (which, in reality, I did not have).

"So, you're from New York?" she asked.

I shook my head. "No. Not from New York," I said. "But I kinda wish I were . . ." If I had been from New York, then maybe I wouldn't have had such a long story to explain. Truth was, I blamed my parents and all of Edward and Centralia for the way my mind had collapsed, or maybe for the way my mind had become too aware of all the collapsing things around me. I blamed them for my disowning of them. I blamed them for bringing me into the world as a person I'd rather not be, in a skin I'd rather not have.

"Where, then?" Maryam asked.

"It's a long story," I said yet again.

We returned to silence and carried on eating our meals.

There's always that point in a date when the conversation drags like a garbage bag filled with a dead body or, perhaps less morbidly, like the train of a bridal gown. The appetizer (none in this case) and the main course (the burgers and fries) have served their purpose, as has the booze (hers), and someone (she) is deciding if it's a date worth staying any longer for.

I smiled awkwardly at Maryam in that moment and later she'd tell me that the indent of my dimple and the way my face lit up did something to her—made her insides "tingle like a shot of whisky." I wiped my lips with my paper napkin and then set the napkin down on the table. It didn't matter that my mouth "looked like a line somebody drew," she'd say.

In any case, in that moment, it seemed to me that she was suddenly aware of herself. Her lipstick was perfectly applied, and her locks were still flawlessly pinned back in that "be sure to take me seriously" kind of way. Still, she checked them both in her pocket mirror, dabbing at the sides of her lips and patting her hair just as the waiter was taking away our empty dishes.

In a few minutes our date would be over, and she'd be gone, and depending on how these last few minutes went, she might never give me the time of day again.

"So, what's your major?" she asked.

"International Relations," I replied.

I saw the celebration in her face. "Aha!" she said. "You finally answered a question!"

I chuckled. "Yours?" I asked.

"Undecided," she said.

23

Manhattan, New York
November 2022

ON OUR SECOND DATE, ONLY A FEW DAYS LATER, AGAIN AT THE Midtown Diner, I saw stories in her dress—in its birds, its flowers, its verdant tree. I admired her accent and her deep velvety voice and the way her hair was rolled up in thick strands. And her lips, I imagined kissing them; I had never kissed a pair of lips before.

"You live in the dorms?" she asked.

"No," I replied. "A studio uptown."

"Better than the dorms, I'm sure," she said. "Do you like it?"

"It's fine enough," I said. "But hopefully one day I'll move into a bigger place."

"What do you need a bigger place for? Don't guys usually like tight spaces?" she asked, giggling softly.

I nearly choked on my water and felt my face turn pink.

Where was she from? I'd forgotten to ask her on our first date. I cleared my throat and said, "You're from the continent?"

She nodded. *"The* continent," she said. I'd learn later that whenever anyone asked Maryam where she came from—schoolmates, cabdrivers, pedestrians, metro riders, especially those in the Chelsea or

Greenwich Village stops—she simply told them abroad. If they pestered her for more, which they often did, she'd say Nigeria. They always followed by asking after her family, and she'd simply say she was the daughter of a doctor and a stay-at-home mom. No matter what their reaction was to her answer, she seemed to think that they were making a judgment about the state of her country—based on something they'd watched or heard on their mega televisions or computer screens—or sometimes, she wondered if they didn't miraculously know something about her personal life—about the doctor and her Mumsi, and the devastation that was her home.

So it made sense that when I asked the question that day, she was as vague as possible. She nodded in a way that seemed to say, *Let's just keep it moving.* I had to pause and ask the question more precisely, for in that moment, it seemed to me, rightly so, that we both had a past we'd rather soon forget, and this could be a point of deeper connection.

"Where exactly?" I queried, recalling my time in Tanzania. Thinking that perhaps she might be from there or close by.

"Congratulations," she said. "You've passed this round. You're clearly aware that Africa is not a country."

I laughed shyly. "What's the next round? Also, you still haven't said what country."

"Nigeria," she replied.

"Nigeria?" I repeated, trying, as I said it, to recall just what I knew of the country.

She must have read my mind because she said, "It's OK if you don't know much about it. Some say it's the reemerging pride of Africa. Only time will tell."

"What once was can certainly be again," I said in what I deemed a supportive tone.

She nodded. "So, you won't tell me where *you're* from?"

"You ask a lot of questions," I said.

"Do I?" she asked. "Well, your turn, then. What other questions do you have for me?"

"Are you committed to dismantling white supremacy?" I asked. I still don't quite know exactly where the question came from, but I do know that I was very much in the midst of embracing my true self, and so it was perhaps only natural that a question like that would emerge. Suffice it to say her shock was undeniable.

"You're serious?" she asked, her eyes widening, her forehead furrowing.

"Yes," I said. "Very serious. Are you committed on behalf of *all* people of color?"

She looked flabbergasted.

She was a Black woman. Of course she was committed to the cause on behalf of all people of color. I should have thought of this at the time. But then again, being a person of color didn't mean that one was committed to dismantling white supremacy. There was, after all, the issue of internalized racism. Still, what business did I, a neophyte, have asking such a question?

"So, you're really into Blacks or Africans or what? Or just me?" she asked.

"Umm," I said honestly, "I've never thought about it in those terms."

"So, you won't just dump me in like two days?" she asked.

I must have seemed surprised at the question because she said, "I don't mean to presume, but becoming an item would be the natural progression of things, don't you think? Or are you one of those guys who's just into hooking up?"

"Yes, yes," I said, nodding. "I mean, no. Yes to becoming an item, I mean."

She chuckled at me. For a moment I had an out-of-body experience in which I found myself nodding, so fiercely that my head might very well have fallen off. What an idiotic sight. I collected myself and smiled at her and held my head with a bit more restraint. Of course I wouldn't just dump her in two days. I'd heard the stories. I knew that for some men, dumping a woman was nothing. But I was not that kind of man. I imagined that it would have been like dragging a pitchfork across his flesh for a true African man to dump his African queen.

When the waiter arrived with the check, before Maryam could even so much as glance in its direction, I picked it up. The music in the diner was louder, Celine crooning, the lyrics to that ancient but enduring song "That's the Way It Is" billowing into the easy diner air.

As we exited the restaurant, I wrestled with questions: Should I offer to walk her home, or offer to take the subway with her home? Or only offer to walk her to the subway, like last time? And if she said yes to any of them, should I offer to hold her hand? And if and when we arrived at the subway stop, or at her doorstep, should I lean in and kiss her? The thought of all the points that had to align in order for a kiss to happen made my palms sweat, never mind the thought of the kiss itself.

At the front of the restaurant, I wiped my palms on my pants and cleared my throat to speak. "You want to come back to my place?" I asked, then immediately scolded myself. Where had that come from? Of all the questions on my mind, that had not been one of them.

"Your place?" she asked, grinning. "Well, maybe another time," she said flatly. "I have to meet Tyler and Justine tonight. Group project."

I had no idea who Tyler and Justine were. Didn't matter. I took that as a rejection and said, "Of course. Anyway, it's far too early for me to be inviting you to my place. I completely understand. Not a problem at all." I wiped my palms on my pants again and raised my hand for a handshake.

She giggled. "Really? A handshake?"

I felt heat rise in my face. Thank God for the evening's darkness. I pulled my hand away and leaned in to hug her. The scent of rosemary oil filled my nostrils, and for a moment I took in the aroma as a symbol of victory, an indication that I was after all still on my way to winning her over. But just as my arms were about to encircle her, she pulled away.

I gazed, confused, at her. Suddenly I was fractured—a young adult man and a helpless little boy at once, or a snail, shrinking back into its mollusk shell. The situation had made itself crystal clear. This was certainly a rejection. I'd bombed this second date. Without saying another word, I turned around and bolted.

24

Manhattan, New York
November 2022

THE HOURS FOLLOWING OUR SECOND DATE SIMMERED WITH anxiety. I crouched in the corner of my apartment where my kitchen met the laundry closet. Thus far, it seemed to me that I'd at least semi-successfully molded myself into my new identity— that at the very least, I was a solid work in progress—but now I wondered. I had imagined things like dates would be much smoother in this new identity, but alas. I was not any less certain of my decision to become this new man, and yet there was a nagging pain in my heart from failing at this first attempt at dating as the new me.

In those days, there was a restaurant directly beneath my apartment. When I returned from my date with Maryam, the restaurant had just closed its doors. The noise of the customers slowly dulled to silence. The cigarette smoke that crept in between the hours of 4 p.m. and 9:30 p.m. through my badly sealed windows had not yet begun to dissipate and should have bothered me like it usually did. But I was engaged with the phone in my hands. "Restraint in an App," the motto under the Dignity logo read.

"Turn on Dignity," I said determinedly into the smartphone.

Turning on Dignity, G-Dawg, the sultry female phone voice replied.

I breathed with relief as I waited for the next step. I had, a long time ago, memorized the Dignity commercial:

> Dignity will assist you in taking charge of your life. Dignity can be purchased at full retail price or leased. Additional features include custom curating and grooming. When not in use, Dignity can be silenced or placed on vibrate, or turned down to its lowest volume setting. If so desired, it can also be stored away or discarded, as you wish. Do note that even when discarded, Dignity will continue to run in the background. In the event of a new crisis, Dignity will be only a finger's reach away. Not to worry. A reliance on Dignity is by no means an indication of being any less capable. Take heart and be brave: Trust Dignity to work for you.

I replayed the commercial in my mind as I waited.

To which of your contacts would you like to apply Dignity? the sultry female voice asked.

"Maryam," I replied, emerging from my musings.

Duration of application?

"Forever," I replied, and returned to crying. My nose became cluttered with snot. Shame was a winding road whose end I could not see. Forever was how long it would take me to get over my broken dream. I needed Dignity for forever, or else I might be tempted to call Maryam, to beg her to give me just one more chance. She could, of course, based on the app's parameters, be the one to contact me. But I would be forever banned from initiating any contact. Banned even if I were to delete the app. At the time, that was fine by me.

If I sat perfectly still, I hoped I could conjure the aroma of her rosemary scent. I tried once. Twice. Thrice. The scent was as elusive as sleep for an insomniac. I tossed and turned and still could not conjure it.

I rose from where I crouched and began pacing around the apartment. My phone still rested in my hands. I placed it on the kitchen counter and walked toward the bed in the corner of the room. The clock on the nightstand flashed 11:11 p.m. I tore off my clothes, leaving only my boxers on.

I sat on the edge of my bed, my shoulders sloped. I heard a rustling sound coming from the kitchen. I ran for my phone, but the screen was unlit. No new messages. No new calls. I left it where it lay.

Earlier that evening, as I cried my way back to my apartment, I'd managed not to pass any police checkpoints. Near my building, I'd stepped into a bodega and bought a pack of Rolling Rock—the first beer I had laid eyes on. At the register, I'd made an awkward excuse about having forgotten my ID. The clerk called the manager, and just when I thought I did not stand a chance, the manager relented. "Next time I'll bring my ID," I said gratefully. "There'll be no next time," he replied. I plopped the pack into the fridge upon arrival. "Chill," I told myself. "Have a beer."

I snapped open a can and guzzled half its content at once. It only occurred to me after I had drunk the first half that I had not wiped the top of the can. It was too late by then, but I wet a paper towel and wiped it all the same. I walked over to my bed with the remainder of the beer can. The clock flashed 11:17 p.m.

I had forgotten my phone on the counter. I rose to retrieve it. As I did, I knocked over the remainder of my beer, which spilled all over my boxers. I squealed in frustration. I wiped myself off the best I could with a paper towel and finally retrieved my phone. Back on my bed, I tempted the app. I dialed her name, but the phone flashed bright red and made a sound like a police siren. I dialed her name a second time to the same effect.

"How dare you?" I shouted at Dignity. I threw the phone at the wall. It crashed to the floor. "Who needs Dignity!" I moaned.

✱

When morning came, I opened my eyes to bright daylight. My phone lay on the floor where I'd left it. My sheets were disheveled and smelled of beer. My chest hurt—that old, familiar burning that started from my stomach. Something in my mind was troubled, but as my mind was still cloudy with beer and sleep, it wasn't until I picked up my phone and saw her text (You ran off so fast last night. Hope you're OK. Let me know.) that I remembered. I felt the heat rise sharper in me. I typed back, elated, almost frantically: So good to hear from you! Very sorry for running off!

I deleted the text and retyped: Very sorry for running off. I was concerned that I had bombed the date.

I erased again and retyped: Sorry about that! If you're available soon, I can explain.

Finally content with the text, I hit send. The phone flashed bright red and made a jarring sound. I stared at the phone. I pushed several keys at once. The phone shrieked, shrilled. Police siren colors swirled ferociously. Heat prickled my cheeks, blossomed to the skin of my neck, to my chest. I exhaled forcefully and then the tears rushed out. My shoulders heaved.

Dignity had seized me by my proverbial lapels and stripped me of all my strength, of my initiative, of my ability to respond to the most important text I'd received in a very long time. My surroundings began to close in on me. The love seat, the bed, the metal barstools by the kitchen counter—they all grew gigantic as if to drown me, and then promptly they shrank away into a gray void.

When I came to, I looked around, found my phone by my side. My wrinkled boxers were pushed up against my hips so that my flaccid penis stuck out past the hem. The smell of beer on the undergarment was now noxious and so I stripped it off. I stood up. Even with the quick rise, my head felt astonishingly clear except for the faint cloud of an almost-forgotten worry.

I remembered. I walked over to my desk, opened the lid of my MacBook Air, and sighed with relief when her Gmail address popped up in the compose message screen.

SUBJECT: I got your text

I'M SO sorry not to have gotten back to you earlier. My phone is having some technical difficulties. Can we meet again and I can explain why I ran off?

I held my breath and hit send right away. Sending, the email screen said. Then: Message Sent. I waited a few minutes. If Dignity had a loophole, a blind spot, it would have to be my computer. How could the app control my computer when I'd never supplied it with Maryam's email address? I stared at the screen. Nothing. Dignity had to be overrated. Desperation would surely always prevail.

A few more minutes and still no alarm. The joy that flooded me was a thick ray of gold light, a mixture of relief and desire, a billowing heat gathering and throbbing in my groin. I felt the erection like an ache inside of me and then looked down to see myself large and spitting slightly from my tip. I brushed my index finger over the wet peak, but that was it. I would let the rest be. It was nothing a warm bath wouldn't soon subside.

THE FOLLOWING DAY, Sunday, as I groomed myself in the bathroom, still listening to *The Vegetarian,* I wondered why a man would be so troubled by his wife's decision not to wear a bra. In a few minutes, I would be meeting Maryam and I could only hope that she was not in fact wearing a bra. More than that, I found myself hoping that her bralessness would be plainly evident to me.

But, of course, I was nothing like the fictional husband in *The Vegetarian.* I hoped to always be respectful of my partner—in this case, Maryam. Even if nothing came of my dates with her, I was grateful for this opportunity to try again.

I leaned toward the bathroom mirror, peered at my reflection in the glass, said loudly to myself, "Good morning! Good morning! It's a good day to be alive because there's beer in the fridge and not on you!"

Maryam flashed again in my mind, and I added, "Good morning! Good morning! It's a good day to be alive because there's a woman in your life, in place of your hands!"

★

IT WAS ANOTHER strangely warm November day. Vaccination and bubble checkpoints notwithstanding, I arrived at the park on time and in good condition. As I reached the meetup spot that Maryam had suggested, an orange ball rolled out of nowhere, which made me remember something I'd read somewhere: If ever you catch sight of a rolling ball, go slow, because a child is sure to follow. I was not in a car but on my feet, and this was a park where no cars were permitted, but just as expected a little blond pigtailed girl emerged, chasing the orange ball. Only a few steps behind the girl was Maryam, calling out, "Sophie! Remember, you have to stay close!"

To me, Maryam said, "If anything ever happened to her, her parents would kill me. I mean, she's a fine kid and all, and I wouldn't want anything happening to her . . . but I also need the money. My scholarship only partially covers room and board!" She smiled anxiously at me, and I remembered the husband in *The Vegetarian*. I peered as inconspicuously as possible at Maryam's chest, at her short blush-pink chiffon dress with its low V-neck. Though I was somewhat able to see the bulge of her breasts through the décolletage, her locked strands of hair hid the area where her chest rose. I was not able to see her nipples.

I should mention here that Maryam was a full year younger than me. I must have seemed less confident than she would have expected of a person older than her, but perhaps she found something beautiful about my bashfulness. Later, she'd tell me that she liked the juxtaposition of the two things: the shy, sweetly hesitant youngish guy that I was and the towering, masculine man that I was becoming. I was indeed basketball player tall, and she might have imagined this made me a voracious, passionate lover. I was on the lankier side, but I could have picked her up off the ground with only a little more effort than I could have a basketball. But I did come off as quite gentle, so it is possible that she did not think of me as the kind of man to pick a girl up off the ground.

"So why did you run away?" she asked, peering at me.

I stammered, "I . . . I thought maybe you—"

"You thought what?" she asked.

"You'd pulled away—" I said.

"I pulled away?" she asked, and then she seemed to remember it. "Oh," she said. She went on to explain that right after I offered her a handshake, it had occurred to her that she was sweating. She'd pulled only a little away, just out of the embarrassment at the possibility of my smelling her sweat. But even before she could really register her thoughts, I was running off. "I didn't mean to do that. It's just—" Her voice broke. "I'm sorry. I wasn't actually pulling away from you."

"Oh," I said, feeling a bit silly at my overreaction.

"Anyway," she said. "I have to drop Sophie off with her parents at six p.m. You're welcome to hang out with me and her here at the park until then."

We walked what must have been at least two miles, chasing little Sophie chasing her ball, and finally all three of us settled in a corner of the park where two sides of a tall wooden fence met.

"So, what do you like to do for fun?" I asked Maryam.

"Fun? What's that?" She laughed. Between her jobs and school, she had time for little else.

"You don't have any fun at all?" I asked.

"Not much to do in the city if you have no money," she said. "I looked it up once online: Things to Do When You Have No Money. Want to know what Google said?"

"What?" I asked.

"Babysit a child." She laughed. She couldn't bring herself to mention the HandyMan job at this point. The few guys she'd told had apparently made fun of her for it. "You a dyke?" one had reportedly asked. The idea of a woman being able to fix things was somehow threatening to his masculinity.

She didn't want to bring it up with me, not then. Too soon. Though she also imagined that if I were the right man, then I'd be able to handle her skills. But she needed more time before she could allow herself to be vulnerable with me.

She carried on talking about babysitting. "Google hit the nail on the head, so, here I am, babysitting a child."

"Ha," I replied.

"You?" Maryam asked. "What do you like to do for fun? You seem like you're good with money, so probably no babysitting for you."

I turned away from her. "I do OK with money," I said. "Full scholarship," I said quietly, then regretted saying it. The possibility of being asked what kind of scholarship made my body tingle with pain. I hoped she would not ask. I remained silent.

"Full scholarship?" she asked. "What about the housing part? New York is expensive AF!"

"I do OK with that," I said.

"Are you independently wealthy or something?"

"No," I replied. "Not independently wealthy at all."

"So?"

I remained silent.

After a while, she said, "You don't want to talk about it? No problem. Will you at least tell me what you like to do for fun?"

I breathed a sigh of relief. At first, I felt an urge to brag about how much of an avid reader I was. What could be more impressive than a person who carried an entire library in his mind? But suddenly I was self-conscious about admitting that I mostly stayed home or went to the park and read. It wasn't just about bragging; I actually enjoyed reading. I could have said that, but then I might come off sounding like a loser, so instead I said, "It's true. Not much to be done around here if you have no money."

Not far from us a street performer was playing music on the violin. He had a metal bucket by his feet. The park was increasingly lined with beggars—those willing to share their talents in exchange for cash and those without any foreseeable talents offering only gratitude for a little currency. The air smelled like moistened trash and overripe bananas. Voices of peddlers and their customers somersaulted into one another in the distance. Sophie swayed high on the swing and landed on the cork-paved ground beneath, over and over again like an Energizer Bunny. Time wound itself forward, and before we knew it, it was five o'clock and the sun had begun to disappear.

25

Manhattan, New York
December 2022

It takes a lot to assemble a dresser, Maryam knew this. The name of the dresser was Monarch Valley Poppy by Little Things, but it was a full-sized monstrosity. Maryam had been putting dressers together for the full semester that she had been in the country. All she needed was her tool kit, mostly just the screwdriver and her hammer. What was more interesting to her than the actual assembly work was the various states in which she found her clients. Men three-quarters naked with the crack of their buttocks peeking out from their tattered boxers. Women in sheer nightgowns that flaunted the most intimate curves of their bodies. Stinky unbrushed morning breath. Stinky day-old alcohol breath. Stinky cigarette breath. Eye boogers as big as the fattest nostril boogers.

They were paying her through the HandyMan app. She didn't know why it was called HandyMan. Neither did I, frankly. She was a woman and, yes, there were fewer women in this line of work, but it was 2022 for God's sake, and it could at least have been called HandyPerson, she used to say. She liked the word "person" more than she liked the word "girl" or "woman." She did sometimes see herself as a girl, and so the word applied to her, but each time she used it, she felt as if she were somehow demoting herself. Yet "woman" was a bit much—she felt that "woman" was a performance, and the performance was often for the benefit of a man. "Person" was much more complete, a holistic word that showed that you were valued as a meaningful member of society. HandyPerson it should have been.

This particular man was bald and had red-rimmed blue eyes. The smell of weed smacked Maryam directly in the nostrils, even through her double masks, as soon as she entered the apartment. (Despite having been fully vaxxed, she always made sure to double mask in her HandyMan clients' homes.)

The dining table and chairs were the only furniture in what appeared to be a studio apartment. Otherwise, the room was empty. Maryam followed the man but stopped by the small corridor that connected the kitchen to the living room area. The man retreated to the dining area and slumped on a wooden dining chair, his hands splayed on the table's surface like old, tired rag dolls, his bald head low. Across from Maryam in the distance was a large balcony. The sunlight poured in through the glass door in about half a dozen thin sloping planks of shimmering light. When the sunlight caught the man's teeth, Maryam saw that they were rimmed in gold.

He must have felt her watching him, because he lifted his head from the table. "Lookin' for a hit?" he asked. "You more than welcome," he said, raising his shaky hand in her direction.

"No, sir," Maryam said, noticing the blunt in his hand with a slight chuckle. That was a first. No client had ever offered her a blunt before.

"What's so funny?" the man asked.

"Nothing, sir," Maryam said. "Is this the dresser over here?" She walked into the living room area, near where the man sat. The box of furniture remained in its package, unopened.

"You think my blunt's funny?" the man asked.

"No, sir," Maryam said. "Just that no one ever offered me one before."

"Ain't nothin' funny 'bout a blunt, girl," the man said.

Maryam bent over the box. "Sir, you were supposed to take the pieces out of the box and examine that there was no damage."

"Ain't that what I'm paying you for?" the man asked.

"No, sir," Maryam said. "Company rules. You should have gotten an email about it."

"Too late now," he said, chuckling almost diabolically. "What you gonna do 'bout it?" he asked. "Forfeit your money and leave?"

She'd had enough of the man. She looked around the room. Clothes strewn in heaps and all over the floor. By the time she was firmly in the apartment's center, she smelled it. No longer just the weed, but a mixture of what reeked like horse manure and dirty, moldy wet clothes.

"Stupid useless prick!" she muttered under her breath, then bent down and began opening the box with her box cutter. The sooner she finished, the sooner she could be out of there. "Sir, I'll help you out just this time, but in the event that I find any damage, you'll have to call the company and let them know. I won't be able to fix broken parts, and I can't be held responsible for them."

It was like talking to a wall. The man had already returned to slumping on the table and was now smoking the blunt.

She pulled the beams carefully from the box. She laid them down on the floor. When all the items lay in an orderly fashion, Maryam looked up and saw the man passed out on the table. She called out to him, but he would not wake up. She went ahead and completed the examination of the parts on her own. Luckily, she did not encounter any damage.

She lifted the planks of the dresser and began to put it together. Even when she hammered, the man did not wake up.

When she was done, she walked up to him and patted him on the shoulder to try to wake him up. But he didn't wake up. She tapped harder and raised her voice. "Sir." The man still did not budge.

She tried the third time, raising her voice and shaking him even harder, and then it dawned on her that maybe this was another first—witnessing those last moments before a man died, and the early moments of death.

"Oh my God!" Maryam said. Guilt crept up her conscience for having called him a prick. Now he was a dead prick. She looked around the room and wondered if anyone would miss him.

To whom should she report the death? The company? 911? What if the cops thought that she was somehow involved in his death?

She went back to him, shook his shoulders once more.

"Wake up!" she cried. "Wake up!"

"Got ya!" the man screeched. Maryam fell backward and hit the floor.

"What the hell?" she asked, getting back on her feet, angry now.

"Girl, just playin' with ya!"

"What kind of joke is that? That's not funny!" she said. She caught her breath, then said, "I'm done. That'll be ninety dollars." The man had registered with a cash-pay option. In those cash cases, it was her duty to collect the pay herself.

"You gonna take those boxes out into the trash?" the man asked.

"Sir, trash service is not included in assembly," Maryam said.

"Then you don't want your money," he said.

"Sir, please pay me so I can leave," Maryam replied.

She looked at the time on her phone. It was nearing noon. Three hours assembling the dumb dresser. It was a Friday. As soon as she was done, she would run home to drop off her tools then freshen up, before going back out to meet me at the park.

"Sir, I need to be on my way," Maryam said.

"You gon' be well on your way when you take them boxes out."

"Sir, pay me or I'll—"

"Or you'll what?" the man asked. He stood up from the table and walked over to her like a threat. She knew then that she had to leave. An entire morning wasted. All that work on the giant ugly dresser and no pay. This was not the first time.

"Or you'll what?" the man asked again, towering above her. Maryam backed away from him and out the door.

Every once in a while, Maryam would later explain to me, there was someone who argued about the payment, or someone who forgot to bring the money. Luckily these were the exceptions. The only recourse was to call the company to report the incident.

Back in her dorm room, she sat at her desk, still trembling from the experience, and called the company line to report the incident. Her roommate was splayed on the bed listening to music on her headphones. Maryam knew well that reporting the incident would not lead to an immediate resolution. It would be some time before she saw the money. They'd have to do a thorough investigation, and depending on how that went, she might not ever see her money.

She tried to clear the incident from her mind as she washed her face at the bathroom sink. Despite the way her morning had gone, she was keen to have a better remainder of the day. She was keen to see me. But before she could see me, she had to steady herself from the experience, then pick up Sophie from school. She was still shaky when she finally arrived at the park, where she broke down and told me, in great detail, what happened. As she told the story, she wrapped her arms around herself, that is, over her puffy winter coat. Even with such a warm coat, she seemed to be shivering from the cold. Meanwhile, Sophie swung gleefully on a swing. It was in this way, during our first December together, I found out that, in addition to being a student and a babysitter, Maryam worked also as a handyman.

26

Manhattan, New York
April 2023

ONE DAY IN APRIL, WE AGAIN MET AT THE PARK. BY THIS
time, Maryam and I had registered ourselves as a designated bubble
on the CDC national pandemic bubble registry, so that if we ever
passed a checkpoint together, we were not each fined the $250 for
being caught with someone outside of our registered bubble. We,
of course, had grown accustomed to always carrying our vaccination cards with us, and even Sophie's, who had also already been
registered as part of Maryam's bubble. We even made sure to carry
our masks with us (Maryam always careful with extras), just in case
we should find ourselves in a situation in which we were somehow
required to put them on. But outdoors at the park, we never did
bother to put them on.

Sophie busied herself on the swing of the outdoor playground
while Maryam and I watched her. Sophie's parents were working
late again, and Maryam would not have to have her home until after
7 p.m.

At first, Maryam and I stood awkwardly by the swing, just watching Sophie play. But at some point, Maryam looked in my direction

and said, "Your legs must be getting tired. Why don't we sit for a bit?"

We found a spot in the grass, at the same corner of the park where we'd sat before, the secluded area where two sides of a tall wooden fence met. I made sure to sit across from her, rather than by her side, so that we could see each other's face.

She was wearing a beautiful spring dress, longer than the last dress I had seen her wear. Not as dainty. More casual. I myself had come as casually as I could—a T-shirt and jeans, freshly laundered. And I'd, of course, made sure to grease my hair and to shave. Now, as I settled on the grass, I worried a bit about dirtying my jeans.

She lowered herself to the ground too. Behind her was the shield of a hulking cedar tree. She drew her knees up to her chest awkwardly. I, still new to dating, was abashedly grateful when, as she tugged at her dress to tuck it around her legs, my eyes landed on that intimate portion of her body. Her tugging stopped midway when she caught my eyes. I instinctively felt a mix of embarrassment and repentance. I looked apologetically into her eyes, then looked away, unable to hold her gaze any longer. But even as I tried to control myself, my unruly eyes descended once more upon that part of her body that I had been trying so hard, out of decorum and respect, to turn away from. "Stupid, stupid, stupid!" I scolded myself silently. "You ruin everything!"

I dared to look back up, but my eyes landed there again! I'm ashamed to admit it. The astonishing thing, however, was that she opened her knees wider, and before I knew what was happening, she'd moved the fabric of her dress out of the way, permitting me to look freely at the unguarded space between. Bald brown smooth skin displayed itself with a groove-like slit at its center from which a slice of pinkish flesh peeked out. All of her and all of it in plain view for me to take in! I wanted to capture the image before me and store it in a private place—a golden safe I could always return to. The whole of her was a language so beautiful, so stunning that I was too dumbfounded to utter a word.

My mouth grew dry. I forced myself to take a deep breath. She was my life's calling and I would do anything to answer. And yet . . . I resisted. For one, I had no idea what to do in a situation like this one. Second, I was historically (and still am) quite timid. Third, there was the matter of the distance between us, seated as I was, across from her. Fourth, we were in a public park, with a child and strangers nearby! Anything too intimate would have been rather distasteful, tactless, offensive, perhaps even criminal. Although, sheltered as we were in the corner within the two sides of the fence, and shielded as we were by the tree, no one, not even Sophie, would have seen us without our first seeing them. We did, for all intents and purposes, have adequate privacy. But again, I resisted. "I don't know if you should—" I whispered.

She stared apprehensively at me. "No?" she asked.

I remained quiet, as if my words were the very thing to be hidden.

"Why don't you come over here?" She summoned me over. Dumbly, I rose and sat by her side. Her brown fingers took my pale freckled hand and guided me to the center of her warm moistness. Sophie was still busying herself at the swing. The closest passersby were a great distance away, but I did wonder if they would somehow intuit what Maryam and I were up to. In any case, my hand lingered on her naked body. I was unsure of what to do next, and afraid to do anything more. Yet I was unwilling to pull my hand away. After a moment, almost of their own volition, my fingers moved slowly, back and forth, a movement of only a couple of inches, as I timidly settled into a rhythm and acquainted myself with the ridiculously soft presence that was perhaps her body's most precious and inti-mate member. Her breath became faintly louder, more weighted. The wetness from her body spread across my fingers. My touch on her was now as slippery as a road in a rainstorm. I felt myself grow hard with desire for her.

When her breathing was loud enough to no longer be so faint, she seemed to catch herself, seemed suddenly to become aware of her surroundings, and she reached for my hand again, this time to remove it from her body. "I'm so sorry," she said in a whisper. "I don't know what came over me."

"Don't be sorry," I whispered back. Sophie's voice was wafting and curling and bulging and shrinking somewhere in the background.

Maryam heard the girl's voice and grew distraught. After pulling her dress down, she stood up and looked frantically around her, calling out to Sophie. Then she looked me in the face and said, "Oh God. What have I done? I have to get . . . Oh God . . ."

"I promise, it's fine. She didn't see anything."

"You're sure?" she asked, looking anxiously around.

"Hey," I said softly. "It was . . . really nice . . ."

She looked up at me. "OK," she said. "OK," as if she were trying hard to convince herself that it was.

"Maybe . . ." I said. "Maybe . . . we can pick up here next time? I mean, maybe just not at the park?"

She smiled weakly at me, and it seemed to me a smile of relief.

27

Manhattan, New York
June 2023

IN THE SPRING AND SUMMER OF 2023, YOGA SESSIONS WERE held on the Fountain Plaza weekday evenings at 7:30 p.m. and were free to the general public, no masking or social distancing required. All one had to do was bring a mat. Of course, there were always those extra-cautious yogis who chose to wear their masks throughout the entire session.

Yoga with Maryam on the Fountain Plaza had been my idea. I'd been curious about it for some time yet had never tried it. Once, I'd gone as far as purchasing a gray plush mat and carrying it with me to the class, but when I walked up to the crowd of lithe, bendy participants and saw the way the passersby ogled the yogis doing their sun salutations and goddess poses and downward-facing dogs, I became self-conscious—the stiffness I was certain would be manifest once I attempted even the most basic of poses. I dolefully carried my mat back to my apartment. To be on exhibit like that—*that* was reserved for the brave.

But when I casually mentioned the class to Maryam, I found out that she went every Tuesday and Wednesday—Zumba on Tuesdays, yoga on Wednesdays. She was already uptown on those days for her babysitting job, which was to say that she would have loved nothing more than for us to attend the class together.

To my surprise, I was quite supple, or maybe it was that I was experiencing a levity of physique borne of a bottomless kind of bliss. Maybe this was the miracle of my life, this ability to subvert previously held beliefs of myself and, in doing so, arrive at a more profound understanding of my being. Identity as transformation. Transformation in the form of unexpected pliability. From my third eye to yours, I see you. Namaste. I bow to the divine in you.

As we walked together up Park Avenue after our session one June evening, I only wished Maryam didn't have to babysit Sophie. I'd have much rather spent the entire night with her—take her out to a nice dinner, perhaps at Francesca, the elegant Asian fusion vegan café that she'd been wanting to try. And after the dinner, I would have loved to catch the sunset in Central Park. In the absence of those options, I resigned myself to walking her to the Keatings' in Lenox Hill.

We'd just turned the corner of 61st Street and were almost at the gates of the Keatings' Upper East Side luxury apartment building when Maryam's phone rang. She picked it up. Mr. Keating's voice on the other end was loud. "Where are you?" he asked.

"On my way, sir," Maryam replied.

A homeless man held out a white bucket with yellow-and-red stripes near its rim. All of New York was teeming with them, Purist migrants from towns all over the country that had already been turned off by the government, and those on the verge of being turned off—as a result of a natural disaster, an economic downturn, large-scale torpescence, excess waste, a garbage dump fire, or whatever the case. Soon, Edward would surely also be turned off. One day, maybe even New York. Sometimes it seemed to me that the whole country was in danger of being turned off.

Purists had been adamant about taking down the entire country in their quest for racial dominance, and in their desire to have the nation's wealth concentrated in their pockets, they seized control of most of the nation's industries and resources—agriculture, transportation, pharmaceuticals, energy, tech. They had not had enough foresight to see the extent of the repercussions: unprecedented income inequality; historic deterioration in infrastructure, education, and health care; unchecked gun violence; record-setting environmental degradation; an all-around disenfranchised majority. Now, with so many cities and towns failing, even the Purists were paying for it.

I pitied the man, with his sleek brown hair and his thin white hands. But I wouldn't give him any money. He was a Purist, just like Chevy and Wayne. Bring me a Black man, and I would gladly give a dollar or two. But there was a limit to my sympathy for the Purist homeless man.

The voice on the phone was reproachful. "When I say eight thirty p.m., I mean eight thirty p.m. American time, not African time . . ."

"Yes, sir," Maryam replied. "I'll be there on time, sir," she said.

"The dishes will need to be done, Sophie's shower, and, of course, she'll need to be read to before bed."

"Yes, sir," Maryam replied.

When she hung up, she glanced anxiously at her phone's clock. It was 8:23 p.m. If anything, she'd be a few minutes early, and yet it seemed to me that she was now worried about being late.

At the gate, she said a hasty goodbye to me, barely giving me a moment to bestow her with my usual goodbye peck on the lips, before she put on her mask. I watched her hurry into the building. Afterward, I lingered at the gate, strolled aimlessly around the building and the general area for what must have been no less than an hour and a half, then, not knowing what else to do with myself, I also put on my mask.

✳

IT WAS EASY for me to gain access into the building. All I had to do was go determinedly to the concierge and say I had an urgent message for the babysitter from Sophie's father. I was immediately granted access to the elevator. I was even given directions to their particular apartment unit, as I had also been forthcoming about never having been in the building before. I strode right on through the hallway, no questions asked, and when I arrived at the door, I knocked eagerly.

The place looked like a museum someone curated and was using as a part-time home. The framed art pieces on the walls were elaborate paintings of a three-member family: a dark-haired white man who appeared to be in his forties and his curly-haired blond wife, and, of course, Sophie. Floor-to-ceiling glass windows encircled the apartment, and the city lights shone through like something from a movie.

"You can't just walk in here," Maryam was saying. "How did you even get in?"

"The concierge," I explained, removing my mask and sticking it in my pocket.

"That can't be," Maryam said softly, pushing me away by my elbow. "Come on," she said. "You gotta go."

"Why can't that be?" I asked.

"Doesn't matter," Maryam replied. "You just have to go. You shouldn't be here."

"Tell me," I said.

"Well," she said, finally ceasing to push me away. She looked me directly in the eyes, and in a careful voice, she said, "Let's just say that the first time I came here, the concierge wouldn't let me in. Even after Mrs. Keating called down to instruct him to let me in, he made her come down to confirm that I was the right person."

"Oh," I said, understanding what she was getting at.

She looked around to make sure we were still alone. "You know how much trouble I'll be in if they find you here?"

"I'm sorry," I said.

I saw in her eyes the instant that her resolve weakened. Yes, even by her own admission, she should have continued to insist on my going away. But therein lay the issue of longing. She'd begun to long for me. More than that, she'd begun to care for me, enough that she didn't want to do or say anything that would leave me feeling rejected.

She entertained the possibility that the Keatings had some kind of camera to watch her. I managed to convince her that the camera was just a figment of her anxious imagination. I assured her that I would be as unobtrusive as possible. I would restrict my movements to the living room and bathroom only. Or, if I got thirsty, then also the kitchen. But certainly not beyond that.

"Well, OK," she replied, hesitantly. "You're here now, so it's fine. But you also have to be very quiet. Sophie's in bed."

She took me by the hand and led me to the living room, where she instructed me to make myself comfortable on the Eames lounge chair and ottoman. I could read the entire stash of *The New Yorker,* but I should make sure not to touch anything.

She settled into the love seat not far from where I sat.

"But tell me one thing, does he always speak to you like that?" I asked, after some silence had passed between us.

She stared blankly at me.

"Never mind," I said.

I didn't know any rich folks, but I imagined that many of these rich folks, especially the rich Purist ones, often spoke in entitled and condescending ways. I resented Mr. Keating on her behalf.

Without giving it much thought, I rose from the Eames chair where Maryam had instructed me to sit and began walking in the direction of the kitchen, opening doors and peeking into rooms as I went.

"What're you doing?" Maryam's faint steps approached me from behind. It rattled her enough that I was inside the apartment, but now to be walking around freely!

"You know I have to be extra careful," she whispered. "The last thing I want is to be labeled as the poor African immigrant who 'we'd tried to help out financially, but owing to her disreputable ways had no choice but to let her go.'"

It was a fair point. I could hear Mr. Keating's voice as he explained this to his colleagues. Maryam had told me about visits from his colleagues while she was tending to Sophie. She did her best never to give them any ammunition with which they could potentially denigrate her character. "G-Dawg," she said again. "What are you doing?"

"Just looking," I said. "Checking out how the rich and famous live." Gold finishes on the cabinets and doors. Crown molding in each room.

"I wouldn't necessarily say they're famous, G-Dawg," Maryam replied brusquely.

"But definitely rich!" I marveled.

In the next room, tucked away in one of the four corners, was a white life-sized inflated balloon doll wearing a sash that read "Michelin."

"Whoa! What the heck is that?" I asked.

Maryam, on tiptoes, peeked into the room from above my shoulders. "A collector's item is my best guess," she said, looking at the doll. "I think he used to work for Michelin back in the day."

The next room was expansive. "Have you ever been in here?" I asked. She scurried after me and pulled me out of the room by my elbow. "You can't go in there," she said. "That's *their* room!"

"Looks like the entrance to a small palace!" I exclaimed.

"Come on," Maryam said. "We can't go in there."

I turned and watched Maryam with probing eyes. When my voice finally came, it was lithe, feathery. "Ever heard of the story of the old man and the tiger?" I asked. I must have read it at some point in elementary or middle school.

"No," she said, still tugging at my elbow. "You can tell me later."

I pulled away from her and stepped farther into the room.

"Come on. Let's go," she said in a whisper.

"There once was an old man wandering in the forest," I said. "He hadn't gotten very far before he realized that he was being followed by a tiger. He began to run, but the tiger pursued him. Soon, the old man reached the edge of the cliff. Not knowing what else to do, the old man leapt off the cliff, barely managing to cling onto a thick green vine. Meanwhile, the tiger had arrived and simply waited, watching the man from above. The old man considered jumping off the vine to the ground below, but the distance was too great, and anyway, even if he were to survive, another tiger, he saw, was waiting for him down there. Also, a pair of mice was munching on the vine." I laughed softly now. "Bottom line, the man was in a terrible bind. One way or another, things were not looking good. Just as he was losing hope, he saw a beautiful, wild strawberry on an opposite-facing vine. He could leap for the vine, but the vine was so weak that if he were to make the leap, it'd surely snap as soon as he grabbed hold of it . . ."

"So what did he do?" Maryam asked from the doorway.

I walked toward her and pulled her gently by the waist into the room.

"The last line of the story is 'How sweet it was.'"

She looked questioningly at me. We stood together for a moment.

✷

IT WAS HER first time. She knew enough to grab an oversize towel from the bathroom closet to spread over the bed. It was my first time too, and I stood awkwardly and watched her. But there was no more awkwardness when she returned to me because I knew to defer to her.

Two doors down, Sophie slept. Many blocks and avenues away, at some swanky New American restaurant in Columbus Circle's Time Warner Center, Sophie's parents ate. And there, in the Keatings' gilded Upper East Side apartment, Maryam and I made love, our first time going all the way with each other, in the most sprawling bed I had ever seen. I relished the presence of her body on mine, warm, like a weighted blanket.

Did she relish my body as I did hers? At first it did not seem she did, for her brow furrowed and her body seemed to grow rigid under mine. I was not selfish enough to let this go unnoticed. I cared so deeply for her. "Should I stop?" I asked, and I did in fact begin to pull out, but Maryam spoke.

"Don't!" she said softly. "It's fine. Just keep going."

I urged myself to be gentle. She groaned a bit, I imagine out of discomfort, and yet she urged me on. "It's fine," she said. "Just continue," and so I did.

Finally, the crash of pleasure. When I pulled out of her, she was shocked by the sudden emptiness of her body. It hadn't always felt this hollow, she said. She would at some point in the future feel whole again without me in her. The hollowness was only a sensation, and yet she wanted to be once more filled up by me. But I had already moved away, out of bed, and was starting to put on my shirt.

She slowly put on her blouse, and then her jeans. It occurred to her that what had just happened was a sort of transgression, and for a moment she panicked, rising rapidly from the bed, carefully but quickly pulling up the towel that she'd spread. As she straightened up, it was clear to me that she was in a bit of pain. She stumbled, gasped, then brought a hand to her pelvic area. I went to her, but she said, "I'm fine. Don't worry about it, I'm fine."

I took the towel. There was only a trickle of blood, and in a cold cycle it would wash off with no trouble. I finished throwing on the rest of my clothes and began remaking the bed, fluffing and re-arranging the pillows. In less than an hour, the Keatings were set to be home. I ran the full wash but did not wait for the dryer to complete its cycle. I rushed out the door long before Mr. Keating and his wife returned.

28

Manhattan, New York
August 2023

By the middle of August 2023, the pandemic was truly, truly over. Rarely did you find anyone wearing a mask around the city. Checkpoints were still in existence, slowly fizzling away, and Maryam and I were learning the fundamentals of each other's bodies with more freedom than ever—all the contours and grooves and arrangements of our limbs and their potential for reaction. All these months together had allowed us the time we needed to understand intuitively what to do to cause a tickle or a gasp, or a complete and silent stun. We knew the basic hiding places of the university libraries too: the silent study rooms and the conference rooms and the information technology section and the stacks and, of course, circulation. Public versus private was our primary categorization system. When hunger seized our stomachs (aside from our early splurging dates, we were both practicing the asceticism of studentship—she by necessity, me by choice), we munched on each other's lips, and sucked on each other's tongues and fingers, and bit softly into thighs and arms, and somehow our hunger abated.

One morning, I arrived at her dorm to find her humming along to Yemi Alade while doing the Zanku. Her roommate had already left for the day.

"Wanna practice with me?" she asked. She belonged to the University's African Students Association, and Yemi's music was part of a dance that the group had recently choreographed.

"The best dancer in the group is Carine, but don't let Monsurat hear it. She thinks she's the best," Maryam said, laughing.

"I'd have thought you were the best," I said.

She laughed some more. "Anyway, come on. Let me show you," she said.

She pulled me to her. We kicked up our heels and gamboled our first dance steps together. To my surprise, I could actually dance! Then again, perhaps it should not have been surprising; as I have said before, I was, after all, in the wrong skin.

We should have been studying—she, for her Intermediate Statistics exam, and I for my Economics exam. But instead of running numbers, we were running dance moves. Somehow it felt imperative that we dance, perfectly synced, future man and wife. This was a magical and surprising new shared interest. I could see it: my life and hers, two thin parallel roads coming together in one sturdily paved union of dance.

The sun was beginning its descent when it finally occurred to us that we should eat. "Let's make it good. A real homemade meal," Maryam said.

I agreed. "Something exotic maybe?" I asked.

She looked curiously at me. "OK. Yeah, something homemade would be nice."

We packed our books into our bags, stopped at the C-Town supermarket, where she picked up some carrots, potatoes, ground beef, thyme, basil, cilantro, butter, and flour, and all the other ingredients she needed to make meat pies in the small but manageable kitchen of my little studio apartment.

Hours later, we stood together in the kitchen, I, putting away dishes, she, chopping carrots and potatoes.

"Look," she said, and showed me what to do next with the carrots and potatoes. "Get it?" she asked.

"Got it," I said.

Her phone rang. "I wonder who that is," she said, but she continued chopping. The ringing stopped but began again seconds later. "Babe, my hands have food all over them. Can you check who it is for me?"

"I hear the ringing but where's your phone?" I asked.

"In my bag," she said. The bag was at the foot of my bed. My only hesitation was that a bag—somebody else's bag—had the potential to be a petri dish of germs. I imagined all the bacteria- and virus-infested receipts, dollar bills, coins, tissues, pens. All the dirty hairbrush bristles and grimy makeup applicators.

"Did you find it?" Maryam asked.

I stood frozen, unable to reach for the bag let alone pull out her phone.

Maryam came to me. She had washed her hands and was wiping them with a hand towel. She reached into the bag herself.

"Oh, it's just Justine," she said to the screen. "Let me call her back quickly."

She sat on the bed and dialed. Her bag lay open enough that I could see some of its contents—lipstick, pocket pack of facial tissues, her laptop in its slim case, a notebook, and some pens—all had their compartments, everything in its place.

"Oh, you shouldn't worry about that!" Maryam was saying. "I'm sure it will all work out fine!"

I turned to go back to the kitchen.

"Oh, he's just fine. We're cooking together," Maryam said, giggling. She puckered her lips toward me. Then she said, "Hey, babe, come say hi to Justine."

"Hi!" I called out to Justine.

"Hi!" Justine called back.

Back in the kitchen after finishing up her call, Maryam continued as if nothing had happened. I stood awkwardly by her side, coming to terms with my inability to go into her bag.

"It's not that I don't like to cook," she was saying. "It's that it's not my portion to be stuck in anybody's kitchen, not even my own, so I'm preparing you now. You can take over in the future."

I laughed distractedly.

"Babe, are you all right?" she asked, looking at me.

"You're preparing me to be your personal chef?" I asked.

"Precisely," she said. "But you know, it's not by force. Most things in life are not by force."

Inside the silverware drawer, there were no spoons left.

"In the dishwasher," I said.

She opened the dishwasher and noticed the row of rusting metal trays.

"Hmm," she said. "What happened to these?" She bent down, examining the points where the jagged red-brown metal tips met the plastic of the wiring.

"Oh, these?" I said. "It's no big deal. Just load carefully."

"Safety hazard, G-Dawg," Maryam said. "It could give you a puncture wound."

"Pretty sure my shots are up-to-date," I said. "Yours?" I admit that there was something almost challenging in my tone. But then I softened. "It's no big deal, like I said."

She nodded and carefully removed the dishes.

"I can replace the racks for you," she said.

"Like I said, it's no big deal."

She finally let it go.

After we ate, she rose and cleared the table and made to load the dishes into the dishwasher, but I stopped her before she began. "Just leave them," I said. "I'll get them myself."

✱

IT IS WITH great shame that I admit that the next evening, when Maryam returned to my place after class, the dishes were still in the sink.

I, too, had been busy with classes, and washing dishes sometimes took great mental preparation for me. Occasionally, I could do it with no problem. Other times, I had to steady my mind in antici-pation of tackling all the dirty dishes, all the nasty food remnants. But I had at least made sure, before my classes, to tinker with the dishwasher and fix the rust problem. I wanted to be the kind of man who took care of business.

Maryam did not nag me about the dishes that were still left in the sink when she returned. She simply went about loading them into the dishwasher. As she did, her fingers must have brushed across one of the edges of the top rack. Flecks of dried paint fell off, revealing rusted sections.

Maryam peered at the racks before turning to me. "You painted them?" she asked, dismay written all over her face.

I nodded. "Why? What's the matter?"

"Oh my," she said. "First of all, what kind of paint?"

"Does it matter?" I asked.

"Of course it does!" Maryam said. "Also, G-Dawg, paint peels. Especially in a place where it will come into contact with water and heat. It will just flake away, and then you're back to square one."

"It'll be fine," I mumbled with irritation. "I should know. I once rebuilt an entire town! I know a thing or two about how things work!"

"Oh, G-Dawg," Maryam sighed.

"What are you, now, a handyman?" I joked, trying to ease my own tension.

"As a matter of fact, and as you already know, yes," she replied.

"So, you know how to fix a dish rack?" I asked.

"I mean, I know a thing or two, too," she said with a smile.

I studied her.

"You're impressed by my handyman skills?"

"Depends," I said.

"On?"

"On if you actually fix it or not."

"Putting together beds, dressers, tables, and chairs. A little plumbing too. A dish rack is nothing," she said.

"OK. I'm impressed in advance," I said.

"Cool," she said, smiling broadly. She turned back to figure out what to do with the dishes, but less than a minute went by before she turned back to me and asked, "But why, though? Would you be impressed if a man told you he could fix it?"

I hesitated. There was suddenly a palpable tension in the apartment. "Woman! You want me to be impressed or not? I don't know what you want from me!"

"Forget it," she said. "Just forget it."

After a silence, she said, "So you really renovated an entire town?"

"It was nothing," I replied.

The hardware store on 167th sold universal dishwasher racks, she said. Any luck and it would have racks the correct size for my dishwasher. She put on her shoes and sweatshirt and headed out the door.

When she returned, I watched as she replaced the old racks. I didn't want to feel any type of way, but my ego was beginning to feel a little hurt.

"Just leave the dishes," I said, after she was done replacing the racks and about to begin reloading the dishes. "It's my place. Let me take care of them."

"But I've already started. I can finish," Maryam said.

"I said I'll do it."

She turned to look at me. "But why?" she asked, each syllable scrupulously articulated. As if she already knew the real reason why.

"Just because," I said.

"But why?" she asked again, that same careful enunciation.

"Because I already told you," I said. "It's my place. I'll take care of them."

29

Manhattan, New York
September 2023

THE WAY MARYAM TELLS THE STORY, SHE APPROACHED THE counter for the umpteenth time that September. Inside the nail salon, the air reeked of polish and acetone. Three staff members clad in white aprons stood huddled together, gossiping at the far corner of the counter. Their voices rose and fell in varying degrees, and their hushed laughter trickled out the way that ash spreads over the sea—first a buildup and then the dispersion. It was hot inside and Maryam wiped the sweat off her forehead and neck. On the counter, a fly had died in the vase of a purple orchid—Maryam could see its inert bluish body—but the plant was thriving. After ten minutes of Maryam standing there, the eldest of the women in the group left the huddle and approached her. "Can I help you?" she asked, fingering the yellow-and-red elephant sticker on the counter. Her eyes widened in a smile that Maryam recognized as counterfeit, practiced, condescending.

"I'd like a manicure. Gel, please," Maryam said. She began to remove the silver bangles and rings that she was wearing on her hands.

"Three hours' wait," the woman said.

Maryam looked around the store. It was 1:30 p.m. on a Wednesday. The chairs were empty, except for an older-looking white man whose feet were being scrubbed.

The last time Maryam came to this particular salon, it had been a two-hour wait. She had forced herself to wait it out. She had wandered around aimlessly on the streets, and she had succeeded in killing time that way. But when she returned to the salon, the nail technician had added an additional hour. "One hour more," the woman had said, like a challenge. Eventually, Maryam had decided to return home and forgo the manicure.

"But the place is nearly empty," Maryam said on this particular day, putting back on her bangles and rings.

"Three hours' wait," the woman said again, filing her nails languidly, blowing on them defiantly. She was begging for a verbal altercation.

Maryam did not feel like arguing. She only wanted to get her nails done. "You're sure it won't be more than three hours?"

The woman nodded. "Three hours," she said for the third time, with a straight face.

I was supposed to meet Maryam at her dorm room for an early dinner at 4:30 p.m. that day, but if she waited the three hours, she'd just be beginning her manicure when I arrived at her dorm. As she walked away from the salon, she sent me a message. (Dignity still prohibited me from initiating contact with her, but Maryam knew that I would at least receive her messages.) She gave me the address of the salon and asked me if I wouldn't mind meeting her there instead.

To kill time, she walked toward Saint Marks Place, passed the corner store on Second Avenue, stopped by the falafel store and grabbed a sandwich, past the bookstore, and into the café, where she grabbed a coffee and took out her books.

She divided her time among her books: the first hour, *Intermediate Statistics*. The second, *Essentials of Psychology*. The third, *History and the World of Art*.

People in light-colored rompers and flowery sundresses walked in and out of the café, and the door chimed upon their entry and exit. At first, she said, the chiming kept her from sinking into her books, but eventually she acclimated to the sound and managed to concentrate so deeply that she did not even realize when the clock struck 4:30 p.m. She had just finished with Statistics and was beginning Psychology. She packed up her things and headed back to the salon.

At the desk, the same woman from earlier met Maryam. "Sorry, another hour," the woman said immediately. She appeared to, if not own the store, then be in charge of its management.

There were at this point a handful of people in the salon, none Black, but several chairs were open and at least two technicians were unoccupied.

"Another hour?" Maryam said. She could have asked about the unoccupied workers, but instead she said, "But I asked if you were sure it would be three hours and you said yes."

"Sorry, my mistake. One more hour."

A younger technician came to the desk now and offered to take Maryam but was immediately ushered away by the older woman.

I entered the salon at the precise moment that the younger technician was being reprimanded for her offer. Before I reached Maryam, the initial front-desk woman had already left her spot behind the desk to greet me. "Sir, can I help you?" she'd asked. "Manicure or pedicure?" She pulled out a menu of more complete options for me to choose from.

I was more than a little confused about what was happening, and the confusion showed on my face. But the older technician soldiered forth, pointing me to one of the empty seats and beginning to walk me to it. "She can help you over there," she said.

I waved away her offer. "No, thanks," I said, walking up to Maryam. "Did you finish already?"

Maryam shook her head, distress evident on her face. My eyes fell on the elephant stickers on the front desk. "Did they take you in at all?" I asked.

Maryam shook her head. The anger welled up in her throat, then the words tumbled out. I could tell that she was trying to keep her voice even. "They always have a two- or three-hour wait each time I come. I thought maybe if I actually waited them out, they'd finally give in . . ." Her voice drifted off.

I took her hand.

"Sir!" the older technician was saying. "Sir? Are you coming or not?"

Behind her, the younger technician looked apologetically at Maryam and mouthed, "So sorry."

"OK," I said to Maryam, taking her hand. "Let's go. We'll find somewhere else uptown."

"What if I don't want to go uptown?" she replied. "What if I want to get it done here? Why can't I be allowed to get it done here?"

I ushered her out of the store, and the door chimed behind us.

Outside, it was stiflingly hot, just like the days when everyone was wearing masks and it seemed that there was no end in sight. I struggled to catch my breath. After about a half-mile walk, my rapid heart rate eventually calmed. But what of Maryam? I turned to her and saw that she had yet to regain her composure.

The truth is that it wasn't just the terrible salon experience. She had also felt a premonition of something bad. In the minutes that followed the incident at the salon, she had even nudged me to go a different route home, but I had insisted that the route we were taking was the quickest way to my place.

At first, things were exactly as to be expected in the city—more homeless people than ever. At one point we had to tiptoe around the lined-up bodies of half a dozen homeless people, their clothes and belongings and blankets taking up most of the space on the sidewalk. I would have thought them corpses except that every once in a while, they moved. This level of destitution was not a thing that I had seen in my earlier days in the city. But with the housing market having spiraled out of control, and the majority of homeowners no longer able to afford their homes, the situation was not exactly surprising. Stray cats and dogs roamed the streets, having been abandoned for fear that they might carry and more aggressively transmit the mutant strains of the virus. Many people (excluding the super wealthy) could no longer afford to own pets.

We first took notice of the man because of the shouting. His greenish hospital gown hung slightly open in the back and he had to stop and tug at the strings every so often to make sure that it didn't come all the way open. The plastic slippers on his feet dragged, each step barely lifting from the ground as he carted a metal pole on wheels, an IV bag dangling from it. The guard's hollering voice was at first fuzzy, muffled because of the distance and the noise of the city. In the skinny, disheveled, sick-looking man, Maryam could probably not have seen herself, but in the mahogany brown of his skin, she certainly did. As she and I walked by the hospital, the guard's voice grew louder. "What the hell do you think you're doing with that equipment?" he shouted.

"Sir, I'm just a patient going on a walk," the sickly man said.

"Like hell, you're from inside. What room? What doctor?"

Maryam stopped before the gate to watch. I stopped with her.

"Sir, I'm just out walking on doctor's orders," the sick man said. "Doctor said I needed to get out and move around a little."

"Like hell he did!" the guard said. "When the cops get here, you can explain to them on which black market you were planning to sell the equipment."

"Sir, I didn't—"

A grotesque and unexpected tackling followed. Maryam and I watched as the guard bounded for the hospital patient, forcing him to part from the IV that hung on the pole.

If you see something suspicious, say something, I thought immediately. "G-Dawg," I muttered to myself, "say something." All the signs in the subway stations and bus stations and train stations counseled as much. But that day, I did not say anything. And I certainly did not do anything. It was, instead, Maryam who ran toward the gate and screamed, "Leave him alone! Let him go! I'll report you for this!"

The police arrived shortly after that, and the noise that ensued was louder than I could bear. I stuck my hands over my ears. By my side, Maryam carried on screaming for the guard to let go of the patient. Eventually, when they had wrestled the sick man onto the ground, Maryam turned to look at me. I stood dumbfounded.

"You can't just stand there!" she said to me. "Help him! We have to do something!"

She turned back to the scene and continued to scream at the guard and the police officers. The patient was now flat on the ground, surrounded by cops.

Some time passed before my arms came around Maryam and I pulled her away from the gate. "You're OK," I said. "Just breathe. You're fine. You're fine. You're gonna be fine," I said, escorting her across the street and down the block from the hospital. In front of the corner store, I finally stopped and looked into her face.

"Are you OK?" I asked with great concern.

She shook her head feverishly.

"OK," I said a little desperately. "OK. Just breathe," I said.

"But we should have—" Maryam began.

"Shhh," I cooed. "Just let it wash over you," I said. Then I grabbed her arm and led her away from the hospital.

Days later, when we talked about the man—the way he looked almost like a corpse; the way he made sure to explain why he was out walking even though it must have been hard for him—when we wondered aloud what had happened to him (Had the cops investigated and had they eventually dismissed the guard's accusation? Or had the cops taken the patient hostage? Was he OK?), Maryam's eyes somehow took on a lifeless quality, glossed over with tears. Each time this happened, I held her and urged her again, "Just let it wash over you." Years later she'd ask me, very pointedly, what such a washing was supposed to look like anyway. "Like rain over a windshield? Like bathwater over skin? Like a false accusation washing over and ruining a life? Just let it wash over you . . . such a cruel way to soothe," she'd say.

It never escaped me that I could have done something to help the sick man. If there had been someone with the power to change the outcome, it might have been me. But instead of speaking up, I stood there bewildered. Only when we were at a safe distance had I spoken, simply advising her, with the best of intentions, of course, to let the incident wash over her. These days, I do see her point. About the cruelty of the exhortation, I now know that she was right.

30

Manhattan, New York
September 2023

At the HandyMan job on the Lower East Side, Maryam knelt over the long golden side frames of a metal queen bed. The bedroom door was wide open. A gray-headed man sat in his small home office, a little nook within the living room, visible from the open bedroom door. The voice on the line spat out via speaker-phone, "You're not hearing me!"

Immediately Maryam recognized the voice. The syntax. "Nigerians are everywhere," she whispered to me. It was my first time accompanying her to her HandyMan job. We had been together all morning, and I was hesitant to leave her.

At the door, she presented me to the gentleman as her assistant. The man waved us in. He was too busy with his phone call to have cared. The call was on speaker, but this did not seem to faze him.

"What do you want me to do?" he asked the woman on the phone. This was, I mused, the typical retort of any man who found himself in a heated conversation with a woman.

"What do you mean 'what do I want you to do'?" the woman shot back. "I need fresh sperm, that's what I need!"

Maryam and I immediately looked at each other and did our best to hold in our laughter.

"And how do you propose I get fresh sperm to you?" he asked evenly.

"I don't know. You do what you have to do!"

"It's difficult, what you're asking. I ca—"

"It's difficult for you?" the woman said. "What about me? Ehn? What about me? There's the fuel scarcity again! That means no generators! How do you expect me to refrigerate the medicine when I haven't seen light in over a year? And you can imagine, without electricity, all the sperm you left is already dead! Na so o! Yenagoa with all its thirteen oil wells, and I don't remember the last time we saw light!"

"I'm sorry," the man said after what seemed to be a thoughtful pause. "But what do you want me to do about it? There's nothing I ca—"

"Am I talking to a wall?" the woman screamed. "I said I need fresh sperm! All that money in your bank account, and you don't think you can afford to fly here or bring me there for the sake of the sperm? Corona times are over! International flights have been running for years. You can't keep using it as an excuse."

"It's not the Coro—"

"So, then, what is it?" she asked. "Is your penis broken or what? Frozen only lives a maximum of twelve hours. How long do you want us to be caught up in this?"

"Baby, I'm doing my best here," he said.

"Maybe I need to get back in touch with Ikenna and make him an offer of free sex. I don't know . . ."

"Who is Ikenna?" the man asked.

"You already know—the guy who delivered my mattress and wanted to 'hang out' in my flat, but I said the flat wasn't set up so . . . Anyway, point is, we never did hook up. But at this rate . . . I have a photo of his dick on my phone. Pathetic excuse of a man, really, but again . . . at this rate . . ."

————————

The whole conversation grew tedious. I began wishing for a little peace and quiet, but the woman's voice droned on, a prick on my temples. I looked up from the bed that Maryam was finishing and watched the man pace the room at a distance. He was a white American man, well-put-together in his perfectly ironed polo shirt and khaki trousers. Well-put-together but not intimidating: his house shoes were fuzzy and almost girlie; his mannerisms were weary and ordinary and far from the loftiness I might have expected from a man who lived in this neighborhood. He appeared user-friendly.

I remembered Wayne's talk of power cuts back when he spoke of the villages in Tanzania. As a tourist, I had not experienced any of it, but surely the lack of electricity had its costs. I imagined them now: patients dying in the gaps between the electricity turning off and on. And if this woman were to be believed, sperm were also dying.

I pitied the woman. I imagined the man's frozen sperm dying with each power cut. I imagined the doctors still inseminating the woman with the dead sperm. No wonder the woman sounded desperate. Nothing frozen stood a chance in a country of steady power cuts. Nothing that wanted to live, anyway.

31

Manhattan, New York
September 2023

Rᴏsᴇᴠɪʟʟᴇ Cᴏɴᴅᴏᴍɪɴɪᴜᴍs ᴡᴀs ᴛʜᴇ ɴᴇᴡ ᴄᴏɴsᴛʀᴜᴄᴛɪᴏɴ project across from Highbridge Park, on the banks of the Harlem River. Two restaurants stood near it, the best of which was the hole-in-the-wall Punta Cana, which I could have sworn had the tastiest shrimpanadas in all of New York. Punta Cana was a bit of a hike from where I lived, but for fresh shrimpanadas, I was willing to make the hike almost every day. Maryam and I sat eating our shrimpanadas on the curb outside the restaurant one day when we saw the child dangling from the third-floor balcony of the condominiums. It was late September, still summer-hot, and the city smelled of litter, metal from the subway grates, and laundry detergent.

A small crowd of at least half a dozen people had gathered in front of the Roseville Condominiums. Maryam stood up, crossed the street, and joined the crowd. I followed.

She had already kicked off her shoes and was heading toward the side of the building when I realized what she was up to. "What the hell do you think you're doing?" I called, running after her.

When she began writhing her way up the beam along the side of the building, I stopped my questioning and watched.

The child was still dangling. I felt my heart pound. I looked back at the crowd. Someone was saying that they had already called 911.

By the time I looked back up, Maryam had scaled the first floor of the building. One hand clung tightly to the steel beam as the other swung forward, and then she was at the second floor. She climbed on top of the second-floor balcony railing and began making her way horizontally on it as if on a tightrope until she was directly below the child. Slowly she lifted herself so that she was on tiptoes. She grabbed hold of the child and leapt back down, landing with bent knees on the floor of the balcony.

The fire truck did not arrive until Maryam had already led the child down the interior stairs of the building. The child's parents had arrived by then and had made their way through the crowd. We all waited with bated breath as the ambulance approached, its siren growing louder.

When the EMTs parked and poured out of the vehicle, the parents rushed toward them. A paramedic had already met with Maryam and was leading her and the child away. In the near distance, two stray dogs barked.

I made my way to the ambulance. From where I stood, I saw that another paramedic was beginning to clean what must have been a cut on Maryam's hand.

"No entry beyond this point," an officer said, catching me by surprise.

"I need to get through," I said.

"And how are you related to the child?" the paramedic asked.

"I'm her boyfriend," I said, pointing to Maryam.

"Then, like I said, 'No entry beyond this point,'" the paramedic said.

I stood there, restlessly and idly regarding the crowd. Several minutes went by and then I heard the moniker, first a whisper, then a forcefully articulated fact. "Spider-Woman!" a little boy said.

"Incredible what she did, wasn't it?!" his father replied.

It had indeed been incredible what Maryam had done with her mere hands. I looked at my own hands. I was carrying Maryam's yellow flats, which I had picked up after she'd tossed them aside to scale the building.

Her shoes were the first things I offered her when the paramedics discharged her.

"Thank you," she said, stretching up to kiss me on the cheek before bending over to put them back on.

I could not help myself. The question basically flew out of my mouth: "What the heck were you thinking?"

"Pardon?" Maryam retorted, surprised by my tone.

"You heard me," I said. "What were you thinking?"

"There was a child about to fall to her death," Maryam replied. "I had to do something about it."

"You know I'm your number-one ally," I said, "but you really shouldn't have. Anything could have happened to you or to that child! What if you had fallen, or what if you had somehow dropped the child and then she died anyway? You're—"

"I'm what?" she asked.

"You're on a visa!" I said. "Now don't take this the wrong way . . ."

"I'm on a visa, and . . . ?" Maryam asked. "What the hell does that have to do with anything?"

"Do you know what it means when someone on a visa is accused of murder?" I asked. "Chances are you'd be deported straightaway." I should know—this was what we'd been studying in my Intro to US Immigration Law course.

"So, I should have just allowed the child to fall to her death?" Maryam asked. "God knows you weren't going to do anything!"

I was appalled at her for speaking this way to me. Her words felt like an accusation. I weighed them in my head before finally realizing that she had spoken the truth. "Okay. Fine," I said. "But where did you learn to climb like that?" I asked.

"I don't know," she said, visibly weary of me.

"You don't know? Come on! There must have been lots of opportunities on the continent. You know, trees and all . . ."

She looked contemplatively at me. "There weren't any big trees where I grew up, if that's what you mean. I didn't spend my life climbing trees." She sighed.

"Well," I said.

She had been shocked to hear me attack her for trying to save the child. But she was more stunned by this question about climbing trees. In all the time we'd spent together, she had probably never imagined me as the kind of man to ask this question, to make these sorts of associations.

"I'm your greatest ally," I said reassuringly. I really believed it.

Maryam looked at me, opened her mouth, perhaps to tell me off, but it seemed she could not find the words. She closed her mouth back up. When she finally spoke, she said, "You know what I'm learning? Never have an ally. Allies are always loyal to their politics and never to you, never even to themselves."

We did not speak to each other for the rest of the evening. Not while we walked together to my apartment. Not as we took turns cleaning ourselves off. Not as we climbed together into my bed and fell asleep. All those tasks, we performed automatically, no words exchanged, as if the events of the day had somehow snatched our voices away.

32

Spider-woman scales roseville condominiums to save
falling child! the headline on the university's main page read.
I clicked on the link and read the article. I clicked on other related
links. heroine saves child! one story read.

I picked up my phone to call Maryam. The phone screeched its
alarm. I slammed the phone on the desk and opened up FaceTime
on my laptop. The Dignity alarm went off again.

I reverted to my email and composed a note to her. No greeting,
no subject.

Have you seen any of this? (I copied and pasted the links to a few
of the articles.) You're all over the news.

I went back to browsing the Internet. I was still browsing when
her response came.

It's a little crazy, isn't it? It's really not all that's serious.

Any plans for this evening? I typed.

For the first time, I felt truly in the doghouse, restless, strung
out with guilt, lonely. She'd resumed staying at the dorms, instead
of with me at my place. I'd invited her over several times, and each

time she declined. I had an inkling of what was the matter, and yet I felt defensive: Wasn't it true? She was, after all, a student on a visa. And, surely she had learned to climb in Africa. I had not exactly said anything wrong. But when I thought on it harder, I could understand why my words could be taken in an offensive way.

I made up my mind to apologize. If she would only agree to meet with me, I'd do it in person, so that she could see—in person—that I was genuinely sorry.

I'm hungry, I typed. You want to meet up somewhere to grab food?

Time passed as I waited for her response, tense with anticipation. I tried to return to browsing, but I could not get myself to focus on anything.

Are you there? You don't have to come here. I'll meet you anywhere.

I had begun to close my browser when I saw her response:

Sure.

I breathed with relief. If I could convince her of my remorse, then perhaps things would go back to the way they used to be.

I opened a new tab to read more about the incident. It impressed me how quickly the news spread. I didn't own a television, but Maryam's face must have been all over TV screens as it was all over computer screens. On one of the sites, there was footage of her climbing the building. I watched it with equal parts awe and jealousy. What would have happened if the balcony railing had broken off, taking her chocolate-colored lithe body with it? I envisioned her falling, metal and bones and flesh crashing at once to the ground, her blood spilling out in spools like perfect silk.

I shook my head, banished those glamorously morbid thoughts from my mind. I knew that this was just me getting carried away with jealousy.

That evening, walking into campus, I paced myself so I wouldn't break into a sweat. It was October, but blistering hot, and though I had taken the subway from uptown, I still had a few blocks to walk. I wore a pair of old jeans, but I'd made sure to put on my nice white short-sleeved Oxford button-up. Maryam loved the way I looked in the shirt, and I wanted to remind her that I was handsome.

Through the library doors, I spotted a crowd of people. The closer I got to them, the more their voices shrilled, as if in a congested open-air bazaar, the kind I'd have seen in Stone Town had I followed my parents on that fateful excursion all those many years ago. A pair of fat flies buzzed around my head. I swatted them away.

I counted at least fifty people, and the commotion of the crowd made me sweat. The sweat made my hair gel drip, and soon, like melting ice, I was excreting liquid from my head, forehead, and face. I felt an urge to run away. Instead, I found myself rubbernecking.

Imagine my surprise when I found Maryam in the center of the mob! I took several steps back, and my eyes landed on the giant MicroLED screen that took up the entire left wall of the library entryway. The news ticker at the lower portion of the large digital screen read: University to honor heroine who saved small child with University-wide Hero Award. A photo of her flashed above the news ticker. I took another step back. She was magnified, and I—I had somehow become invisible, a transparent, hollow thing of a man, relegated to the background where nobody could hear or see me.

I wiped my forehead with my handkerchief, straightened my shirt, and braced myself to enter the crowd. After much effort, I found my way to her side. A man was holding out his iPad in Maryam's direction, as if to say, "Over here, may I have a photo of you?"

When I took her hand in mine, I held her like I was holding the most valuable gemstone in the world, rare like my tanzanite gift from the darkest man. I loved the soft center of her palm, and I held it with all the love I could muster.

Maryam pulled away and my breath caught. I didn't know the meaning of the withdrawal. What I knew was that it had happened. I understood it as a betrayal. It brought back memories of my childhood, during which a retraction of touch from Chevy had been a staple, a source of permanent anguish, a source of shame. I loved Maryam, but I suddenly hated her too, because she must have stopped loving me, must have become like Chevy and taken back her love. Love, hate, resentment, abandonment, desire for acceptance. I looked into her face just as she smiled widely, but the gaze in her eyes was blank, like a corpse groomed for public viewing.

A flash went off. Someone else took a picture. All the ruckus exasperated me, but I couldn't see my way out, not with the crowd as large as it had become.

It wasn't until her head fell on my shoulder that I understood that encounters like these must have been ongoing for days. She had not bothered to mention them to me. They must have been the reason she was so worn out, enough to let her head fall on my shoulder. Out of spite and envy, I at first refused to indulge her. I stepped away so that she was forced to lift her head from my shoulder.

Seconds later, guilt swelled in me like shouts to a roar. I stepped back toward her, closing the gap I'd made between us. A few minutes went by. It's funny the way love is like a sedimentary rock, accumulating and cementing over time from intense heat and pressure. Or the way time chips away at resentment like erosion on the side of a mountain. After an hour or so, I found myself growing less envious of her, and more full of love. She became once more my star and moon.

"Stay the night with me?" I asked in a whisper.

She nodded.

I had not in the end gotten the opportunity to apologize to her for my comments on the visa and the trees, but she seemed to have dropped her grouse with it, so I made up my mind not to bring it up lest I resuscitate her ire.

Looking back, it occurs to me how seamlessly the rest of the night should have gone, how easily we should have been able to return to a more romantic state of affairs. But as we headed in the direction of my place, I caught a glimpse of a nail salon. "Want to try again for a manicure?" I asked. It was that time between evening and night; salons were still open, but they were rather empty. If she were willing to give it another try, then she might finally get her chance.

"Nah," Maryam said. "You already know how that goes."

I tossed her refusal aside. I wanted to be able to give her this gift, to be able to be there when she finally got this thing she'd been wanting so much.

"Come on," I said, nudging her by the elbow. "This might be your day! With all that fame, they might be more reasonable . . ."

"I doubt it," Maryam said.

At the street corner across from the nail shop, a couple of students cheered "Spider-Woman!" They walked up to Maryam and asked for a photo. Maryam smiled as the students took the photos.

"You see?" I asked, whispering it in her ear. We continued to walk. "The salon technicians have likely seen your face all over their screens too! And you know how the saying goes," I said. "Success has many fathers . . . My treat. Just give it a chance. See if they won't take you this time. See if the whole thing hasn't just been a big misunderstanding."

Maryam stopped midstep, looked at me. "Really, G-Dawg?" There were things, she said, that I really didn't seem to understand. And how could I? "They aren't in your experience," she said. And perhaps it was true. My experience, according to her, was one where technicians rushed to service me, no matter what salon I walked into. Sometimes she wondered just what I understood about the politics of race. There were parts of me that she still could not quite put her finger on. She looked more closely at me and asked, "You really think people are that vacillating with these sorts of things?"

I shook my head and said I was no longer sure.

"Trust me," she said. "They won't change their minds. It's not a misunderstanding. None of it has been a misunderstanding. Watch," she said, like a dare.

She took my hand and led me into the salon. Inside, only half of the chairs were occupied. A staff member approached us. Maryam said hello, biting her bottom lip nervously, something a little girl could have done. I saw that the whole situation was unnerving for her, but I also saw that she was eager to prove her point.

The technician smiled knowingly at Maryam, and for a moment I thought that Maryam might be wrong. But instead of giving her the usual long wait time, the technician said brightly, "Sorry, no opening." I didn't know which emotion took the trophy—infuriation at the salon technicians for being so shameless about their racism, or respect for them for not being swayed by her celebrity.

I was baffled and offended on her behalf. So why was a part of me also a little relieved that she had been brought back down to reality by the nail technicians? In fact, if I had to say it, I was more delighted than I wanted to be when the technician looked condescendingly at Maryam and then turned away. My guilt for having had the thought promptly trickled out like syrup, and I felt it spread through my mind and build up at the perimeter of my conscience into something like shame. Shame, because while I had never understood myself as competitive, I now sensed a sort of competitive spirit in me. If I could not make her happy, I did not want anyone else to have that power. I reasoned that this desire to be the only one to please her was why I inappropriately gloated at her disappointment. Moreover, this strange sort of competitiveness, surely, was a remnant of my white self. I had to do something about it.

That evening, shortly after we arrived at my place, I begged permission to run an errand. I did not tell her where I was going, and I knew that she was too tired to ask. As she crawled into bed, I left.

Through the doorway, down to the basement of the nondescript coffee shop. DBT FOR SELF-ACCEPTANCE, the tiny sign still read. The place smelled of wet concrete and old wood and dead cockroaches and mold.

NO MORE GUILT.

I wanted to rise above the pettiness of my white self. I wanted the freedom of mind to embrace other people's superiority over me. I wanted the grace to lend my support to those who outperformed me. I had a terrible sense that I was becoming something like Wayne, a man who saw others as less than, a man who allowed others to take the blame for his own shortcomings. Or was I becoming more like Chevy? A person who distanced even loved ones by virtue of her own insecurities. None of it was my fault. I was a product of my upbringing. But I acknowledged, too, that I had the power to change that.

"Looking at one's white self in the mirror can often be a stressful experience," the facilitator said to the group. "Emotional regulation techniques will help you identify your primary emotion and block out secondary emotions. Using praise and encouragement, I will reinforce your use of DBT skills. Let us begin again with positioning ourselves before our mirrors."

Standing before the mirror, all of us participants exhaled. We stared at our reflections.

"What are you all feeling right now?" the facilitator asked.

"Jealousy," I said.

A silence.

"Fear," I said.

"What are you afraid of?" the facilitator asked.

"Of not being good enough," I said. "Of not being strong or capable enough. Of being inferior."

"How do those feelings affect your daily life?"

"I engage in destructive behaviors. I say and think hateful things because of those feelings."

"Any other feelings besides jealousy and fear?"

"Superiority," I said. "I feel like I am superior. And when I'm not, I feel a miserable sort of discomfort that causes me to want to lash out."

"When's the last time you did things to stop yourself from lashing out?"

"I'm always holding myself back," I said.

"Ah, excellent! So, you've entered into the next stage!"

"But it hasn't worked," I said. "I feel the emotions all the time, and what if one day I do lash out?"

"Then perhaps it's because you have not fully confronted the white self in the mirror. Is that possible?"

"Anything is possible," I said.

"I understand how hard it is for you right now," the facilitator said. "But try to move toward your white self, toward the emotions. Go toward the fear and jealousy. It is a big, bland white body reflected back at you. But look at it. Confront it. If you run away from it, your fear and jealousy will grow, and you'll never be able to fully transition into your Black self. If you stare at it enough, over time your discomfort will decrease, you will be able to let go of the behaviors and feelings associated with it, and you will be able to transition more smoothly. So, can we all move closer to our reflections and try to sit with them?"

Fifteen minutes passed. The bald man was crying.

"Perfect," the facilitator said. "Now, tell me. How does that feel?"

"Painful," I said.

"I get it," the facilitator said. "But you did it!"

"Yes," I said. "Yeah, I suppose I did it."

A woman had joined the bald man in crying.

"Good," the facilitator said. "A two-minute break and then let's try again. Begin from the top. Everybody together. Remember, the longer you sit with the discomfort, the greater the chances that your discomfort will eventually decrease. That's the first step—accepting the role that whiteness has played in history. After you've made your peace with it and are no longer terrified of your white selves, then we can work toward becoming your new Black selves. This will involve more elaborate steps. We can get into that later."

"Could you walk us through the next steps again?" someone asked. I wanted to know too—it had been a while since I'd been there last.

"Sure," the facilitator said. "Let's see. First, there's psychotherapy for racial reassignment. This takes anywhere from a few months to a couple of years. Followed by physical transformation support— voice training and dialect coaching, hair texturizing, tanning injections or complexion creams for skin darkening and toning. Cultural competency courses for your official racial reassignment certificates. And finally, support groups, which I highly recommend you attend for at least a couple of years. Ideally, you will have a lifelong support group. Research shows that the greater support you have from your community, the greater your rate of success." A pause. "I believe that covers it. Any other questions?"

We all shook our heads.

"Great, so let's get back to it!"

33

Manhattan, New York
November 2023

IF THEY KEEP COMING UP TO YOU AND YOU GET TIRED OF IT," I
said, "I'm more than happy to be your escape route."

The whole month of November, Maryam had refused to go out,
not even for food. She hated the cold, but this wasn't just due to
the cold. She even refused to venture back to Punta Cana. She
only left my apartment to go to class. She stopped her HandyMan
job altogether. And this particular day, she was also refusing to go
babysit Sophie.

"Just send me an alarm emoticon if anything bad happens, and
I'll know to call you and act as if it's an emergency."

"It wouldn't be acting," Maryam said. "It would be an emergency. I
feel like I'm in a constant state of emergency," she said. "Anyway,
G-Dawg, that plan won't work," she said. "You still can't call me.
Remember?"

"So, you'll just skip babysitting altogether?" I asked.

"They'll figure it out," Maryam said. "I need some time off. It's not
as if they really need me. These days I'm just a show animal for them.
They take turns inviting over their friends, colleagues, whatever, and

they won't let me leave until each of them has drilled me with their questions. 'So, what did you say you're studying? Where did you say you were from again? That's the place where those girls were kidnapped, not so? Oh, you're so lovely. How are you finding your time in the city?' G-Dawg," she said, "I'm tired of it all. I'm tired of the fake smiles and the small talk. I'm tired of hearing myself referred to as 'Maryam, our very own heroine.' It's all very exhausting."

I wasn't entirely surprised. The headlines that week had announced even more honors and awards.

"As if I'm some spectacle. When I'm in their house, I feel a little like Ota Benga must have felt."

"Ota who?" I asked. Maryam shook her head wearily. "Never mind," she said. It seemed as if she was also finding me exhausting. I knew that this wasn't about me, but didn't my feelings also count? This tension between her feelings and my own would be a struggle that I would have for years to come, I knew. If I remained with her, I'd have to choose—to sympathize with her or with myself? The two were not exactly mutually exclusive, but somehow in my mind, they often seemed to be.

"I'm sure we can find out how to override Dignity if we just Google it," Maryam said. "Google has everything."

It was a good idea and, truth be told, I had not wanted to spend money on a new phone and had had every intention of Googling it, but for one reason or another had just not gotten to it. Now, it was a matter of Maryam's sanity, and for her sanity, I was eager to conquer Dignity.

I lifted the lid of my laptop, revived it from sleep. I opened my browser, and then the university news page. Before I could switch to Google, I saw a photo of Maryam.

"Not again," she sighed. "It's into the second month now. You'd think they'd have moved on." She walked away from the screen, tired of reading about herself.

I remained at my desk and read the news on the page. This time something looked different.

COPYCAT SCAM! the subheading read.

I opened a new window and typed in "Spider-Woman Maryam." A series of search results popped up, many seeming to be the same blogs that had run the story previously. Only now, many of them had changed their tune and seemed to have spun a new story.

I gasped, and Maryam must have heard because she asked, "Are you OK?" and walked over to me.

We read the words on the screen together:

IMMIGRANT FAKES RESCUE TO GET ACCLAIM!

WOMAN RE-CREATES PARISIAN FEAT IN ORDER TO GET AWARDS AND MONEY!

REMEMBER THE STORY OF MAMOUDOU GASSAMA?

"Who the heck is Mamoudou Gassama?" Maryam asked, shouting.

I typed the name in a new window, and the first image that came up was one of Gassama, scaling four, rather than three, balconies to reach a dangling child. The eeriness of the coincidence was not lost on me. But I knew that Maryam had not faked the rescue. I had been there with her. I had witnessed the rescue from start to finish. The parents also must have known that there had been no scandal, no fakery involved, and yet they had remained silent. Or maybe they weren't the kind of people who were always online, or maybe they'd simply chosen not to speak to no-name blogs.

Maryam began crying.

"It's nothing to worry about," I said. "Just some people who are confused and others who are bored, or troublemakers trying to make unnecessary trouble."

She cried harder. Something in my heart broke.

"Why would they make these assumptions?" she asked. "They weren't there. They don't know what happened. How could they . . ." Her voice trailed off.

She rose from my side and went to the couch. She curled up in a ball. Jealous as I had been of her recognitions, and eager as I was to bring her back down to my level, this was not what I ever would have wanted for her.

Hours passed and she remained curled up on the couch. I needed to do something to ease her suffering. I needed to help her feel better. It occurred to me that she must be hungry. I had some left-over pizza in the fridge. I heated two slices up on a plate and brought them to her with a glass of water. "Here," I said. "You should eat something."

She refused the plate.

"Come on, Maryam," I said. "You really should eat."

Still, she refused.

After a couple more hours, I took the plate, washed my hands, and ate the slices of pizza myself. Maryam did not eat for the remainder of the day.

✷

WITHIN TWENTY-FOUR HOURS, the accusations had spread like wildfire. Maryam had still not eaten and, with the exception of a couple of bathroom breaks, had not left the couch.

Sometime around 7 p.m., she finally stood up, found her purse, walked over to the entryway, put on her shoes, and left the apartment. Fifteen minutes later, she returned with a brown bag, a bottle neck sticking out of it. As she filled up a large tumbler with the Muscat wine at the kitchen counter, she mumbled to herself that finally she understood why people turned to alcohol.

I listened to her talk to herself, and then I watched as she took the tumbler with her and returned to her blanket on the couch. She chugged the wine between loud agonizing sobs. In all the time that I had known her, with the exception of our first date, she'd not drunk any alcohol.

I wanted to be strong for her. I wanted to force her to be strong for herself. I sat next to her and said, "What exactly are you whining about? What exactly are you falling apart for?"

She looked blankly at me and then began sobbing again until her face was as puffed up as the Keatings' Michelin Bibendum, until her eyes and lips turned an almost cayenne red.

Her phone buzzed. She ignored it. It began to ring. "Mumsi" flashed on the screen. Her mother had called several times that afternoon and Maryam had ignored the calls. Now that it was evening, her mother was calling again. Maryam shook her head at the phone. "I can't talk to her, not in this state. I don't want her to worry."

"What if she's already heard something?" I asked.

Maryam wiped her face, cleared her throat, cleared it again, then picked up the phone. "Hi, Mumsi," she said, a false cheerfulness in her voice. "How are you? Are you keeping well?"

I paced around the apartment.

"Yes, yes. I'm fine. No, nothing is wrong. I'm just getting up from a nap."

Her mother said something, but I could not decipher it.

"Yes, I'm sure," Maryam said. "And you? You're keeping well too, no?"

I walked and sat by Maryam's side.

"Any news from the doctor?"

I stroked her thigh as a sign of solidarity.

"OK. Yes, no news is good news. At some point we will eventually hear something. Someone will eventually know something."

I continued to stroke her thigh.

"Yes, Mumsi. Yes. You, too. Continue to take care of yourself."

When she hung up with her mother, she put down her phone and burst into tears.

"Oh, Maryam," I said. "Did she hear anything?" I asked.

Maryam shook her head. "No, thank God. But, G-Dawg—" Her voice broke.

"Well, that's at least one less thing to worry about," I said.

"It's all just terrible," she said.

I took her by the shoulders and, shaking her gently, I allowed myself to speak words that I only half-heartedly believed. "There's no such thing as bad publicity," I said. "In the words of Oscar Wilde, the only thing worse than being talked about is not being talked about. The point is, babe," I said, "none of it matters. It will all work out fine."

"You really think so?" she asked, wiping her face.

"I firmly believe so. Things like these always work out."

She was all ears now. Her attentiveness gave me the fuel to continue: "I never met a successful person who didn't have enemies," I said. "Let them talk. It's just talk. People need someone to take their frustrations out on, and your story was convenient."

I still remember the look on her face. It would be no exaggeration to say that she looked at me like an expectant mother seeing her baby for the first time on an ultrasound machine. Her look was full of hope, full of the sudden recognition of the possibility of new life! Her words came out softly: "You really think so? You really think all of this will pass?"

Truth be told, I had no idea. I really did hope that the trolls would eventually move on. But even so, how long until then? A month? A year? Half a lifetime? No way to know. I decided to err on the side of optimism. "Yes, Maryam. I really think so."

In that moment she appeared filled with gratitude. "Oh, G-Dawg," she said. "Thank you for saying that." She wrapped her arms around me. "I hope you're right." She pushed her body with such tenderness into mine. I felt powerful, full of pride, for I had managed to convince her that the greatest disaster of her life—her own personal Armageddon—was nothing that could not be overcome with me by her side. I had managed to convince her that the wickedness of the world could not really touch her, that the current murkiness of her circumstances could do her no real or lasting harm. After all of my convincing, she was so relieved that she began to cry again.

When she finally fell asleep, I returned to my laptop. I scanned the websites to see what they were now saying. My eyes fell on the comment section of one blog:

ANONYMOUS 12:51 P.M.: I knew of a man who killed himself after something like this. I wonder if she will kill herself now that she's been found out.

G.I. JOE 1:17 P.M.: As soon as the criminal nature of the "heroic act" is proven, she will be in jail.

JORDAN 5:37 P.M.: The lengths people go to get money and fame. What a terrible human being! But these immigrants can be like that! Nothing is beneath them!

G.I. JOE 7:18 P.M.: We should demand she gives any money she received back! Give the money back! Give the money back! Give the money back!

ANONYMOUS 11:59 P.M.: Isn't it a breach of Son of Sam's? Making profit from your crime?

G.I. JOE 2:06 A.M.: Hold on, just hold your horses! For fairness sake, we're not 100% for sure yet that it's a crime. But yeah, I'm with you on that too! Give the money back!!

ANONYMOUS 3:13 A.M.: If it's not a crime, I don't know what is! Didn't it say she was from Nigeria? Nigerians are the biggest criminals out there! It's a wonder we let them into our country!

I tore my eyes from the comments. They truly were reprehensible, inhumane! If they made me sick, I couldn't bear to think what would happen to Maryam if she stumbled upon them.

I spent the rest of the day revisiting Gassama's story. In one interview a journalist asked him about his newfound celebrity. "I did what I had to do and that's life. I'm still the same person that I was before. When you become a celebrity, it's because there are people around you who say that you are," Gassama said. "But people can just as easily say that you're not a celebrity, that you're nothing."

With respect to Maryam, Gassama had spoken with astute foresight. At least in the gauzy abstract world of blogging, she had now been pronounced a fraud, and no matter that they were nonreputable, obscure sources, she felt the blow sharply.

I suspected that the owners of the blogs as well as their commenters might have been mostly Purists or people who were in some significant way unhappy with their lives, looking for ways to make themselves feel superior, looking for ways to make someone else more miserable. At least I rationalized it in this way.

34

Manhattan, New York
December 2023

B𝗒 late December, Maryam had at least stopped her constant sobbing, but outside of attending classes, she remained cooped up in my apartment. Even when Monsurat and Carine called, leaving messages in which they asked when Maryam would be returning to the African Students Association, Maryam did not bother to get back to them. Several times, Justine called asking when she and Maryam would hang out next ("We have so much catching up to do!" she said), but Maryam did not respond.

As a show of solidarity, I remained cooped up with her. My time was a sacrifice I was willing to make. (Though if I'm being completely honest, it wasn't as if I had anything much better to do.)

One Friday, as noon was approaching, I suggested that we go out and clear our heads. "How about a walk to Punta Cana for some shrimpanadas?" I asked, trying to sound as cheerful as possible.

I was lying down in bed by her side. She was disheveled, locks dangling lifelessly around her face. She'd stopped taking the time to pin her hair up. Her lips were permanently swollen from crying, in a way that I felt made a woman appear even more beautiful. But she was sad. I wanted her no longer to be sad. I drew myself close to her, kissed her on the tip of her shoulder. "What do you think? A little fresh air can't but help do the body good."

We had been practically home-locked since the attacks had begun. I took care to order or prepare our meals, most of which she did not bother to eat. I took her hand in mine. "What do you say?"

She turned to face me. Her brown eyes glistened with tears, but the tears did not fall. She nodded and off we went.

We'd hardly made it halfway to Punta Cana when an older man, seated on his patio off 168th Street, whistled at her.

Maryam turned frantically around.

"Beautiful," the old man said.

Now, I know that the man was out of line whistling at her as if she were some kind of animal. But truth be told, I was proud to be standing by her side, and it seemed to me such a negligible infraction. If anything, it should have reminded her that life kept going. An old man found her attractive and that was that. I squeezed her hand and smiled at her. I had expected to see her smile back. Imagine my surprise when I saw the look of panic on her face.

"It's just a compliment," I said, trying to calm her down. This was certainly not the first time that a man had whistled at her while we walked around the city, I reminded her. "Try not to worry so much. There's really no need."

She exhaled deeply. "All right," she said.

At the corner of 173rd and Broadway, a woman crossed the street with her child and was waiting to cross the adjacent street when she looked lengthily at Maryam. The woman's face appeared thoughtful, and it seemed a struggle for her to tear her eyes away. At one point, she looked as if she were going to say something, but then her child in his navy-blue shorts and blue-and-white plaid shirt tugged at her hand, and she became aware that the walk sign was on.

"Did you see that?" Maryam asked me.

"See what?" I responded. I had seen the woman's dawdling, but I didn't admit it to Maryam for fear it would make her more anxious. Besides, the woman could have been reacting to anything. What if, I reasoned, it was something as simple as Maryam reminding her of her sister, or a cousin, or an old friend?

"She looked at me weird," Maryam said.

"Don't be silly," I replied.

"She was thinking something," Maryam said, "and whatever it was, it wasn't good."

"We don't know that," I said. "Let's just take things one step at a time. We'll cross this street and the next, and then the next. But, please," I pleaded, "try not to cross them carrying the weight of other people's thoughts in your head."

Finally at the restaurant, I breathed a sigh of relief and ordered four shrimpanadas, which I carried carefully back out. Maryam waited for me in a quiet corner outside. We did not sit along the sidewalk as we used to do; Maryam wanted nothing more than to head right back home.

In my apartment, we sat together at the kitchen counter. I ate my shrimpanadas hungrily, almost inhaled the two patties, but Maryam simply held hers, awkwardly shifting them between her hands. "Sometimes I just want to disappear," she said.

"Disappear to where?" I asked.

"I don't know," she said. "All I know is that I need to be somewhere else. Anywhere else but here."

I thought about my own life. I had once wanted to be somewhere else too, and now I was there. I had succeeded in escaping my old life. But sometimes when the memory of my parents resurfaced, I felt a sadness, a vague nostalgia. Had they truly been as terrible as I'd believed them to be? Sometimes it seemed to me that I missed the idea of them, if not the people that they were. I missed the notion of having parents. I wondered about Maryam. She never talked about her parents, and I'd never pushed because I, too, had not brought up my parents with her. Only once had I told her that I carried a great resentment for Wayne, but when Maryam asked me why, I stumbled over my words and then altogether stopped trying to explain. She didn't push. And I didn't want to push her. To prod her would only open myself up to being prodded too.

Parents or not, former life or not, this life was the hand that we'd been dealt, and we must make the best of it.

"One day you will look around," I told her, "and all of this will be in the past."

"I don't know about that," she said. She stood up from the counter and walked over to the window. "Look around us," she said. "All of this wahala!" She extended a hand as if to point me to it. As if on cue, a shout came, and then a sound like glass shattering. It was true that tensions were continuously rising with the Purists. Another election was around the corner, less than a year away, and everywhere there was a sense of impending retaliation. But I was hopeful.

"Things will eventually settle," I said, though if I were being honest, I would have said that there was a good chance that things would not.

"All I know," she replied, "is that right now, I want to be somewhere else. If not home, then somewhere like home."

An understandable sentiment, of course. The way things were going, I myself would have wanted nothing more than to see my way out of the country too.

PART IV

35

Cape Coast, Ghana
January 2025

Bʏ ᴛʜᴇ ᴛɪᴍᴇ ᴡᴇ ᴘᴀᴄᴋᴇᴅ ᴀɴᴅ ʟᴇꜰᴛ, ᴛʜᴇ ᴜᴘʀɪsɪɴɢs ᴡᴇʀᴇ painting the days gray. Night seemed perpetual, so much ambient darkness from all the fire and smoke and all the burning and burnt things. The never-ending tensions with the Purists were a sure in- dication that the natural tendency of history was to repeat itself. Which is to say that Maryam and I were very happy to escape.

The first time the flight attendant came to us, she offered us drinks, but Maryam declined. She had spent every day since the Roseville Condos debacle slowly uncoiling herself from the experi- ence, like a small, injured animal emerging from a cold dark space into the bright glow of the sun. She was living again, which meant that she had released herself from that relative oblivion induced by alcohol. Which is to say that she had returned to her usual disinter- estedness in it. I was also disinterested on her behalf.

The flight attendant was serving food—chicken with rice or pasta with eggplant—when the plane hit turbulence. I held on to the armrests. My mind wobbled. Once, long after my trip to Tanzania, I had read somewhere that turbulence was the collective souls of the departed grasping for the plane, grasping for another chance at life. I imagined the souls. The possible repercussions of their grasping: more dead souls and never a soul revived. I turned to Maryam for reassurance.

Maryam kept her gaze fixed out the window. She made no move to reassure me. For the last couple of months, she had returned to something vaguely like herself, and yet I could tell that she still felt the weight of the Roseville Condominiums debacle.

We were by then in the spring semester of our junior year. We had embarked on this study-abroad trip together in an attempt to leave behind all vestiges of a difficult sophomore year. This trip should have been our greatest joint decision. We were, after all, a team.

But already, my confidence in us was faltering. As the plane continued to jerk, Maryam stayed looking out the window. The flight attendant's words billowed like a thin cloth in heavy wind. I rejected her offer and shut my eyes. I sank my body lower into my seat, and before I knew it, I had fallen into a deep slumber. The next thing I knew, the landing preparation announcement was going off and we were soon disembarking the plane.

✳

ON THE BIOMETHANE bus from the airport to the university campus, we passed the towns of Winneba, Apam, and Mankessim, and all the old Compass Oleum and Frimps and Humano former fuel stations a person could find, but instead of fuel, they had been converted to solar-powered electric charging stations. We passed a series of billboard advertisements, which the professor-cum-tour-guide who was in charge of leading us to campus explained had formerly advertised Enzomie noodles but now advertised fruits of the land—coconut and palm kernels, bananas and plantains, cacao.

Cape Coast sat on a knoll, like a sprawling goddess seated at the edge of the earth, mulling over the Atlantic.

The road was a winding thoroughfare lined with tall coconut trees equidistant from each other; two miles of neatly arranged sentinels.

The university's east entrance was across from Jemima Elizabeth Taylor Memorial School.

"Someone must have really loved Elizabeth Taylor," a student said.

"Who is Elizabeth Taylor?" another student asked.

"And what of the Jemima part of the name?"

"Do they mean Jemima as in Aunt Jemima?"

"That would be perpetuating that terrible stereotype, wouldn't it?"

"Can't names be allowed to be just names? Why are we assuming that they named the school after anyone in particular?"

"Names are never just names," a thin voice said.

As we approached our dorms, the professor explained that the university was divided into two sections, but I didn't exactly catch the explanation. I was distracted by the distance I'd been perceiving between Maryam and me.

Eastern and Western campus? Or was it Northern and Southern? What I did catch was that the university housed lecture halls and libraries and even a zoo. Like any other university in the States, I was stunned to see, and then I registered my surprise at being surprised.

★

IN HER DORM room on the second floor of her building, the first thing Maryam did was blast Yemi's "Johnny." My own dorm room was in a different building from Maryam's (we had not been given the option of rooming together), but as her roommate had not shown up, it appeared that she might have the room to herself. This pleased me immensely, for I could park myself by her side.

And yet, the silence between us was killing me. Chevy used to get this way with Wayne. Was it possible that what Wayne used to say was true—that women were an entire universe unto themselves and there was no use trying to understand them?

I equated Maryam's mood to a heavy, transient gust of rain. I made up my mind to simply wait this one out.

On her bed, I lay down listening to an audiobook on my phone. But as listening to the audiobook added one more level of separation between us, I rose from the bed and went to where she stood folding her clothes into a small chest of drawers. Dancing, I knew, could bring back the intimacy. I moved my body against hers and began moving my hips until I saw her face stretch slightly with a smile. At this point, I dedicated myself fully to the Git Up. I slid to the right, and she followed. I twirled around and ended with the butterfly, and she did the same. I slid to the left and dipped into a curtsy. She slid to the right and spun. We both leaned back to the left, leaned back to the right, freestyle, freestyle, and then we began it all again.

We startled to a stop when we heard the students' voices outside, followed by the sound of a horn. It reminded me of the sound of the ambulance's siren when we had boarded the A Train for the airport back in New York. There had been the smell of something burning, and smoke billowed from the subway entrance like a cloud touching ground. The street vendors who had lined the road were selling honeydew melons and sweet cherries and apricots, and yellow-and-pink apriums, and purple king pluots. What bothered me was the way they stayed, as if they'd grown used to toxins. The effusion billowed and subsided and billowed again until everyone was gagging and coughing and covering their noses and mouths with their hands and collars and hankies. This noxious stench was the last smell I had of New York.

My body stiffened with fear in Maryam's dorm room and I prayed that the chaos of home had not managed to follow us. Was the world falling apart here too? At least Maryam was standing by my side. I leaned into her, happy at least to be in her presence. Regardless of her broken spirit, she was the only home I could lean safely into, rest safely inside of.

The sound of footsteps grew louder and then we heard a voice say, "Let's go before we're marked late!"

And suddenly Maryam and I remembered: the siren was the meeting call. This very first meeting would be the one where we'd receive itineraries for our excursions as well as our course schedules for the semester. We raced down the hallway and through the building's large doors, our eyes catching the glare of the naphthalene whiteness of the morning light.

36

Cape Coast & Kwahu-Aduamoah, Ghana
January 2025

Mondays in Ghana started with breakfast and then led to excursions. The rest of the week we focused on coursework.

This particular Monday, we set off in the biomethane van to Kwahu-Aduamoah very early in the morning at what must have been no later than three o'clock. I met Maryam in her room at a time when we should have been eating breakfast. But we were both always running late, and anyway, it was too early for breakfast.

I do not exaggerate when I say that when I arrived, her bedroom was a hot mess. It turns out that earlier she'd been trying on several sets of clothes and had settled on a leopard-print jumpsuit with a zipper, which she said would still allow her to use the bathroom without too much trouble.

Standing in front of the mirror, she said, "A photo every morning for my Gram. A good way to keep a record, don't you think?"

"Sure," I said, taking a seat on her bed.

"A sbooty!" she said. "You get? A selfie of the booty! I coined it myself," and she giggled like an elementary school girl. Since we arrived, her mood had steadily improved.

A sbooty required at least one mirror. Possibly two, to play off the ricochet effect of mirrors and phones. They didn't matter—the physics and effort involved. What mattered was the way her backside looked next to mine, both in the camera's reflection and in the mirror. When I had finally captured the perfect photo, I cupped one of her buttocks in my palm. She playfully slapped my hand away. Truly, when I think back to this time, I can say that this was the good life, and we were living it!

★

OUR GROUP ARRIVED in Aduamoah at the edge of dawn, when the dew was still fresh and the sun had hardly risen, but already the drummers were out, beating their barrels and dancing around the villagers, the elders at the front of the group.

Two jerry cans with liquid in them sat in the middle of the crowd, near where the elders stood. The presiding elder summoned me with a broad smile. "You are welcome, oburoni!"

I knew the meaning of the word, and it startled me to have been referred to by it. Had I heard correctly? "Excuse me?" I asked.

The elder said it again. "You are welcome, oburoni!"

Horror-struck at this repeat affront, I managed to say, "I'm not an oburoni!"

The elder looked carefully and intensely into my face. He could have been looking at some reincarnation of his ancestor, so intense was his stare. Or maybe he perceived that I had borrowed an ancestor's eyes, and he was searching my face to make sense of things.

Maryam sighed. "G-Dawg," she whispered. "Just let it go."

The elder shook his head as if shaking away a pesky thought, then he presented me with a traditional kente cloth. "Your new name shall be Kwesi," he said. "Kwesi, because you were born on a

Sunday." I had indeed been born on a Sunday and had told the man as much.

"Why can't I be Nana or something," a young woman was saying. She twirled the ponytail of her brown hair with her fingers as she spoke. "It's royal, from what I heard. I want to have a royal name."

Another young woman said, "There's nothing especially royal about you. Just stick to the name you were given."

The first young woman sulked and walked away from the group, guzzling down the cup of drink in her hand, then began pressing buttons on her phone. "So it's like this . . ." she said into the phone. "They don't even . . ."

Maryam pulled me aside from the group and said, "You know, he wasn't trying to insult you."

"But I'm not . . ." I began, then I thought better of it and stopped. I had not completely transitioned yet.

The young woman was now walking around screaming into her phone, laughing madly, twirling around in an intoxicated manner. One of the drummers went to her. "Madam, please calm down. Please follow me."

"The drink was supposed to be sipped not guzzled," someone whispered.

"Americans," another said.

On our return, the bus weaved around numerous pedestrians and street vendors and bicyclists. Earlier when we had been in Aduamoah, the road had been clearer and nature had asserted itself, the leaves of the teak and kusia trees flanking the roads, and the pale green fruit of the mansonia tempting us to stop and have a taste. But now the roads were crowded with people, and one could hardly notice the trees. The air smelled of guavas and only a little dust. And then there were the sounds of High Life. The bass of the outside music appeared to make the bus vibrate.

The intoxicated young woman had sobered and was napping in the seat in front of me and Maryam.

"Is it really true that the bus is run on human waste?" I asked.

Maryam nodded. "I read that there are sewage stations all over the city and in the villages. It makes a good alternative to diesel. A huge savings in CO_2 per year."

"Incredible," I said. "So many wonderful developments. The continent never ceases to surprise."

Maryam looked through the window and did not respond.

37

Cape Coast, Ghana
February 2025

How the sun spread its wings that Monday morning in February, like a shower of grace! If I had the mental space to notice the weather, then I just knew the day would be excellent. I walked through the tree-lined pathway from my building to Maryam's. I had become her de facto roommate. No one had batted an eye about our dorming arrangement; however, for the last week or so, it occurred to me to give her some space, out of respect. Also to keep myself from becoming like stale fish, my presence no longer welcome.

Well, I had given her space, and in two days' time, she had actually sent me a message, asking how I was and if she would ever see me again. And of course she would! She only had to say the word!

Students were cavorting in small groups all around the campus grounds as I walked to her dorm building. A pair of young women were doing cartwheels on the main lawn. At the bench near the dormitory entrance doors, a group of young men sat eating their kelewele. The aroma of their food caused my stomach to growl.

Inside the dorm, I'd barely knocked before Maryam opened her door. "Hi, babe," I said, greeting her with a peck on the cheek. Music was already playing as she drew me by the arm inside.

We began a slow dance, and then I was spinning her, and soon we were both out of breath. We switched gears to taking sbooties. The sbooties, like the dance, had fast become part of our early morning ritual. Every Monday, so long as we were not having a quarrel, we took time for a brief morning dance and a photo. While she prioritized the sbooty, my heart lay in the dance—in the comfort of our bodies swishing together like two integrating bodies of water. There was a lot to love about days like that one— mornings when, even after the music had stopped, we continued to slow dance in each other's arms. That Monday indeed held the promise of an excellent day.

We carried ourselves to the bus to meet the group, and then we were off. We passed empty roads, crowded roads, colorful roads. The bus stopped us at Jamestown for the walking tour, which led us past the lighthouse in a direction that seemed to close the distance between the harbor and Bukom district. The air smelled of salted fish, and it wasn't hard to imagine how the place must have been those many decades ago, at least half a century ago—the corrugated shacks, the wooden pirogues, the vendors selling kenkey and mackerel and barracuda and squid. But now everything was shiny and prepossessing, nothing like the history books described things to be. The food, at least, remained.

At a vendor stand, after our group had dispersed for a quick break, Maryam and I fingered through trinkets—a necklace and some earrings for her. We scooted close to each other on the sidewalk to make way for the hordes of people.

"Good quality, good prices. Perfect for you," the female vendor said.

"What do you think?" Maryam asked me, holding up a gold set of earrings.

"Your skin goes with anything," I said honestly.

"Lovely man," the vendor said. "How long have you two been together?"

"A long time," I said, laughing.

"You're happy?" the vendor asked.

Maryam looked at me, and I smiled and nodded eagerly. "Very happy. Never been happier."

"You heard the man," Maryam said, laughing.

We moved on from that vendor, and Maryam whispered, "A bit nosy, wasn't she?"

"Maybe she saw something in us that made her ask," I replied. "Maybe we have the kind of relationship she wished she had. You never know."

Maryam scoffed at that.

"What's that supposed to mean?" I asked.

"Nothing," Maryam said. "Just that she wouldn't really know what kind of relationship we have."

"I guess," I replied reluctantly.

For lunch, the university chaperones laid out a picnic table and giant flasks of food and served the group waakye with a side of chicken on the bone. The Monday before we had eaten a lunch of fufu and groundnut soup by hand, all of us careful to swallow, not chew the soup-covered starch.

We sat together again this time. I looked forward to both learning about and assimilating into the culture. Perhaps I was too eager because, out of the blue, I found myself saying, "I wonder if there are any native Mandingos around." I had read of the Mandingos in preparation for the trip.

No one responded to my musing, but it did not at the time occur to me that this silence was a form of rebuke.

Things only got worse. When the food came, I laid aside the silverware that had been put on my place mat. "It'd be nice to see a real Mandingo," I said again, as I eagerly dug into the plate of food with my fingers despite my incredible discomfort with eating that way. Inside, my mind revolted against the act. I was terrified of the germs, but my desire to belong trumped my fear. Maryam looked at me aghast.

"What're you doing?" Maryam whispered, looking at my hands. I was in the middle of lifting up clumps of rice and beans with my fingers in preparation to stuff them into my mouth.

"Eating like the locals," I said. "When in Rome . . ."

"But the locals don't eat it this way," she whispered. "Are you trying to embarrass yourself?" She bit her lips nervously. What had I done wrong? Nothing that I could see. I continued to eat. When I was done, I lifted my bottle of water and slurped it all down in one go, convinced that she would soon come to see that my actions were simply a way of showing her that I was in fact one of them.

Imagine my shock, when, for the rest of the day, Maryam did not speak to me. Later that night, back in the dorm, when things were still tense between us and she was still not speaking with me, I retreated to my own dorm room and listened to my audiobook. Exasperated—a mixture of angst and boredom—I fixed my ears on a new book, Steinbeck's *Winter of Our Discontent.*

38

Mampong & Aburi, Ghana
March 2025

Up the mountains into Aburi and past the cliffs of Mampong we went. When we arrived at the Tetteh Quarshie cocoa farm, sage-green entry gates greeted us. In the pagoda where the group gathered, the tour guide rang his bell to silence the crowd and began his speech, his voice clean and sharp like a perfect recording. "Tetteh Quarshie was a blacksmith turned cocoa farmer, born in Accra, of the Ga peoples, who lived between 1842 and 1892. As a young man, he took a blacksmith job in Fernando Po, now in Equatorial Guinea, and returned with a handful of beans. It was not permitted to transfer plant seeds at the time, but Quarshie managed to do just that. Rumors say that he swallowed the cocoa seeds in order to smuggle them by sea. Keep in mind that a trip between Ghana and Fernando Po would have taken six weeks. Have you ever tried forcing yourself not to defecate for one week, let alone six?"

The crowd snickered.

"No one can be at sea for six weeks without using the bathroom," the guide said. "So, it's more likely that he put the cocoa pods in his blacksmith toolbox, under the tools, and for lack of more exquisite technologies, he was able to get away with it. He brought six yellow cacao pods, the Amelonado variety, which has a long gestation period and does not start to bear fruit until after six and a half years. But Quarshie was a patient man . . ."

By now the group had already been led through a grove of plantain, cocoyam, banana, and avocado trees, which all formed shades. The gliricidia were the most abundant of these shading trees, providing canopy-like support for the cocoa plants.

The group arrived in front of a labeled tree: *One of the originals; planted in 1879.* Nearly 150 years old, the original tree had grown several offshoots that had continued to sustain it.

"It's thanks to Quarshie that Ghana has become the number-one exporter of cocoa in the world, but, as with many things in life, history is a bit complicated. We all know that white politics and ego get in the way of Black recognition."

The tour guide winked knowingly at the crowd.

The crowd was a mixed group of students. Some of them snickered and others winced uncomfortably.

"But he basically stole the pods," someone said.

"Don't you believe that seeds of the earth should belong to everyone equally?" another person asked.

I nodded my head vehemently; I couldn't have agreed more.

"In any case," the guide continued, "the story goes that the British colonial judge at the time disputed the claim that Quarshie was the first to bring cocoa to Ghana. He argued that the first person was in fact his own father."

"Who won?" a voice asked.

"The white man always wins," someone muttered reproachfully.

"Not this time," the tour guide said. "After a full investigation by the British governor of the Gold Coast at the time, it was determined that the credit belonged to Quarshie."

I looked at the guide in happy astonishment. Maryam, who stood by my side, stroked my arm, which I then proceeded to wrap around her shoulders. The farm was bursting with yellow pods of cocoa, which hung down from each tree. The guide grabbed a go-to-hell sickle and hooked one of the yellow pods. He went on to demonstrate the fermentation process, describing the different methods: heap, basket, box, and tray fermentation. "Fermenting must be done on plantain leaves," he said. The yeast, the insects, the bacteria, the acids, and the alcohol, he explained, all play their various roles. Seven days of fermentation, three weeks of drying, he said. Fermenting and drying were crucial in creating the cocoa liquor that would then be used for soaps, lipsticks, creams, drinks.

The group dispersed, cutting through the greenery and tall branches of the farm, taking a look at the different stations that had been set up around the tour site. Maryam and I moved about the farm in an unhurried way, and then not entirely all of a sudden, I pulled her to a stop, leaned in close, kissed her on her cheek, then on her lips. There were the sounds of Twi mixed with English in the distance, and I thought, "A place like paradise still exists in this world!" I laughed that I should have found myself in such a place and not alone, but with Maryam to share it. "Maybe we could have our very own farm here," I said, stroking her arms. "Have our children. Start our own small army of cocoa farmers."

She looked thoughtfully at me.

"Wouldn't it be wonderful?"

"Yes, maybe," she said, and then it looked like she was about to add something else. But she must have seen the longing in my eyes because she leaned toward me and kissed me back. When she pulled away from the kiss, she said, "It would be wonderful, yes, G-Dawg. But why don't we focus on finishing school first, then we can revisit this idea?"

If she had been forthcoming in that moment, she might have said that while she did think that our time in the cocoa farm was wonderful, home was what she had begun to long for. This farm in the middle of a beautiful, serene little town was a place close to home, but not at all like her old home. The home she knew was more bustling than this almost-sleepy little town. And, anyway, home was where her family resided. The distance away for school had been brutal, distance compounded by the daily reminders that she was in fact in someone else's country.

There was also the matter of the passage of time. She ached every day at the thought of her mother getting older. She knew well that loss was the risk of love, but the weight of her mother's mortality hung heavily on her shoulders. Never mind that their relationship had been turbulent and that there had been times when she had considered severing all ties with the family. But she knew that the woman was like a shadow to her, always one backward glance away, and the fact remained that one could not run away from her shadow.

She called her Mumsi that night.

Of course, I would not find out that it was her mother Maryam had called until years later, after I'd finally managed to track her down on the continent. On the actual night of the phone call, she gave no indication that it was her mother. I only heard her say on the phone, "Don't worry. Everything will work itself out. He's gone now. He can't do that to you anymore. I don't think you have any more reason to be afraid. I know . . . I know . . ."

The woman's voice on the phone was loud enough that it was somewhat audible from where I sat. She said, "Thank you, my dear. I thank God for you every day." And then she added something along the lines of Maryam being better than any child she could ever have prayed for.

But hours before that call, earlier while we still stood in the cacao fields, the faint scent of cocoa and green leaves and earth wafted around us, and I closed my eyes. The desire for a life with her in a place as simple and pure as this one was so strong in me, but so was the roadblock that I was now perceiving she might be in the plan—she, like a block of cement in my chest.

★

ON THE RETURN trip from the cocoa farm, the driver stopped again, and the group descended from the van at the Aburi garden. Not far from where we convened, other visitors had also gathered. The temperature had dropped, and the weather had cooled with the rise in elevation, and then all of us stood in the midst of enormous kapok trees and thousands of epiphytes.

Late morning grew into a full afternoon. Maryam walked away to look at some species of plants. I stood back, watching her. When she returned, she wrapped her arms around me, and I rested my cheek on the rugged bed that was her hair. I loved the feel of my cheek on her twists, and when I kissed her on her head, she leaned into me more.

As soon as we alighted from the bus at the Boti Falls, our final stop for the day, the guide explained that the twin waterfalls were the closest falls to Accra and were referred to as male and female.

I circled my arms around Maryam, pushed my body into hers, and whispered, "Ha! Man and woman. Perfect spot for us."

She shifted away from me for a reason that I could not have explained, but just as I began to worry, she moved closer.

"The falls are known because of the magic that happens between them," the tour guide explained. "You see, in the right season," he continued, "the two of them actually become one, and when this union happens, a rainbow appears."

"Incredible!" I said quietly.

"If you ask anyone from this area," the guide said, "they will tell you that the rainbow forms because they are mating."

Some of the group members snickered.

"Now, now. Wipe away all your blushing!" the tour guide teased. "Mating is a natural part of the circle of life! Even the mountains know it!"

The group snickered some more, and then we were dismissed. Tour over.

We entertained ourselves for the next couple of hours. Some chose to do the one-hour hike up the rocky forest to Umbrella Rock; others walked to the nearby bead market. Another set of lovers in the group got on one of the small green-and-red canoes that were available on-site.

Maryam and I walked around the waterfalls for some time, then down to the bead market, where we haggled with vendors and filled our backpacks with bottled water and pouches of Capri Sun.

Back near the waterfalls, we got in a canoe and paddled out. The shore had cleared, and all the other group members seemed so far away. I hummed softly to myself the melody to an almost-forgotten song. *"Tell me something, girl,"* I sang. *"Are you happy in this modern world?"*

"Pretty song," Maryam said. "Never heard it before."

"'Shallow,'" I said. "It's old now."

"You sing beautifully," she said.

"Thank you," I said, recognizing something in her—something dreamy and nostalgic in her eyes, a look I'd come to understand as a signal that she wanted me close. We looked awkwardly at each other. When we were farther out from the shore, and after I'd sung the song one more time, I scooted carefully over to her. The water was calm, and far from us, I could see where the cyan waters appeared to drop into the deep. She was wearing a floral sundress that flared down from her waist. I knelt in front of her and asked, "May I?" She nodded, and I gently pulled up her dress, allowed my tongue to trail the skin on the inside of her thighs. That skin. That chocolate, chocolate skin. The boat swayed, and for a moment, I might have been deterred from our lovemaking. But the wobbling quickly calmed, and the boat steadied itself in the water. I kissed her greedily but tenderly, enjoying the flavor of her beautiful skin.

By the time we were done, the sky was growing dark. The sun, which had been heavy on our heads and backs all afternoon, was now a faint glow, distant and sinking fast into the purple horizon. A nice evening breeze had replaced the heat. The palm trees stood tall. By this time, Maryam and I had begun to feel a tussling in our guts, hunger pangs knocking on the walls of our stomachs. We paddled our way back to shore and stepped off the canoe, content in each other's embrace.

39

IN APRIL, WE BEHELD THE BEAUTY OF THE 1,600-FOOT WATER-fall from the high peak of Mount Afadja. I felt the power of nature's beauty rush through my body. The sky was an electric blue, the kind of color that obliged people to relax a little, to obliterate their inhibitions and bare their souls in the bright open air.

Not far from where our group stood, a little local girl with her hair in two symmetrical large puffs cried for her father. "Papa?"

The man that Maryam and I believed to be her father was standing right before her, only he was occupied, talking to another adult. The girl tugged lightly at the tail of the man's shirt.

"Grown-ups hardly ever have their priorities straight," Maryam whispered to me with irritation before walking over to the little girl, who stood sulking in her little yellow pinafore with her dusty little legs. Her socks peeked out of her brown sandals; once upon a time, they must have been white, but they had by now turned almost the same sandy brown of the shoes.

Maryam patted one of the puffs on the girl's head. She would tell me years later that she used to wear her hair that way when she was a small girl back in Lagos.

The man whom we assumed was the girl's father had walked a little farther away but was still close enough to check on her. The little girl turned to face Maryam with some apprehension.

When the girl began sobbing, the sound of her cry was something Maryam must have recognized from her own past, as if the small girl that Maryam used to be existed in this little girl.

The girl's cries for her "Papa!" were now softly ringing, and the tour guide paused in the middle of his spiel and said, "Everyone, by the way, this is Jojo, the apple of her father's eye."

The group members *Aaawww*ed almost on cue, and all the while, the little girl's jaw trembled until tears fell down her cheeks like tiny raindrops.

Maryam knelt down to her level and opened her arms, and the girl went in for the embrace. Meanwhile, her father was throwing watchful eyes at them.

I knelt down by Maryam's side. "She's adorable," I whispered to Maryam. Pulling out my phone camera, I said, "Photo time! Let me get a photo of her."

Maryam at first seemed to glare at me, but then she let go of the girl to make space for me to take my photo. "Brilliant!" I said. "Like something straight out of that old magazine!"

Maryam flinched.

"What old magazine?" she asked.

"*National Geographic!*" I said. "Remember it?" I peered at my camera, scanned through the photos I'd taken, then held the device to Maryam. "Do you mind getting a photo of us together?"

Maryam took the camera. I knelt next to the girl, a wide grin on my face. Maryam snapped the photo. She must have already been wondering what the older version of the little girl might think of a person like me, who saw her as an object to be admired, a magazine photo or intriguing wall art, something a person could own. She must have also wondered what the little girl's older self would think about a woman who loved a man who thought of the girl in that way.

To Maryam, my assessment of the girl was distasteful, almost sinister, but as with many things in life, I would not find this out for a while.

Later that afternoon, when a group of the most beautifully dark-skinned kids I'd ever seen gathered around playing a game with polished pebbles and holes dug into the earth, I exclaimed, "Beautiful children! So exotic looking!"

Immediately I observed Maryam's discomfort in the sudden stiffness of her manners. She hesitated a bit before she spoke. "Exotic?" she asked pointedly. And then the series of questions followed: Was it that I thought that I myself was not exotic? Or maybe I thought that these African kids were from an altogether different universe? Or what? "Which one is it?" She really wanted to know.

My instinct told me to carry on as if nothing had happened. If I engaged, her questions might grow into a full-blown altercation. And no one ever truly won a battle by fighting. All they had was the illusion of victory.

I could, of course, have answered her simply, palliatively, but the truth is that I didn't have answers to her questions, for I hadn't exactly thought of things in those terms.

Before Maryam could have known what was happening, I was gathering the children from their game and arranging them so that I could carry on taking photos.

"Please?" I asked Maryam, handing her my phone for the photo-op.

The children were already smiling widely and posing. Some were chanting, "Cheese!"

"To have so little," I whispered to Maryam, "and yet be so happy. It's always amazed me how people in Africa can be so happy with so little. We should all aim to be this way."

Maryam looked around as if checking to see if anyone had heard me. Or maybe it was that she was looking for an escape. It's only recently that I've come to realize the possible implications of my comment and, in fact, of many of my running observations during that trip, even the supposed compliments among them.

"Maybe they have more than your eyes can see," Maryam said, candidly.

She stared at my hand as I held my phone for the photo. Rain began to fall.

I glanced up at her, begging her with my eyes to please take the phone. But she would not. Instead, she looked into my eyes like a dare—as if to say that I could let my hand hang there and allow the phone to get drenched in the rain for all she cared.

The sky opened up. The downpour pelted our skin. The lithe tree branches whistled. Leaves stirred. Dips and holes in the muddy earth filled with rust-colored water. Petrichor rose and hovered around our nostrils.

She continued to stare coldly at me. It occurred to me that she might even end things with me right there and then. I called for her to come out of the rain, but she would not budge. All the other tourists shrieked and scuttled off into the rain shelters. Maryam remained there under the howling havoc of the storm, allowing the rain to wash over her.

40

Cape Coast, Ghana
April 2025

CLASSES AFTER THE MOUNT AFADJA EXCURSION WERE AN abyss of silence as Maryam and I waged a battle of wills against each other. Who would have thought that my sweet Maryam was capable of such extreme coldness? Yes, she had her moods. But this was something else altogether.

In our Politics of West African Development course, the desks were arranged in pairs, and we were each other's partner, but partnership had never felt so solitary, seated side by side, barely speaking a word. The weekend was a buckling of our commitment to each other. We stayed separate, each in our own dorm.

When the next excursion Monday came upon us, there was no morning dance and no morning sbooty. A profound and unmistakable distance had arisen between us, and we arrived separately to the biomethane bus.

Our group first alighted at the main tro-tro station at the main Ho–Hohoe road. Just when many of the group members had begun to complain that they'd soon fall over from fatigue, we finally arrived at the Tafi Atome Monkey Sanctuary in the Volta region.

The first thing our group did was to go on a tour of the surrounding forest, making stops to examine the flora and fauna. At the gate to see the mona monkeys, the tour guide paid a collective entrance fee of several handfuls of bananas. Inside the monkey sanctuary, a troop of about a dozen Old World monkeys swung from branch to branch through the canopies, their brown agouti fur sharply contrasting with their white rumps. Those that were eating their meals—of beetles and butterflies and ants, and sprouts and leaves—carried the food in their cheek pouches. Time went by as swiftly as the monkeys' flights. The furry animals frolicked, hung by their tails, and reached for the banana offerings. "Incredible!" I declared to no one in particular. I had decided to enjoy the forest, despite the situation between Maryam and me, or perhaps because of it. "Just like the zebras! Did you know that zebra skin is also black and white, shadow and light to absorb and reflect the light, which in turn is to protect the zebras from predators? I wonder if it's the same for these monkeys."

"It very well might have been nature's idea," the tour guide responded. "But this is a sanctuary, so the monkeys are relatively safe from predators. Anyway," the guide continued, "there's the matter of the dark stripes across the monkey's faces and their other coloring." He pointed out that their tails and legs were black and their faces a bluish gray. The insides of their limbs were a beige white—browns and blues and blacks and grays and whites—so it was quite a bit different from the zebras.

"But it's also rather the same," I insisted. "Isn't it?"

The tour guide smiled a placating smile, like a mother firmly assuaging a misbehaving child.

We followed the Cemetery Trail to the kente-weaving village, hiking the six kilometers over the course of an hour, the trails thinning and thickening like women's hips. The oburoni among us lathered on their sunscreen, and we all tugged at our sun hats before trudging through the muddy road and the tall elephant grass. "Look at us!" I burst out in the middle of the hike. "Just like wildebeests crossing the Mara!"

No one seemed to hear me.

"Did you know that zebras have horns in their upper and lower teeth and lead the way, eating all the tall grass, and the wildebeests follow? The wildebeests don't prefer the tall, tough grass like the zebras do, so the symbiotic relationship is necessary."

"This is Ghana, not Serengeti," a tall male Black student groaned.

"Yeah, no one cares about your zebras and wildebeests," a white woman muttered. She was almost as tall as the Black man, and as she uttered the words, she flung her hair with annoyance over her shoulders.

Maryam must have felt the pain of the rebuke on my behalf because she came to me, held my hand in hers. It seemed to me that she had grown increasingly lonely without my company. In which case, the gesture was a little exploitative. Still, I didn't blame her for it. Nobody knew better than I that loneliness was a beast, and the tools people employed to ward off that beast should never be mocked.

Across the street, a vulture was picking at a dead sheep, tearing through the carcass with its beak.

"The sheep's body," I said, wearily. "It looks almost like what the rhinoceros looked like in the Mara. The way we only see the top of it? Almost like the shape of a termite's mound."

I realize it now, years after the fact, that I was lecturing like a know-it-all. All those animal descriptions. Why? Nerves? Retaliation for Maryam keeping her distance from me? Even I do not understand why I behaved in this way. What was my endgame, my telos? What I now speculate is that being a child of weak constitution who suffered a certain oppression of self, I needed a path to fitting in. Like those Purist kids all over the city who got Purist tattoos to be a part of a recognizable community, I wanted to be a part of that old Serengeti community. Benson and his colleagues. Everyone should have a community. Everyone deserves to belong somewhere.

As if she'd read my mind, Maryam asked, "Why all this animal talk? Does this place remind you that much of Tanzania?"

"Animal talk?" I asked as if unsure of what she meant. But then I replied, "I don't know. Serengeti was a good childhood memory, I guess. Maybe I enjoyed the animals more than I realized."

We continued with the group, and after a while my feet began to ache. "Soon, I'll begin limping like a hyena," I said, teasing.

Maryam looked blankly at me.

"But seriously," I explained, "did you know that they run like they're limping?"

"All right," Maryam said, shaking her head in defeat. "Good to know, I guess."

At Tafi Abuife, while pouring water over our faces to cool ourselves off, we watched a demonstration of how kente cloths were made. We followed the demonstration with a tour of the village, and then finished off with shopping for keepsakes from the vendors along the main road.

By the time we arrived at the fantasy coffin tour the following week, Maryam would have probably liked to bury me in one of those fantasy coffins.

We took the Accra-Tema Beach Road down to the Tema sub-road and arrived at the Teshie Mobile area. For most of the drive, the Atlantic Ocean lined the road on one side, glinting in shades of silver and blue. Markets lined the other side of the road.

"Akwaaba!" the coffin maker said. "My name is Anders Nkrumah Ansong, alias 'Goodbye.'" He laughed. He was a jovial-looking man with puffed-up cheeks. It seemed paradoxical that such a lively, happy man had chosen to deal in death.

"Now, you might ask about 'Goodbye.' The story goes that there is no story! My mother called me that way," he said, "and I don't even know why!"

The group laughed.

"Now, as we all know, the hoe of death does not weed in one place, but in a million places at once. Shall we sit around moping and crying? No! My philosophy is that any funeral should be a celebration of life!"

He led us to the first casket. It was gold and shaped like a woman, with a large scale hanging from each ear. "She was into astrology," the coffin maker said. "Her family wanted to celebrate her life by burying her in a coffin that represented her astrological sign, so I made them a set of scales. She also loved her gold jewelry . . ."

The next two coffins were a cobalt-blue Rolls-Royce Sweptail and a silver Mercedes-Benz Exelero. "One method of celebrating is to send off our loved ones in style," the craftsman said. There were also several eagle caskets. "The eagles took me one month to complete. One month for the lobster too. Very detailed work. I'm making it for a former fisherman."

"And the truck?" someone asked.

"Three weeks to a month. For a commercial truck driver."

He led us to the fetish priest coffin, then to the silver hair dryer for a former hairdresser. "Three weeks to a month for the fetish priest coffin, three weeks for the hair dryer."

"How many of these do you make a year?" someone asked.

"Anywhere from ten to fifteen," the craftsman replied. "But fewer people are dying in the country these days, so most of our products end up being exported to the West. Did I tell you your former president—President Carter, if any one of you knows your history—purchased two coffins from my father back in the day? Another former president of yours also came—the one who took advantage of that young woman? What was his name?"

"That could have been almost any of them," a Ghanaian woman muttered from the crowd.

"Yeah, but definitely not our African brother president," her friend said. "That one has always been a good family man."

"And very handsome too."

"Tell me about it," and the two women chuckled among themselves. The rest of the crowd was stiffly silent.

The coffin maker cleared his throat. "What I was trying to say is that I have all the old photos of my father and Carter." He used his handkerchief to wipe the sweat off his forehead to demonstrate the awkwardness of the situation.

As the group dispersed, I brushed shoulders with the coffin maker. "My brother," he said. "Akwaaba," and he wrapped his arm around my shoulder. That small moment filled me with more happiness than I can explain. I immediately felt a bond with him. He hadn't called me oburoni; he'd simply called me his brother.

Later, as Maryam and I stood examining the hair-dryer coffin, I said to her, "Do you ever meet someone and just feel like you identify with him?"

"What do you mean?" Maryam asked.

"The coffin maker," I said. "There's a kind of person you meet, and . . ." My voice shook. I inhaled deeply then exhaled slowly to steady my breath. I must have been terrified to say it so straightforwardly to her. ". . . You just know that if you could be born again as a different human being, you might choose to be born . . ." I couldn't finish.

We stood looking at each other in silence. For the first time, I felt that she was truly seeing me, seeing who I was beyond my skin.

"You want to be reborn as him?" she asked, looking penetratingly at me. "Why?"

"Well, forget humans," I said awkwardly. "Did I ever tell you that if I could be any animal, I'd be a klipspringer?"

She shook her head. "No, you never told me."

"They're, of course, native to Africa, and also one of the most monogamous creatures on earth. In my heart, I'm A—" My voice broke. I laughed from the discomfort of the situation. "Well, you and I both know that I'm as monogamous as they come. One partner is enough for me."

"So, you're a klipspringer now?" she asked, watching me with genuine curiosity.

"Yes, as monogamous and . . . African . . . as they come," I said. "A klipspringer at heart."

"But you know that, historically, many African men are anything but monogamous, right?"

I wrestled with this thought momentarily. "Well," I said. "I suppose I'm the monogamous kind of African man."

41

Cape Coast, Ghana
April 2025

VISITORS THIS WAY, READ A SIGN AT THE ENTRANCE. THE grand closing tour, the last week of our semester abroad, was at the historic Cape Coast Dungeon.

The amber sun scorched. My clammy skin burned. Now more than ever in this country, I felt my entire body as a betrayal, as a site of menace, something to be wary of. At the dungeon, the skin on my body mattered far more than it ever had. The locals would surely identify me, and if they were unlike the coffin maker (and very likely they would be), then I would certainly be made to feel like an outsider. Accusatory stares might descend upon me, a rebuke for the violations that my supposed ancestors had committed. These grounds, and the people, who could not see who I really was, might turn on me. And of course, it'd be no fault of theirs. Who I was could not be seen by ordinary eyes. What I appeared to be, this skin that I wore, was merely a trick of the light.

I held Maryam's hand tight like a lifeline. An ocean breeze tousled sand and leaves in the near distance. The dungeon's veneer shined deceptively white. The group walked past the piles of red, rusting cannonballs, past the ruddy black army of cannons that hung like divers on their marks, getting set to leap into the depths of the ocean.

The guide stopped to allow us a moment to peruse the museum. The tall black-and-white prints of the trade routes and photos of the shackled queues of people stared accusingly at me, or at least I perceived them this way. I tried to catch my breath. My hands were musty and wet, and I pulled away from Maryam's grasp. My head swirled with discomfort. What a horror their lives must have been, and yet my life in that moment felt somehow more miserable.

To acknowledge the pain that had been caused on these grounds was to somehow implicate myself, and I certainly felt the implication. But I really wasn't to blame. What infuriated me was that I was not one of *those* ancestors; I was not even white.

I used the back of my hand to dab sweat off my forehead.

"The locals like to say that the white man came with three things: booze, guns, and Christianity," the tour guide said with a playful look on his face. "Got us all intoxicated so we could kill one another while they pretended to care by preaching the Bible to us." Just as I had feared, it had already begun.

My heart raced. I examined the group. I was not alone. Others with skin paler than mine stood among us. No one from the group spoke.

"You see, initially, there had been a barter system," the tour guide continued, "between the Africans and the Westerners. Ceramic dishware for gold. Booze and tobacco for gold. This area was known for its gold, hence its former name, the Gold Coast. But one day gold was no longer good enough, and before you knew it, they were capturing and selling human beings."

How had we so quickly arrived at the branding tools? There, before my eyes, was a rod used by one of the slave masters to brand his slaves.

At the entrance to the female dungeon was a gate made of steel, rusted by time and ocean breeze. Inside was a floor of red bricks leading into yellow bricks. You could see the colors from the entrance, but only if you looked closely. The vault was dark except for a thin sliver of light by the entrance. Some of the group members turned on the flashlights on their phones, and though the vault was more illuminated with the added light, the darkness appeared to win.

Inside the dungeon, piles of pink and red and purple burial wreaths wrapped up in plastic and tied at their tops with ribbons littered the floor.

"People who have traced their family members back to this place have come to pay respects to their ancestors who died here. Each year they visit and leave these gifts for the dead," the guide explained. Handwritten notes were attached to each gift.

"Take your time," the guide said. The air was stiff. A cry came like a baby's sob, but there was no baby in the group.

I walked over to the wall where the sound had come from. Did anyone else hear it? It didn't seem so. They were all going about the tour like nothing had happened.

"Hello?" I whispered in the corner of the dungeon. "Who's there?"

But the cry did not come again. Reluctantly, I returned to the group, to Maryam's solemn side.

"We are standing on feces, urine, blood, tears, sweat, and, to some extent, human flesh," the guide was saying. "You see, on average, slaves had to spend three months waiting in the dungeon, because ships took three months to get from the Gold Coast to Europe and the Americas and back.

"The drainage system was a simple continuous dip in the brick of the flooring, which meant that the slaves, their bodies piled up in the dungeon as they were, were forced to stand in place to urinate and defecate. The smell of their excretions hung in the air and spread disease among them.

"At one point it appears that there were buckets hidden at the corners of the dungeon, but as the slaves were from all different parts of the country, even from different African countries, they spoke different languages, making communication difficult. And, given that they were shackled so tightly, they would have needed to communicate about accessing the buckets. They had no choice but to bleed and urinate and defecate in place."

I looked at where my feet stood. The thought of standing on ancient feces and urine made me sick to my stomach. My entire body trembled in the darkness. Before I knew it, I was running out of the dungeon, nearly retching as I did.

In the open space between the cannonballs and where the cannons stood in a line, a misty breeze blew with force. In the distance, ocean waves crashed into the glistening bluffs. I counted numbers: One . . . two . . . three . . . four . . . . five . . . six . . . I continued on like a small child learning to count. Even after I reached a hundred, I could not get my heart to stop racing.

I stayed there, unable to bring myself to return to the group. If things between me and Maryam had been perfectly fine, she would certainly have come to check on me. But, perhaps already turning against me by virtue of what she was learning on these grounds, she had not. This added insult to injury and hurt me almost as much as my having to withstand the ghastliness of the dungeon and of history.

When the group reconvened and began walking over to the governor's residence, I rejoined them.

"You OK?" Maryam asked, a little too nonchalantly. Then she looked more closely at me. "You don't look so great. Everything OK?"

I nodded, grateful for her sudden attention. "I'll be OK," I said.

"OK, good. Come on, then," she said. She took my hand.

We climbed up the stairs into the governor's parlor. A breeze blew in through all seven windows of the room, sunlight shining brightly, pleasant. Through the parlor, we made our way into the expansive governor's dining room, its windows bursting like gold with light. An original stone-carved oven took up an entire wall of the kitchen, and the lime-green spirogyras twisted on the whitewashed walls like decoration. We were still in the kitchen when I heard praise songs coming from the room next door. But when we entered the room, there was no music. A row of pews sat in neat order in the middle of the room. An age-worn blackboard hung on the front-facing wall. Above the blackboard, the lines from Psalm 132:

The Lord has chosen Zion; he wants to make it his home:
"This is where I will live forever: this is where I want to rule."

"This church is just above the female dungeon," the guide said. "While they were sermonizing above, the slaves were being tortured just below. A lesson for us all that religiousness is not equivalent to goodness. Goodness does not come from religion; it comes from the soul."

"Do you think the whites have souls?" someone asked, out of the blue. To this day, the question still astonishes me. Although I did not identify as white, it felt like an assault.

"Like I said," the guide replied slickly, "the locals like to say that they preached us the Bible to make us feel that they cared, and then they stole our people and our land from right under our noses."

I looked around the room with discomfort.

"Some people are of the opinion that they were only sharing," the guide said.

"I was just about to say it!" a gray-haired white American woman from the group said. "After all, didn't we bring formal education into the continent?"

"That age-old argument," another woman said, a Ghanaian. "Don't forget trade! They like to claim they brought formal education and trade! As if we didn't have our own form of education and our own barter system!"

"Abi?" a Nigerian male student said. "Why does formal education have to look the way *they* think it should?"

"It wasn't just education and trade," the gray-haired white American woman said. "What of religion, the churches?"

"You think Africans didn't have their own religions?" a bald-headed Ghanaian young man with a squeaky voice said. "You think we didn't have our own forms of worship, our own equivalent of churches before the Westerners came?"

There was a silence.

"Maybe the fault was ours, sha," a Nigerian-Ghanaian student said, a young woman I recognized as one of the women who lived on the same floor as Maryam. "You go converting to somebody else's God simply because they tell you that you should? Foolishness! Don't you know that someone else's God will always have their own interest at heart instead of yours? Look around! The white man's God clearly had the white man's interest at heart! Even the Jesuits supported the slave trade. Immanuel Kant and Hegel—think the master-slave dialectic—two philosophers whose teachings greatly influenced Jesuit philosophy. They both supported slavery in their beliefs that Blacks were inferior. In fact, Kant believed all non-Europeans were inferior. Native Americans and Africans, especially. Isn't he the philosopher widely known as one of the originators of race-based differentiation of humans? Jesuits functioned under these same principles. You're from America, abi?" she said, looking at the gray-haired white woman. "You name all your formerly great universities. From Harvard to Georgetown—they were all built on money earned from slavery, weren't they?"

I stood stiffer than ever.

"So, what are you saying?" Maryam asked.

"Am I speaking Chinese or what?" the Nigerian-Ghanaian woman asked. "Isn't it clear what I'm saying? I'm saying that we create our gods. Yes, we've all grown to think it's the opposite, but believe me, the gods don't create us; *we* create our gods. In the case of the white man, he created his God very cleverly, so as to ensure that his God would have only his interests at heart!"

"You're overanalyzing the whole thing," some man said. "It's simply a matter of wickedness versus goodness. Gods have nothing to do with it."

"So, I ask again, do you think white people have souls?" the same person from before asked.

"Of course they have souls," I said, unexpectedly. My voice had exited my mouth without my permission. I rebuked myself for entering the conversation. I was shocked by my defensive stance.

"But what kind of people commit such atrocities against other humans? Put them in dungeons and let them die in their own feces?" that same person asked.

"But weren't we the greedy ones to fall for their tricks? We wanted more—wanted their money, booze, ammunition. We were just plain greedy, and out of greed we sold our own brothers and sisters to them. All in the name of greed!"

"Is it that simple? Think power differential. If a man stands in front of you with guns and cannons that you know can kill you far quicker than any of your bows and arrows . . . If a man comes with guns and cannons that can kill far more people than your little bows and arrows . . . you think it's easy to say no? Even the most well-meaning people, if they have any sense, would know that they couldn't fight a person holding a gun to their head. And if they give you an ultimatum while holding a gun or cannon at your head, betray your brother and live—"

"My sister!" the Ghanaian man said. "Greed is what the white man has trained us to blame it on, which also means that we self-blame. Meanwhile the white man sits back and laughs, still winning in their mission to divide and conquer."

"Yes," the budding psychologist in the group said. "I am thinking that we need to look deeper. Yes . . . Yes . . . I am thinking that this accusation of greed is part of their propaganda. But if any accusation should be hurled, it's that it was mental manipulation on the side of the whites—to make us think, under threats of imprisonment and death, that they were better, and their ways superior, and that everything they brought was for our own benefit. It was in many ways, then, a lack of confidence on our part to think they were indeed better and their ways superior. Quite a bit of naïveté on our part. They are not better. Their ways are not superior. What they brought was for their own benefit, and hardly ever fundamentally for ours."

"So, you're saying . . . ?" the white American woman asked.

"I'm saying, look deeper," the psychologist said. "I'm saying that the mental manipulation of the whites was so strong that even today they have managed to get us to assume the guilt for what they did— for their crimes. I agree that it is wrong for us to blame ourselves and carry on with talk of our greed, our culpability; all the while they smile and nod with satisfaction. If Stockholm syndrome can happen between individuals, in marriages, for instance, why not between nations? We are manipulated into identifying with the abusers, into excusing their behaviors, into blaming ourselves for their behaviors. That is the very essence of their abuse. That particular form of mental manipulation is the very strength of the West. Why have we chosen to remain so gullible, so naïve at the game, that we play right into their script? Foolishness, perhaps. Or is it simply that we have an erroneous deep-seated belief in the goodness of all humans, and therefore of all nations?" She shook her head as if shaking away a fly. Then she continued: "We do know that sociopaths exist. If individuals can be sociopathic, why not nations? Are nations not merely a collection of individuals? At the very least, why not their governments?"

"Isn't that a bit harsh?" someone said.

"A person is never so fully bad that they are irredeemable," someone else added. "Likewise, an entire nation—and by extension, its entire government—cannot be declared entirely and irredeemably bad."

"If you believe that, you'll believe anything," the Ghanaian young man said.

"If white America and white western Europe were a person," the Nigerian-Ghanaian woman said, laughing, "they certainly would be sociopaths."

Awkward silence.

"That's a judgment," I muttered. "No need for name-calling."

"I am thinking that the question is," the psychologist said, "or at least should be, what kind of childhood trauma caused white America and white western Europe to be the way they are? We all know that these social disorders are often a result of childhood traumas—parental abandonment, for instance. Consequences of abandonment include the inability to feel guilt. It is possible that America and western Europe would benefit from looking deeper into their own histories and their own traumas to examine the ways their histories have rendered them a generally sociopathic society, at least where many of their governments are concerned. The younger generation is not exempt; we all know that these traumas are inherited genetically. Studies show generational genetic changes related to trauma. Epigenetic inheritance of sociopathy is, thus, a possibility. And I am thinking that there is no cure for sociopathy."

At this point the floodgates opened and I found myself in a body-shaking cry.

"G-Dawg!" Maryam exclaimed softly. "What . . . are you . . . ?"

For the second time that day, I ran out of the room.

★

WHEN I FOUND the group again, the guide had finished touring the male dungeon and was leading us toward the slave exit to the waiting boats. We walked up to the archway, up to the dark entrance of the tunnel that led to the tiny skeletal-sized Door of No Return.

"Here was the last time they ever stepped foot on the Gold Coast. Once they passed this door, their journey to the Caribbean and the Americas began, and they never saw home again."

"But the door is so small. How did they fit?"

The guide laughed. "By the time their three months of waiting was up, believe me, even the fattest of them were skinny enough to fit."

"But they fed them, didn't they?" the Ghanaian young man asked.

"Barely," the guide said. "Just enough to keep them alive. And in fact, some women refused to eat. They'd have rather died than continue living in such inhumane conditions. Incidentally," the guide said, lifting a tool now, "say hello to this wicked invention also known as the 'mouth opener' which they used to force the slaves to eat so that the slave owners didn't lose their products. Speculum orifice," he said, and held up the tool for all to see.

Outside the Door of No Return, the ocean opened up like an embrace. Fishermen lined their canoes along the beach, flags waving in the air.

"And so, ladies and gentlemen, this brings us to the end of our tour," the guide said. "May we remember and may we grow in our humanity and love for one another."

A blond-haired family from another tour group passed by. Two curly-haired primary-school-aged children walked with their mother, who appeared to be cajoling them in Dutch. Their father trailed behind, looking seriously into his camera, taking a photo of the backside of the Door of No Return.

"Such small children," someone whispered. "Why would you bring them to a place like this?"

"Clearly, to learn about history too!" the gray-haired white woman from the group snapped.

"Well, you never know with them," the Nigerian-Ghanaian woman snapped back. "For all we know, maybe it's more like they are taking notes and training their young ones on how to do it again, only this time with the aim of getting away with it!"

The tour guide laughed. "May we remember and may we grow in our humanity and love for one another," he said. "As you head out, please be careful walking down the steps. The wood is slippery. Be sure to hold on to the railing."

"There's too much wickedness in the world," Maryam said, sighing.

"How old is the railing that we are holding on to for safety? I hope not so old that it will break on us, o!" a Nigerian woman said.

At the estate's exit, local children engrossed themselves in activities: a group of boys and girls stood playing a clapping game. Closer to the beach, teenage boys played ball. Two small girls sat together, drawing a face, taking turns with a stick, carving the silhouette into the wet sand.

"Such cute little monkeys!" I whispered warmly to Maryam.

"Oh God," Maryam said, like a gasp. Then she quickened her steps, leaving me behind.

"Maryam!" I called to her, racing after her.

"I have to go," she said to me, almost to herself. "Let me go. I just have to go."

She walked off. Something tells me that, as she did, she must have done a mental review of our history together. Something tells me that she must have thought of me, understood me, at the very best, as a man who was nothing but a parasite on her selfhood, siphoning her identity and the identities of those like her, trying to latch on and live off of them so as to keep from fading into nothingness. And at the worst, well . . . I was the very stereotype of whiteness, a man who saw her and people like her as less human than himself.

PART V

42

Manhattan, New York
May 2025

ON THE RETURN TRIP TO THE US, THE RIDE WAS SO TURBULENT I was certain the souls of the departed were indeed grasping for the plane. It should have scared me as it did on the arrival flight. But not this time. The terrible and steady stream of turbulence jostled the plane as it crossed the Atlantic, but I surrendered to it. My mind was instead weighed down by the burden of how to win Maryam back. She sat by my side, but everything had changed between us. I assuaged my fears by telling myself that it was only a matter of time. That is, in the fullness of time, I could in fact make amends.

That first day back at home, after the flight, after baggage pickup, after the train rides, after making my way past a crowd of Purists who stood erecting their gallows, calling for the hanging of government officials, I sat on my bed and was glad to be back in my apartment. Certainly, I was startled at returning to a country in such a state. That was panic enough, but another kind of panic was rising in me—panic at the possibility of having to return to a life without Maryam, a lonely life, an empty life. It was only the first day back and the loneliness was already cutting through my soul.

Chevy and Wayne returned to my mind. Panic turned into melancholy because, maybe, just maybe, I missed them. Maybe I was their son, and, whether I liked it or not, they were my parents. Panic reared its ugly head again when I considered the fact that I was longing for people I'd fought so hard to leave.

Melancholy returned as I remembered the way Maryam had said, "I have to go."

"I just have to go." And of course, she did pick up and go. Would she ever return?

If I could make peace with Chevy and Wayne, perhaps I would not need Maryam the way I currently needed her. And yet, my desire for her was so sharp; Chevy and Wayne would always be a sorry consolation prize.

I wanted to get up and wash myself after all the traveling, but the weight of my melancholy was too heavy. "Get up, G-Dawg!" I said to myself, but I could not bring myself to rise. "Get up and make yourself useful!" But I sat in my misery, staring into the blank wall. At some point I must have lowered my body into sleep.

THE FOLLOWING DAY, after I had finally mustered the energy to get up and unpack, I wrote to Maryam:

> Hey, M,
>
> I know it's only been a day, and you're probably still jetlagged, but I was thinking maybe we could go see Medea. Tomorrow or Sunday evening? Let me know if you'd like that, and if so, what night works best for you.
>
> ~G-D

I paced my apartment for the next hour, waiting for her response. After that first hour, and no response from her, I told myself that she was probably still sleeping. I played Yemi Alade's greatest hits loudly from my computer and jumped into the shower.

I dried myself and could not help tapping my foot. Any other time I might have broken out into dance. But the only meaningful relationship I'd ever had in my life had somehow shattered. The last thing I wanted to do was dance. What could I possibly have said to push her so far away? Or was it simply that she had grown tired of my company?

I raked my mind to understand how I could have done things differently. I tried to inhabit her mind for answers. But wasn't it the saying that if you're in their head, then you're out of your mind?

I left my apartment for a long, miserable moseying walk from Washington Heights in the direction of Midtown. The leaves hung limply from the branches as if too tired of the heat. The trees looked like old, shriveled heads of broccoli. The sun looked like a bleeding half orange. The city had morphed into something ugly. My view of the world, which only a few weeks ago had been relatively bright, had suddenly grown dimmer, as if oversize sunshades had been placed permanently over my eyes. I dialed Damian on the phone.

Only one ring, thankfully, and Damian answered. "Yo, what's good?" he said.

"You got a minute?" I asked.

A few minutes later, he joined me on my walk. The streets crawled with beggars. I explained that something was awry between me and Maryam. I recounted everything in as much detail as I could.

"What do you think I did wrong?" I asked.

Damian shook his head. "I don't know, man. I don't know her side of the story so no way for me to know."

"I just want to fix it," I said.

We continued to walk silently. After some time, Damian turned to look at me. "Did I tell you about my sister and the woman who hit her car?" he asked.

"I didn't even know you had a sister," I said.

Damian laughed. "Yeah, well, now you know. Anyway, my sister was on her way to her doctor's appointment, driving her new white VW Passat that she paid over $30K for . . ."

I imagined it, the car, the sun shooting glints off the pearly white of the vehicle's body.

"She entered the parking lot and was about to pull into her spot when, get this, this old Purist woman backs up into my sister's car. Backs right up into the passenger side. The woman's car was covered with those yellow-and-red Purist bumper stickers, so my sister knew to be on guard. Anything could happen. So, the woman gets out of her car and walks up to my sister's window and says, right away, 'I'm so sorry I did that.' My sister doesn't say anything. But she gets out of her car, too, and walks around to take a look at the damage. The woman looks with her and says, 'Sweetie, I don't think it damaged anything. It looks fine. Don't you think, sweetie?'"

The way Damian said it, I could just imagine the woman's voice, the way "sweetie" came out, the way all the other words flowed out, like honey.

"But my sister squints her eyes," Damian said, "and she can see that there's a little dent on the neck of the passenger door. So, she says to the woman, 'You're right, it's not too bad, but I need your license and insurance information, just in case the damage is somehow worse than what we can see.' The woman's voice turns to gravel and she says, 'I'm in a hurry. You're wasting my time. I really have to be getting to DC. I don't want to be late.' So, my sister stops her inspection and looks the woman square in the face and says, 'You don't think I had anywhere to be when you slammed your car into mine? You don't think *you* might have inconvenienced *me* by hitting my car? Accidents happen, but your rudeness is unacceptable.' The woman now says, 'All right, all right, you're right. If it were my car that got hit, I'd probably be the same way.' But before she goes to get her license and insurance information, she pauses midstep and says to my sister, 'So, you mean you didn't see me backing out? Why didn't you honk when I was about to back into you?'"

"OK," I said. And I really did get it. "Your sister was already there before the woman started backing out. The woman should have been the one to check to make sure there was no car there before backing out. But what's the point of this story?"

"Point is," Damian said, "the woman said she was sorry. Sorry, you get? But she didn't really see what she had done to my sister. Why? Because she didn't really *see* my sister. All she saw was herself. How the accident was affecting her. How the accident was keeping her from getting to DC. Bro, you can't see what the problem is if you don't even see the person. And if you don't see the person, then you can't care. And when you don't care, you make empty apologies and engage in empty gestures. Somewhere in all of those empty apologies and empty gestures, the person will understand that you don't really see them. You love Maryam, right?"

I nodded.

"Then make sure you *see* her."

Needless to say (but I'll say it anyway), this outright accusation made me irritated at Damian. But somewhere in all of Damian's tedious poetics was a glimmer of meaning: Maryam and I were each other's destiny, so I must do my best to see her.

We walked for four hours that afternoon, Damian and I, and when I finally returned home and opened my laptop, there was still no response from Maryam.

It was a miracle that sleep came to me that night. My tired mind welcomed it, this opportunity to temporarily escape reality.

The following day, I wrote again.

Hey, M,

Just checking to see that you got my email. I know you're upset, but maybe we can talk things out? It'd be good to see you.

I repeated my cycle from the previous day, and by early afternoon when I returned home, she'd still not responded. Where previously I had felt some remorse and was even a bit self-flagellating, at this point, I was angry with Maryam for being a big baby, for being so vengeful as not to respond.

I got ready and headed out to see *Medea* on my own. Who needed Maryam, anyway?

In the darkness of the theater, *Medea* faded in and out of my view. I faded in and out of worry, in and out of tears, and then in and out of sleep.

The last utterance I remember hearing before the audience burst out into applause were Medea's words: "Remember that those you oppress will rise and their defiance will shatter you." Was there a chance that there was an oppressor in me? Was that the reason Maryam had distanced herself from me? I needed her back because I was shattering, and this shattering, I was sure, was nothing compared to what would ensue if I did not succeed in winning her back.

The following Monday, I bought flowers and took them to her dorm. School was in its final days and students would be leaving soon for the summer holiday, but she was staying to take summer classes and resume her work with the Keatings. I would also be staying because financial aid and my scholarship covered both my summer tuition and rent.

She did not answer my buzzing or, after I had made my way into the building behind a student, my knocking. I knocked a number of times, and then eventually left the flowers at the foot of her door.

The next day, I returned to her dorm room to find the flowers still sitting on the floor where I'd left them. I knocked again but still no answer.

On Wednesday, I returned much earlier in the morning. The flowers were gone and I heard voices inside. I turned the knob without knocking and when the door flung open, her roommate and a couple of other people I didn't recognize looked up at me in surprise. The flowers peeked out from the trash bin by the door, and Maryam's empty bed announced itself, the sheets ruffled, as if someone had been tousling in them with her. I wanted to find her, wherever she was. She was close by, I could tell. If she were gone for the day, she would have properly made her bed.

I walked briskly down the hallway, opening the doors of the lavatories, sticking my head into the doorways, calling her name.

At the fifth door, after I had exhausted all the bathrooms on the floor, I heard their voices. I did not need to open the door to know that she was inside. I paused and listened. "Harder!" Maryam's voice was saying. "Harder," she said again.

I mustered courage and pushed open the door enough that I could peek in. Seeing Tyler there was all the proof I needed. Tyler, tall and handsome, the rough and edgy kind of white, with stringy brown hair down to his shoulders and tattoos snaking his forearms. He was standing with his front to Maryam's back, and Maryam stood, her back to him, half bending over the sink.

"How dare she?" I muttered angrily to myself. How dare she choose Tyler over me? For all anyone knew, Tyler might even be a Purist! I was better than he could ever dream of being. The faucet was running, or maybe it was the sound of the sex, I could not tell. Heat rose in me and rendered my face on fire. I tried to speak, but no words would come out. I slammed the door and raced out, letting the betrayal snake its way and find a home deep in the innermost part of my chest.

Greenwich Village was a blast of color and noise. In one corner of Washington Square Park, at a distance from the marble arch, about two dozen protesters were raising their poster boards. I regarded them as I walked past the water fountain. Off and on, I heard some Spanish and Chinese interspersed with English. From what I could see, the majority of the protesters were African Americans, but there were also a good number of Asians and Latinos in the group.

The fountain only dripped those days. There was a time when its water used to rise lushly in beautiful arcs, and children and grown-ups ran happily through it. Now, mold and algae and weeds and mildew crept along its perimeter.

Down by the edge of the fountain, as I inched closer to the group, a small yellow-and-brown-spotted newt scrambled up to me, turned his little head upward to examine me with his bulbous eyes, and then scrambled off into a crack in the plaza's concrete base. Little bubbles of mouse droppings speckled the ground. I could wager a big red apple that these days this was a city that only an eremite would be proud of. Everything looked better from a distance—from your own protected paradise. The same way a rainstorm looked more beautiful through glass windows than when you were standing in it, your pant legs drenched and mud-stained, the cold wetness sending chills up your spine.

"Purists must be stopped. This nation belongs to all of us!" the crowd cried.

I called Damian on the phone. "Damian," I said, when he picked up. "Can we talk?"

There was a rustling on his end.

"The Purists have destroyed the world! Put the Purists in their place!" the protesters chanted. A young couple joined the protesters. They appeared to be white, with his blond hair and with her red hair. They raised their signs emphatically and chanted loudly too. Their performance seemed so genuine that for a moment I wondered if they did not realize that they were the very issue that the protesters were raging against. And then my mind went back to Damian.

"Damian?"

"Man," Damian said in a hushed tone. "I'm in the middle of something here. But all right," he said. "You got me, just for a minute. What's up?"

How could I even begin to explain Maryam's betrayal? My shoulders heaved. The sun's heat was heavy on my back. I felt perspiration all over my forehead, my neck, my underarms—all over my body.

"Man, are you OK?" Damian asked.

When the tears arrived, I allowed myself the indulgence. After I finished crying, I wiped the tears cleanly from my face.

★

I SPRINTED MANIACALLY home and slammed the door of my apartment shut. I stood unmoving at the entryway, my hands at my sides. I hated her. I had an obligation to hate her because she had broken my heart, and she was still breaking it. She had exposed me to such indecency! I'd never thought of her as indecent, but there she had been, as indecent as I never could have imagined.

I'd caught her mid-act! It was her voice; I was sure of it, her breathless throaty voice, crying for Tyler to give it to her harder. Had I ever really known her? No, I was sure now that I had not. How strong my love had been for a person I had not truly known! That was the tragedy of love! No matter now. My first obligation was to myself. I had to protect myself from her. She, a self with no soul. Did Maryam know that she had no soul? Was it possible for a person to live their whole life pretending to have a soul? All this time that I'd known her, had she simply been mimicking the love, the care, the humanity of those with souls? Was that how she slunk her way into my heart?

Memories of my past flooded back. The crawling ivy, the leather sofa, Chevy's purple-scented perfume. Chevy and Wayne. Chevy and Lucinda. The glint of the sun in the Centralia sky. That old Centralia man. My breakdown.

Memory was a psychological and physiological jolt. I had to tell myself that I was no part of that past, that my parents were no longer a part of me, that Edward and Centralia were no longer a part of me, that I could forgive myself for ever having been a part of them. After all, I'd gotten out! Wasn't it the same thing now with Maryam? Rather than wasting precious time, invaluable energy arguing over what she'd done, I could find my way out of her clutch. Don't get stuck. Just get out!

But then my reasoning changed course. I could not allow myself to continue to think so poorly of her. She must also be a good person. How could I have ever loved her if not? How had I ever found her to be the most beautiful and lovable woman in the world if not? *I* must be somehow mistaken, then. *I* must be the one who was somehow not understanding, committing a crime against her integrity. A false accusation. My head felt as if a giant rock were crushing it, and I could hardly stand. I walked toward the wall and let my back drag down it until my bottom reached the floor. My keys jangled beneath me. I slumped and tucked my head into my thighs. I was wrong, I decided; I had to be. I had to try to forget everything I had seen. I stood up, walked into my bathroom, tore off my shirt, washed my face, dabbed my neck and chest with my towel. I looked at myself in the mirror and practiced what I would say to her. What combination of words had the greatest shot at winning her back?

I pulled out the Dark and Luscious™ cream that I had been hiding in my cupboard all the years since I'd been in the city. I spread it first on my arm, rubbed it in until it seemed to have set. I rubbed it onto my face, my neck, my shoulders. My skin became almost exactly what I'd spent a lifetime wishing for. And yet, I was still unsatisfied. My dark body and my Black soul ached.

✴

THE CROWD AT Washington Square Park was slightly thinner by the time I headed back out. Each of the huddled figures held their hands up in protest. Blue masks shielded their noses. There was an odor of something burning in the air, and gasoline. When I got closer, I saw a pile of debris ablaze. Yellow flames rose in dark clouds of smoke. I thought of Centralia. What if these protesters somehow set the entire city on fire? What would become of New York? My mind couldn't handle the thought, so I brushed it aside as I walked past on my way to her dormitory. Somewhere in the distance, a pack of dogs barked.

Maryam answered the knock right away and invited me in. Her roommate looked up at me with irritation, flinging her brown curls off her shoulder, rolling her eyes, and sighing exasperatedly. Maryam sat on her bed, stuffing clothing and other items into a set of polka-dotted luggage.

I knelt by her side and said, "I'm better than he is. Can't you see it?"

"Better than who?" she asked, looking genuinely confused. "What's wrong with your face?"

I explained the bit about Tyler, that she had a moral obligation *not* to choose Tyler over me.

"Effin' hell!" the roommate exclaimed. It startled me. "Why don't you just let her go back to where she came from?! She and her people, they all just need to go back to where they came from! It's high time!"

I stared at the roommate, astonished. I'd never imagined that she felt this way. All this time I'd reasoned that her irritated demeanor was a result of regarding me as a nuisance. I'd not realized that the roommate's anger was directed toward Maryam and "her people."

Maryam shook her head and returned to her folding.

The roommate stormed out of the room, slamming the door shut.

After a moment of silence, Maryam sighed lengthily and said, "You really thought I was choosing Tyler over you?"

"I saw you two," I said. "Why him?" I asked. "He's a white man, for God's sake!"

Maryam looked at me and then one amused burst of laughter escaped her lips. She shook her head and examined my face some more. All her questions came out in a fury: Was this my white self or my Black self speaking? Which one? She didn't know how to take my argument. Was I being racist in making this comment, or was I being pro-Black? Did I resent Tyler because I perceived that I had lost to another white man, or because I perceived an injustice of being Black—of being pushed to the back burner in favor of a white man? Which self was feeling affronted? She could not decide.

"You know what?" she said, after she had asked all the questions. "Doesn't really matter anymore. It's good. You're good. Just forget about it."

The scent of incense—smoky but floral—wafted through the room, and for a moment I thought we'd make amends.

Maryam looked me firmly in the eyes and said, "But, G-Dawg, it's over. Look around us. Don't we have greater things to worry about now?"

I took her hands so that she had to let go of the shirt she was folding. "Please," I said.

"What's this you have all over your hands and face?" she asked. But then she moved her mouth in a way that shook away the question—the answer didn't even matter. She said, with resignation, "G-Dawg, you should leave."

I remained standing, grasped her hands tighter in mine. She pulled away.

I begged again, "Please."

She said austerely, "I think it's best you leave now."

My hands hung limply at my sides. I faded into my mind, searching its nooks and crannies for something I could say to upend her resolve, but I found nothing. When I came to, I saw that she was angry.

"G-Dawg, are you deaf?" she was asking. "You really don't hear me? Please leave."

The last couple of years with her flashed through my mind like a scenic film viewfinder. All the memories we'd made, our first date, the tenderness in her eyes when I took my seat at the diner, our babysitting rendezvous with Sophie, the moments I watched her sleep, the moments I watched her cry, the moments I had the honor of assuaging her even in my envy, our hand-holding, our dances. No music I'd ever listened to with her would ever sound the same. How could I even bring myself to listen to any of those songs again? It was all over. I saw it now. Our whole relationship billowed like a large garbage bag floating away. She had been everything to me, an extension of my body. I had loved her the best way I knew how, with my flawed, imperfect love. I did love her. But I suppose it's true: people cannot love anyone any more than they love themselves. And of course, there had always been that part of myself that I did not, could not, ever love.

The last thing I heard her say was "G-Dawg, if I open my eyes and you're still here, I will slap you into tomorrow!"

I ran away devastated, cutting through the burning park. The fire had risen, red-hot and sweltering flames expanding and bursting into tiny translucent embers, radiant marks of an ardent protest. The city was always burning in those days, with passion and, always, a fire. All the while a different kind of fire was consuming me. Breathless and panting, my mind wobbled and for a moment I wondered if all of Maryam's behavior—her ending things between us, her screaming at me to leave—was not, perhaps, a trick of my mind. Did she really ask me if I was deaf? At what point exactly did she say the bit about slapping me into tomorrow? What was the tone and cadence of her voice when she said it? What if the riot in the park was all a figment of my imagination, just an extension of my grief? But no—my clothes, hair, skin, flesh, even my memory held the burning scent in them, like blood in veins.

★

THE INSTINCT TO decontaminate had clearly existed in me for a long time. Perhaps it had been in me as a mere baby, and then as a boy, even as I resented my mother for her own compulsions. It must have been there with me throughout my teenage years. It was there throughout the Centralia renovation, and certainly afterward—those breakdowns leading up to and after the pandemic. That same instinct was certainly with me still, manifest and obvious so that I could not name it otherwise.

If our universe were just one line of existence in a series of long, parallel, and sometimes intersecting universes, then perhaps there was an iteration of the multiverse—a different dimension of existence—

in which I did not find Maryam in the bathroom with Tyler. And if I had not found Maryam in the bathroom with Tyler, then I would not have found myself feeling corrupted by her betrayal. And if I did not feel corrupted, then I would not have ever returned to the rinsing and the cleaning and the inability to stop. So much desire to rinse away the memory of the betrayal.

But this was the universe in which I existed, and so I found myself back in my bathroom, in Washington Heights, bringing water to my mouth. I rinsed and I spat, but my mouth still did not feel clean. Slime coated my tongue, and even when I managed to rinse it off, there was the problem of the water, which refused to pour out gracefully. It splattered onto the sink's basin and the bubbles ricocheted and splashed at me like an attack, and there I was, hours passing by, my lower back aching, my shoulder muscles tense. I began to rinse again. Again and again, and again, I rinsed.

43

Manhattan, New York

THE TRUTH IS HARDLY EVER AS WE PERCEIVE IT. WHEN I HAD finally managed to get ahold of Maryam online months later, I learned what had actually happened with Tyler.

At the sink that day, as Maryam was bent over, she had been pondering the trajectory of her life. She had come to the decision that she would be returning home. Any day and she would be gone, and it pained her that I would not know anything of her disappearance. But she could not have brought herself to tell me this news. True to my suspicions, she had been struggling with how to accept the man that she was recognizing me to be. More than that, she was struggling with her place in a country that was not her own. She had decided that she would have to leave this place that seemed determined to suck all of her dignity from her through a thin and hollow straw, to erase her humanity. And I was part of that place.

I tend to agree with her evaluation of things. The city, especially in those days, was a ball of chaos. And anyway, she'd later ask, "Don't you think it's good to take care of what we have at home instead of running away to somewhere new? We never really escape, you know? It always follows us."

Those words continue to haunt me.

She went on to explain that—imperfect and as full of painful memories as it was—home was now a siren luring her back. "Do you ever think about maybe doing the same?" she asked. "About going back home to Edward?"

"I'm not sure about that," I said.

In any case, that particular day, even Tyler did not know of her plans.

He stood behind her, close enough to run his hands over the hair and the dye, to rinse them out according to her instructions.

"Harder, harder!" she had said, simply because she did not want any dye residue in her hair. She was cautious with chemicals, afraid that they might lead to "some kind of brain cancer or something." Last time she dyed it, the color had still continued to run for days.

The bathroom smelled intensely of Dark and Lovely® hair colorant and radiant peroxide, and I should have known. If I'd only stayed to watch, I might have heard the moment when Tyler said, "I'm rinsing as hard as I can!" I didn't know anything of Tyler at the time, but I'd later learn that he would have been a licensed beautician but for his parents.

He was dyeing her hair as a birthday gift. Her birthday was around the corner, and she'd mentioned to him that her gray hairs had multiplied. For all the time we spent together, I had not noticed them. But she wanted them gone.

"We wouldn't want you looking too much older than your boyfriend," Tyler had teased.

Maryam didn't laugh. Instead, she confessed that she did not see things working out with us.

"Trouble in paradise?" Tyler asked.

She could have kept her explanation efficient with stock terms like "White Savior" and "body dysmorphia," she said, but "White Savior" seemed too much an accusation and "body dysmorphia" did not completely capture the conflict that she sensed had arisen between us.

"It was good while it lasted," Maryam said. "No condition under the sun is ever permanent."

"Except death," Tyler said, as if that settled it.

It wasn't until after I'd already shut the door and left that she realized that I might very well have been the one at the door. She felt some guilt, knowing that what she'd told Tyler could be misconstrued as gossip. True that she no longer believed in our union, but she still did care about me. Owing to her care, she knew—had known for some time—that the kindest thing she could do would be to break things off. To leave someone you love is sometimes the greatest act of love.

44

Manhattan, New York
August 2026

I WALKED THROUGH THE DOORWAY, BACK DOWN TO THE BASE-
ment of the nondescript coffee shop. Maryam's rejection had hit
hard, and I found myself running for comfort to the first place of
safety that I could think of.

DBT FOR SELF-ACCEPTANCE, the tiny sign read. Out of desola-
tion, I had arrived early. The television news broadcast was coming
from somewhere in the back of the room. The newscaster's voice
boomed. "Continued job losses are no doubt fueling the homelessness epidemic. So far, while the measures that were implemented
globally to bring the virus under control continue to be successful,
the pandemic did cause three times as much homelessness as the
Great Recession of 2008 . . . The president continues to work on his
plan to stimulate the economy . . . There appears to be no end in
sight with the clash between the protesters and the Purists. At the
United Nations, world leaders have met to discuss plans for aiding
the United States in dealing with the political clashes. Eleven reso-
lutions were put forth from many different nations, but so far none
has been undisputedly agreed upon . . ."

The place smelled of wet concrete and old wood and dead cockroaches and mold.

No more guilt. I wanted no more guilt. After all, I had done my best to love her and show her that we were meant to be.

Other group members arrived. The facilitator turned off the television.

"Looking at one's white self in the mirror can often be a stressful experience," the facilitator said. "Emotional regulation techniques will help you identify a primary emotion and block out secondary emotions. Emotional regulation techniques will help you validate your primary emotion. Emotional regulation techniques will help you treat your primary emotion. Using praise and encouragement, I will reinforce your use of DBT skills. Let us begin again with positioning ourselves before our mirrors."

Standing before the mirror, all of us participants exhaled then stared at our reflections.

"What are you all feeling right now?" the facilitator asked.

"Repulsion," the bald-headed man spat.

"Sadness," the woman said.

"Uncomfortable," another man said.

"What are you repulsed by?" the facilitator asked.

"My body," I said. "It still doesn't match who I see in my mind."

"Any other feelings besides sadness, repulsion, discomfort?"

"I'm afraid of what will happen if I remain this way and don't start to match the version of myself in my mind."

"When's the last time you did things to match the self in your mind?"

"Not since I was a child," the bald-headed man said.

"I don't remember. Such a long time ago," the woman said.

"I've been using Blue Magic pomade for some time now," I said. "And last year, I began using the black-market Dark and Luscious™ skin colorant."

"Progress! You've entered the next stage!"

"But it hasn't worked," I said. "Some days I still don't believe myself."

"Then perhaps it's because you have not fully confronted the white self in the mirror. Is that possible?"

"Anything is possible," I said.

"I still just see whiteness, a big, bland, destructive soul," a man said.

"That's a judgment," the facilitator said. "We always aim to steer clear of criticism and judgment. Remember, simply describe."

"I wish I could drop this mirror and get out of here right now," I said.

"I understand how hard this is for you," the facilitator said. "But try to move toward your white self, toward the emotions. Go toward the fear. It is a big, bland white body reflected back at you. But look at it. Confront it. If you run away from it, your fear grows. And you'll never be able to fully transition into your new Black self. If you stare at it enough, over time your discomfort will decrease, and you will be able to transition more smoothly. So, can we all move closer to our reflections right now and try to sit with them?"

Fifteen minutes passed. The bald man was crying again.

"Perfect," the facilitator said. "Now, tell me. How does that feel?"

"Painful," I said.

"I get it," the facilitator replied. "But you did it!"

"Yes," I said. "Yeah, I suppose I did it."

"Good. A two-minute break and then let's try again. Begin from the top. Everybody together. Confront your white selves again. Make sure not to run away. The longer you stay with the discomfort, the greater the chances that your discomfort will eventually decrease. That's the first step. After you've made peace and are no longer terrified of that self, then we can work toward becoming your new Black selves."

Mirrors scraped the floor. All of us participants stared at our reflections again, and in that instant, I saw the futility of my efforts. I was like a waterbird trying desperately to feed, head submerged in a stream. But the food was elusive, and the more I sought it, the more my pale, unclothed bottom jutted, naked in the open for passersby to mock. Despite my best efforts, I had failed to become the man I saw myself to be, and it was unlikely that I would ever succeed unless I tried a different method.

I made up my mind firmly that I would go after her. Maryam, so far away from me. She was the solution. She was the closest that I had ever come to my self-actualization, and so I must reclaim her. Without her, the profound emptiness in me would only continue to grow. Whatever it took, I would make my way back to the continent, to that place where my heart and soul and identity resided—there, in the people of the land and, ultimately, in her. My heart itself was an expanse of land, a forest full of love. She was my beautiful rose. But if the forest is burning, how can you expect a rose to take root? And yet, I would try.

In reanalyzing my past, I'm allowing myself to pinpoint where I made my biggest mistakes. But I have not yet come to a firm verdict on that. I suppose it remains to be seen, even as I speak. All these many years later, I'm, in essence, still on my journey to win back Maryam's love.

In any case, I gathered myself, up the basement stairs, out the café, into the streets. The Purists were still vexing over their loss, a full year and a half after inauguration. There they were, burning down the country. Whether they won or whether they lost in the coming years, it was clear that there would only be more burning, more dissension and, if I stayed, more tension within my soul. Although I had renounced them, I was still the de facto offspring of Chevy and Wayne and was still filled with a fear of one day becoming like them. The futility of change. The inevitability of torpor. Time carries forward, but people—and, by extension, countries—dig in their heels. History repeats itself and the world continues its spiral . . .

And in this way, my next journey began.

Acknowledgments

My heartfelt gratitude to:

Bucknell University's C. Graydon and Mary E. Rogers Faculty Fellowship and the Margaret Hollinshead Ley Professorship in Poetry and Creative Writing.

United States Artists, for your generous financial support.

Angelina Nwaudeafor Okoye, Ifeyinwa Irene Okoye, and Chibundo Juliet Onyejepu: we are missing you.

Aunty Nora Etoniru, Aunty Gloria Godwin Enwere, Aunty Obianuju Okoye, Aunty Linda Obimma, and Aunty Uchenna Amanchukwu: who fed us; who gave us shelter; who shared your stories with us; who spent many hours on the road with us.

Ernest and Kobe in Ghana, and Elisante William and the entire team at Asilia's Olakira, who also spent endless hours on the road with us; and what amazing inspiration you were.

Jennifer Sy, Rachel Phillips Anderson, for your lessons on managing the mind.

Jin Auh and Jacqueline Ko at the Wylie Agency, for believing in my work. Jackie, for bringing *Harry* to life. You are magic.

Pilar Garcia-Brown, for seeing the heart of my work.

Jenna Johnson, for your professional friendship and support.

Rakia Clark: I can't wait to see what the future holds!

Eliza, Kelly, and Katie from marketing and publicity, for your hard work on *Harry*. I'm so grateful for your championing of this book.

Erin DeWitt, for your fantastic copyediting!

Aham Maduchukwu, my dear father, for helping me to sort through all of my ngwongwo.

Chibueze Okparanta, Chinenye Okparanta, Chidinma Okparanta, Lennox Okparanta, Lincoln Okparanta, Liam Okparanta, Carys Okparanta, and Penelope Woodruff-Okparanta. You are my heart. You have my heart.

Constance Okparanta: There's nothing like a mother's love. Thank you for your stories, your songs, your hugs, your laughter, your unfailing love. Thank you for your strength. Surely goodness and mercy shall follow you, all the days of your life.

THE EXECUTIVE'S QUOTATION BOOK

THE
EXECUTIVE'S
QUOTATION
BOOK

A Corporate Companion

Edited by James Charlton

St. Martin's Press   New York

Design by Laura Hammond

Library of Congress Cataloging in Publication Data
Main entry under title:
    The Executive's quotation book.

    Includes index.
    1. Business—Quotations, maxims, etc. 2. Management—
Quotations, maxims, etc. 3. Money—Quotations, maxims,
etc. I. Charlton, James, 1939-   .
HF5351.E95   1983   650   83-16067
ISBN 0-312-27431-9

10 9 8 7

FOREWORD

I like quotations. There is something about the short form that appeals to me. Maybe it has to do with our diminished attention spans—"Quotations are the literary form of the '80s," to quote one wag—but I prefer to think that quotations are a distillation of wit and thought imposed by the brevity of the form. Quotations are not only entertaining to read, they can be provocative and useful. Nothing shores up an argument or provides an authoritative cap to some conversation like the proper quote; it reflects our education, our erudition. Many times a quote can substitute for a sentiment or sentence that we ourselves would not dare utter. But put quotation marks around it and attribute it to Twain or Wilde and you can get away unscathed.

"Every quotation contributes something to the stability and enlargement of the language," said Samuel Johnson, and I agree. *Good* quotes—those that make their way into the consciousness of a people—seem almost to spring up on their own. Oftentimes they are attributed to people who never said them, or who said them in quite a different form or context. We take them up and edit, shape and polish them to fit our needs. Whether Leo Durocher ever said, "Nice guys finish last," when referring to the Dodgers, doesn't matter. The phrase was too perfect, too useful in a variety of situations, to let die.

The financial and business worlds are particularly rich fields for quotations, since they are areas that touch all our lives. Opinions, reflections, regrets, gloatings, admonishments, warnings and advice abound. Some are pompous; others are humble and reflect a very non-corporate view of the world. Many of the wittiest come not just from the established humorists such as Mark Twain, Will Rogers and Oscar Wilde, but from unexpected sources such as Robert Frost and J. Paul Getty, both of whom are marvelously funny on the subject of business.

The Executive's Quotation Book is not meant to be all-inclusive, even in the subject areas we've staked out for it. I have been a collector of quotations for years, clipping favorites from newspapers or magazines and stuffing them in folders and drawers. Many of those included here are a result of those efforts. A number of others have been sent along by friends and acquaintances, and to them I owe a debt of gratitude. Then there are a number of larger sources of quotations, wonderful compendiums such as *Bartlett's Familiar Quotations*, *Peter's Quotations*, *The Fitzhenry and Whiteside Book of Quotations*, that I acknowledge, respect and recommend for everyone's library. To those books I leave subject lists, key words, first line indexes and such. At the request of Barbara Anderson and Nina Barrett, two patient and supportive editors who shared my enjoyment of the subject, there is an index of names. While the quotations are arranged loosely according to subject matter, they need not be read in any particular order. Whether you start at the beginning or dip in at the middle doesn't matter—as long as you enjoy the book.

THE EXECUTIVE'S
QUOTATION BOOK

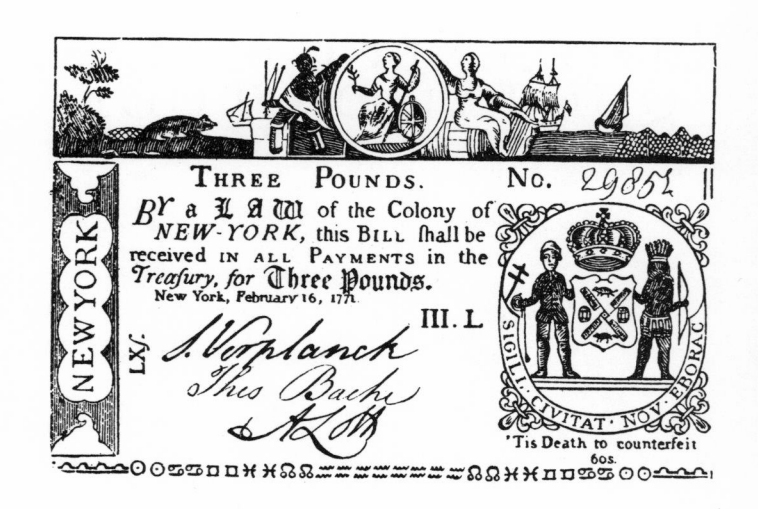

THREE POUNDS. No. 29852

BY a LAW of the Colony of NEW-YORK, this BILL ſhall be received IN ALL PAYMENTS in the Treaſury, for Three Pounds.

New York, February 16, 1771.

NEW YORK

III. L

LX.

S. Verplanck

Theo Bache

A. Lott

'Tis Death to counterfeit 60s.

SIGILL · CIVITAT · NOV · EBORAC

Money is the wise man's religion.
EURIPIDES

Money, which represents the prose of life, and is hardly spoken of in parlors without apology, is, in its effects and laws, as beautiful as roses.
RALPH WALDO EMERSON

You can be as romantic as you please about love, Hector; but you musn't be romantic about money.
GEORGE BERNARD SHAW

Money, it turned out, was exactly like sex; you thought of nothing else if you didn't have it and thought of other things if you did.
JAMES BALDWIN

Money is like manure. You have to spread it around or it smells.
J. PAUL GETTY

Money is the poor people's credit card.
MARSHALL MCLUHAN

I've been in trouble all my life; I've done the most unutterable rubbish, all because of money. I didn't need it. . . the lure of the zeros was simply too great.
RICHARD BURTON

I

"WHAT A FALL WAS THERE, MY COUNTRYMEN!"

If women didn't exist, all the money in the world would
have no meaning.

ARISTOTLE ONASSIS

Make money and the whole world will conspire to call
you a gentleman.

MARK TWAIN

The greater the wealth, the thicker will be the dirt. This
undoubtedly describes a tendency of our time.

JOHN KENNETH GALBRAITH

So you think that money is the root of all evil. Have you
ever asked what is the root of money?

AYN RAND

Not to be covetous is money in your purse; not to be
eager to buy is income.

CICERO

The covetous man never has money; the prodigal will
have none shortly.

BEN JONSON

I would rather have my people laugh at my economics
than weep for my extravagance.

OSCAR II OF SWEDEN

3

Who needs money when you're funny.
RANDY NEWMAN

The petty economics of the rich are just as amazing as the silly extravagances of the poor.
WILLIAM FEATHER

Money is a terrible master, but an excellent servant.
P.T. BARNUM

The use of money is all the advantage there is in having money.
BENJAMIN FRANKLIN

The value of money is that with it we can tell any man to go to the devil. It is the sixth sense, which enables you to enjoy the other five.
W. SOMERSET MAUGHAM

Money may be the husk of many things, but not the kernel. It brings you food, but not appetite; medicine, but not health; acquaintances, but not friends; servants, but not faithfulness; days of joy, but not peace or happiness.
HENRIK IBSEN

I believe in the dollar. Everything I earn, I spend!
JOAN CRAWFORD

There are three great friends: an old wife, an old dog, and ready money.

BENJAMIN FRANKLIN

Money and time are the heaviest burdens of life, and the unhappiest of all mortals are those who have more of either than they know what to do.

SAMUEL JOHNSON

Too much of a good thing can be wonderful.

MAE WEST

Everything in the world may be endured except continued prosperity.

GOETHE

The entire essence of America is the hope to first make money—then make money with money—then make lots of money with lots of money.

PAUL ERDMAN

The highest use of capital is not to make money, but to make money do more for the betterment of life.

HENRY FORD

The more money an American accumulates, the less interesting he becomes.

GORE VIDAL

A feast is made for laughter,
And wine maketh merry,
But money answereth all things.
ECCLESIASTES 10:19

The man who damns money has obtained it dishonorably; the man who respects it has earned it.
AYN RAND

When a fellow says, "It ain't the money but the principle of the thing," it's the money.
FRANK MCKINNEY "KIN" HUBBARD

Finance is the art of passing currency from hand to hand until it finally disappears.
ROBERT SARNOFF

Finance is the art or science of managing revenues and resources for the best advantage of the manager.
AMBROSE BIERCE

Where large sums of money are concerned, it is advisable to trust nobody.
AGATHA CHRISTIE

Those heroes of finance are like beads on a string—when one slips off, the rest follow.
HENRIK IBSEN

I don't want to make money. I just want to be wonderful.
MARILYN MONROE

I don't want to be a star, I want to be a millionaire.
"KINKY" FRIEDMAN

Surplus wealth is a sacred trust which its possessor is bound to administer in his lifetime for the good of the community.
ANDREW CARNEGIE

Prosperity is only an instrument to be used, not a deity to be worshipped.
CALVIN COOLIDGE

Make money your God, and it will plague you like the devil.
HENRY FIELDING

There is nothing wrong with men possessing riches but the wrong comes when riches possess men.
BILLY GRAHAM

You know, Ernest, the rich are different from us.
F. SCOTT FITZGERALD

Yes, I know. They have more money.
ERNEST HEMINGWAY

Paying attention to simple little things that most men neglect makes a few men rich.

HENRY FORD

As a general rule, nobody has money who ought to have it.

BENJAMIN DISRAELI

Sudden money is going from zero to two hundred dollars a week. The rest doesn't count.

NEIL SIMON

The only way to keep score in business is to add up how much money you make.

HARRY HELMSLEY

If you can count your money, you don't have a billion dollars.

J. PAUL GETTY

The end is easily foretold,
When every blessed thing you hold
Is made of silver, or of gold,
You long for simple pewter.
When you have nothing else to wear
But long for cloth of gold and satins rare,
For cloth of gold you cease to care
Up goes the price of shoddy.

W.S. GILBERT *(Gilbert & Sullivan)*

I've been rich and I've been poor, and believe me, rich is better

JOE E. LEWIS

I've never been poor, only broke. Being poor is a frame of mind. Being broke is only a temporary situation.

MIKE TODD

I have tried to become conservative. In 1958 I resolved to be simply a piano player. That was the year I lost $800,000.

LIBERACE

That money talks
I'll not deny,
I heard it once:
It said, "Goodbye"

RICHARD ARMOUR

Neither great poverty nor great riches will hear reason.

HENRY FIELDING

Poor people know poor people and rich people know rich people. It is one of the few things La Rochefoucauld did not say, but then La Rouchefoucauld never lived in the Bronx.

MOSS HART

The chief problem of the lower-income farmers is poverty.

NELSON ROCKEFELLER

There is a serious tendency towards capitalism among the well-to-do peasants.

MAO TSE TUNG

The trouble with being poor is that it takes up all your time.

WILLIAM DE KOONING

Poverty is uncomfortable; but nine times out of ten the best thing that can happen to a young man is to be tossed overboard and compelled to sink or swim.

JAMES A. GARFIELD

Almost all the noblest things that have been achieved in the world have been achieved by poor men, poor scholars, poor professional men, poets, and men of genius. A certain staidness and sobriety, a certain moderation and restraint, a certain pressure of circumstances are good for men. His body was not made for luxuries. It sickens, sinks and dies under them.

HENRY DAVID THOREAU

I'd like to live like a poor man with lots of money.

PABLO PICASSO

I never wanted to be a millionaire. I just wanted to live like one.

WALTER HAGEN

Mamma may have
Papa may have
But God bless the child that's got his own.
That's got his own.

BILLIE HOLIDAY

Money is always there but the pockets change; it is not in the same pockets after a change, and that is all there is to say about money.

GERTRUDE STEIN

Most people seek after what they do not possess and are enslaved by the very things they want to acquire.

ANWAR EL-SADAT

Property is the fruit of labor; property is desirable; it is a positive good in the world. That some should be rich shows that others may become rich, and, hence, is just another encouragement to industry and enterprise.

ABRAHAM LINCOLN

Government has no other end but the preservation of property.

JOHN LOCKE

It is preoccupation with possession, more than anything else, that prevents men from living freely and nobly.
BERTRAND RUSSELL

Possessions, outward success, publicity, luxury—to me these have always been contemptible. I believe that a simple and unassuming manner of life is best for everyone, best both for the body and the mind.
ALBERT EINSTEIN

In God we trust, all others pay cash.
Sign used in retail stores during the Depression

Neither a borrower nor a lender be;
For loan oft loses both itself and friend,
And borrowing dulls the edge of husbandry.
WILLIAM SHAKESPEARE

It is better to give than to lend, and it costs about the same.
SIR PHILIP GIBBS

Let us all be happy and live within our means, even if we have to borrow the money to do it with.
C.F. BROWNE (ARTEMUS WARD)

I get by with a little help from my friends.
JOHN LENNON & PAUL MCCARTNEY

Credit buying is much like being drunk. The buzz happens immediately and gives you a lift. . . . The hangover comes the day after.
DR. JOYCE BROTHERS

Economy is in itself a source of great revenue.
SENECA

The human species, according to the best theory and form of it, is composed of two distinct races, *the men who borrow, and the men who lend.*
CHARLES LAMB

Do you know the only thing that gives me pleasure? It's seeing my dividends roll in.
JOHN D. ROCKEFELLER, JR.

Never invest your money in anything that eats or needs repairing.
BILLY ROSE

There is nothing so disastrous as a rational investment policy in an irrational world.
JOHN MAYNARD KEYNES

There are only two times in a man's life when he should not speculate; when he can't afford it, and when he can.
MARK TWAIN

There is scarcely an instance of a man who has made a fortune by speculation and kept it.

ANDREW CARNEGIE

There is no moral difference between gambling at cards or in lotteries or on the race track and gambling in the stock market. One method is just as pernicious to the body politic as the other kind, and in degree the evil worked is far greater.

THEODORE ROOSEVELT

One of these days in your travels a guy is going to come up to you and show you a nice brand-new deck of cards on which the seal is not yet broken, and this guy is going to offer to bet you that he can make the jack of spades jump out of the deck and squirt cider in your ear. But, son, do not bet this man, for as sure as you stand there, you are going to wind up with an earful of cider.

DAMON RUNYON

The bulls make money
The bears make money
But the pigs get slaughtered.

Wall Street axiom

With an evening coat and a white tie, even a stockbroker can gain a reputation for being civilized.

OSCAR WILDE

Wall Street. A thoroughfare that begins in a graveyard and ends in a river.
ANONYMOUS

October is one of the peculiarly dangerous months to speculate in stocks. The others are July, January, September, April, November, May, March, June, December, August and February.
MARK TWAIN

There is no more mean, stupid, pitiful, selfish, ungrateful animal than the stock-speculating public. It is the greatest of cowards, for it is afraid of itself.
WILLIAM HAZLITT

It is a socialist idea that making profits is a vice; I consider the real vice is making losses.
WINSTON CHURCHILL

There is much more hope for humanity from manufacturers who enjoy their work than from those who continue in the irksome business of founding hospitals.
ALFRED NORTH WHITEHEAD

The worst crime against working people is a company which fails to operate at a profit.
SAMUEL L. GOMPERS

There are poor men in this country who cannot be bought: the day I found that out, I sent my gold abroad.
COMTESSE DE VOIGRAND

Buy land, they're not making it anymore.
MARK TWAIN

Invest in inflation. It is the only thing going up.
WILL ROGERS

Inflation is the one form of taxation that can be imposed without legislation.
MILTON FRIEDMAN

We have a love-hate relationship. We hate inflation, but we love everything that causes it.
WILLIAM SIMON

Inflation can be conquered by the continued application of public and private restraint, and by attention to long-run political policies that increase supply and productivity.
CHARLES SCHULTZE

If people believe that there will be a marked decrease in the rate of inflation, that might be a self-fulfilling set of beliefs.
WILLIAM BAUMOL, *president of the American Economics Association*

A nickel ain't worth a dime anymore.

YOGI BERRA

The way to stop financial joy-riding is to arrest the chauffeur, not the automobile.

WOODROW WILSON

What's money? A man is a success if he gets up in the morning and gets to bed at night, and in between he does what he wants to.

BOB DYLAN

All you need in this life is ignorance and confidence, and then success is sure.

MARK TWAIN

It is no wisdom ever to commend or discommend the actions of men by their success; for oftentimes some enterprises attempted by good counsel end unfortunately, and others inadvisedly taken in hand have happy success.

SIR WALTER RALEIGH

The best thing that can come with success is the knowledge that it is nothing to long for.

LIV ULLMANN

Success has always been a great liar.

FRIEDRICH NIETZSCHE

The success of each is dependent upon the success of the other.

JOHN D. ROCKEFELLER, JR.

Nothing succeeds like success.

ENGLISH PROVERB

It is not enough to succeed. Others must fail.

GORE VIDAL

The moral flabbiness born of the bitch-goddess SUC-CESS. That—with the squalid interpretation put on the word success—is our national disease.

WILLIAM JAMES

The most successful businessman is the man who holds onto the old just as long as it good, and grabs the new just as soon as it is better.

ROBERT P. VANDERPOEL

The successful people are the ones who can think up stuff for the rest of the world to keep busy at.

DON MARQUIS

The toughest thing about success is that you've got to keep on being a success. Talent is only a starting point in business. You've got to keep working that talent.

IRVING BERLIN

Every successful enterprise requires three men—a dreamer, a businessman, and a son-of-a-bitch.

PETER MCARTHUR

The secret of Japanese success is not technology, but a special way of managing people—a style that focuses a strong company philosophy, a distinct corporate culture, long-range staff development, and consensus decision-making.

WILLIAM OUCHI

No man lives without jostling and being jostled; in all ways he has to elbow himself through the world, giving and receiving offense.

PLAUTUS

Each citizen contributes to the revenues of the State a portion of his property in order that his tenure of the rest may be secure.

MONTESQUIEU

The power to tax . . . is not only the power to destroy but also the power to keep alive.

UNITED STATES SUPREME COURT

The nation should have a tax system that looks like someone designed it on purpose.

WILLIAM SIMON

When there is an income tax, the just man will pay more and the unjust less on the same amount of income.
PLATO

Taxes are what we pay for a civilized society.
OLIVER WENDELL HOLMES, JR.

There is nothing sinister in so arranging one's affairs as to keep taxes as low as possible.
JUDGE LEARNED HAND

The hardest thing in the world to understand is the income tax.
ALBERT EINSTEIN

The income tax has made more liars out of the American people than golf has. Even when you make a tax form out on the level, you don't know, when it's through, if you are a crook or a martyr.
WILL ROGERS

The entire graduated income tax structue was created by Karl Marx.
RONALD REAGAN

From each according to his abilities, to each according to his needs.
KARL MARX

I have no use for bodyguards, but I have very special use for two highly trained certified public accountants.

ELVIS PRESLEY

There have been three great inventions since the beginning of time: fire, the wheel, and central banking.

WILL ROGERS

Banking establishments are more dangerous than standing armies.

THOMAS JEFFERSON

Banking may well be a career from which no man really recovers.

JOHN KENNETH GALBRAITH

A sound banker, Alas! is not one who foresees danger and avoids it, but one who, when he is ruined, is ruined in a conventional and orthodox way along with his fellows so that no one can really blame him.

JOHN MAYNARD KEYNES

A banker is a fellow who lends you his umbrella when the sun is shining and wants it back the minute it begins to rain.

MARK TWAIN

BLACK FRIDAY.

One rule which woe betides the banker who fails to heed it . . . Never lend any money to anybody unless they don't need it.

OGDEN NASH

It is rather a pleasant experience to be alone in a bank at night.

WILLIE SUTTON

If you owe a bank enough money you own it.

ANONYMOUS

The banks couldn't afford me. That's why I had to be in business for myself.

SAMUEL GOLDWYN

It's so American to start one's own business.

ANNE MCDONNELL FORD

I'm self-employed.

PRINCE PHILLIP

In soloing—as in other activities—it is far easier to start something than it is to finish it.

AMELIA EARHART

Consultant: any ordinary guy more than fifty miles from home.

ERIC SEVAREID

The real problem is what to do with the problem solvers after the problems are solved.

GAY TALESE

Management consultants are people who borrow your watch to tell you what time it is, and then walk off with it.

ROBERT TOWNSEND

The ability to deal with people is as purchasable a commodity as sugar or coffee. And I pay more for that ability than for any other under the sun.

JOHN D. ROCKEFELLER, JR.

The greatest ability in business is to get along with others and influence their actions. A chip on the shoulder is too heavy a piece of baggage to carry through life.

JOHN HANCOCK

When two men in business always agree, one of them is unnecessary.

WILLIAM WRIGLEY, JR.

It were not best that we should all think alike; it is difference of opinion that makes horse races.

MARK TWAIN

Every kind of peaceful cooperation among men is primarily based on mutual trust and only secondarily on institutions such as courts of justice and police.
ALBERT EINSTEIN

Nice guys finish last.
LEO DUROCHER

An eminent lawyer cannot be a dishonest man. Tell me a man is dishonest and I will answer he is no lawyer. He cannot be, because he is careless and reckless of justice; the law is not in his heart, is not the standard and rule of his conduct.
DANIEL WEBSTER

I don't want a lawyer to tell me what I cannot do; I hire him to tell me how to do what I want to do.
J. P. MORGAN

The first thing we do, let's kill all the lawyers.
WILLIAM SHAKESPEARE

What's the first excellence in a lawyer? Tautology. What the second? Tautology. What the third? Tautology.
RICHARD STEELE

Necessity has no law; I know some attorneys of the same.
BENJAMIN FRANKLIN

I think we may class the lawyer in the natural history of monsters.

JOHN KEATS

An oral contract isn't worth the paper it's written on.

SAMUEL GOLDWYN

He is no lawyer who cannot take two sides.

CHARLES LAMB

It is the trade of lawyers to question everything, yield nothing, and to talk by the hour.

THOMAS JEFFERSON

Lawyers have been known to wrest from reluctant juries triumphant verdicts of acquittal for their clients, even when those clients, as often happens, were clearly and unmistakably innocent.

OSCAR WILDE

Lawyers make a living trying to figure out what other lawyers have written.

WILL ROGERS

Whether you're an honest man or whether you're a thief depends on whose solicitor has given me a brief.

W. S. GILBERT *(Gilbert & Sullivan)*

Discourage litigation. Persuade your neighbor to compromise whenever you can. As a peacemaker the lawyer has a superior opportunity of being a good man. There will still be business enough.

ABRAHAM LINCOLN

Work is love made visible.

KAHLIL GIBRAN

The labourer is worthy of his hire.

NEW TESTAMENT

Business underlies eveything in our national life, including our spiritual life. Witness the fact that in the Lord's prayer, the first petition is for daily bread. No one can worship God or love his neighbor on an empty stomach.

WOODROW WILSON

Man matures through work which inspires him to difficult good.

POPE JOHN PAUL II

Don't tell me how hard you work. Tell me how much you get done.

JAMES LING

When your work speaks for itself, don't interrupt.

HENRY KAISER

As others toil for me, I must toil for others.
ECCLESIASTES 2:20

If he works for you, you work for him.
JAPANESE PROVERB

The man who is employed for wages is as much a businessman as his employer.
WILLIAM JENNINGS BRYAN

It is not the employer who pays wages—he only handles the money. It is the product that pays wages.
HENRY FORD

There are two things needed in these days; first, for rich men to find out how poor men live; and, second, for poor men to know how rich men work.
E. ATKINSON

People of privilege will always risk their complete destruction rather than surrender any material part of their advantage.
JOHN KENNETH GALBRAITH

It is easier to do a job right than to explain why you didn't.
MARTIN VAN BUREN

Work is of two kinds: first, altering the position of matter at or near the earth's surface relatively to the other matter; second, telling other people to do so. The first kind is unpleasant and ill paid; the second is pleasant and highly paid.

BERTRAND RUSSELL

In a hierarchy, every employee tends to rise to his level of incompetence.

LAURENCE PETER

If A equals success, then the formula is A equals X plus Y, with X being work, Y play, and Z keeping your mouth shut.

ALBERT EINSTEIN

The world is full of willing people; some willing to work, the rest willing to let them.

ROBERT FROST

It never fails: everybody who really makes it does it by busting his ass.

ALAN ARKIN

I worked for charity all my life and now it's kind of fun to work for money.

CHARLOTTE FORD

I've always worried about people who are willing to work for nothing. Sometimes that's all you get from them, nothing.

SAM ERVIN

Those who work much do not work hard.

HENRY DAVID THOREAU

I never knew a man escape failures, in either mind or body, who worked seven days in a week.

SIR ROBERT PEEL

My rule always was to do the business of the day in the day.

DUKE OF WELLINGTON

There is more to life than increasing its speed.

MAHATMA GANDHI

Opportunities are usually disguised as hard work, so most people don't recognize them.

ANN LANDERS

Small opportunities are often the beginning of great enterprise.

DEMOSTHENES

Luck means the hardships and privations which you have not hesitated to endure, the long nights you have devoted to work. Luck means the appointments you have never failed to keep; the trains you have never failed to catch.

MAX O'RELL

Progress in industry depends very largely on the enterprise of deep-thinking men who are ahead of the times in their ideas.

SIR WILLIAM ELLIS

There is hardly anything in the world that some men can't make a little worse and sell a little cheaper, and the people who consider price only are this man's lawful prey.

JOHN RUSKIN

The man who will use his skill and constructive imagination to see how much he can give for a dollar, instead of how little he can give for a dollar, is bound to succeed.

HENRY FORD

I should never have made my success in life if I had not bestowed upon the least thing I have ever undertaken the same attention and care that I have bestowed upon the greatest.

CHARLES DICKENS

If you want to succeed you should strike out on new paths rather than travel the worn paths of accepted success.

JOHN D. ROCKEFELLER, JR.

Technological progress has merely provided us with more efficient means for going backwards.

ALDOUS HUXLEY

You can't sit on the lid of progress. If you do, you will be blown to pieces.

HENRY KAISER

Punctuality is the soul of business.

THOMAS HALIBURTON

Patience is a most necessary quality for business: many a man would rather you heard his story than granted his request.

EARL OF CHESTERFIELD

The better work men do is always done under stress and at great personal cost.

WILLIAM CARLOS WILLIAMS

The reason why worry kills more people than work is that more people worry than work.

ROBERT FROST

Few enterprises of great labor or hard work would be undertaken if we had not the power of magnifying the advantages we expect from them.

SAMUEL JOHNSON

If you aren't fired with enthusiasm, you'll be fired with enthusiasm.

VINCE LOMBARDI

I am a friend of the working man, and I would rather be a friend than be one.

CLARENCE DARROW

Don't be misled into believing that somehow the world owes you a living. The boy who believes that his parents, or the government, or anyone else owes him his livelihood and that he can collect it without labor will wake up one day and find himself working for another boy who did not have that belief and, therefore, earned the right to have others work for him.

DAVID SARNOFF

Like every man of sense and good feeling, I abominate work.

ALDOUS HUXLEY

I do not like work even when another person does it.

MARK TWAIN

My own business bores me to death. I prefer other people's.

OSCAR WILDE

Idleness is only the refuge of weak minds.

EARL OF CHESTERFIELD

The brain is a wonderful organ; it starts working the moment you get up in the morning and doesn't stop until you get into the office.

ROBERT FROST

Anyone can do any amount of work, provided it isn't the work he is *supposed* to be doing at that moment.

ROBERT BENCHLEY

I find that two days' neglect of business to give more discontent in mind than ten times the pleasure thereof can repair again, be it what will.

SAMUEL PEPYS

One must work, if not from inclination, at least out of despair—since it proves on closest examination that work is less boring than amusing oneself.

CHARLES BAUDELAIRE

Work is the curse of the drinking classes.

OSCAR WILDE

Employment, sir, and hardships, prevent melancholy.
SAMUEL JOHNSON

Wanting to work is so rare a want that it should be encouraged.
ABRAHAM LINCOLN

Men can do jointly what they cannot do singly; and the union of minds and hands, the concentration of their power, becomes almost omnipotent.
DANIEL WEBSTER

The workingmen are the basis of all government, for the plain reason that they are the most numerous.
ABRAHAM LINCOLN

When large numbers of men are unable to find work, unemployment results.
CALVIN COOLIDGE

It's a recession when your neighbor loses his job; it's a depression when you lose yours.
HARRY TRUMAN

The long range solution to high unemployment is to increase the incentive for ordinary people to save, invest, work and employ others. We make it costly for employers to employ people, and we subsidize people not to go to work. We have a system that increasingly taxes work and subsidizes nonwork.

MILTON FRIEDMAN

The taxpayer—that's someone who works for the federal government but doesn't have to take a civil service exam.

RONALD REAGAN

You will find men who want to be carried on the shoulders of others, who think that the world owes them a living. They don't seem to see that we must all lift together and pull together.

HENRY FORD

Men always try to keep women out of business so they won't find out how much fun it really is.

VIVIEN KELLEMS

Being a woman is a terribly difficult task, since it consists principally in dealing with men.

JOSEPH CONRAD

The man flaps about with a bunch of feathers; the woman goes to work softly with a cloth.

OLIVER WENDELL HOLMES

All women are ambitious naturally.
CHRISTOPHER MARLOWE *and* GEORGE CHAPMAN

All ambitions are lawful except those which climb upward on the miseries or credulities of mankind.
JOSEPH CONRAD

Just as war is too important to be left to the generals, so is an economic crisis too important to be left to the economists or "practical men."
JOHN KENNETH GALBRAITH

Business is a combination of war and sport.
ANDRÉ MAUROIS

The business of America is business.
CALVIN COOLIDGE

Agriculture, manufactures, commerce and navigation, the four pillars of our prosperity, are most thriving when left most to free enterprise.
THOMAS JEFFERSON

The business of government is to keep the government out of business—that is, unless business needs government aid.
WILL ROGERS

As soon as government management begins it upsets the natural equilibrium of industrial relations, and each interference only requires further bureaucratic control until the end is the tyranny of the totalitarian state.
ADAM SMITH *of Glasgow (1776)*

In all that the people can individually do well for themselves, government ought not to interfere.
ABRAHAM LINCOLN

The best minds are not in government. If any were, business would hire them away.
RONALD REAGAN

In business, the competition will bite you if you keep running; if you stand still, they will swallow you.
WILLIAM KNUDSEN

The business system is blessed with a built-in corrective, namely, that one executive's mistakes become his competitor's assets.
LEO CHERNE

Forget your opponents; always play against par.
SAM SNEAD

The trouble in American life today, in business as well as sports, is that too many people are afraid of competition. The result is that, in some circles, people have come to sneer at success, if it costs hard work and training and sacrifice.

KNUTE ROCKNE

Who gives up when behind is cowardly. Who gives up when ahead is foolish.

DR. WILLIAM ARTHUR WARDE

If the spirit of business adventure is killed, this country will cease to hold the foremost position in the world.

ANDREW MELLON

Blessed are the young, for they shall inherit the national debt.

HERBERT HOOVER

The only good budget is a balanced budget.

ADAM SMITH *of Glasgow (1776)*

The only good rule is that the budget should never be balanced—except for an instant when surplus to curb inflation is being altered to a deficit to fight deflation.

WARREN SMITH *of Ann Arbor (1965)*

No nation was ever ruined by trade.
BENJAMIN FRANKLIN

No nation was ever ruined on account of its debts.
ADOLF HITLER

Any government, like any family, can for a year spend a little more than it earns. But you and I know that a continuance of that habit means the poorhouse.
FRANKLIN DELANO ROOSEVELT

There is no art which one government sooner learns of another than that of draining money from the pockets of the people.
ADAM SMITH *of Glasgow (1776)*

The Congress declares that it is the continuing responsibility of the federal government to . . . promote maximum employment, production and purchasing power.
EMPLOYMENT ACT OF 1946

There is no doubt that the real destroyer of the liberties of any people is he who spreads among them bounties, donations, and largess.
PLUTARCH

We work not only to produce but to give value to time.
EUGENE DELACROIX

I have succeeded in getting my actual work down to thirty minutes a day. That leaves me eighteen hours for engineering.

CHARLES STEINMETZ

What we call "creative work" ought not to be called work at all, because it isn't. . . . I imagine that Thomas Edison never did a day's work in his last fifty years.

STEPHEN LEACOCK

Everything comes to him who hustles while he waits.

THOMAS ALVA EDISON

The average person puts only 25% of his energy and ability into his work. The world takes off its hat to those who put in more than 50% of their capacity, and stands on its head for those few and far between souls who devote 100%.

ANDREW CARNEGIE

Work expands so as to fill the time available for its completion.

C. NORTHCOTE PARKINSON

In the ordinary business of life, industry can do anything which genius can do, and very many things which it cannot.

HENRY WARD BEECHER

Life is work, and everything you do is so much more experience.

HENRY FORD

Don't bother about genius. Don't worry about being clever. Trust to hard work, perseverence and determination. And the best motto for the long march is: "Don't grumble. Plug on!"

SIR FREDERICK TREVES

Most of life is routine—dull and grubby, but routine is the momentum that keeps a man going. If you wait for inspiration you'll be standing on the corner after the parade is a mile down the street.

BEN NICHOLAS

Concentration is my motto—first honesty, then industry, then concentration.

ANDREW CARNEGIE

The workingmen have been exploited all the way up and down the line by employers, landlords, everybody.

HENRY FORD

What is work? A way to make a living? A way to keep busy? A glue to hold life together? Work is all these things and more. As an activity and as a symbol, work has always preoccupied us. We do it and we think about it. I go on working for the same reason that a hen goes on laying eggs.

H. L. MENCKEN

Perhaps it is this spector that most haunts working men and women: the planned obsolescence of people that is of a piece with the planned obsolescence of the things they make.

STUDS TERKEL

Until you understand Capitalism you do not understand human society as it exists at present.

GEORGE BERNARD SHAW

In these days a great capitalist has deeper roots than a sovereign prince, unless he is very legitimate.

BENJAMIN DISRAELI

I think that Capitalism, wisely managed, can probably be made more efficient for attaining economic ends than any alternate system yet in sight, but that in itself is in many ways extremely objectionable.

JOHN MAYNARD KEYNES

The craft of the merchant is this, bringing a thing from where it abounds to where it is costly.

RALPH WALDO EMERSON

It is well-known what a middleman is: he is a man who bamboozles one party and plunders the other.

BENJAMIN DISRAELI

The by-product is sometimes more valuable than the product.

HAVELOCK ELLIS

Make three correct guesses consecutively and you will establish a reputation as an expert.

LAURENCE PETER

The successful businessman sometimes makes his money by ability and experience, but he generally makes it by mistake.

G. K. CHESTERTON

Be awful nice to 'em going up, because you're going to meet 'em comin' down.

JIMMY DURANTE

Hitch your wagon to a star.

RALPH WALDO EMERSON

The best executive is the one who has sense enough to pick good men to do what he wants done, and self-restraint enough to keep from meddling with them while they do it.

THEODORE ROOSEVELT

A man is to go about his business as if he had not a friend in the world to help him in it.

LORD HALIFAX

A friendship founded on business is better than a business founded on friendship.

JOHN D. ROCKEFELLER, JR.

Business is business.

GEORGE COLEMAN THE YOUNGER

Business is the oldest of the arts, the newest of professions.

LAURENCE LOWELL, *first president of the Harvard Business School*

Avarice, the spur of Industry.

DAVID HUME

Nothing is quite honest that is not commercial, but not everything commercial is honest.

ROBERT FROST

Men of business must not break their word twice.

THOMAS FULLER

Nothing is illegal if a hundred businessmen decide to do it, and that's true anywhere in the world.

ANDREW YOUNG

It is no secret that organized crime in America takes in over forty billion dollars a year. This is quite a profitable sum, especially when one considers that the Mafia spends very little for office supplies.

WOODY ALLEN

Whatever may be the case in the court of morals, there is no legal obligation on the vendor to inform the purchaser that his is under a mistake, not induced by the act of the vendor.

JUSTICE BLACKBURN

What recommends commerce to me is its enterprise and bravery. It does not clasp its hands and pray to Jupiter.

HENRY DAVID THOREAU

There are no new forms of financial fraud; in the last hundred years there have only been small variations of a few classic designs.

JOHN KENNETH GALBRAITH

The first man gets the oyster, the second man gets the shell.

ANDREW CARNEGIE

Eats first, morals after.

BERTOLT BRECHT

The secret in business is to know something that nobody else knows.

ARISTOTLE ONASSIS

Few people do business well who do nothing else.

EARL OF CHESTERFIELD

Too many executives tend to follow the road proved safe, rather than the dynamic approach of self-reliance, individualism and initiative.

LOUIS E. WOLFSON

Business has only two basic functions—marketing and innovation.

PETER DRUCKER

A man is known by the company he organizes.

AMBROSE BIERCE

If ignorance paid dividends, most Americans could make a fortune out of what they don't know about economics.

LUTHER HODGES

The age of Chivalry is gone; that of sophistry, economists, and calculators has succeeded.
EDMUND BURKE

A businessman is a hybrid of a dancer and a calculator.
PAUL VALÉRY

A computer does not substitute for judgement any more than a pencil substitutes for literacy. But writing without a pencil is no particular advantage.
ROBERT MCNAMARA

Economists are the great imperialists of the social sciences.
GARDNER ACKLEY

What we might call, by way of eminence, the dismal science.
THOMAS CARLYLE, *on economics*

An economist is a man who states the obvious in terms of the incomprehensible.
ALFRED A. KNOPF

Booms and slumps are simply the expression of the results of an oscillation of the terms of credit about their equilibrium positions.
JOHN MAYNARD KEYNES

John Stuart Mill,
By a mighty effort of will,
Overcame his natural bonhomie
And wrote *Principals of Political Economy.*
EDMUND CLERIHEW BENTLEY

If all the economists were laid end to end, they'd never reach a conclusion.
GEORGE BERNARD SHAW

The instability of the economy is equaled only by the instability of the economists.
JOHN H. WILLIAMS

I am now a Keynesian.
RICHARD NIXON

We are all Keynesians now.
MILTON FRIEDMAN

In the long run, we are all dead.
JOHN MAYNARD KEYNES

Whenever there are great strains or changes in the economic system, it tends to generate crackpot theories which then find their way into the legislative channels.
DAVID STOCKMAN

Very dangerous things, theories.
DOROTHY SAYERS

Advertising is a valuable economic factor because it is the cheapest way of selling goods, especially if the goods are worthless.
SINCLAIR LEWIS

Advertisements contain the only truths to be relied on in a newspaper.
THOMAS JEFFERSON

Anything you do to enhance sales is a promotion.
BILL VEECK

Promise, large promise, is the soul of an advertisement.
SAMUEL JOHNSON

Advertising is the modern substitute for argument; its function is to make the worse appear better.
GEORGE SANTAYANA

You can tell the ideals of a nation by its advertisements.
NORMAN DOUGLAS

You can fool all of the people all of the time if the advertising is right and the budget is big enough.
JOSEPH E. LEVINE

Advertising is 85% confusion and 15% commission.
FRED ALLEN

The guy you've really got to reach with your advertising
is the copywriter for your chief rival's advertising agency.
If you can terrorize him, you've got it licked.
HOWARD L. GOSSAGE

The codfish lays 10,000 eggs,
The homely hen just one;
The codfish never cackles
To tell you that she's done.
And so we scorn the codfish,
And the homely hen we prize.
Which demonstrates to you and me
That it pays to advertise.
The Toronto Globe

Nothing except the mint can make money without advertising.
THOMAS B. MACAULAY

It is a great art to know how to sell wind.
BALTASAR GRACIAN

To sell something, tell a woman it's a bargain; tell a man
it's deductible.
EARL WILSON

Everyone lives by selling something.
ROBERT LOUIS STEVENSON

Buying is cheaper than asking.
GERMAN PROVERB

People will buy anything that's one to a customer.
SINCLAIR LEWIS

Business is never so healthy as when, like a chicken, it must do a certain amount of scratching for what it gets.
HENRY FORD

To lead the people, walk behind them.
LAO-TZU

Executive ability is deciding quickly and getting someone else to do the work.
J. G. POLLARD

A man who has to be convinced to act before he acts is *not* a man of action.
GEORGES CLEMENCEAU

Young men are fitter to invent than to judge; fitter for execution than for counsel; and fitter for new projects than for settled business.
FRANCIS BACON

68

Leadership appears to be the act of getting others to want to do something you are convinced should be done.
VANCE PACKARD

Good management consists in showing *average* people how to do the work of *superior* people.
JOHN D. ROCKEFELLER, JR.

The secret of successful managing is to keep the five guys who hate you away from the five guys who haven't made up their minds.
CASEY STENGEL

You take all the experience and judgement of men over 50 out of the world and there wouldn't be enough left to run it.
HENRY FORD

The man who builds a factory builds a temple; the man who works there worships there; and to each is due not scorn and blame but reverence and praise.
CALVIN COOLIDGE

The question "Who ought to be boss?" is like asking "Who ought to be tenor in the quartet?" Obviously, the man who can sing tenor.
HENRY FORD

The big salaries in business always go to those who have what it takes to get things done. That is true not only of those executives who guide the destinies of a business, but it is true of those upon whom executives must depend for results.

J. C. ASPLEY

Power means not having to raise your voice.

GEORGE WILL

Power is the greatest aphrodisiac.

HENRY A. KISSINGER

A friend in power is a friend lost.

SAMUEL ADAMS

A chief is a man who assumes responsibility. He says, "I was beaten," he does not say, "My men were beaten."

ANTOINE DE SAINT-EXUPÉRY

The employer generally gets the employees he deserves.

SIR WALTER BILBEY

When you get right down to it, one of the most important tasks of a manager is to eliminate his people's excuse for failure.

ROBERT TOWNSEND

Never give up a man until he has failed at something he likes.
LEWIS E. LAWES

Big shots are only little shots who keep shooting.
CHRISTOPHER MORLEY

No man ever manages a legitimate business in this life without doing indirectly far more for other men than he is trying to do for himself.
HENRY WARD BEECHER

Committee—a group of men who keep minutes and waste hours.
MILTON BERLE

Nothing is ever accomplished by committee unless it consists of three members, one of whom happens to be sick and the other absent.
HENDRIK VAN LOON

You know, if an orange and an apple went into conference consultations, it might come out a pear.
RONALD REAGAN

Having served on various committees I have drawn up a list of rules: Never arrive on time; this stamps you as a beginner. Don't say anything until the meeting is half over; this stamps you as wise. Be as vague as possible; this avoids irritating the others. When in doubt, suggest a subcommittee be appointed. Be the first to move for adjournment; this will make you popular; it's what everyone is waiting for.

HARRY CHAPMAN

Men are never so tired and harassed as when they deal with a woman who wants a raise.

MICHAEL KORDA

Suffer women once to arrive at an equality with you, and they will from that moment become your superiors.

CATO THE CENSOR

To be successful, a woman has to be much better at her job than a man.

GOLDA MEIR

Try not to become a man of success but rather try to become a man of value.

ALBERT EINSTEIN

Always mistrust a subordinate who never finds fault with his superior.

JOHN CHURTON COLLINS

The only way to get the best of an argument is to avoid it.
DALE CARNEGIE

Good fellows are a dime a dozen, but an aggressive leader is priceless.
EARL "RED" BLAIK

Few great men could pass Personnel.
PAUL GOODMAN

A 10,000-aspirin job.
Japanese term for executive responsibility

America is the country where you buy a lifetime supply of aspirin for one dollar, and use it up in two weeks.
JOHN BARRYMORE

When you can do the common things of life in an uncommon way, you will command the attention of the world.
GEORGE WASHINGTON CARVER

Most employers these days are more interested in performance than conformance.
HENRY FORD II

Whenever you're sitting across from some important person, always picture him sitting there in a suit of long underwear. That's the way I always operated in business.

JOSEPH P. KENNEDY

The most successful highest-up executives carefully select understudies. They don't strive to do everything themselves. They train and trust others. This leaves them foot-free, mind-free, with time to think. They have time to receive important callers, to pay worthwhile visits. They have time for their families. No matter how able, any employer or executive who insists on running a one-man enterprise courts unhappy circumstances when his powers dwindle.

B. C. FORBES

The first-rate man will try to surround himself with his equals, or betters if possible. The second-rate man will surround himself with third-rate men. The third-rate man will surround himself with fifth-rate men.

ANDRÉ WEIL

They tell me I often go out on a limb. Well, that's where I like to be.

HENRY J. KAISER

When you say that you agree to a thing in principle you mean that you have not the slightest intention of carrying it out in practice.

BISMARCK

In all matters of opinion, our adversaries are insane.

MARK TWAIN

When people agree with me I always feel that I must be wrong.

OSCAR WILDE

I don't want any yes-men around me. I want everyone to tell me the truth—even though it costs him his job.

SAMUEL GOLDWYN

I have heard your views. They do not harmonize with mine. The decision is taken unanimously.

CHARLES DE GAULLE

All business sagacity reduces itself in the last analysis to a judicious use of sabotage.

THORSTEIN VEBLEN

A corporation is an artificial being, invisible, intangible, and existing only in contemplation of law.

JOHN MARSHALL

Corporation: an ingenious device for obtaining individual profit without individual responsibility.
AMBROSE BIERCE

Corporations are invisible, immortal and have no soul.
ascribed to ROGER MANWOOD, *chief baron of the English Exchequer, 1592*

Corporations are people, too.
WILLIAM SIMON

Corporations . . . are many lesser commonwealths in the bowels of a greater, like worms in the entrails of a natural man.
THOMAS HOBBES

Capitalists are no more capable of self-sacrifice than a man is capable of lifting himself by his own bootstraps.
LENIN

What is good for the country is good for General Motors, and what is good for General Motors is good for the country.
CHARLES E. WILSON

A big corporation is more or less blamed for being big; it is only big because it gives service. If it doesn't give service, it gets small faster than it grew big.
WILLIAM S. KNUDSEN

Big Business is basic to the very life of this country; and yet many—perhaps most—Americans have a deep-seated fear and an emotional repugnance to it. Here is monumental contradiction.

DAVID LILIENTHAL

Big Business is not dangerous because it is big, but because its bigness is an unwholesome inflation created by privilege and exemptions which it ought not to enjoy.

WOODROW WILSON

We demand that big business give people a square deal; in return we must insist that when anyone engaged in big business honestly endeavors to do right, he shall himself be given a square deal.

THEODORE ROOSEVELT

One cannot walk through a mass-production factory and not feel that one is in hell.

W. H. AUDEN

Going to work for a large company is like getting on a train. Are you going sixty miles an hour or is the train going sixty miles an hour and you're just sitting still.

J. PAUL GETTY

One way to avoid having industrial troubles is to avoid having industries.

DON MARQUIS

Retirement at sixty-five is ridiculous. When I was sixty-five I still had pimples.
GEORGE BURNS

He's no failure. He's not dead yet.
WILLIAM LLOYD GEORGE

The man who dies rich, dies disgraced.
ANDREW CARNEGIE

There is a great deal of truth in Andrew Carnegie's remark "The man who dies rich, dies disgraced." I should add, the man who lives rich, lives disgraced.
AGA KHAN III

When you have told anyone you have left him a legacy, the only decent thing to do is die at once.
SAMUEL BUTLER

There's no reason to be the richest man in the cemetery. You can't do any business from there.
COLONEL SANDERS

When I die, my epitaph should read: *She Paid the Bills*. That's the story of my private life.
GLORIA SWANSON

INDEX